holy hearts

USA TODAY BESTSELLING AUTHOR
AMANDA RICHARDSON

Holy Hearts
Amanda Richardson
© Copyright 2025 Amanda Richardson
www.authoramandarichardson.com

Copy/line editing: Rumi Khan
Proofreading: Michele Ficht
Cover Design: Moonstruck Cover Design & Photography
Cover Photography: Wander Aguiar
Cover Model: Valerio Logrieco

NO AI TRAINING: Without in any way limiting the author's exclusive rights under copyright, any use of this publication to "train" generative artificial intelligence (AI) technologies to generate text is expressly prohibited. No generative AI was used in the creation of this book.

This is a work of fiction. Names, characters, businesses, places, events and incidents are either the products of the author's imagination or used in a fictitious manner. Any resemblance to actual persons, living or dead, or actual events is purely coincidental.

All rights reserved. This book or any portion thereof may not be reproduced or used in any manner whatsoever without the express written permission of the author except for the use of brief quotations in a book review.

BLURB

Bound by holy vows, undone by sinful desires...

Malakai

I've spent years hiding my depraved deviances behind my roles as pastor and headmaster of Saint Helena Academy.
When Julian—my former best friend—returns to my life, the tension between us is impossible to ignore.
He's married now, and I try to keep my distance.
Until he confesses his secret: he wants me to sleep with his wife, Sophie, while he watches.
It's their arrangement, their game—and now, I'm the one they've chosen.
I should walk away, but I can't—I'm just as drawn to her as I am to him.
What starts as curiosity spirals into something far deeper–something that could destroy everything I've worked to protect.

Julian

He kissed me once. Then he disappeared.

Seventeen years later, Malakai is back, and my unresolved feelings soon evolve into a new obsession: watching him with Sophie.

It consumes me.

Sophie is a hotwife, and watching her with other men has always been my kink.

But with Kai, it's different—he prefers a darker, more intense experience.

He's also used to being in control, but now it's my turn.

But only if my marriage can survive opening up to him–and if I can maintain control without falling for him all over again.

Holy Hearts is a full-length MMF billionaire romance with BDSM themes. It is the fifth and final book in the Ravaged Castle series. All books can be read as standalones.

Warning: This book contains explicit sexual situations and strong language. There is no cheating, and there is a HEA between all three characters.

There once was a castle, so mighty and high,
With large, gilded gates, it rivaled Versailles.
To all those below, it was splendid and lush,
But to those inside, it was ravaged and crushed.
Five Ravage boys born amongst old, rotted roots,
Their father ensured they'd all grow to be brutes.
Some said they were cursed, sworn off of desire,
But they turned into men and found what they required.
Forbidden, illicit, they had to work for that love,
They questioned that castle when push came to shove.
The curse and the rot gave way to unsavory tastes,
Dark proclivities and sick, messed up traits.
Five stories of five men with sinfully dark tales,
The Ravage brothers prove that love does prevail.

AUTHOR'S NOTE

This book contains themes that may be problematic for some people. However, please note that Holy Hearts is not a dark romance.

For a complete list, please visit my website here:
www.authoramandarichardson.com/triggers

Happy reading!

For all the bookworms who understand that being the filling in a possessive alpha sandwich is the only proper way to be devoured.

PROLOGUE
THE EXPERIMENT

MALAKAI

Seventeen Years Ago

"If I were in this movie, I'd definitely trip while running away from the killer."

"You'd trip and then look back like, 'Why is this happening to me?' Classic Malakai move," Julian adds, laughing. It makes me smile. His laugh is something I've heard a thousand times, but lately, it hits differently. I don't know why. "If I were in this movie, I'd be hiding under the bed instead of running toward the sound. Survival 101."

"But we wouldn't have a movie if everyone was smart. Where's the drama in that?"

"Touché." Julian passes the popcorn to me. "If the killer from this movie doesn't get them, I'm pretty sure the awful dialogue will."

"Come on, Julian. It's a classic."

"You Americans and your proclivity for god-awful slasher movies. I'd take a chainsaw-wielding killer over this plot any day."

I'm grinning as I take another handful of popcorn. "You're such a menace."

The movie plays in the background for another few minutes, the only sounds our chewing and the overdramatic screams of the clowns on-screen.

"Hey, I got an email about housing next year," Julian says casually. "If you want to be roomies next year, we should fill it out so we don't lose out on a room."

The popcorn turns to lead in my mouth as I attempt to swallow. The sound of pouring rain outside sounds louder all of a sudden. "Yeah. Okay."

I hate how my chest tightens. Moving into seminary housing isn't the end of the world, but leaving this dorm—leaving him—feels heavier than it should.

Julian must notice the shift in my tone, because he turns to face me. "Hey, no pressure. I know things are a bit up in the air for you because of the seminary application—"

"I got accepted into the program," I blurt, sitting up straighter. "I got the email this morning, and I was going to tell you—"

"I fucking knew you would," he says, his gaze lingering a little too long. His grin falters for just a second. It's quick—so quick I could've imagined it. But I didn't. "I'm so proud of you, Kai. When does it start?"

I hand the popcorn back to him, taking a deep breath. "January."

His brows pull together. "Oh, so we'd—"

"You'd have to get another roommate for next semester," I tell him at the same time, ignoring how my chest aches.

"But you got into the program!" Julian says brightly, though his smile doesn't reach his eyes. "I suppose I can find another roommate who doesn't snore."

I punch his shoulder. "Screw you. I don't snore."

He chuckles. "Whatever you say."

"I'll still be at Crestwood University, but we have to live with the other seminary students," I explain, reaching over to get some more popcorn. I can't remember if I'd explained that part of the program, but apparently not considering his pinched expression.

"I see," Julian concedes. "Makes sense."

We both watch the horror movie in silence for a few more minutes, finishing the popcorn.

"Seriously? This heroine... Ugh. Instead of calling for help, she's going to investigate the noise?" I ask, trying to diffuse the situation a bit. I didn't expect Julian to react poorly to me moving out of our shared dorm room, but as I study his serious expression and tense jawline, I realize I might've underestimated the impact my leaving would have on him.

"Horror movies and common sense don't mix," he says drolly.

"Do all these characters have a death wish? They're literally running into danger," I grumble, reaching the bottom of the popcorn bag as one of the heroines begins to explore the dark woods alone. Julian shifts slightly, and his knee brushes against mine.

Something inside of me shifts, but I tamp it down before I can acknowledge it.

"Maybe they're just trying to distract themselves from their feelings. Works for some people, right?" Julian answers, sounding almost bitter.

My brows pinch. "Hey—"

"I'm going to go heat up another bag of popcorn in the common room," Julian says, hopping off the bed and throwing the empty popcorn bag into the trash. "Want anything else?"

"I'm good," I tell him, watching his weird behavior with narrowed eyes.

After he walks out of the dorm, I sigh and lean back against the wall of Julian's bed. Is he really that worried about getting another roommate? I'm not easy to live with—I'm antisocial and I go to bed at ten p.m. He's the life of the party, and he has, like, a thousand friends. Everyone loves Julian Ashford. I figured he'd be happy to find a roommate more predisposed to his night-owl tendencies. We're only in our freshman year, so it's not like we're short on time to hang out. We still have three and a half more years here together. Plus, it's not like we'd never see each other. I'm only going across campus.

I don't have long to contemplate the out-of-character behavior of my best friend, however, because a second later, Oscar is knocking on the door and peeking his head inside.

"Hey, Kai," Oscar says, giving me a fist bump.

"Sup, Oscar?"

Aside from Julian, Oscar and the rest of my friends from theology have been a saving grace this semester. Julian likes to call them my "God friends"—they're all religious, and they attend church every Sunday. There's just *something* about being in church, surrounded by like-minded people. It's so different from how I grew up. There's light and goodness in church. Warmth. *Community*. It's a stark contrast to the silence and tension that always hung heavy in my house growing up.

"Not much. We're going to watch a movie and make some popcorn in my dorm. Want to join us?"

I shake my head. "Thanks, but no thanks. I'm introducing Julian to some of the classic American slasher movies."

"Ahh. Sounds fun. Hey, did you give any more thought into the ministry conference next month?"

I rub my mouth and imagine what I'd tell my father if I decided to spend my winter holiday at church camp, let alone what he'll say when I tell him I'm dropping out of the business program at Crestwood University in lieu of seminary school. The ministry conference would be a really good way for me to get to know the others in the seminary program before it started, but I hadn't decided yet. The two-week conference in Mexico City could be life-changing. Mom would be thrilled—she was always encouraging us to travel. But my dad? If I didn't get a return on my investment, he'd call it a failure. The man didn't have a charitable bone in his body.

And I'd decided from a very early age that I didn't want to be anything like him.

"Sort of. Can I let you know by Monday?"

"No rush, man. But we'd love to have you. Have you told Julian the news about seminary?" he asks.

I nod. "Yeah. I told him a few minutes ago."

"And? How'd he take it?"

Shrugging, I rub my mouth with my hand. "Fine."

"Really?" he asks. "Huh. I would've expected him to be devastated."

I laugh. "Devastated? Why?"

Oscar shuffles his feet uncomfortably. "Aren't you—I mean—" He rubs the back of his neck. "He's your boyfriend, right?"

My chest feels tight with... something... shame, maybe. But then the absurdity of the situation hits me, and I burst out laughing.

"What? No!"

Oscar's face turns red. "Fuck, sorry, man. I just assumed." He holds his hands up. "But if you were together, it wouldn't matter, just so you know—"

"Well, we're not," I say a little too loudly.

Oscar opens and closes his mouth before he crosses his arms. "I know this isn't my place, but are you sure *he* knows you're just friends?"

Shock rolls through me. "Yes," I tell him sternly.

"Okay. It's just that he talks about you nonstop in biochem. It's kind of adorable," Oscar adds.

"Are you sure we're talking about the same Julian? *My* Julian?"

"Yeah. I just assumed..."

That uncomfortable, tight feeling returns. "No," I stammer, feeling a rush of warmth in my cheeks. It's not just the absurdity of the idea that rattles me. It's how quickly I'm dismissing it—like I'm afraid to sit with it for too long, for fear of the idea sinking in too deeply. "You're wrong."

"Sorry, man. I didn't mean to make you uncomfortable."

"No, it—it's fine," I stutter.

"I should go. Let me know about the conference before Monday, okay?"

I nod and wave him away, but it feels like I'm dreaming or drowning... and I'm not sure which, or why an innocent assumption threw me off my game so much.

My heart is racing, and I rub my chest with my hand. Julian and me? The thought is laughable.

I'd never even considered the idea...

A minute later, Julian returns with two bags of popcorn. "Got you your own bag so we don't have to share," he mumbles, handing it to me.

"Thanks," I say slowly, observing him as he climbs into the bed next to me. He purposefully positions himself farther away, too, and my mind races.

I study his profile as I look over at him, wondering what he's thinking. His white-blond hair is flipped over to one side, and his day-old, ash-blond scruff makes him look older than his eighteen years. I've been trying to grow my beard for years unsuccessfully, and I have to shave every morning so that no one can see how patchy it is.

I've always been envious of it.

I mean... yeah. He's good-looking. I've noticed. But I don't really think of him that way.

"Why are you staring at me?" he asks, chewing popcorn. His eyes don't leave our tiny television screen.

"You're acting weird," I tell him truthfully.

He shrugs. "I'm fine. Just tired."

He's lying, but I don't understand why. We continue to watch the movie until it ends with the heroine stabbing the serial killer in the neck. He puts another DVD in, and I don't see what it is. I don't really care. The rain continues to pour outside, so much so that Julian gets up and looks out of the window.

It reminds me of something an old man would do, and I have to try not to laugh. His moods are *so* apparent, and when Julian is happy, everyone is happy.

When Julian is miserable...

"It's pissing down outside," he mutters, but he doesn't look at me as he gets back into the bed. Every time he gets back in bed, he situates himself a little farther away.

And I can't help but think of what Oscar said—about the way Julian talks about me in class. What does he say? Maybe Oscar is just misreading the situation. We're close, sure, but Julian has never said or done anything to make me think he's anything but straight.

I can't shake the feeling that when it comes to Julian, there's something deeper I'm not seeing.

I usually go home on the weekends since Crestwood University is only a short drive away from Ravage Castle, where I grew up. My father had called Julian a word I'd never heard him use last weekend, and while it made me angry, it also confused me—now more than ever. I'd brushed it off last weekend, but now? That's twice someone's mentioned it.

Julian dates women.

He likes women.

We even check out girls together sometimes.

And, as his roommate, I've *definitely* caught him jacking off to porn.

I suppose it's possible he's bi... or lying to me.

I don't like how that thought makes me feel. Not that I would ever judge Julian for who he's attracted to—despite being interested in religion, I keep an open mind. But the thought of Julian being anything other than straight makes my heart race in a way I'm not sure I understand.

And what about me? I'm straight, so why am I having this reaction?

Maybe I'm not as certain about my own sexuality as I assume. Especially when a sex scene comes on the screen, and my neck burns. I imagine the couple on-screen is Julian and me, and I think about how it would feel to run my hands over his chest, to feel his breath mixing with mine, to feel his calloused hands on my bare skin—

No.

This isn't me.

"My dad wants me to come home," Julian says, interrupting my thoughts. "Since you're not going to be here next semester, maybe I should take him up on his offer."

His words cut through my existential crisis, and I swing around to face him fully. "Back to England?" I ask, my voice hard and accusatory. "I'm moving across campus, not across the world," I add.

Julian's jaw hardens. He still won't look at me. "Oh, so it's okay if you move out, but it's not okay if I do?"

I scowl at him. "What? That's not—"

"Duty calls, Ravage. You should know that better than anyone," he says, and his voice is so... melancholy. *Unfriendly.*

My chest aches as I stare at my best friend.

I knew he'd have to go back to England after college. As the eldest Ashford son, and a baron or a viscount, I think—not that it mattered—his responsibility to his title is inevitable.

"I don't want you to move back," I say.

Julian's jaw feathers as he stares at the TV screen. "What's the point in staying in an empty dorm room, or applying for a room next year? I don't really want to live with anyone else."

"But your degree—"

"My degree?" he asks, scoffing. "I can finish a liberal arts program anywhere. In fact, I'm sure Oxford or Cambridge would be happy to oblige another Ashford," he adds, sounding almost disgusted at the prospect. "It's not like I need to get a job after university with my connections."

I swallow hard, my thoughts spinning. This feels wrong. I only intended to tell him about seminary. I thought we'd discuss housing. It was supposed to be *simple.* And yet, it's somehow spiraled into something deeper. Rubbing the ache in my chest, I tell myself it's not a big deal, though it feels like a turning point, somehow.

If Julian goes back to England, I won't see him every day. The thought grips me harder than it should, twisting in my chest.

I can't even make sense of it, but the idea of him being gone feels unbearable, like more than just physical distance.

What the hell am I so afraid of?

"It feels like you're punishing me for moving across campus," I offer.

Julian finally turns to face me, and his eyes flash with fury. "You're being a hypocrite."

I huff out an outraged laugh, climbing off the bed. "You wouldn't be leaving if I wasn't. If anything, you're the hypocrite," I accuse, nostrils flaring.

Julian climbs off the bed too, and the movie drones on behind him.

"A heads-up would've been nice," he says through gritted teeth. "I spoke to my father yesterday and told him to fuck off, just so you know."

"Then don't go!" I say. My voice is too loud, because Julian's eyes widen just a fraction. "No one is making you go back to jolly good England, Julian. I'll be a five-minute walk away. I don't understand what the big deal—"

"I already told you I don't want to live with anyone else," he offers, narrowing his eyes and walking closer to me.

For years, I was taller than him. But in the last year or two, he's gained a couple of inches.

It suits him. Julian's personality is larger than life, so it makes sense that his physique would follow suit.

"Why? They might not even assign a new roommate for next semester, and then you can get one of those single rooms next year."

He looks away, and I watch him as he shuffles his feet. The Julian Ashford I know could talk to a frog for hours. He gets along with everyone. People love his accent, his charisma, his charm. Any future roommate would be lucky to have him.

An unexpected pang of jealousy flares through me.

I imagine someone else watching slasher flicks with him on Friday nights, or his future roommate throwing their pillow at him when he snoozes through his alarm for the fifth time.

Mental images of another guy bringing him his favorite chocolate bar float through my mind.

Those are *our* things.

Then I think about how, because of seminary, we might drift apart naturally.

It's such a horrible thought that I briefly squeeze my eyes shut before opening them again.

"Just... it's nothing," he says, thumbing his nose and walking over to his desk. He picks up his keys and wallet, shoving them into his pocket. "I'm going for a walk."

He turns and walks past me, and I don't know what compels me to do it, but I reach out for his arm and wrap my hand around his wrist.

"Julian, talk to me," I urge.

Julian slowly drags his eyes up to mine. "I'm sorry. I need fresh air."

I don't let go—instead, I curl my fingers tighter. His pulse is racing against the tips of my fingers, and his eyes flick between mine as if he's searching my face for something.

"I'm your best friend. You can tell me anything," I say, my voice softer.

A sad expression drags his features down. "Yes. We're the best of friends," he says, sounding sarcastic. *What the hell?*

The corner of his mouth curves up slightly, and I can't help the way my eyes track the movement. He tugs out of my grip and pulls the door open before disappearing through it.

"Fuck," I whisper, running a hand through my short hair.

Quickly turning off the TV, I begin pacing the dorm room. I'm not sure what just happened. Everything was fine until I told him about seminary.

No, he was fine until you said you had to move out.

The thought nags at me.

But why? Why does it matter if we live together or not? We can still see each other all the time when I'm not busy.

I walk in circles as my mind races.

Is... is it possible that he has feelings for me? Is that why he's acting out? There's no way he'd willingly go back to England otherwise. He hated the pomp and circumstance of his title. Julian made *sense* in California. The long-ish, blond hair. The jeans and flannels. The friendly attitude. He was more of a native Californian than I was.

A flash of lightning is immediately followed by a clap of thunder.

Chewing on my lower lip, I deliberate between staying put or going to make sure Julian is okay.

Another flash of lightning has me slipping into my boots and grabbing my jacket. Pulling the door open, I almost walk right into Julian, who is standing there, soaking wet. His chest rises and falls as his eyes sweep across my face. Neither of us moves. Instead, he takes a step forward just as we're both plunged into complete darkness.

Power outage.

"Fuck," I whisper, looking around.

"Kai," Julian says, his voice husky.

"Flashlight," I add, twisting around and stumbling back into the dark room. I nearly trip over something and catch myself on one of the beds, and my hands skim over the wood before my fingers curl around the desk drawer. Pulling it open, I fumble inside for the flashlight and pull it out.

After I switch it on, I look over at Julian. He's still standing by the door, still out of breath, still soaking wet. His hair lands over his forehead and rivulets of water fall down his face, bouncing off his scruff onto his wet, long-sleeved shirt.

"You okay?" I ask, clearing my throat.

Julian rubs the back of his neck and looks away. "Yeah. Just needed some air. Got more than I bargained for, I guess," he adds, shaking his hair slightly.

I watch my best friend as he takes a tentative step back into the dorm room.

"You're acting weird. Are you sure everything's okay?"

"I'm fine," he says quickly. *Too* quickly. "Just... trying to process everything."

I stand up straighter. "I told you, the only thing that has to change is us rooming together. We can still hang out."

"I know."

"Then, what? This feels like more than that," I add, gesturing to him.

He sighs. "I'll be fine, Kai. Really."

The concern from earlier turns into something nagging and irritable. He's avoiding me, and I want to know why. If what Oscar said is true, we should talk about it. The last thing I want is to lose him as a friend.

Julian steps into the dorm room fully and begins stepping out of his wet shoes.

"I know you, Julian. I know something's bothering you. Please just talk to me. Whatever it is, you don't have to hide it from me. You know I've always had your back, no matter what."

Julian pauses, and a shadow of annoyance crosses over his expression. "It's complicated."

I take my chances and decide to make a playful joke. "No offense, but when is it ever *not* complicated with you? Remember that time you tried to charm your way out of three different speeding tickets in one day? You can't even keep a road trip simple. Or the time you organized that spontaneous weekend trip to Vancouver—only to forget your passport and sweet-talk the customs officer into letting you through. Everything with you turns into an adventure."

Julian smirks and looks down at the floor. The storm rages outside, and somehow, the dim room seems smaller in the dark. Julian is standing still, dripping wet, clearly struggling internally.

And for some reason, my heart is racing.

Julian runs his hand through his wet hair. "It's just... everything's changing, Kai. England, my family, us. I don't know how to deal with it. I want everything to stay the same. I'm happy here."

With me, I think.

I swallow. "You mean me? You don't know how to deal with me leaving?"

He freezes, and his eyes flick up to mine. "That's not what I—"

"Then what?" I cut in, taking a step closer. I know I'm pushing him. The truth is, I'm scared of his answer. But I *need* to know. Can't stand the thought of not knowing. "Because you've been acting weird since I told you I'd be moving out. And I don't think it's just about you going back to England."

The corner of Julian's mouth twists with exasperation. "What do you want me to say, Kai? That I'm scared of leaving? Of losing this—us?"

My heart thumps against my ribs, and it feels like I can't breathe. "That'd be a good start."

There's another tense pause. The air feels heavy, charged with more than just the storm outside.

"I'm scared of everything. What happens next... and what I'm feeling."

My throat tightens with anticipation, and I ball my fists at my sides. "What are you feeling?"

Julian stops moving. One shoe is off, and his face and hair are still wet. He's drenched and vulnerable, and his guard is down in a way I've never seen before. It's disorienting, and my mind is reeling with confusion.

If someone had asked me if Julian was attractive, I'd have said yes. He's my best friend... of course I noticed the way people's eyes tracked his features, his muscular build, his bright smile.

But now?

Now I can't help but notice the way the stark light from the flashlight catches the blond scruff along his angular jaw, the sharp cut of it softened only by the faintest shadow. His thick brows frame those piercing blue eyes, cool and stormy beneath dark lashes that brush his skin when he blinks.

"I don't know what to do with this. With... you. Every time I'm around you lately, it's... different, and I can't figure out how to deal with it." His voice is uncharacteristically unsteady, as if he's struggling to find the right words. "I don't know how to handle it."

I attempt to steady my voice, but my hands are shaking. "Maybe you don't have to handle anything. You can just... let it be what it is."

Julian takes a deep breath, finally meeting my eyes. There's something raw and desperate in his gaze.

"And what if what it is... isn't what I thought it'd be? What if it's something I can't take back?" His voice breaks on the last word, and I unconsciously take a step closer.

"Then maybe it's something you don't need to take back."

The words are out of my mouth before I can contemplate them.

Julian stares at me, and the distance between us suddenly feels like too much. He takes one step forward, then another, his chest rising and falling quickly. I don't move, watching Julian's internal battle play out on his face and letting it happen.

Because maybe I want it to happen.

"Can I try something?" Julian asks, his voice quiet.

The air between us suddenly feels different. *Heavier.* His eyes, barely visible in the dark, search my face like he's waiting for me to say no.

I don't.

Instead, I swallow and answer. "Yeah."

"Turn off the light. I can't—I can't look at you while I—"

I flick the light off before he can finish his sentence. My pulse rages in my veins, and a strange ripple shoots down my spine. I shift slightly, attempting to ease the knot tightening low in my stomach, but the movement only makes me more aware of him. It sparks something—a ripple of heat that catches me off guard. It's as if my body knows what's happening before my mind does, and before I can stop it, a warm, heady ache unfurls low in my gut.

It's unmistakable now—spreading, insistent. My cock feels heavy... half hard at first, like it's testing the waters.

And then it gets achingly rigid.

My mind is racing, bouncing between the fear of what this could mean and the hope that it's exactly what I want, though I can't even admit that to myself yet or explain this wild fucking turn of events. I can feel the weight of the silence between us, heavy, charged. But what if this is a mistake? What if I'm wrong, and everything changes for the worse? He's my best friend. If this goes wrong, what happens to us?

But... the thought of him being this close, of something happening... it makes my chest tighten with anticipation.

The sound of his ragged breathing gives me goosebumps, and I can smell the shampoo he uses—it's herbal and minty and *familiar.*

A split second of lightning illuminates the room for half a second, and the look on Julian's face makes me inhale sharply. Determination. Courage. But also... fear.

I hear him take a step closer, and he's close enough now that I can feel the heat radiating from him. Everything inside of me is burning—probably because the jackass in front of me has the heater set to eighty.

Or maybe he's the one making me feel like I'm about to spontaneously combust.

"Please don't be scared," he murmurs, almost whispering. "I just... I need to know. But you can tell me to stop."

The connotation of his words, of what he's about to do, sends a wave of anxiety through me.

"Okay," I say softly.

He takes another step closer. *Julian.* My best friend. The bizarre situation before us almost makes me laugh, but it feels too serious to laugh. I feel heavy and grounded, almost like I'm going to implode from wanting—*needing*—to see what he's going to do.

One of his hands finds my jacket, and he slowly tugs me closer to him. Everything inside of me is pulsing, hinging on this one strange moment with him. He pulls me even closer so that we're standing chest to chest, and I can smell the sweet, buttery scent of his breath, and the musky scent of *him*.

I'd never considered how he smelled before this moment, but I don't hate it. In fact, the smell of him—of something rich with hints of bergamot—brings me comfort. I'm desperately trying to see his face, but it's still too dark to see anything.

I need to know if he's about to do what I think he's

about to do. I need to prepare myself, and I don't like not knowing.

"Seriously," he whispers, his breath fanning across my face. He's close. "Just tell me this is a fucked-up idea and we never have to talk about it a—"

I fist his shirt and pull his mouth to mine.

We both go still, and I swear he must be able to hear how hard my heart is hammering in my chest. His lips are hard and unmoving, and the only thing I can hear is the sharp, surprised staccato of his breathing through his nostrils.

Fuck.

I kissed him.

I made the first move.

And now he's too stunned to move, and *holy shit* what if I got it all wrong—

He moves his tongue over my lower lip and parts my lips with it. White-hot heat flares through me, and my whole body tingles as his warm hands come to my torso. I don't know what I'm doing, but my body does.

I pull him closer like I've done it a hundred times before.

He tastes like the popcorn we were just eating, but also something minty and wild. The second my tongue lashes against his, it's like a fire has been lit beneath me.

I pull him into my torso by his shirt, gripping it for stability. He lets out a surprised sigh against my lips before pushing me back against my desk. My thighs hit the edge, and then he's knocking my legs apart with his foot so that he can step between them.

Julian taking charge shouldn't surprise me, but it does.

Only because it's laughable that he thinks *he'd* be in charge.

I push him backward until he hits his desk, and the sound of something falling has us both huffing laughter as we fight to stay connected. He tries to push me backward, but I move one hand to the base of his throat, and I feel him go still underneath me before he groans.

It's a husky, deep sound that has my whole body tingling.

"Kai," he whispers. "Fuck."

I move my hands to his hips. I'm not even sure what I'm doing—I've only kissed a girl two times, never had sex, and *never* felt like this.

Like I'm already addicted to something I've never tasted before.

Arousal crawls down my spine, sinking into my balls and causing my cock to throb. Well, this is... *new*. I press into him harder, feeling frenzied and frantic. Julian's tongue sweeps along my lower lip again, and then he pulls that same lip between his teeth, and I...

"Fuck," I hiss, dragging his hips against mine and rocking myself against his hard length.

He releases a heady moan. "Stop doing that unless you want to take this further than you're willing to go," Julian says into my mouth.

The shock of his words, commanding and intense, causes me to stumble back.

My eyes have adjusted enough to see the outline of his body, but I can't see his expression.

"Sorry," he mutters, lifting a hand to his lips.

I huff a nervous laugh. "For what? I kissed you, Julian."

"I— Yeah. You did." He places a hand at the back of his neck. "Why?"

"Just saving you the trouble of making the first move."

He blushes. "Fair enough."

His face starts to become visible, and he's watching me with a disoriented expression. I don't move. I can't. Everything feels charged, like we're standing on the precipice of something life-changing.

"I'm not gay," he says, his voice frayed.

"I know," I say, though I'm not entirely sure why I'm trying to placate him. "But you're not straight, either."

He laughs again. "Is anyone one hundred percent straight? You're not either. *Obviously*."

My lips quirk. "Fair enough."

"How long?" he asks, and I know what he's asking. He's buying time, and I'm not sure if it's from nerves, or something else.

I shrug. "An hour? I dunno. It never occurred to me that you'd…" Looking down, I'm not sure what I'm trying to say. "What about you?"

He doesn't answer. I look up, and he's watching me with narrowed eyes. "This doesn't change anything, right?"

"One kiss? Nah."

"You sure?"

I nod. "We're cool."

"I really do need some fresh air," he says, walking over to where he stepped out of his shoes. "I'll be back later. Don't wait up."

He's gone before I can think of something to say.

Something to stop him.

Something to get him to kiss me again.

I stand frozen, lips still tingling. The dorm feels bigger, emptier, and the space between us has never felt so wide. Letting out a shaky breath, I run a hand through my hair and try to quell the unease and confusion that I'm feeling. I drop my head back until I'm staring at the ceiling.

What the hell was that?

I'm still trembling, so I close my eyes and take several deep breaths. My first instinct is to call Liam or Miles, my older brothers, but I don't even know what they'd say. When I open my eyes, I look around the dorm room. Flicking the flashlight back on, I change into sweatpants and a T-shirt before grabbing my toothbrush. The walk to the communal bathroom is eerie in the dark, but the voices behind the door are comforting. I quickly brush my teeth and wash my face, and just as I'm drying my neck with a hand towel, the lights flicker back on.

I can't help but stare at my reflection.

I'm not gay.

I know. But you're not straight, either.

I'd never really contemplated my sexuality before tonight. I just assumed I was straight. I took a girl to homecoming and prom. I had a girlfriend for a couple of months junior year of high school. But I wasn't like Chase, my younger brother. He's the popular guy in high school, and all the girls flock to him. And me? I preferred to watch everything from the sidelines. I stuck to hanging out with Julian and his friends.

I think back to senior year, and how Julian and I had been dubbed "Best Bromance." We'd laughed it off, and I never even thought about if it bothered him. Why would it? He dated around a lot. He loved women.

He might not be straight, but he's not gay.

But… am I?

I blow out a slow breath of air. I got *hard* for my best friend. I can still feel his lips on mine, taste the butter and mint, hear the frenzied way he said my name.

Kai. Fuck.

It had been supplicant and desperate. Just the thought of Julian saying my name like that…

It makes me want to scream.

I flick my eyes up to my reflection, and I look haunted. My short, dark hair is messy as always, and my gray eyes have dark circles underneath them. I've been told I'm attractive, and I suppose I've always just accepted it, but now… now I'm not sure what I see. There's something different. Maybe it's in the way my lips still tingle, like they're betraying me with memories I shouldn't have.

His lips. Julian's lips.

I can't stop thinking about it. It wasn't supposed to feel like this—this deep, gnawing confusion in my chest, like something's come undone inside me and I don't know how to stop it. I'd kissed him. And in that moment, it felt like everything clicked into place... and shattered all at once.

It was just a kiss. Just a silly, impulsive kiss.

But my head's spinning, and I can't stop replaying it over and over, searching for something that makes sense. Something that tells me what I want it to mean.

What should it mean? I can't even tell if I want it to mean anything, or if I'm terrified that it does.

No.

This isn't me. It can't be me. I'm not... like that. I've never been like that. I like girls. *I'm supposed to like girls.*

My reflection comes back into focus.

I don't even recognize the person staring back at me.

Why can't I just stop thinking about it? Why can't I stop thinking about him?

About him. *Him.*

I grit my teeth, gripping the edge of the sink until my knuckles turn white, trying to shake off the feeling. Julian's my friend, and that's all he's ever going to be.

That's all I can ever give him.

I'd kissed him. *I'd kissed him.*

His lips—*Julian's* lips.

It doesn't mean anything.

It can't mean anything.

It was just... just a mistake.

A ridiculous mistake.

I push myself away from the sink, trying to shove the thoughts down, and bury them deep where they can't reach me. As I walk out of the bathroom, I catch a glimpse of Julian coming down the hallway, his eyes meeting mine, hopeful, maybe even confused.

But I can't face him. Not now... not after what happened. I twist around and walk the other way. My heart pounds in my chest. *Don't look back.*

Not now.

Not ever.

Every step feels heavy, like I'm not just walking away from Julian.

I'm walking away from our friendship: everything we were, every memory, every secret.

But I can't stop.

I have to keep moving.

Even if it means losing him forever.

CHAPTER ONE
THE ATTACHMENT

Sophie

Present

"Honey, I'm home!" I say cheerfully, removing my leather riding gloves and setting my keys on the marble table next to the front door. I like the way the words echo through the empty house. It feels... satisfying. A reminder that this house is mine as much as it's his.

Even if I still don't know what to do with all this space.

The house is quiet, but Julian's car is in the driveway, so I know he's home. Walking through the foyer full of plastic sheeting from the renovations, my boots clack against the floor lined with cardboard. My riding helmet is hanging on my arm, but just as I set it down on the table, a deep voice floats down the stairwell.

"Put it back on. You look so fucking adorable in it."

I smirk when I twist around to find Julian gliding down the stairs in a three-piece suit that fits him impossibly well. My heart squeezes at the sight of him, and I stand there trying not to smile as he walks over to me. Julian has always been larger than life. And sometimes I wonder if I blend into the background of our picture-perfect marriage. The devoted, doting wife. The calm to his storm. It's not a bad thing... but some days, I want to be more than just the reflection of his light.

I place the helmet back on and clip the strap together to appease him. "Oh? Do you happen to have a thing for sweat? Because I'm sure I smell like the bollocks of the horse I was riding—"

He grins as he picks me up by the waist and lifts me over his shoulder. "My wife? Smell? Never." He smacks my arse and I slap his in retaliation as I squeal with surprise and laughter. "Even if you do, you know I like it when you're a little... musky."

"You're disgusting," I tell him, the blood rushing to my face from being upside down.

He chuckles as he carries me up the stairs at a jog like I weigh nothing at all.

It's one of the things I love about him—one of the reasons I agreed to the marriage. The way he touches me, the way he handles me, still gives me fanny flutters even now, almost ten years on.

"Come on, wife. Let's get you undressed so I can ruin you for all other men."

"Ha ha ha."

He walks down the hallway and into our bedroom before depositing me on our hand-embroidered bedding.

"At least have the decency to take my bloody boots off," I huff, glaring up at him from under the helmet.

"At your service, my Lady."

My lips twitch but I don't allow a smile as Julian kneels before me, sliding the riding boots off one at a time. His hands then work their way up my sore calves to my thighs, where he pushes my knees apart and leans forward. My breathing hitches as his hands come to my hips and skim along the waistband of my tan breeches. I inhale sharply as he tugs the trousers down slowly, and I lift my arse so that he can get them down my legs. He removes my sweaty socks and I reach up to unbuckle my helmet.

I could stop him right now. I probably should—my hair is plastered to my forehead, and my breeches smell like leather and sweat. But I don't. I like the way he looks at me when I let him take charge.

"If you're going to act like a savage brute, at least let me shower beforehand."

My helmet falls off the bed, and I begin unbuttoning my navy riding jacket. Tugging it off and unbuttoning my white blouse, I remove them quickly, leaving me clad only in my white knickers and bra.

"No," he says simply.

"Julian, I've been out there all day, and it's hot—"

"Don't care."

I huff a laugh. "Stubborn mule."

"Yes, but I'm your stubborn mule."

I run a hand through his soft, blond hair affectionately. "Yes, you are."

He groans as he nuzzles his nose along the inside of my thigh. "I've been waiting for you for hours," he says in a faux-whining tone.

"You've been working."

"And? I can still miss my wife while I work. Plus, work is not that important anyway. Not as important as your cunt."

I smile because I know he means it. But I can't help but wonder if loving me is too easy for him. Would he love me as much if I became someone else—someone who didn't need him as much? The thought unsettles me, and I push it away.

"Julian—" His lips graze the seam of my knickers, and I wince.

"Shh," he whispers, moving them to the side with his teeth.

"Please let me shower first," I beg, inhaling sharply when his tongue slides through my seam.

"Mmm. Imagine how much fun we'll have with our shower bench. So much potential for shower fucking."

"If it ever gets built," I mutter, gasping when he inserts one finger inside of me. My back arches, and he curves his finger just so... "Fuck," I whisper, looking down at him with heavy eyelids. "It's hard to imagine something that might never happen," I add quickly and sarcastically.

"Shh, pet. No renovation talk while my tongue is on your pussy."

His dirty words make me bark a laugh. "You're shameless." He inserts another finger, and that effectively shuts me up. "Holy shit. Yes. Right there—"

"I love how vocal you are, Soph. Drives me mad," he says against my labia.

"Yes, well, you're just very good at your job."

"I know."

His tongue slowly explores me, swirling over my sensitive bud with the practice and ease of someone who knows my body like the back of his hand.

"Fuck." I circle my hips as he continues. Everything inside of me draws tight, and my eyes squeeze shut. "Julian—"

He withdraws his fingers and my eyes snap open as he stands up. "That's it," he says, chin wet. He licks his lips salaciously and loosens his tie. "Take off your knickers."

I do as he says with a scowl, tugging them down a little too roughly and flinging them at his face. He pulls the tie loose from his collar, and then he shrugs off his suit jacket. My eyes track the crumpled wool and mohair, and I narrow my eyes.

"Only you would discard a custom-made suit on the floor."

"Promise to pick it up after we're done, pet," he murmurs, unbuttoning the sleeves of his white Oxford shirt.

I smirk as I pull my white sports bra over my head. "Done? Doing what?"

His blond hair falls over his forehead, and my heart skips a beat as he begins unbuttoning the front of his shirt. When he's playful like this, he reminds me *so* much of the man I fell in love with ten years ago.

"You know what."

I twist my lips to the side as I lean back on my elbows. "Well, then, hurry up."

He huffs a laugh as he discards the white shirt onto the floor, and I roll my eyes. Julian has a lot of fabulous, positive traits, but being tidy is not one of them.

As he steps out of his trousers and boxers, I can't help but admire his physique. He's muscular but not chiseled and obsessed about it. His arms are corded, and his biceps could put some of these younger fit guys at his gym to shame. His blond hair makes him look younger than his thirty-five years, but there's a sprinkling of gray in his scruff which gives his age away.

My stomach clenches as my eyes drag down to his hard cock.

"Spread your legs for your husband," he says, arching a brow. "Or do I have to do it for you?" he adds, moving my legs apart. "My God. Look at that gorgeous cunt."

I bite my lower lip as he pushes me flat on the bed and crawls on top of me. Placing quick kisses along my stomach, breasts, and neck, his lips finally find mine just before he pushes into me.

"Oh God," I gasp. His eyes bore into mine as he

begins to fuck me relentlessly. "Yes, just like that," I hiss, loving the feel of him inside of me like this.

Loving the look on his face when he drives into me.

If I ever doubted how much Julian Ashford loved me, it wouldn't be during those first few moments of sex. He always looks at me like I'm something to be cherished and revered, and I hope I never take this for granted.

His movements are smooth and familiar, and I move my left knee higher so that he knows I want it over his shoulder.

"Please," I whimper.

He gives me a cocky smile as he positions my left leg so that it's over his shoulder. My nails pierce into his biceps as he pounds into me, and I groan.

"Harder."

He grunts and leans down to kiss me before he slowly drags his thick cock out.

"Now, now... how do you ask politely?"

I roll my eyes. "Pretty please."

Giving me a lopsided smile, he places one hand around the base of my throat as the other one holds himself up on top of me.

"Who fucks you the best?" he asks, nuzzling his mouth onto the place along my collarbone that sends shivers down my spine every time. That, mixed with the possessive tone of his voice...

It sends me reeling every time.

"You," I whisper, panting.

"Who knows exactly what you want?"

"*You*," I moan. "It'll always be you, Julian."

"That's right, baby. *Me.* Don't ever forget it."

He squeezes his hand a bit tighter around my throat, just enough to cause my orgasm to shatter through me unexpectedly.

"Yes," I hiss, arching my back as waves of pleasure light me up from inside. My toes curl and my eyes roll back as Julian moves his hand down between my legs, extending the pleasure with his thumb on my clit, dragging it out until I'm twitching and gasping.

"That's it," he says, his voice ragged. "Fuck, Soph—"

The low, heady groan that escapes his lips is a holy experience. His jaw goes slack as he comes inside of me, and his arm next to my head trembles.

When he's done, he pulls out of me and lays down next to me, breathing hard.

I look over at him as my chest rises and falls, and then we both laugh.

"That was unexpected," I tell him, kissing the scruff along his jaw as I wrap an arm around his warm torso. "But I know what you're doing."

He smirks as he kisses my nose. "And what is it that I'm doing?"

"It's Saturday."

"And?" he asks, turning to face me.

"You're being territorial," I say softly, propping my head up on my elbow.

His smile starts slow and grows as the seconds pass. "Territorial? Perhaps. But I'm also excited." He takes my hand and brings it to his still-hard cock. "See? Just thinking of another man fucking my wife makes me lose my mind with lust."

I pull my lips to one side as I study his expression. "You'd tell me if you felt otherwise, right?"

He leans over and kisses my forehead. "I would. I promise."

"Okay. Because I'd give it up right now if you decided you didn't enjoy it anymore."

"Mmm, look at us having such a healthy conversation like adults. Communication, baby."

I laugh. "I love you."

"I love you too, pet."

He sits up and walks to the en suite bathroom that only has a working sink. The shower and toilet are still under construction, as is most of the house. I suppose that's what we get for buying a house that needed a lot of repairs.

He walks out a few seconds later with a warm washcloth, and my heart squeezes as he slowly runs it between my legs to clean me up.

"Now I really need a shower," I tell him.

"Me too. Care to join me?" he asks, discarding the washcloth onto the floor.

I click my tongue, and he sighs before he picks it up and walks it to the laundry basket a few feet away. He even makes a show of plucking our dirty clothes off the floor and walking those to the laundry basket after.

"I'd love to join you," I tell him, but before I can stand up, he picks me up from the bed and carries me out of the bedroom in his arms.

"Julian! There are workers in the garden—"

He chuckles. "That's all the way outside. There's no one here."

We walk into the small guest bathroom—the one we're using for the time being—and we step into the shower together. Julian begins washing my hair, his fingers gently massaging my scalp. The motion is practiced, something he enjoys doing whenever we shower together. I lean back into his touch, letting the warm water wash over me.

"This okay?" he asks, his voice low and soft.

"Perfect," I murmur.

Once my hair is rinsed, he reaches for the soap, lathering it carefully before he begins to wash my body. His touch is familiar, yet grounding. Firm yet tender.

When we're done, he dries me off, and I look up at him with a shy smile.

"God, Soph," he murmurs, kissing my forehead. "When you look at me like that..." He trails off, and his eyes go watery. "I'm the luckiest fucking man alive."

"I love you," I tell him, placing my cheek against his chest.

"I love you more."

After we get dressed—he in another three-piece suit, and me in loose jeans and a cashmere jumper—we walk downstairs hand in hand to survey the progress of the renovations. My hair is still damp, so I shake it out with my hand as we walk between sheets of plastic to the kitchen.

"The cabinet handles came in today," he tells me as we walk into what looks like a woodworking shop.

There are large pieces of raw wood everywhere, bits of sawdust, cans of paint, and more of that plastic fucking sheet material. I knew a renovation of this size would take a long time, but as I survey the damage, I can't envision an end.

I can't visualize myself here yet.

I can't *see* the picture Julian is always trying to paint of the finished project.

All I can concentrate on is the mess.

And I hate when things are messy.

Julian sees it—the finished house, the perfect picture. But I struggle. I don't want to just live inside someone else's vision. I need something that feels like mine. A room, a project, a purpose. Something that isn't plaster and marble.

"This brass will look nice against the brown cabinets," Julian says, handing me a piece of what I'm assuming will be a handle.

My thumb brushes over the high-quality metal. I know, from what the designer showed us, that this kitchen will be state of the art.

Only the best for my husband, Lord Julian Archer Ashford, Viscount of Brookshire.

I sigh as I lean against the marble island. "I'm excited to see it all come together. Right now, it just feels... excruciatingly slow going."

Julian presses me into the island and steps between my legs as he takes my other hand.

"I've been thinking... maybe we should throw a party when it's all done. Something big and grand. A way to celebrate what we're building here."

Julian smiles. "I like it. Obviously the best champagne, Michelin-starred chefs, live music—"

"Imagine how gorgeous the staircase would look with some of those fresh magnolia flowers from the tree outside," I chime in, my heart racing with excitement. "Fresh seafood... we have to take advantage of living so close to the ocean," I explain. "And once your art and my books arrive..." He grins. My eyes flick between his eyes. "What?"

He kisses me—long, deep, and slow. When he pulls away, he lets out a tortured sigh.

"That sounds perfect."

"Now we just have to find some friends to fill the place up," I say sarcastically.

"What about Stella Ravage?"

"Yes, but she's my *only* friend. And I'm pretty sure she only took pity on me because she designed the dress I wore to that gala last year, we both happen to be British, and we live in the same city."

"But you like her, right?"

"Oh, she's fabulous. But..." I look around. "I don't know. I know we've already been here for two months. It's just that reality is setting in, and I miss my friends in London."

Julian smooths a hand over my hair as he pulls me into his hard body for a hug. His hand continues to stroke the back of my head, and I hum contentedly, going completely limp in his arms.

"I know."

"Do you have any friends we can invite to this hypothetical housewarming party?"

He stiffens slightly—enough for me to notice.

I pull away. "What about that friend you had growing up? Isn't he related to Stella, somehow?"

Julian's blue eyes narrow slightly. "Malakai Ravage? Yeah, he's Stella's husband's younger brother. We used to be close, but it's been almost two decades."

"You guys didn't keep in touch after you moved back to London?"

"No."

The change in his temperament is apparent, but just as I open my mouth to ask about Malakai, he takes a step back.

"I should get back to work. Need anything before I go?"

I shrug. "Another expensive hobby? A career? Perhaps an invisible friend?"

He huffs a laugh. "You know I'd fully support anything you wanted to do. I've been telling you for years to get a job or go back to school."

I place a hand over my heart. "And send my mother to an early grave? Never," I add, speaking in my mother's posh, aristocratic accent.

He gives me a roguish smile. "Fuck her."

I snort. "For now, I'll settle for toiling away with

riding, reading, renovations, and this housewarming party."

He winks as he begins walking out of the kitchen area. "It's going to be the best party ever if you're the one holding the reins."

"You know it will be."

"Love you," he calls as he walks through the house.

"You too," I say to myself.

Once he's gone, I sigh and look around the mess. Grabbing the brass handle, I pass it between my hands. I let my thumb brush over smooth curves before setting it down again. I know I can't hurry up the renovations. I can't force the workers to show up faster or make the house look like the magazine spreads Julian envisions. But I can do *something*. A drawer. A room. One small thing at a time.

I set the handle down carefully—like I've made a decision, even if I'm not sure what it is yet.

Walking out of the kitchen, I make my way up the stairs to my office.

It's one of the only finished rooms in the house, and it's a soft, pink color. I love it, but I have no idea what to do with it. My stomach does that fluttery, butterfly thing when I think of what I *want* to do. I want to start my own business. I want to work my way up, put in long hours, and attend meetings. I want to *create* something I'd love as a consumer.

I just don't know what that is yet.

Maybe that's what scares me the most—the not knowing. I'm not afraid of hard work. I'm not afraid of starting from scratch. But the thought of never finding that *thing*? That terrifies me. I want to matter. I want something that feels like *mine* in a way this house, this marriage, can't give me.

My mother had made it very clear that when I married Julian, there'd be no reason to get a job. And since we'd been married right after I graduated college, there was no time to dabble in anything.

I grew up the only child in an upper-class, English family. That meant my father worked and earned money, my mother spent her time at brunch and shopping, and the nanny raised me.

And when I learned that my parents planned to marry me off to Lord Julian Ashford? It seemed like a dream. He was a bit older, handsome, titled, and he'd take care of me forever.

I don't think they ever expected Julian to turn his back on his aristocratic duties, or for him to take my side over and over and over.

I don't think they expected us to walk away from everything in England to move to Southern California, but here we are.

In the end, we chose happiness over heritage. The freedom of being selfishly, recklessly in love, and finding a place that was all our own—without the weight of his title and estate holding us captive—felt like the first thing we'd ever truly owned.

No expectations. No duty. Just us, carving out a life that wasn't dictated by bloodlines or obligations.

That's why he built this office for me. *One day,* he'd said.

I sit down in my white chair and spin around a few times. I remember what I said about the magnolia tree, and suddenly, I have a thousand ideas for the housewarming party.

Grabbing a fresh notebook and a pen, I begin writing things down with a large smile on my face.

I don't know what my business will be yet, but as I stare out the window, I have to hope it'll come to me soon. Maybe I just need a sign.

Or maybe it's time I stop waiting for signs and create one myself.

CHAPTER TWO
THE REUNION

Julian

I grimace as I lift the barbell again, grunting as I finish the set.

Setting the weight down, I do the other arm as I focus on my form in the mirror. I *fucking* hate this. I swear this gym is filled with masochists. There's no other explanation. Every time I pick up a barbell, I mentally draft a resignation letter to fitness, but then I remember the smoothie bar and suck it up. It's the only thing keeping me from skipping out entirely.

At least with cardio, I can zone out and watch TV. But weight training? It requires my full attention, which is extremely hard, and it's boring. My mind keeps flitting between ten different things I'd rather be doing, but counting reps helps to yank my focus back to what I'm doing. I promised myself I'd work out more regularly for my mental health, so here I am—at Crestwood's most exclusive VIP gym. I had a gym in our town house in London, but I never used it. I figured if I paid for a membership, I'd come more often.

So far, so good.

Tracking every weight increase, every rep—as if the numbers mean something more than just strength—helps keep me sane. It's ridiculous, I know, but I enjoy seeing tangible progress.

Toweling my face off, I walk over to where I set my phone down.

> SOPHIE LOVE <3
>
> I just learned people microwave their tea here. I think I'm experiencing culture shock. Help. Me.

I laugh as I text her back.

> That has to be a cardinal sin.

I shake my head, picturing Sophie's horrified face as she holds a mug like it's been cursed.

> Should I call the embassy? You could claim asylum.

> SOPHIE LOVE <3
>
> I'll look into it. ;)

> I just need to do some presses and then I'll be home.

SOPHIE LOVE <3

Mmm. Sounds hot. See you soon.

Pocketing my phone, I walk over to the bench press and set my things down. It's late afternoon and today is Saturday, which means...

I swallow as I towel my face off again. No use in thinking about it now, or I'll be sporting a very inconvenient erection.

As always, that brief moment of internalized shame washes over me.

I mean, I love Sophie so *fucking* much.

But I also love watching her *fuck* other men.

It doesn't make sense. I can't reconcile the two halves of myself—the man who was taught to protect and the man who finds pleasure in letting go. But maybe that's the point. Maybe I like the idea of breaking rules I never agreed to in the first place.

It's the kind of thing I shouldn't like. Not with the way I was raised—straitlaced, taught to keep things proper and respectable. The idea of *sharing* anything like that, of getting a thrill from it, goes against everything drilled into me growing up. Saturdays always bring that wobble, the knot in my gut tightening just enough to remind me that part of me still clings to what I was supposed to believe.

Lying down on the bench, I push those thoughts away. I focus on lifting, on the fact that I've added weight to the barbell every day I've been here this week.

Sometimes it's nice to see concrete progress in one

aspect of my life, especially considering the house is still up in the air. I've never been huge on working out, but I feel so much better physically and mentally since prioritizing it. It's fucking hard in the moment, but there's no glory without hard work.

I'm breathing heavily when I finish, so I sit up slowly and towel myself off.

Movement in the mirror catches my eye, and I see a man with his back to me lifting a fuck-ton of weight on the shoulder press. He's shirtless, and the muscles on his back ripple with every controlled, up-and-down movement. I can't help but appreciate the wide shoulders, corded forearms, and tapered waist. *That* is why I work out—to look like that guy. My eyes peruse a bit lower, taking in his muscular calves and black trainers. His hair is dark and short, and though I can't see his face, I can appreciate the even, golden complexion of his skin.

Reminds me of—

I close my eyes and shake that thought from my head.

Standing, I walk over to the smoothie bar. It's my treat after every workout, and the best part of becoming a member of this gym, if I'm being totally honest.

As a young woman begins to blend my kale and mango smoothie with extra protein, I let myself think about Malakai Ravage.

I'd give anything to go back to that night in the dorms—to rein my feelings in a bit better, to keep my emotions in check. He was my bisexual awakening, and despite only ever sleeping with two men before Sophie, Kai was my Achilles' heel.

The one that got away.

Sophie knows about my sexuality, but she has no idea that Malakai started it all. It never felt right telling her about what happened—and to be honest, I'd pushed that night so far back in my mind. I was angry at Kai for years, but now? I'm better. I've forgiven him. I *mean, for the most part at least.* Sophie makes me happy. And I hope Kai is, too, wherever he is. We don't follow each other on social media, so I don't even know if he still lives in Crestwood, but I'd be lying if I said I wasn't curious.

Especially since Sophie and Stella Ravage are friends now.

"Kale and mango with dragon fruit," the woman calls, letting me know it's ready.

"Thanks," I tell her, tapping the virtual tip jar with my phone and depositing one hundred dollars.

Her eyes go wide, but I'm already walking to the locker room and sipping the delicious smoothie.

As I walk into the locker room, I notice the same guy from earlier changing. I nearly stop walking as he tugs his shorts down and I get a full view of his perfectly sculpted arse. *Damn.* Smirking, I walk to my locker nearby and begin grabbing things for my shower. When I turn around, the man is gone, but the sound of a shower starting around the corner tells me he hasn't gone far. We seem to be the only two people in here, which is only minorly creepy.

I shower quickly, rinsing the sweat off and letting the

hot water run down my face and chest. The showers here are the cleanest I've ever seen, and it doesn't feel like a locker room shower. It feels like a nice hotel shower, and considering Sophie and I are living out of a tiny guest bathroom with a capsule shower, this feels luxurious in comparison.

Shutting the water off, I grab my towel and open the door of the shower room, running smack-dab into another body.

"Fuck—"

"Sorry—"

I stumble back, blinking the water from my eyes. I look up, and my heart stops dead in my chest before hammering out of control.

Malakai Ravage.

Time slows in that shitty cinematic way I hate. I notice everything—the water dripping down his collarbones, the faint nick on his jawline from shaving.

I hate that my brain still catalogs him like this.

He's staring at me, his gray eyes wide with surprise, and then recognition clicks into place. Drops of water trail down the scruff on his neck, over his bare chest, all the way down to the hard lines of his abs. He looks… different. *Older*. Rougher around the edges. But it's him.

It's Kai.

My pulse spikes, not from shock but from everything I've buried for the last seventeen years, and God, I hate that. I thought the next time I saw Malakai, I'd be able to control my emotions, but… a fiery maelstrom burns through me instantly.

For a moment, I'm frozen. My breath catches, and all the anger, the confusion, the *hurt*—it all rises up again, clawing at the walls I've spent years building. But it's dulled, worn down by time. It's not sharp anymore, not like it used to be. I guess I'm thankful for that.

I have no right to be angry anymore. Life moved on. I moved on. I have Sophie now. I'm happy. *Really happy*. But damn if it doesn't still sting, seeing him here, like this, like nothing's changed when everything has.

I swallow hard and pull myself together, wiping away whatever shadow of emotion might've crossed my face. I won't give him that. Not anymore. I grip the towel tighter around my neck, like that's going to do anything to stop my pulse from racing.

"Malakai."

I say his name like I'm trying it on for size, but it doesn't fit right anymore. Too tight. Too worn in all the wrong places. My voice is steady, but there's an edge to it, one I can't quite hide. I nod, forcing some semblance of civility, even though every part of me feels like it's vibrating with tension.

Kai blinks again, taking me in, and his lips part as if he's about to say something. He doesn't, though. Just stares at me like he's still trying to figure out what to do with me being here.

But I'm not giving him the satisfaction of asking. He lost that chance a long time ago.

"Julian? You... look different," he finally manages, voice lower and rougher than I remember.

"So do you." My lips twitch into a humorless smile,

and I let my gaze flick over him again before I snap it back to his face. I won't let myself linger. *Not again.*

The silence stretches, heavy, as if neither of us knows what to say next. Or maybe there's too much to say, and neither of us knows where to start. It's almost suffocating, this unspoken weight between us, the years, the memories, the *kiss* that never got a chance to become anything more.

He clears his throat, shifting on his feet. "What are you doing here?" His words are careful, like he's walking on glass, unsure of how thin the ice is beneath us.

I offer a half-smile that doesn't quite reach my eyes. "Funny, I was about to ask you the same thing." I don't mean for it to sound as harsh as it does, but it slips out before I can stop it. It feels easier to deflect than to explain the knot tightening in my chest.

His expression falters, and I know he catches it. The sting beneath the surface. I see something like regret cross his face, but I won't fall for that either. Not now.

I sigh, forcing myself to release the tension in my shoulders. "We just recently moved back from London," I explain.

"We?" he asks, brows knitting together.

"My wife, Sophie, and I."

I say it like I'm laying down a card in a game we're both pretending not to play. Kai watches me carefully, but I flash him the same grin I give everyone.

Unbothered.

Easygoing.

Like it doesn't matter.

Except my fingers won't stop drumming against the water bottle in my hand.

I shift, leaning casually against the lockers as if we're just two old friends catching up. As if my pulse isn't still trying to break free of my chest.

This is what I do—what I've always done. Keep it light. Don't let anyone know when something cuts deeper than I want to admit. It works everywhere else. It always has. But standing here in front of Kai? I can feel the edges of that easy grin start to slip.

He nods slowly, his throat bobbing as he swallows. "That's great," he says, voice soft, almost hesitant. "And you... go to this gym?"

"I do. I've been a few times a week since we moved here."

"I see."

The words hang there between us, and for a moment, I wonder if he's waiting for me to say something more. Maybe ask him *why* he left. Maybe confront him with the hurt I buried a long time ago. But I won't. That door was closed, locked, and I'm not opening it again. I hold his gaze, searching his face for any sign of the boy I once loved, but all I see is a stranger standing in front of me, soaked and silent.

"I should go. See you around," I say quietly, stepping around him, our shoulders brushing for just a moment as I pass.

I begin to walk away without looking back, leaving Malakai standing there with whatever weight he's carrying. It's not my burden to bear anymore. But even as I get to my locker, the sting of it all still lingers, a dull ache that time hasn't quite erased. And maybe it never will.

"Wait," Malakai calls, and I hear him come after me.

I turn back to face him, clenching my teeth to stop myself from saying something I might regret. Malakai's standing there, a little unsure, but there's something in his eyes—maybe hope or desperation, I'm not sure. And part of me wonders what he could possibly want after all this time.

He shifts awkwardly before he finally speaks. "I have an hour before I have to be somewhere. Want to grab a coffee and catch up?"

I cross my arms, narrowing my eyes at him. Do I have an hour? Not really. But I could make the time if I wanted to. The question is, *do* I want to? Should I give him the satisfaction of sitting down with him like nothing happened, like we're just two old friends reconnecting? I'm not sure if I'm ready for that—or if I even want to be.

What does he think a coffee is going to fix?

And yet, before I can stop myself, the word comes out. "Sure." The word leaves my mouth before I can snatch it back. I'm not sure if I said it because I want closure or because I'm still the same clown who can't say no to him.

Malakai's eyes light up, a small glimmer of triumph flashing across his face before he clears his throat, trying to play it cool. "Cool. Meet you out front in five?"

I nod, and we part ways without another word. As I walk off, towel still slung over my shoulder, I can't shake the feeling that this is a really, really bad idea.

The ache in my chest, the one I thought time had dulled, flares up again. Seeing him after all these years has kicked up dust I thought had long settled. And now I'm about to sit down with him, have coffee, and pretend like none of it ever happened?

What the hell am I doing?

I text Sophie so that she doesn't worry.

> Ran into Malakai at the gym. Going for a quick coffee, so I'll be home a bit later.

Her response comes in immediately.

SOPHIE LOVE <3
Okay, babe. Love you.

I stare at her response for a moment, the warmth of her words tugging at me, grounding me. *Love you.* Simple. Steady. Safe. It's everything I have with Sophie—everything I should be focusing on right now. But instead, I'm about to sit down with the one person who once shattered all of that before I even had the chance to know what it felt like.

CHAPTER THREE
THE CLASH

MALAKAI

I thumb my nose as I lean against the exterior wall of the gym. My workout bag is between my boots, and when I see Julian walk out of the gym a few feet away, I take a single, steadying breath.

Julian Ashford.

The one person I never expected to see again.

The one person I never expected to *speak* to me again—not after what I did.

But that's neither here nor there, because there's only one thing from our brief conversation earlier that keeps circling around in my mind.

We just recently moved back from London.
My wife, Sophie, and I.
Wife.

In all the scenarios that played out in my mind, I

never imagined Julian would get married to a woman. And I suppose that assumption is on me, because I should've known that just because he kissed me didn't mean he wasn't attracted to women.

I mean, I enjoyed that kiss seventeen years ago. *A fucking lot.* But I hadn't been with a man after him. I enjoyed women and I was sexually aroused by them.

It makes sense that perhaps Julian was the same.

In the last decade, I'd convinced myself I'd made peace with it. Now, I enjoyed the opposite sex and being the one in control—taking the lead, especially when it came to certain... extracurricular activities.

Saint Helena Academy would burst into flames if they knew what I got up to in my free time.

What happened between Julian and me—*the kiss*, the confusion, the way I left—was just the fumbling curiosity of two teenagers. At least, that's what I've told myself over and over again. We were friends, we were young, and for me, that's where it ended.

But as Julian walks toward me now—in a crisp white button-up and black trousers that cling a little too well to the muscle he's clearly built since I last saw him—I'm suddenly questioning how true that really is.

His damp, light blond hair falls messily over his forehead, and I can't help but glance at him, even though I keep telling myself not to. I take in the sharp cut of his jaw, the scruff that's grown in over the years, the way he's filled out.

It's purely objective.
It doesn't mean anything.

Just noticing the difference in him, that's all.

But even as the thought crosses my mind, I can't help but let my eyes trace the broadness of his shoulders, the way his chest has filled out under the fabric of his shirt. The Julian I knew at eighteen was all limbs and smiles— lanky, easygoing, with a lightness about him that made everything feel simpler.

But the Julian standing in front of me now? *He's all man.* Brooding, rough around the edges in a way he never was before, and when his blue eyes meet mine, there's a weight there I don't remember. A tension that wasn't there when we were young.

Something unspoken settles between us, and for a moment, I forget that I was the one who walked away. All I can think about is how much time has passed, and how much has changed—and whether or not I made the right choice all those years ago.

I shake my head as I push off the wall.

Of course I made the right choice to walk away.

The eighteen-year-old who got hard when he kissed his best friend wasn't me.

I know who I am now.

"Hey," I say, walking up to him.

"Hi."

His voice is clipped—polite, but not warm. He stands too straight, like he's bracing for something, and his grip on the strap of his gym bag is too tight. Back then, he was a bit taller, but now I have maybe an inch on him. It feels... strange to be standing before him after so many years.

"I don't have a lot of time," Julian says, face unsmiling. "Do you know of a place?"

So we can get this over with...

He doesn't say it, but all those years learning his nuances clue me into how he's really feeling about all of this.

"Yeah. Let me just drop my bag in my car and we can walk over. It's just down the street."

We walk through the parking lot, and Julian seems distracted. He points a key fob at a black Range Rover parked three spaces away from mine, so I walk to my white Audi Q6 and set the bag in the trunk. When I lock my car, Julian is standing a few feet away as he texts someone on his phone.

Crossing my arms, I wait until he finishes. It's a beautiful day out—clear, warm but not too hot, with just a whisper of wind from the ocean. A small part of me regrets not going on the hike Stella invited me on this morning, but I'd wanted to get a full-body workout in.

Joke's on me, I guess.

"Sorry," Julian mumbles, pocketing his phone. "It's work."

We walk toward the main road in one of the more suburban parts of Crestwood. The coffee shop down the road is decent, albeit usually very crowded. It's not the first place I'd choose to catch up with my ex-best friend, but it's better than nothing.

"And what is it that you do for work?" I ask.

I'd somehow resisted googling Julian for all of these years, so I have no idea how he occupies his time now.

"I'm an art consultant."

We begin walking down the street. Julian walks a step ahead of me—not by much, but enough to notice. He's always been like that. If he can't control the situation, he'll control the pace. I don't call him out on it, but I let him have it.

"Really? That sounds cool. What does it entail?"

He shrugs. "Most people have no idea what kind of art they want in their homes. I'm the person they come to when they want to invest, but they don't know what they want. I match them with meaningful pieces, and we go from there."

He rattles off the details too fast, like he's reading from a brochure. I watch the way his eyes flick to the ground—calculated, as if keeping his gaze there will stop me from seeing whatever's hiding behind his words.

"How'd you get into that?"

"I've always had a passion for art, and after graduating with an art degree, I decided to channel my energy into helping others find investment pieces for their home."

It sounds like he's answering interview questions.

Which means he's probably not super comfortable being around me.

Should I apologize? For the kiss, and for walking away?

I'm quiet for several seconds, trying to place this version of Julian. I never even knew he liked art—it must've been something he picked up after going back to England.

"Do you have a favorite artist?" I ask.

Julian laughs and looks away. "You haven't changed."

I stop walking—we're standing in front of the coffee shop anyway—and cock my head.

"How so?"

"You were always so curious about other people. Notice how you haven't offered me anything about your life?"

My lips twitch with a hint of a smile. "Well, what do you want to know?"

He sighs and runs a hand through his hair. I rub my mouth with my hand, and his eyes catch on my tattoo.

I can hear the question before he even asks.

"That tattoo..." he says slowly. "I noticed it earlier. You could start there."

"Let's get coffee first."

His eyes narrow slightly, but he follows me inside the small café. It's crowded, so we wait in line as Julian takes in his surroundings.

"Much different than London," I muse, as we creep forward in the long line.

"Very."

I don't say anything in response. A minute later, we place our order, and I pull out my card to pay before he has a chance to.

"Thanks," he says, blue eyes boring into mine.

"Welcome."

Once my coffee and Julian's tea is ready, we walk to one of the only free tables in the back.

As we sit down, I sip my coffee and look up at my old friend. "So, how'd you and Sophie meet?"

His face completely relaxes, but he doesn't smile. She's special to him, that much I can tell. I can see the love in his soft expression.

"In university. We were both in an art program at Oxford, though she was a first year and I was a graduate student. It was love at first sight."

"I'm really happy for you," I tell him.

"Thanks. And you?" he asks, looking at me warily. "Married? Kids?"

Not quite.

"I'm the headmaster at Saint Helena Academy. Before that, I was a pastor." I hold my hand up. "Hence the tattoo," I say, showcasing the cross on my left middle finger.

Julian's brow lifts, but the corners of his mouth tug down. It's subtle, but it's there—that flash of something tense.

"Huh," he says, tapping his fingers once against his mug. "Didn't see you in that role."

Neither did I, but the way he says it makes me wonder if he expected me to stay the same.

My eyes trace the lines of his face, the way his fingers rest on the table. Then he looks away, fiddling with his wedding band.

"What's Sophie like?"

"She's... kind. Strong. She has a big heart."

Julian says it without hesitation, but there's something guarded in the way the words land—like he's holding back the rest, keeping the best parts of her for himself.

I nod. "She sounds wonderful. Good for you, Julian."

He shifts in his seat, not really meeting my gaze. "Yeah. I got lucky."

The silence stretches, but I press on, trying to reconnect. "So, do you two travel much? I remember you always talked about going places. Spain, wasn't it?"

His hand stops moving. "We went to Spain for our honeymoon."

"Nice. How was it?" I ask, smiling, though I notice the way his jaw tightens.

"It was fine," he replies, too curtly for something that should've been a happy memory.

I can feel something shifting, like I've touched a nerve, but I can't quite put my finger on it.

"It's nice to catch up," I tell him honestly.

His eyes flash with something—frustration, maybe. "Nice." The word falls from his lips like it's sharp.

There's a chill in the air now, but I keep going, my smile faltering. "So what does Sophie do for work?"

The muscle in his jaw flexes the longer we sit there. His fingers drum once, twice, then stop abruptly, as if catching himself. I can feel the weight pressing down on the table between us, the unsaid things stretching wider by the second.

I know that look. It's the same one he had the night he kissed me. Right before he pretended like it hadn't happened.

"I know what you're doing," he says abruptly, cutting me off as he stands up.

I blink, taken aback. "Julian, I wasn't trying to—"

"You think you can just come back after all this time, ask a few questions, and everything will go back to how it was."

"I wasn't—"

But he's already walking away, his voice tight with anger. "I should go."

I watch him leave, still trying to figure out what the hell I did wrong.

"Hey!" I call out, chasing after him. "Did I say something to offend you?" I ask as I catch up with Julian a few doors down.

Julian stops walking and turns to face me. "You're exactly the same. Asking questions to put me at ease, but instead it feels like a smooth interrogation. You always were so good at manipulating the situation."

I narrow my eyes. "I was asking a question to be nice. To see what you've been up to for the last seventeen years." My tone is harsher than I anticipate, and Julian's eyes widen just a fraction.

"Well, now you know all about my life, and like always, I know next to nothing about yours. Which is fine, I suppose, because I've spent the last seventeen years trying to forget about you."

He storms off before I can fully comprehend his words.

I've spent the last seventeen years trying to forget about you.

I've spent the last seventeen years trying to forget about you.

I've spent the last seventeen years trying to forget about you.

It hits me as I stand there, watching him disappear down the street. I spent years convincing myself that walking away was the right thing to do. That Julian was better off without me and whatever confusion we felt that night. But maybe... maybe I wasn't the only one confused.

I walk down the street until I get to the parking lot for the gym, but his Range Rover is already gone by the time I get to where he was parked.

Fuck.

My heart sinks as I lean against my car, rubbing my face as if that'll somehow erase the last ten minutes. I thought seventeen years was enough time to bury one kiss. But the way Julian looked at me today, like he's still holding on to something he doesn't want to name, makes me wonder if I ever really let go either.

I have to fix this.

I have to apologize.

But for what?

CHAPTER FOUR
THE OFFER

Sophie

"Babe, someone's at the door!" I shout from the pantry. Chappell Roan is blasting through the surround sound speakers, and my arms are covered in wet paint. I probably shouldn't be painting in my favorite spandex shorts, but here we are. At this rate, half the clothes I own are destined to become 'painting outfits,' and honestly, I'm fine with that. Julian keeps threatening to toss them out, but I've caught him staring at my arse too many times for him to follow through. "Julian, can you hear me?"

The doorbell rings again, and when I glance down at my phone, I see an unfamiliar man standing at the front door according to the security camera.

Setting the paintbrush down, I quickly wipe my hands on my shorts and walk through the house to the front door. It's probably the tree delivery company with the new magnolia trees I ordered for the front garden. As I pull the door open, I place one hand on my hip.

"Hi. Let me go grab my husband and he'll tell you where to plant it. You're from the garden center, right?"

The man before me is incredibly good-looking, and I swallow as I take in his fitted jeans and leather jacket. He's tall, like Julian, and has dark brown hair that compliments his golden skin tone. And his eyes... they're a light gray color that reminds me of molten silver.

"Umm, not exactly. My name is Malakai Ravage."

The name clangs through me, and it takes me a second too long to realize this is Julian's long-lost childhood friend.

"Oh fuck, I'm so sorry," I mutter, before my hand flies to my mouth briefly. "Shit. Fuck. Sorry."

He laughs, and his face softens, the corners of his eyes crinkling as a relaxed warmth spreads across his features. There's something easygoing in his expression —and I realize, in that moment, I instantly like him.

"It's okay," Malakai says, a smirk tugging at the corner of his lips. "I like it when people don't filter themselves. Keeps things... real." His eyes glint with something mischievous as they flick briefly over me, and then back to my face. My cheeks heat slightly when I realize I'm only wearing spandex shorts and an old, too tight T-shirt—the paint in my hair and all over my face notwithstanding. "Besides, I think the more honest someone is, the more fun it gets."

I raise an eyebrow, matching his playful tone. "I'll be the judge of that. Are you good at planting trees or does your specialty lie in charming unsuspecting homeowners? Because I really am expecting a delivery from the garden center and I just picked up some baked goods from downtown, and if you're good with a shovel, there might just be a warm cinnamon roll in it for you. I'm also completely in over my head with the renovations."

He chuckles and the sound is low and smooth. "Now that's an offer I'd be a fool to pass up." His grin widens, and for a second, the air feels lighter between us. I bite back a laugh, my pulse quickening at the easy way he's bantering. His eyes flick over the exterior of the house in all of its half-painted glory. "Really, though. I'm more than happy to help out. I spent a few summers building houses in college."

Relief washes through me. "Oh my God, that would be incredible. And I'm sure Julian would appreciate the help, too."

Malakai's expression tightens for a fraction of a second, and then one of his hands comes to the back of his neck.

"Yeah, we'll see about that. We sort of got into an argument last weekend."

My brows pull together. I'd asked Julian about the coffee date with the infamous Ravage brother, and all he'd said was that Malakai hadn't changed one bit in the seventeen years they'd gone without speaking. I'd assumed that meant they'd drifted apart naturally, not that there was any lingering bad blood between them.

"Oh, well, I'm sure if you offer your services, he'll be quick to forgive," I say quickly. Holding the door open, I gesture for him to come in. "He's just painting the games room."

Malakai whistles as he steps inside and does one full circle as he looks around. "Wow."

I sigh as my eyes take in the plastic sheeting that could fill a football field at this point. That's not even including all of the dust and grit from the drywall and plastic sheeting over the original stained glass window we've decided to restore.

"I know. It's a work in progress. Trust me, I stay up late in bed just tossing and turning about if it'll ever be done—"

"It's fucking fantastic," he says, walking through the foyer before turning around to face me. "This is a great house. I'm kind of jealous," he says, walking until he reaches the grand staircase. Running a hand over the smooth wood, he turns to face me. "Sebastian Hale Whitlock?"

My mouth drops open at how easily he names the architect who built the newly renamed *Ashford Palace*—a name my husband chose, obviously.

"How on earth do you know who Sebastian Hale Whitlock is?"

Malakai chuckles. "Because he built the house I grew up in, too."

A smirk plays on my lips. "Right. Ravage Castle. Did you know he only built the two houses before dying in a plane crash?"

Malakai nods. "I did. It's kind of a grim thought. Two masterpieces and then *bam*."

Sebastian Hale Whitlock was known for his grand yet intimate designs that blended European influences with California's natural beauty. His designs were a hallmark of luxury in the late 1800s. Not a lot of people know about him, and the fact that Malakai does pleases me.

"He was really ahead of his time—"

"Malakai."

My husband's voice resounds through the large, empty hallway, and Malakai and I both turn to face him as he walks over to us.

My eyes flick between my husband and Malakai, and both of them seem to size the other up immediately. Malakai, for example, pushes off the banister and places his hands in the pockets of his jeans. All hints of the smile that was just on his face is gone, instead replaced with scrunched brows and an apprehensive expression.

I glance at Julian as he approaches, noting the sweat still glistening on his skin and the way his eyes immediately flick toward Malakai like he's scrutinizing him.

Huh.

"Julian," Malakai says.

"I see you've met Sophie," Julian says, stopping next to me and placing a sweaty arm around me.

"I have," Malakai replies, eyes twinkling. He looks right at me as he delivers his next line. "And she's even more beautiful than you described."

My neck flushes as I grin up at Julian. "Aww. You told him I'm beautiful?"

Julian's arm tightens just enough around my waist to

make a point. A point I can't quite read yet, but I know it's there. His gaze locks on Malakai, and suddenly the easygoing husband I know is gone. This version of Julian is colder, like someone threw a bucket of ice water over him.

"I did," my husband says, words cold.

"I see you're renovating?" Malakai asks. "Apparently I've volunteered my services." He looks at me briefly before continuing. "I also wanted to apologize for last weekend."

My eyes flick between the old friends, and I remove Julian's arm, stepping back. "Why don't I give the two of you some privacy?"

"Soph—"

I take another step back. "I'm going to make us lunch. Malakai, would you like to join us?" I ask.

"As long as it's okay with Julian."

My husband's jaw tics and he shrugs. "Sure."

Clapping my hands once, I smile at both men. "Wonderful. We don't have much—just some leftover sandwiches from a place downtown. And a couple of cinnamon rolls that I can heat up, as promised."

"Sounds great," Malakai says, giving me a genuine smile. "Thank you, Sophie. I'm really glad we met."

I wink at Julian before walking to the garage, where we have a small makeshift kitchen set up. I plate the leftovers and make a quick salad before bringing it all to the old bar table that Orion loaned to us so that we didn't have to eat our meals on the floor. It's dark in here, so I click the button to open the garage in order to bring some natural light in. A minute later, Julian and Malakai walk into the garage.

Their voices are too low to decipher. Julian is doing his casual-but-not-really posture, the one he uses when he's pretending to be fine. I've seen it before—him keeping his guard up with my mother and his parents, especially—but he's usually very warm to random strangers, let alone people he considers friends.

I set the salad down, watching as Malakai places a hand on Julian's shoulder, only for Julian to flinch, like he didn't expect it. I don't think Malakai notices, but I do. Julian hates people catching him off guard, but he doesn't usually react that way to old friends. I cross my arms as I observe them some more.

This isn't the same banter I usually see when Julian reconnects with old friends. I bite the inside of my cheek, wondering if there's more to their story than the neat little version Julian gave me years ago. Racking my brain, I try to remember what he's said about Malakai over the years. Whenever he talked about living in Crestwood, Malakai always came up. Julian seemed to have mostly fond memories of their time as friends, and I can't recall any sort of falling out.

What really happened between them?

I set the sandwiches down on the table, grabbing a bag of Julian's beloved Flamin' Hot Cheetos from the stash he keeps hidden behind the cereal. He discovered them shortly after moving here, and now he's obsessed.

I toss them onto his plate, catching the quick smirk he tries—and fails—to hide.

"I knew I married you for a reason," Julian says, popping one into his mouth.

"Don't let it go to your head," I tease, nudging him with my elbow.

"Thank you for lunch," Malakai says.

"Of course." I take a seat across from them. "So? Did the two of you reconcile? Because we could really use Malakai's help around the house," I add, cocking my head at Malakai. "That is, if you're still able and willing to help?"

He gives me a dashing smile and removes his leather jacket, his muscles contracting underneath a fitted, gray T-shirt. *Good God.* I swallow and look down as he sets his jacket on the back of a spare chair, mentally chastising myself for checking out another man right in front of my husband.

"I'd love to."

I look over at Julian, and he's watching me with some kind of unreadable expression.

I can't tell if he actually agrees to all of this, or if he's going along with it for some reason I don't understand.

"Great," my husband says, grabbing a sandwich.

"Great," Malakai echoes, narrowing his eyes at Julian as he grabs a sandwich, too.

My lips twitch as I look between them.

This is going to be... *interesting*.

"Great," I tell them both.

CHAPTER FIVE
THE TORTURE

JULIAN

It's been the longest fucking two weeks of my life. Having Kai's help around the house has been immensely helpful. I don't say much to him, and he doesn't push. We move through the same spaces like strangers who know too much—polite and civil, yet distant. I tell myself it doesn't matter. That's all this is—nostalgia. And nostalgia is just the mind playing games. But it's getting harder to ignore how much space he takes up in a room, and how easily Sophie pulls him in with her charm.

Sometimes I catch myself watching him, wondering if he's really the same person I used to know. It's strange to be around him again, to remember the small quirks I used to find adorable. Things like how he holds his breath before he laughs, how his eyes crinkle like he's holding back a secret, and the way his tongue presses against his cheek when he's concentrating.

I like having him here—more than I want to admit. But that's the problem, isn't it? The closer he gets, the easier it is to remember what it felt like to trust him. And I'm not ready to feel that again.

Still, he's been helpful. Not only is he good at this renovation stuff, but he also seems to make Sophie happy. Neither of them stops talking as we tackle one thing at a time—most of which is stuff we agreed we'd do ourselves. We had the money to hire things out, but since Malakai came into the picture, we'd been keen on him helping with stuff we could do without outsourcing to the contractors since it was quicker that way and would save us weeks of work.

Today's project is the master bedroom mattress frame, something I promised Sophie I'd make myself. I enjoy using my hands and working around the house when I'm not on the computer or phone for my job, and I took a few woodworking classes at university, so I know enough of the basics to cobble a nice frame together.

And this frame might be the fucking death of me. Sophie had seen a similar one online a few months ago, but it was fifteen *thousand* quid. Not that we don't have the money—we do.

It's just the principle of it all.

I'd volunteered to make a similar one from scratch without thinking of the logistics—something I'm very prone to do.

And I was determined to finish this one today.

My therapist in London liked to call these little projects my *fixations,* and I couldn't agree more.

If it didn't get done today, it wouldn't get done at all.

Sophie is in the corner of the large room showing Kai the rolls of custom wallpaper she ordered from William Morris while I hammer another fucking nail into the wood. Every minute or so, I look over at them, and Kai is staring down at her in adoration.

Something uncomfortable works through me at the way he's looking at her.

It's not jealousy—I'd be a fool to get jealous, considering the kinds of things we were into.

It's something far more subtle, like the feeling you get when you see an old friend, someone you once cared about deeply, laughing just a little too easily with someone else. Not territorial, not possessive—just... aware.

I should be happy for them. I should want this—should love the way Sophie lights up around him, the ease in her body language when she laughs at his jokes. And I do.

But part of me wonders when I became the observer, not the participant.

It's silly, really. I should be happy they get along so well—but there's something quietly unsettling about watching the man I used to be in love with flirt with my wife, like I'm witnessing a moment I should feel part of, but instead, I'm standing just outside its edges, uninvited. Not quite envy or regret, but a sense of being *left out* of something they share, something I used to understand with regards to him.

It's as though I'm watching two parts of my life thread together in front of me, and somehow, I'm the one fraying at the seams.

I haven't really been myself since Kai reentered our lives. To be honest, I've been more irritable, moodier, and distracted since I started seeing him most days. I know Sophie notices, but because she's polite, she hasn't mentioned anything.

And this past weekend, Sophie and I went to one of the kink clubs in town called Inferno. We didn't advertise our kink, but people could infer it from speaking to us. Couples who swing are immensely popular within these types of clubs, and since what we do is a subset of swinging, we felt like we were right at home. We ended up taking a guy back to a nearby hotel suite, and like always, I settled in to watch my wife undress.

One of the best things about Sophie being a hotwife —where a married couple consensually agrees for the wife to have sexual encounters with other men while I remain monogamous—is the way other men look at her.

The way they drink her in.

I see it.

I am in constant awe of her natural beauty.

I know how fucking gorgeous she is, and that's exactly what I get off on.

But something happened this past weekend.

She'd been straddling a new guy, clothes half off, the condom already on... but the moment he shifted into the shadow, something about the angle—the set of his shoulders, maybe—looked too familiar. Suddenly, all I could see was Malakai beneath her, the lines of his body overlapping with the stranger's until I couldn't separate the two. There was something in the way the man moved—confident, slow, like he knew exactly how to touch her—that pulled the image to the surface and wouldn't let it go.

It wasn't logical. The guy didn't even look like Kai.

I'd told myself that, over and over.

But my mind doesn't give a rat's arse about logic. It cares about the way Kai's hands looked on Sophie's hips in the living room the other day. About how easily he makes her laugh. And suddenly, it's seventeen years ago again, and I'm eighteen, staring at Kai across the dorm room floor, watching him sleep, wondering how much longer I can pretend.

And this past weekend, I'd used the safe word.

I'd only ever done it once before, when we first started down this road. Back then, I was worried that word would get out about our proclivities—about *my* proclivity—or that Sophie would contract an STI. The anxiety exploded, and it took me a couple of months to try again—with safety measures and new protocols in place, of course.

For example, every man she sleeps with has to have been tested recently. A condom is nonnegotiable, and all parties sign an NDA that never expires.

Sophie had crawled off the guy and we'd very quickly and politely said goodbye. We'd talked about it—as we did after every scene. If there was one thing I could appreciate about Sophie and me, it was that we were *solid*. I love her so fucking much, and I know she reciprocates my feelings.

But this recent experience had thrown me.

I was honest—I told her that I wasn't quite in the right mindset. She understood—of course she did.

And I got to spend the rest of the night fucking her bare, like I always did.

Sophie's laugh echoes through the room, pulling me from my thoughts. Kai is smirking as she places a hand on his arm.

His very muscled, corded arm.

An unknown feeling burns my chest, and I clench my jaw. I swing the hammer up and bring it down over and over as I get the foundation for the frame nailed together. Just as I slide my hand down the wood, the fleshy part between my thumb and index finger catches on a massive splinter.

"Fuck," I hiss, pulling my hand back as blood trickles down my palm. I hear Sophie and Kai rush over to me. "Splinter," I murmur, feeling woozy at the sight of the blood.

Sophie knows about my vasovagal syncope, aka how I can sometimes faint at the sight of blood. She got a paper cut on our honeymoon, and I went down like a sack of potatoes.

Now that I think about it, Kai knows, too. And that's on two reckless seventeen-year-olds who thought smashing beer bottles against the side of an abandoned building was a good idea.

"Sit down. I'll fetch the tweezers from my makeup bag," she says quickly, placing a cool hand on my forehead. Looking up at Kai, she opens her mouth, but he holds a hand out.

"I know. I'll make sure he doesn't faint."

I'd laugh, but my vision begins to swim as the blood creeps down my forearm.

Sophie jogs out of the bedroom, and Kai kneels in front of where I'm sitting on a nearby chair.

"Let me see," he murmurs, taking my hand.

Kai's fingers brush against mine, steady and sure, his touch unexpectedly gentle and exploratory. I feel the roughness of his calloused fingertips as they press lightly around the wound, and a weird jolt of calm washes over me, cutting through the dizziness. He's always had that affect—grounding, without meaning to. His hands linger just a second longer than they need to, cradling mine like I'm something fragile, and it does something to the tightness in my chest.

My breathing steadies, even as my heart starts to pound for a different reason.

I know what's coming before it happens. Kai's always been like this—unapologetically physical. He used to sling his arm over my shoulders after swimming practice, drape himself across my bed like he lived there. He doesn't even think twice about touching me, but I do.

God, I do.

"Here," he says, bringing my hand close to his mouth. "I can get it out with my mouth."

My lips part, but I can only nod as he takes my bloody hand and places his lips over the wound.

The suction of his warm, wet mouth goes straight to my cock.

I forget about the blood. I forget about Sophie coming back with tweezers. It's just me and Kai—my hand in his mouth—and the weight of a thousand unsaid things between us.

His eyes lock onto mine as he sucks some more, and *fuck* there's something really arousing and erotic about watching him suck my blood out. I mean, I know he's sucking the splinter, but... it feels *intimate* in a way I can't quite explain.

His lips are warm against my skin, and the pull of his mouth, gentle but deliberate, sends a strange, electric thrill through me.

It shouldn't feel like this. His mouth shouldn't feel this deliberate, like he's taking his time, tasting me. I want to believe it's my imagination—some twisted projection—but I see it in the way his eyes flick up to mine, unreadable and steady. He knows exactly what he's doing.

There's something about it that goes beyond the act itself—this is Kai, the guy I once knew so well, the guy I used to be *in love with,* now impossibly close again, his breath ghosting over my hand. Vulnerability hangs between us, thicker than the tension.

It's not just about the splinter anymore; it's the raw

closeness of it, the kind you don't plan for, the kind that leaves you exposed in more ways than one.

And this is the second time I've been in this situation with him.

His eyes don't leave mine, and instead of pulling away, he scoots closer to place his other hand on my arm. It's disorienting, having him so close, and it stirs something old and familiar, something I've long buried. My pulse quickens, not from the pain, but from the way his touch feels—how easy it is to let him take care of me, even after all these years. There's trust in it, but also something charged, something we've never fully addressed but always felt.

Or, something I've always felt, at least.

That same sort of explosive feeling that happened the first time we kissed.

His lips pull off my hand, and he holds it up with a satisfied smirk, but I barely notice.

My eyes are locked on his lips—bloodied from my wound, swollen from sucking on my skin. He looks almost wild, a little unhinged, with his dark hair falling messily over his forehead and the rough shadow of his short scruff catching the light. His angular jaw is sharp, accentuating his striking features, and those deep, intense eyes—light gray with flecks of silver—seem to burn as they meet mine. His expression glimmers with some kind of dark promise I can't quite infer—like someone on the edge of giving into his primal needs—and it sends a shiver down my spine.

For a second, I forget to breathe. I'm transfixed,

caught between the rawness of the moment and the heat that lingers between us. It feels like he can read my mind but isn't going to say a word. His lips pull up into that knowing smirk again, and it's unsettling how badly I want him to stay this close.

Fuck.

I thought I could do this, but I really, really can't.

Not now—not when I have Sophie.

I stand up and adjust my erection before he can see.

It's nothing. It's just the adrenaline. Or the blood loss. Or maybe I haven't jerked off in a few days.

That's all this is.

He stands and takes a step back just as Sophie walks into the bedroom with tweezers.

"I got it," I tell her, showing her my hand.

"That's a relief," she says, blowing a stray piece of hair out of her face. "Are you feeling okay?"

I nod once and run my good hand through my hair. "Yeah." I kiss her on the forehead. "I need to go clean my hand. And then I forgot I have a client meeting at two," I tell her, feeling instantly guilty for lying.

"Okay, babe." She looks at Kai. "Guess you're stuck with me again. How well can you mix wallpaper paste?"

Kai laughs, and when I look over my shoulder at him, he's still looking at me with that darkened expression.

"I can figure it out," he says, breaking eye contact before giving her a warm smile.

Walking down the hall to the guest bathroom, I remove my old T-shirt with shaking hands. First the blood and then what happened with Kai... I need a minute to get my bearings.

Closing the door, I step out of my clothes and lean against the small vanity. Looking up into the mirror, I stare at myself.

What the hell was that?

After running a hand down my face, I turn the shower on and step inside.

I'm still hard.

Fuck me.

I thought I was past this. I thought I'd forgotten all about my ex-best friend with captivating silver eyes and cheekbones that could cut glass.

I thought I'd moved on—gotten him out of my system. I mean, fuck... I'd slept with two men in the weeks after we kissed. It wasn't exactly a sexual rampage or anything, but it helped. And while I still had fleeting thoughts about men, there's something about Kai that cuts deeply and effectively.

I close my eyes and let the water run over my face, but all I can see is the heavy, hooded way Kai looked at me while he sucked my life force out of my body.

And the way he just took charge?

It was really fucking hot.

I never thought I'd say that, either. I was all alpha, in control of every situation. With Sophie, I liked to be a bit rough. I liked to throw her around, fuck her from behind, pull her hair. It's how I differentiate myself from the guys she slept with.

Suddenly, I imagine Sophie touching Kai's arm again.

I imagine his easy smile as he touches her face, and the way she sucks in a breath whenever I grab her waist.

My cock is heavy and aching as I think of Kai taking control of her, twisting her around and pushing her against the wall, his lips still bloody with *my* blood.

I imagine the gritty way he'd groan when he ripped her little shorts off—and before I know it, my hand is slowly stroking my cock.

This is fine.

This is my kink, after all. I enjoy the thought of my wife fucking other men. So what if it's Kai that I'm envisioning?

My hand moves faster, and I hiss. Grabbing some conditioner, I lube my shaft up and squeeze my balls with my other hand as I begin to pant.

I think of how Kai wouldn't even get undressed—he'd unzip his pants and step between her legs. Maybe he'd even drop to his knees and eat her cunt from behind.

My mouth drops open as I imagine it—the low, heady moan that would come from his lips as soon as he tasted her for the first time. And because I know what she tastes like, it feels too real. The mixture of imagining his *and* her arousal has me working my hand faster.

I think of how he'd unsheathe himself, pumping his massive cock a few times.

And yeah, I knew it was massive from that time we went skinny dipping a few weeks before everything changed.

My toes curl against the tile as I envision his cock pushing into her—and again, because I know what she feels like, I let myself think of how it would feel for *both* of them. I imagine the way she'd look back at him and let her eyes roll into the back of her head, and the way he'd fist her hair as he grunted, driving into her and letting his head drop back just before he came inside of her...

Fuuuuck.

I shouldn't be thinking about him like this. Not with Sophie down the hall, not when I've built a life with her that I love more than anything. But the image doesn't let up—the curve of Kai's mouth, the way his eyes darken when he's focused. It rushes in like a flood, drowning the voice in my head that tells me to stop.

My orgasm creeps up quickly, and my balls pull up as my shaft curves, and then I'm imagining Kai looking over his shoulder at me as he fucks my wife, as he stills and comes inside of her, and I explode in one long, pleading, *tortured* groan. My cum hits the wall of the shower in thick ropes as suddenly Sophie is replaced with me, and he's pounding into my arsehole, hitting my prostate and milking this orgasm with the pink head of his cock—

"F-fuck," I rasp, my whole body twitching as the last of it leaves me.

I'm breathing heavily as my whole body trembles, and I watch as the water washes my cum down the drain. Leaning against the wall, I let the water run down my back as I figure out what the hell just happened.

I mean... I'd definitely wanked to the image of Kai before.

But it had been... *seventeen* years.

I hadn't let myself even think of him in all this time with Sophie.

Somehow, I knew if I let myself think of him, everything would come tumbling down like a house of cards.

This was a slippery slope I'd resisted for that long—something I pushed away again, and again, and again.

I'd shoved all thoughts of Malakai Ravage out of my mind, pushing them so far back until I couldn't even remember what he looked like.

And now?

I'd just had one of the best orgasms of my life.

In all of my fantasies involving Sophie and other guys, I hadn't ever considered what it would feel like to be fucked by them.

Guilt washes over me when I squeeze my eyes shut.

In my little shower wet dream, I'd even imagined *him* fucking *me*—which is laughable.

There was no way in hell I'd ever let Kai top me. I've never been a bottom, and I sure as hell wasn't going to start with Kai.

I turn the shower off, grab a towel, and pat myself dry. Just as I wrap the towel around my waist, I hear Sophie's laugh from down the hall, followed by Kai's low, sensual tenor.

I can't help the image of him fucking her float through my mind.

Scowling, I walk to the closet, closing the door behind me to drown everything out. I lean against the wood, my breath ragged, eyes squeezed shut again. His face floods my mind, sharp and clear, as if seventeen years had never passed.

Sophie's laugh echoes in my ears, but it's his voice I hear—low, dangerous, and far too close.

God, I'm losing it.

I press my forehead against the closet door, the weight of everything crashing over me.

A sickening realization is taking hold: Malakai was never really gone.

I'd buried him deep, but now... now he's clawing his way back to the surface.

And I'm terrified I won't be able to stop him.

I built this life for a reason—to keep that part of me locked away. To keep Sophie at the center of everything. But I'm starting to wonder if Kai's the one who holds the key, and I don't know what happens if that door opens again.

CHAPTER SIX
THE PENANCE

MALAKAI

"Forgive me, Father, for I have sinned."

My lips twitch and I lean back in my chair. The office around me is dimly lit, shadows stretching over the dark wood paneling that lines the walls. It's not the same as my actual office at Saint Helena Academy, but I'd done a good job having the room custom-made for me. I'd managed to replicate each groove of the paneling worn smooth from years of silent witness of everyone's confessions, each dark smoke shadow from a candle burning for too long.

The thing is, my real office—with its symbols of devotion and unyielding tradition—feels like a cage. The thing about that particular cage is that it's carved out of expectation, reinforced with obligation. I used to think I could live inside it, let the weight of it mold me into the perfect shape. But lately, that weight has started to shift, pressing in on the wrong places. Places I don't want to admit are soft.

The crosses, the holy figures in the stained glass—each one stares back at me with a kind of cold, silent reproach. I wonder what they'd say if they could talk.

I wonder what they'd say if they knew about the impulses I've stopped trying to contain.

That's the problem, though. I don't want to contain them anymore.

Which is why I have an office here. *A safe space, in a safe place.* Far away from the prying eyes of the children and staff who attend Saint Helena, and also a safe space for the women who act as my submissives.

"May the Lord be in your heart and help you to confess your sins. How long has it been since your last confession?"

She gives me a pretty, little smile. "Too long," she purrs. "Since my last confession, I have defiled this very desk and had lustful thoughts about you, Father."

"I'm going to assign a penance. You understand what that means, don't you?"

I stand up, and Vivienne looks at me with wide, brown eyes. "Yes, Father. It's something to show remorse and renew my commitment to the Lord."

Walking over to where she's sitting, I stop a few inches away and place my hands in the pockets of my pants. My already-hard cock is at face level for her.

"Suck."

Vivienne goes still. "And this will forgive my sins?"

I cock my head as I look down at her. "We'll see. I might want to assign another penance."

She moans and reaches for my zipper. "I worship you, Father."

"Yeah? You want your face fucked like you're an offering to God himself?"

Humming, she pulls my cock out and wraps her mouth around it. I fist her hair and guide her all the way back until she gags.

She knows the safe words—verbal and nonverbal.

I'm *very* strict about them, and since she's been in the lifestyle much longer than me, I trust her to use them.

"Such a good, faithful servant."

"Yes, Father," she murmurs around my shaft, using her hand to stroke me.

I groan and let my head fall back. "Fuck."

"I want your cum, Father. I need it," she says, gagging when I push myself all the way to the back of her throat.

"I know you do."

"*Please.*"

It's so quiet here... something I've come to appreciate. I don't take submissives back to my apartment, and unless I'm here, at Inferno, I can't chance anyone seeing us out in public.

Like I said... this is my safe space where I can play uninhibited.

Only Orion, the owner and my youngest brother, knows how much time I spend here.

A few years ago—after discovering my ironic worship kink, thanks to a woman I was dating—I decided to keep the experience as authentic as possible and keep all play here, in a room that's identical to my office at Saint Helena.

No one else knows, and no one ever will. Not with the ironclad NDA all the women sign.

So every few weeks, I cycle in a new submissive who seeks moral guidance from a real-life pastor, confessing her misdeeds and accepting the discipline I deem necessary.

You'd be surprised how many people have religious kinks...

"You want me to come down your throat as a sign of your devotion?"

Tears stream down Vivienne's face as she nods up at me, her mouth full of my cock.

"Fuck yes," I tell her, gripping the back of her short, dark hair as I pump into the back of her throat.

My mouth drops open just as my phone starts ringing.

"Keep going," I growl, feeling my balls start to draw up. "I'm close, and you still need to complete your penance."

She groans and uses her free hand to cup my balls, and as I sharply inhale, my phone goes off again.

"Fuck," I mutter, pulling out of Vivienne's mouth to lean over the desk.

Julian's name flashes over the screen.

"One second," I tell her, holding a finger to my lips as I answer the call. "Hey. Everything okay?"

"Malakai. Sorry to bother you, but I have a favor to ask," he says, and there's an announcement of some kind going off in the background.

I run a hand over my mouth as I look down at Vivienne. "Sure. What's up?"

"I'm about to board a five-hour flight to New York. It's a work thing. I'll be back tomorrow, but Sophie's not feeling well. Would you mind going to check on her?"

Alarm bells begin ringing in my mind. "Is she okay?"

"I mean, she's not going to perish imminently, but it would make me feel a lot better if you kept an eye on her."

"Now?" I ask, checking my watch. It's half past six in the evening.

"If you can. She's not answering my calls, and I'm a nervous wreck. I left her in quite a state."

There's something fragile in Julian's voice. I don't know if it's worry for Sophie or hesitation in calling me for help. Maybe both. But I can't shake the flicker of relief I feel at being the one he turns to, even if it feels like standing on shaky ground.

"Okay. Yeah. I'll be right over."

"Thanks." It sounds like he wants to say something else, but he just clears his throat. "Sophie doesn't have that many close friends here, and Stella is styling a photo shoot in Santa Barbara, so..."

"Julian. It's not a problem."

He sighs. "Thanks. I appreciate it. I'll call you when I land."

We hang up, and when I look down at Vivienne, my priorities shift. "I'm sorry," I tell her. "I have to go check on a friend."

Vivienne stands up and straightens her dress. Smirking, she kisses me on the cheek. "I might have more confessions for you next Wednesday. Same time?"

I nod absentmindedly as I tuck my cock away. "Sure. Yeah. Text me."

She turns to go, and I remember my manners as her Dom. "Wait. Sorry. Fuck. Are you okay?"

Her lips tug to one side. "We barely even got started. I'm fine. I promise."

I take her hand. "Are you sure?"

She laughs. "Kai, I literally sucked your cock for five minutes. Last week, you held a knife up to my neck while you roughly fucked me on your desk, and the week before that was the blood play. I'm. Fine. Promise," she adds, batting her lashes and kissing my hand. "Go be a hero."

I nod and watch her unlock the door and walk out of my private room. I'm in a daze, and right now, all I can think about is Sophie and making sure she's okay. Grabbing my things, I close the door and walk out of Inferno. It's a ten-minute walk back to Saint Helena, where I left my car. Just as I pull the passenger door open to set my things down, another car pulls up next to mine. I quickly glance over, groaning internally when Rod Dumplant exits his Escalade and waves me over.

Plastering on a smile, I saunter over to the massive vehicle and wait for Rod to grace me with his presence. There's something about him that I don't like. Unfortunately, seeing as he's a board member for the school, I have to interact with him more than I'd like to.

"Malakai," he says, his teeth gleaming like he's trying too hard to appear charming. His navy suit swallows him whole, hanging off his shoulders like he's playing dress-up in someone else's clothes, but he wears it with the kind of arrogance that makes it seem deliberate. He looks like he's just walked out of a boardroom after crushing someone's career, the kind of guy who's used to firing people with a smile.

"Rod," I say, shaking his hand.

"Do you have a minute?" he asks, frowning.

Not really. "Sure."

He sighs, shuffling from foot to food. "You know I'm a man of God, just like yourself," he says, his voice serious.

A man of God? Perhaps if God loved a man who used the money from his church for a luxury yacht.

I wait for him to continue. "I received two more complaints over the weekend from concerned parents regarding Bradleigh Evans."

Instantly tensing up, I attempt to keep my face neutral. "What about her?" I ask, my voice calm but firm.

Rod looks around as if anyone could overhear us, despite being in a nearly empty parking lot. Leaning in slightly, his voice drops.

"I got two more calls from concerned parents.

Bradleigh's presence is causing confusion among the student body. And discomfort among the parents. You understand."

I glower at him. "No, I'm not sure I do understand. All of the kids have been great with Bradleigh. There were instances of bullying, but as you remember, those students have been expelled due to our zero-tolerance discrimination policy."

He nods solemnly, as if he's about to deliver some divine truth. "Well, the parents are concerned, and one has even threatened to remove their children from Saint Helena Academy. Perhaps the situation would be easier for everyone—Bradleigh included—if she were moved to a different school. Somewhere... more accommodating to her particular needs. I'm not quite sure Saint Helena is the right fit for someone like her."

Someone like her. What he means is transgender. My fists curl at my sides as I contemplate exactly what he's insinuating.

Keep the complaints out of the boardroom meetings.

Send Bradleigh away somewhere more "tolerable."

Except, that solution would never work. It would put Bradleigh, who has attended Saint Helena since she was four, and her mother, who is a hardworking single mother, in an impossible situation. They'd have to trek into Los Angeles, as Crestwood doesn't have a public school, and I know Bradleigh's mom would find that difficult with her work schedule.

"Easier for whom?" I ask, crossing my arms over my chest.

Rod's brows draw together in faux paternal concern. "These situations are always difficult to address within the framework of our institution. I know we have to respect the code of ethics, of course, but this might be best for all parties involved."

"I disagree. I'll talk to the other board members and see if we can have a meeting to discuss the situation. From my vantage point as headmaster," I say slowly, knowing that term is a sore spot for Rod since he wanted the position, "all the children love and respect Bradleigh. If anyone's parents have an issue with her, they can come to me. But I'm not going to consider asking a single mother to uproot her daughter—her *trans* daughter, who's already dealing with enough—to transfer her to another school because it's inconvenient for us to follow our own policies."

Rod stiffens, and to his credit, he looks genuinely affronted. "Malakai, I'm sure you can understand my predicament. I harbor no ill will for the girl, for God loves all of his creatures."

My jaw rolls as I wait for him to continue. He huffs an uncomfortable laugh, rubbing his mouth.

"I'm just trying to consider what's best for everyone. Perhaps we should hold a board meeting. I fear you might be too close to the situation to see the bigger picture."

I take a deep breath, attempting not to say something cruel back. "We should be helping her. Educating parents. Be the leaders that children like her need. But I refuse to push her out, because I promise you, I'll fight that every step of the way."

Rod's jaw tightens, and his eyes narrow. The silence stretches on as neither of us speaks, and the tension grows taut between us.

"I'll pray on this," he says finally, his voice clipped.

"I'll do the same."

Without another word, I turn and walk around to the driver's side of my car, opening the door and pulling out of the parking lot before I say something I'll regret.

I stew the entire drive to Ashford Palace. People like Rod hide their bigotry behind God, and it pisses me the fuck off. Then again, it doesn't surprise me. I've spent the last seventeen plus years listening to my peers tear down anyone different.

I'd have to call Chase and get this settled with the board before Rod got there first.

Once I arrive at Ashford Palace, I'm ushered in without question by the security guard, and the gate closes as I pull up to the front door. Sophie's vintage Mini Cooper sits next to the spot where Julian's Range Rover usually sits, and as I jog to the front door, I shoot a quick text to let Julian know I'm here. Sophie had given me a key last week when I was over doing some work on the crown molding while they were away for the night. I use it as I make my way inside, looking around for any signs of Sophie.

"Hello?" I call out, waiting for her to answer.

She doesn't, so I walk through the ground floor in search of the captivating woman I've been getting to know over the last couple of months. My eyes take in the almost-finished additions, such as the new floors, the massive chandelier in the entryway, and the kitchen that's only waiting for appliances to be installed. It looks good, and a sense of pride fills me. *I* helped with this—my own blood, sweat, and tears are baked into this amazing house. Most notably the latter when Sophie and I realized one of the rooms was built at a very slight angle, and we were ten planks of antique wood flooring short.

I managed to sand, stain, and age ten new pieces of wood to look almost identical, and it became an inside joke.

Still, these renovations aren't for the faint of heart.

But now? I can see the vision Sebastian Hale Whitlock had when he built it. He was a damn genius, and I'm only slightly jealous that Julian and Sophie were able to purchase this obscurely famous house.

"Sophie?" I call out at the bottom of the stairs.

Still no answer.

My pulse spikes at the lack of answer, and I imagine the worst-case scenario—that she's unconscious, or worse. Julian didn't elaborate, but I assume that if it were an emergency, he would've called an ambulance instead of asking me to check on her. She's probably sleeping or something.

I take the stairs two at a time, and I make a beeline for their bedroom. "Sophie? It's Kai," I say, hoping it's enough of a warning if she's indecent.

No answer.

Fuck.

Pushing the bedroom door open, I don't see her—but the bathroom door is cracked. "Sophie?"

"I'm in here," she says, her voice weak from inside the en suite.

I stalk to the door and pull it open, and Sophie is curled up in a ball on the floor.

"Fuck," I murmur.

My pulse jumps. Not from fear, but from the sight of her—so vulnerable, curled up like a delicate thing I shouldn't touch. I kneel beside her, and every impulse I've ever tried to repress slams against the bars of my chest. Not desire, but something more dangerous.

The instinct to protect her.

She's wearing baggy sweatpants and a sweatshirt. Her cheeks are wet from crying, and when I reach out to touch her arm, she begins to sob even harder.

"Oh God, I really don't want you to see me like this," she says, her voice cracking.

"Hey," I murmur, pushing the sweaty hair on her forehead out of her eyes. "What's wrong?"

"It's just—a bad period."

I arch a brow. "You're curled up and crying on the floor..."

She huffs a laugh before sniffling. "I get really bad periods."

"May I pick you up?" I ask.

"Sure. I was just going to run a bath, but the pain got too bad."

"Do you take medication?" I ask.

She shakes her head. "I'm allergic to morphine and all other opioids. The other things won't touch it."

I scoop her up, adjusting her body weight in my arms as she rests her head against my chest. I swallow through the thick emotions clogging my throat as I carry her to the bed, setting her down gently and pulling the duvet over her body.

Looking down at her with a furrowed brow, I run a hand over my chin as I think of how I can help her. I don't want to ask her, because her eyes are closed, and she's already curled up in a ball again, facing away from me, so I take things into my own hands.

"I'll run you a bath," I tell her.

"Thank you," she says, her voice muffled. "Extra hot, please."

I walk to the bathroom and turn on the tap on the large bathtub. While it fills up, I place a delivery order for Sophie and text Julian again that she's okay but in pain, and that I'll stay with her until she's better or he's back.

I add some bubble bath and a few of the essential oils scattered along the shelf above the bath, and once it's halfway full, I walk back into the bedroom.

"Bath's ready," I tell her, unsure if she needs help getting out of bed.

"Thanks," she says, slowly sitting up and walking over to where I'm standing.

"I'll give you some privacy—"

"No, it's okay. Just turn around while I get in."

My heart races for an entirely different reason, and as she passes by me, her arm brushes mine. A skittering, electric current runs from where we touched straight down to my cock.

Fuck.

Once I'm turned around, I close my eyes, but it doesn't stop my mind from drifting. It's not even the thought of her body—it's the trust in her voice, the ease with which she lets me stay. As if there's nothing threatening about me, nothing inappropriate about the way I linger on the edge of this intimate moment. I tell myself that's a good thing. That I should be relieved she doesn't see me as anything more than Julian's friend.

But part of me hates that she doesn't.

The torturous sound of Sophie's clothes dropping to the ground as she undresses behind me echoes in the bathroom. Sophie is naked right behind me, and I'm imagining what she looks like while she's in excruciating pain. Not to mention she's Julian's *wife*.

I hear her step into the water, and a few seconds later, she sighs contentedly.

It certainly doesn't help the situation.

"Okay, you can turn around."

I do, and fortunately the bubbles cover her completely below the neck. "Better?" I ask.

"Very. The temperature is perfect. Scalding but not unbearable," she adds, giving me a small smile.

I walk over to the edge of the windowsill and sit down, which gives her a bit of privacy as I'm lower down.

Over the last few weeks, I've gotten to know Sophie well. She's bubbly and fun, and witty as hell. I can see why Julian fell in love with her. We spend our time together doing various projects around the house while she tells me about her horse, Snickers, and how much she enjoys riding. She's passionate about planning the housewarming party, and she talks about the romance books she enjoys reading. In fact, she's taken a liking to telling me about the elaborate plots and ridiculous things the characters get up to, but I can't help but admire how much she seems to enjoy reading, and how much she lights up when she talks about it.

I just enjoy watching her talk, to be honest. I shouldn't, but I do. And it's not just the way she talks—it's the way she looks at Julian, like he's her whole fucking world. I've never envied Julian for his title or his wealth. But for the way she looks at him?

Yeah. I envy that.

Though neither of them talks about it much, I know Julian and Sophie are much happier here than in England. I don't exactly know what happened, but when I asked how Julian's family was, they shared *a look*. It's almost as though they've agreed to communicate a part of their lives in a way that doesn't need outside validation or permission.

The more I watch them together, the more I notice little signs—fleeting looks, private smiles, subtle touches that linger just a bit too long. It's not that Sophie doesn't trust me; in fact, she's more open and friendly than most people I've met. But there's a part of her that remains inaccessible—a part she's saved just for Julian. Even when she's talking about herself, it feels like she's holding back, as if something essential is just out of reach.

And it's in the way Julian looks at her too—the way his eyes soften when he thinks no one's watching, and the way they seem to communicate just by looking at each other. They're united, but there's also something else there. It's like they've learned to navigate a unique space in their relationship, an arrangement that needs no explanation beyond what they share with each other.

I get the feeling that there's something deeply personal between them that they choose to protect.

And I'm not sure if I'm jealous... or curious.

Sophie groans and leans her head against the back of the bathtub. "This feels so fucking incredible," she murmurs. "Can you do me a favor?"

I perk up. "Sure. What's up?"

"In the drawer to the left of my dressing table is a silver box and a lighter. Can you please pass them to me?"

I stand up and walk over to the antique-looking dressing table in the small room between the bathroom and the closet. Reaching into the left-hand drawer, I pull the small silver case and matching lighter out, walking them back over to Sophie.

"Thanks."

To my utter surprise, she pulls a cigarette out and lights it, setting the case and lighter off to the side.

I contain my laughter as Sophie slips both feet out of the bath, crossing them at the ankle, and takes a deep drag of the cigarette.

"I should quit," she says slowly as she blows smoke out into the air. "Old habits die hard. Now I mix tobacco with marijuana to help with the pain."

"I didn't know you smoked," I tell her, an amusing smile playing at my lips.

"I don't."

"Does Julian know?"

She looks over at me and gives me a sharp look. "Of course." I sit down and lean back against the window. "It's endometriosis, by the way."

My lips part, but I don't ask her to elaborate. I'm scared she's going to realize she's sitting naked in the bathtub with someone other than her husband any second now, and yell at me to get out.

By not speaking, it feels like the spell can remain in place for just a few more minutes.

A second later, she tips her head back and squeezes her eyes shut, inhaling and exhaling a few times. "It means my periods are incredibly painful, and it's not just my periods, either. I get flare-ups periodically, especially right before my period. And since I'm allergic to opioids and I'm of child-bearing age—meaning several doctors have refused a hysterectomy—I can't do a damn thing about it. Besides this, of course," she says, holding the spliff up.

"I'm so sorry," I tell her earnestly.

She shrugs, blowing more smoke out. "It's okay most days until it's not. Julian and I... we tried having children." I swallow. Again, I'm not sure what to say, or even if she *wants* me to say anything. "It was two years of hell, and then... everything with Julian's family happened, and we decided we didn't want biological children. In a way, my endometriosis saved us. Not that I don't want a child... I do. I just don't want to deal with trying to get pregnant again."

My brows knit together. "Would you consider adopting?"

She nods, putting the spliff out in the bath water and placing the filter on top of the cigarette case.

"We'd like to adopt, I think." She sighs and turns to face me. "Julian's been fixed. It's... complicated, I suppose. Julian's title is hereditary and can only be passed down to a biological heir. If we adopt, our children wouldn't inherit it. They wouldn't be recognized in that line of succession, so the title would end with him."

She looks down, almost reflective. "In a way, it's freeing. The title comes with expectations, responsibilities, and endless judgment from people who think they know us simply because of a name. Julian's done his duty. He tried to fit the mold, but we both know it's not what we want for our future children. It's why we left England. To start over."

There's so much vulnerability in her voice, and my hand twitches at my side. I want to touch her, to stroke her hair and make her feel better.

I keep my hands to myself.

"The family, the estate, the legacy—it's all designed to be inherited by blood. It's how these things work. There are centuries of tradition. But traditions like that aren't built to account for love that doesn't fit into tidy boxes. We're more interested in giving a child a home where they're free to be themselves, not bound by outdated rules. Not like we were for so long."

Her voice is light, but the words carry a heaviness that settles in my chest. I recognize that weight—it's the sound of someone pretending they've come to terms with a wound that hasn't fully healed.

I wonder if anyone's ever told her it's okay to still hurt, to still wish for that life.

I clear my throat. "That's very brave of both of you. To walk away from everything and start over, like you said."

She takes another spliff from the box and lights it. "Yes, well, there were things his family would never approve of."

I cock my head, feeling brave. "Like what?"

A faint smile crosses her lips, and she turns to face me. "Married people things," she says coyly.

I tell myself she's in pain, but I can't help watching her full lips suck on the spliff as she lights it—can't help but watch her delicate fingers hold it, can't help but be in awe of how beautiful she is under the soft light of the bathroom.

"What about you? You're a handsome man. Do you want to get married one day?"

I shrug, leaning forward and placing my elbows on my knees. "Maybe. I've never really felt the itch to make anything official, but one day I'd like to settle down, I think."

"And your job? Do you enjoy the religious aspect?"

I pull my lower lip between my teeth as I study her. Because right now? I don't feel religious *at all*. As my eyes skim over her dewy skin and the way her hair curls slightly along her hairline, or the way her bare shoulder is poking out of the water...

"Sometimes. Other times, it feels like God wouldn't approve of me."

She arches a brow. "How so?"

My lips tug into a lopsided smile. "Single people things."

She barks a laugh, a soft, restrained sound that barely escapes her lips, more a controlled exhale than an outright laugh. It's tinged with that effortless aristocratic composure, polished and measured, as though every ounce of mirth has been delicately refined.

In fact, until today, every part of Sophie has been polished and refined.

I smile as I take in the slightly *less* refined version of her, and I wonder if this is the side Julian gets to see all the time.

That sneaky jealousy springs up again.

She's not mine. She's his.

But I wish, just once, she'd look at me the way she looks at him.

"I feel a lot better. I think the worst of it is over," she tells me, her face relaxed. "The bath was a dream, so thank you."

"I have chocolate coming soon," I tell her, checking on the delivery.

Her lips pull into an easy smile. "I knew there was a

reason I liked you, Malakai Ravage. Always keeping me on my toes with your little surprises."

Her praise makes me grin, and I stand. "I'll let you get out—"

"Actually," she says with a playful glint in her eyes, "can you just pass me a towel?" She slowly rises out of the bath, and water cascades down her skin like silk. I'm momentarily frozen—my gaze locked on her. *Fuuuuck.* She catches me staring, a mischievous smile playing at the corners of her lips.

"Maybe I should have told you to turn around again," she teases, tilting her head as if reading my thoughts.

I can't help but feel a rush of heat at being caught in such an unguarded moment.

Or maybe it's from seeing her naked.

That perfect, petite body... the full breasts that would fit perfectly in my palms, the light brown, puffy nipples, the soft-looking stomach, the dark blonde hair between her legs...

I quickly look around for the towel and hand it to her without looking. "Here."

She shifts closer, the steam curling around her in my peripheral vision. I keep my eyes fixed on the floor, but my pulse betrays me, racing beneath my skin. It's not desire that trips me up.

It's the awareness of how *easy* this feels.

Too easy.

"Sorry. Didn't mean to make you uncomfortable," she says, placing a hand on my arm a few seconds later, after she's wrapped the towel around her body.

Temptation doesn't start with desire. It starts with comfort. With familiarity. One step closer, then another, until you're staring over the edge of something too deep to climb out of.

Sophie is the kind of comfort that makes the ground feel steady, even when you're already halfway off the cliff.

I let myself look down at her, and she's watching me with concern. "The marijuana helps with the pain, but it makes me feel a bit loopy sometimes."

I nod. "It's okay." I still feel in a daze as she grabs a nearby robe and pulls it on over the towel, letting the towel drop to the floor. She quickly runs a brush through her damp hair, and I drag a hand down my face, trying to think of anything to break the tension. "I'll go make you something to eat."

Sophie smiles as she tilts her head. "Sounds perfect. Thanks, Kai."

I walk out of the bathroom feeling dizzy, and as I quickly jog down the stairs to the garage, I realize I feel dizzy because my heart is racing a thousand miles a minute.

Penance.

The word clangs around my mind.

This is my penance for getting close to Sophie.

As a pastor, I know all too well about temptation. I used to preach about temptation and tell people it's like standing on the edge of a cliff of the most beautiful beach you've ever seen. Crystal-clear water, colorful coral, white sand. Temptation isn't the beach. It's the pull of desire beckoning you forward while the voice of reason warns you to step back.

Everyone wants to think they'd back away, but for a select few... the temptation of the water is too great, and they want nothing but to feel the free fall.

This attraction feels like a test. With each moment I spend with her, I can't help but wonder if I'm being led astray by the beautiful beach. Here I am, captivated by a woman who's everything I'm not supposed to want.

Plus, it's not like I'm the saint everyone expects me to be.

I've had my moments—thoughts and desires that swirl beneath the surface, hidden in the shadows of my conscience, as well as within the confines of my office, where the burdens of expectation can't touch me.

This, though... this is *different*.

This is Julian's *wife*.

This is just a minor inconvenience, I think as I heat up some water for pasta.

It has to be.

It's just a fleeting distraction that will pass with time. It has to be. Nothing else can happen—I can't think these things about her. She deserves more than a fleeting glance from someone who is supposed to be a moral guide, and the ex-best friend of her *husband*. But what if this isn't just a passing storm? What if this is my punishment for everything I've done to disgrace God? The thought sends a shiver through me, and a mix of fear and exhilaration—the same one I get before my scenes, or whenever I do something I shouldn't—pierces through me.

It only deepens my resolve to keep my distance.

From both her *and* her husband.

But the problem with distance is that it only makes you more aware of the space someone occupies. And right now, Sophie and Julian are starting to feel a little too close, like they're pressing into corners of my life I didn't realize were still empty.

CHAPTER SEVEN
THE MISUNDERSTANDING

Sophie

There's something so satisfying about watching all of my hard work fall into place. The glittering candles, the magnolia blooms spilling over every surface, the carefully chosen linens brushing the floor beneath the tables... it turned out better than I could've ever expected. A large part of me thrives on the chaos of planning—the orchestration, the details, the feeling of coming up with an amazing idea. I like the control of it all. In a way, it's the same reason I learned how to braid horse manes as a girl. Each tiny section woven with precision until there wasn't a single strand out of place.

For the past four months, I've poured myself into planning a night like this. Every tiny decision, from the champagne pairings to the imported truffles, was curated by me. Julian keeps calling me *his little project manager*, and though he's joking, I can't help but wonder if he's right.

My eyes take in how *clean* everything looks, considering how covered in dust everything was yesterday. I sip my champagne, adjusting one of the tall candlesticks that looks a half inch out of line.

The tables are full of our favorite English foods and champagne, the string quartet is playing in the courtyard, and Julian's art arrived last week, which gives the whole place a lived-in feel, despite all the work only finishing two days ago. Plus, my collection of books is perched on every shelf space I could find, making me feel like I'm *finally* home.

What will I do when this is over?

Can I spend my days in the library, getting lost in books? God, that would be a dream come true. I wonder if there's a job that would allow me to work with books all day long—aside from being a writer, because I'm rubbish at writing.

Perhaps I should think about becoming a librarian. I'm sure Julian would love that, too. It's probably a fantasy of his.

I let my eyes drift across the grand room. People are filtering in, and I make note of the attendants. We'd really invited everyone we knew: Julian's art clients, a few friends from my Pilates classes, Kai and his brothers, as well as their partners, and a lot of people Stella had introduced me to over the last couple of months. And then there are also people we'd met at Inferno.

There's excitement buzzing in the air, but something tugs at the back of my mind.

The party feels too perfect. *Too* polished. That same feeling of claustrophobia clings to my throat, and I swallow the panic down.

Maybe that's the problem. This house was supposed to be an escape from the life I left behind in London, but I can still hear my mother's voice lingering in the formality of it all.

The party sparkles under the chandelier's soft glow, but it's like I can still hear her.

A lady never lets her guests see the cracks, Sophie.

Smile, even if the house is burning down around you.

I blink and sip my champagne, but the echo of her voice lingers, curling around the edges of the evening.

What happens after tonight?

The thought feels selfish, like a betrayal of all the work I've done. This is my home now. Our *palace* without the prestige that usually comes with a palace. The name is ironic... a play on his upbringing. It was supposed to be a grand project to nurture and fuss over, but the thought of waking up tomorrow without another party to plan or wallpaper to choose feels... hollow.

Maybe I need more than just parties and renovations.

Maybe I need something that doesn't get packed away at the end of the night.

Julian slips behind me, wrapping an arm around my waist as if he knows exactly what I'm thinking. His familiar scent of bergamot makes me sigh and close my eyes briefly as I smile.

"This looks incredible, Soph," he murmurs into my hair.

"Thanks," I say softly, letting my head fall against his chest for just a moment. "It feels... done. Like there's nothing else to fix."

He laughs quietly. "You've been saying that since we finished the guest room, and then two days later you were halfway through sanding the banisters."

I roll my eyes but grin anyway. "I can't help it. I like when things feel new."

Julian kisses the top of my head. "Well, if you need a new project, I'm always open to suggestions. I quite liked the leather straps you added to the bedroom."

I smother a laugh against my glass. "That wasn't exactly *renovation*, Julian."

He smirks and pulls me in closer, lowering his voice. "It doesn't matter. It's our house, pet. Our rules."

The words are comforting, but they feel like silk draped over something thornier. I know he means them, but it's hard to untangle years of my mother's voice reminding me that *'a proper woman doesn't flaunt her marriage, she* manages *it.'*

That's something Julian says often, that this is our space, our kingdom, free from the prying eyes of family and obligation. I believe him.

Most days.

More people file in, and I take Julian's hand, squeezing it once. "You look very dapper tonight," I say, taking in his neatly slicked-back hair paired with a navy suit and a champagne-colored tie—the exact same color as my dress.

"And you," he says, kissing my forehead. "Look stunning. As fucking always."

I giggle, tucking my straightened hair behind my ear. "Thank you."

Guests greet us—mostly a handshake, or a kiss on each cheek. I have déjà vu from the parties we used to host in Brookshire, and my mouth goes dry when I realize this is the same thing, only in a different location.

I swirl the champagne in my glass, leaning into Julian with a playful glint in my eye. "God, this is starting to feel like one of my mother's parties. Quick—let's sneak into the pantry and eat cake with our hands like heathens. Completely unhinged."

Julian chokes on his drink, coughing through a laugh as he tugs me closer. "You mean scandalize the entire guest list with crumbs on your dress and frosting on my tie?"

I shrug, biting back a grin. "Adds character to the evening. Think anyone would notice?"

His eyes darken with that familiar spark—the one that always means he's tempted by my nonsense. "Oh, they'd notice. But I'd bet good money no one would dare say a word."

"Then it's settled. Meet me by the lemon tart in five minutes?"

Julian laughs, low and indulgent, like I've just suggested something far more indecent. "Deal. But if you get powdered sugar on my suit, you're cleaning it off later with your tongue. Speaking of later..." One of his hands comes around my backside, squeezing my arse.

Clearing my throat, nervous butterflies flit through me when I think of the surprise Julian has planned for me tonight. "Is everything all set for... later?"

Julian nods discreetly, taking my hand. "It is."

"And you want it to happen upstairs?"

"I do."

"Okay." My hand curls around his. "You're sure?"

Julian squeezes my hand back, leaning down so that his lips brush my temple. "What better way to celebrate our new home than to watch another man fuck my wife?" he whispers.

I bite my lower lip to keep from smiling. "As long as you're happy, I'm happy."

"Oh, I'm very happy, pet."

"Are you sure it's a good idea? To invite others... in the lifestyle..."

"I've asked them to wear masks, so we know who is in and who isn't. Should be a fun night of chaos and debauchery if we're lucky."

"And the contract is signed?" I ask, feeling slightly nervous to play with so many people around.

"Yes. He's been vetted, health checked, and he knows exactly what the terms are."

I nod. "Okay, babe."

A second later, I see Malakai walk through the door, and my breathing hitches slightly. For a moment, the party fades into the background. The chatter, the soft clink of champagne glasses, even the weight of Julian's hand on my lower back—all of it dims under the sudden awareness of him. His presence fills the room effortlessly, his dark hair tousled just enough to look like he hasn't been thinking about tonight at all, and yet, somehow, he fits here perfectly.

I don't know why I expected seeing him tonight to feel normal.

It's not.

I glance at Julian. He hasn't noticed yet. But I can feel it, the sharp edge of excitement curling low in my stomach.

And the guilt that follows immediately after.

What the hell is that about?

I press closer to Julian's side, grounding myself in the solid warmth of his body. His fingers trace absent circles along my waist.

This is fine, I tell myself. *This is fine.*

But as I catch Malakai's eyes across the room—his gaze lingering just a little too long before sliding away—I wonder if I believe that.

Julian's lips brush against the shell of my ear. "You've been staring at him for a full minute, pet. Should I be concerned?"

I snort softly, even as my skin heats. "Absolutely not. I'm just marveling at how good he is at pretending he's not looking at us."

Julian chuckles, tipping his glass toward Kai in a

subtle, knowing toast. "Well, let him look. He knows exactly who you're going home with tonight."

And I do.

Malakai's eyes shift toward mine once more, and something dark and dangerous—and hopeful—begins to grow inside of me.

———

An hour later, Julian squeezes my hand three times.

It's his cue to let me know the man he chose for me is waiting upstairs. Julian will take the back stairway up and sneak into the guest bedroom to watch us. Like always, I've been given a picture of the guy and a copy of his records, but I never know what they're like until we start the scene. It doesn't really matter to me, because the best part of it all is watching Julian lose his mind. Watching how his eyes get this sexy, dark color as he watches me. Putting on a show *for him.*

Plus, there's something really empowering about doing something so frowned upon in society. Others might call it cheating, but for us, it has only solidified our marriage and made us stronger.

Also, I can't lie and say it doesn't turn me on that Julian always has a say in who gets to touch me—in who gets to play with me. It makes me feel safe and protected. And while we've never seriously dabbled in the BDSM lifestyle, I've discovered that doing this is my way of submitting to him in the bedroom.

Which is really fucking hot.

Straightening my dress, I walk down the hallway upstairs and place my hand on the handle of the guest bedroom, but before I can open it, a man comes out of the shadows.

It's the guy Julian chose for tonight, and he's wearing a masquerade mask that covers his eyes and hugs his cheekbones.

"Sophie?"

I nod. "Hi."

He takes another step forward, and I know Julian is somewhere nearby, or will be very shortly. Every detail will have been worked out by him, and I trust that I'm in good hands.

The mystery man moves forward, closer to me, and presses me against the wall. With one arm above my head, he pins me in place, taking his other hand and placing it on my hip gently. I hear shuffling in the hallway, and I don't want to break the scene, so I do the only thing that makes sense. I kiss him.

His lips are soft, and his hand grips my hip tightly as his tongue invades my mouth. He tastes like mint, and though he's a few inches shorter than Julian, I imagine it's my husband, just like I always do. As I press my back against the cool wall, the man Julian chose for tonight trails slow kisses along my neck. My heart hammers in my chest, not from nerves, but from the delicious thrill of being seen. The weight of someone's gaze prickles over my skin, drawing heat to my face.

Julian.

I feel him watching. I always do.

I arch into the man's touch, letting my eyes drift open, expecting to catch the familiar silhouette of my husband slipping into the shadows. But when I glance down the hall, my breath stalls.

It's not Julian.

Kai stands there, half shrouded in the dim light, his stormy eyes locked onto me with something I can't place. His expression isn't scandalized or amused—it's raw. Unreadable.

Heat floods my cheeks, shame curdling in my stomach, and I pull back sharply from the man's lips.

"Shit," I mutter under my breath, stepping away.

For one heartbeat, Kai doesn't move. His gaze lingers, tracing every inch of me, like he's trying to make sense of what he's seeing. I can't breathe.

I thought I wanted to be watched.

But not by him.

Never by him.

I force a polite smile for the man beside me, murmuring an apology, but Kai's stare burns hotter than anything else. When the stranger slips away down the hall, I wipe at my lips, trying to erase the sensation of someone else's mouth.

My heart stumbles in my chest. I open my mouth to say something—anything—but no words come. Kai steps closer, slow and deliberate, his hands tucked into the pockets of his suit like he's barely holding himself back.

He looks bloody furious.

"Sophie," he says quietly, but there's nothing soft in his voice.

And just like that, the air between us turns razor-sharp.

"This isn't what you think—"

"Of all the people I know, you're the last one I expected to be a cheater," Kai says, his gray eyes steely and his jaw hard underneath the dark scruff. My whole body rocks back from his words, but before I can respond, he takes a step closer. "But I suppose we all have our secrets, don't we?"

My lips part in surprise as he steps into my space. "I'm not cheating—"

"Oh? Maybe you call it something different in London then," he growls, eyes boring into mine. "Julian deserves better," he adds.

Before I realize what I'm doing, my palm is making contact with his face, and color blooms on his cheek where I slapped him. He barely moves, instead touching his cheek and looking at me with hooded eyes.

"Fuck you, Kai. You know nothing about our marriage."

Gathering my dress with shaking hands, I stalk away from him and jog down the stairs. People say hello, but I'm too busy replaying Kai's words in my head to notice or care. Just as I reach the drawer in the larder that houses my cigarettes, Julian's hand comes around my wrist.

"Hey," he says gently. "What happened? I went upstairs but no one was there."

I lift my eyes to look at my husband—to explain what Kai walked in on—but one of the servers walks up to Julian and whispers into his ear. His face freezes for a second, brow furrowed, and then he groans out a low sound of realization.

"Fuck, I forgot. I have to give the speech because dinner is almost ready. You're okay, right?" he asks, one hand cupping my cheek. His expression is apologetic, and I can't help but smile.

"I'm fine, I promise."

He got so wrapped up in the scene we had planned that he forgot about the speech. I'm used to watching the wobble in his expression as he recalibrates, that same familiar glimmer of frustration crossing his face. It's not at me, it's at himself. He hates when this happens—when he forgets something while in the heat of the moment.

Taking my hand, he gives it a quick squeeze, his thumb brushing over my knuckles in a way that feels almost apologetic. Then he pulls us toward the grand staircase at the center of the room.

When we're a few steps above the crowd, he clinks his champagne flute with a small spoon.

The crowd goes quiet.

My husband is nothing if not effective, and he's always been able to command a room better than anyone I know.

"Thank you all most sincerely for joining us this evening to celebrate our new home. Sophie and I are absolutely delighted to have you all here with us."

I shift slightly closer to him, trying to lose myself in the warmth of his words, but the weight of another gaze lingers somewhere past the crowd.

I already know who it is before I look.

Across the room, Kai's eyes catch mine, and my breath stills in my throat.

"The move back to California has not been without its challenges. It is something we have long aspired to, and now we are beyond pleased to finally be here. There are many individuals to whom we owe a debt of gratitude for ensuring the transition has been as smooth as it has..."

Kai's gaze is heavy—sharp, lingering just a second too long. I can't tell if the tight expression is disappointment, judgment, or something worse. Something more dangerous.

My stomach clenches.

A flush rises to my cheeks, and for a moment, I feel exposed, as if Kai's gaze has peeled back something carefully guarded.

What's worse is the way part of me bristles at it.

I drag my eyes away, swallowing the knot tightening in my throat.

Julian's voice hums next to me, light and full of warmth as he talks about our home, our future.

I chance another glance toward Kai. His eyes haven't moved. That same trace of something unreadable dances behind his gaze, and it's enough to make me look away again, biting the inside of my cheek.

Focus, Sophie.

I straighten my spine, grounding myself in his presence, letting his easy confidence wash over me. Whatever that was—whatever unspoken thing just passed between me and Kai—it doesn't belong here.

Julian's voice lifts, clear and steady.

"And of course," Julian continues, "I would be remiss if I did not extend my heartfelt thanks to my oldest and dearest friend, Malakai Ravage. Kai, would you care to join us?"

Oldest and dearest friend...

It's not like they're enemies, but there's still tension between them. I know Julian is just calling him that for show.

The crowd parts as Kai begins to move toward the stairs, but I don't miss the faint quirk of his lips—like he knows exactly what's going through my head. I quickly flick my gaze over the rest of his family—his four brothers and their partners.

They make a beautiful family.

My chest tightens, and suddenly I feel far too warm under the gaze of the entire room.

Fuck.

A few seconds later, Kai joins us on the stairs, and I feel my whole body stiffen in his presence, especially when his eyes find mine and he gives me an arrogant, knowing look.

Fuck him.

"A long time ago," Julian continues, a lightness in his voice, "I was just a boy in search of a friend. I suspect many of you are familiar with the Ravage family name.

Imagine my astonishment when Malakai Ravage himself decided that we should be friends. We were in sixth grade, and my family had just moved from London."

Julian looks at Kai. Their relationship is still a bit icy in places, but ever since Kai came over to help me while I was in pain, he's been friendlier to his old friend.

"Malakai, in his infinite wisdom, decided to assist with some of the more laborious tasks—patching walls, painting, carpentry... We would not be standing here tonight without the invaluable help of Malakai Ravage," Julian finishes, lifting his champagne flute. "To Malakai."

"To Malakai," the crowd echoes.

"Thank you all once again for joining us. Do enjoy the rest of your evening."

Everyone begins speaking again, and I lean over to Julian. "I need to speak to you. I'll be in our bedroom."

I don't give him a chance to ask why—I don't want to be around Malakai for a second longer than I have to. Not until I can speak to Julian.

Ascending the stairs, I hear someone following me, and a quick glance over my shoulder tells me it's Kai. *Not* Julian—who is currently laughing with a man I don't recognize. He gives me a quick apologetic look, and mouths, *One second.*

I keep going, and at the top of the stairs, I turn to face Kai. "Why are you following me?" I don't bother trying to hide the ice in my words. We're far enough away from everyone that we have some privacy up here, and any second now, Julian will come rescue me and explain everything. "I'm just a *cheater*, right? Leave me alone," I add, my voice breaking.

I turn and continue down the hall toward the master bedroom.

Before I know it, tears are falling down my cheeks. Not because I'm embarrassed, but because I actually enjoy spending time with Kai. I look up to and admire him, and now he thinks I'm worse than the scum on the bottom of his shoe.

It stings—for reasons I'm not sure I'm ready to admit.

Before I reach the master bedroom, I feel Kai's hand close around my wrist, stopping me in my tracks. I spin around, but his face is unreadable, his usual calm replaced with something sharp and simmering beneath his clenched jaw.

"You don't get to just walk away," he says, voice low but intense. "You don't get to act like *I'm* the one who's out of line."

His words cut deep, but I keep my head high, quickly wiping the tears from my cheeks. "It isn't what you think. But considering how *rude* you've been about it, I don't owe you an explanation. Now, like I asked before, please leave me alone."

His grip loosens, but he doesn't let go, searching my face as though he's trying to piece together a puzzle. "Fine. Maybe you don't owe me anything, but it'd be nice to know the truth before you make me out to be some kind of fool. Does Julian know?"

The truth.

I bite back the urge to tell him, to explain that I'm not some thrill-seeker playing games behind Julian's back, that I wouldn't be this careless with people I care about.

People I care about.

The realization that Kai is one of them only makes this hurt more, the sting of his mistrust swelling in my chest.

If he *really* knew me, he'd know that I'd never cheat on Julian.

That, above all else, hurts the most.

I wipe away the remnants of my tears. "Whatever you think you saw... it's not what it looked like."

His laugh is hollow, almost disbelieving. "Not what it looked like? You were kissing another man, Sophie. That's pretty clear. So, explain to me what I'm supposed to think. Because from my viewpoint, it looks like you're betraying Julian—and that..." He runs a hand over his face. "I'm sorry, Sophie, but he's my friend. And I have to tell him."

My shoulders slump. I want to defend myself, want to shout that Julian knows everything, that he's always known, that there's nothing underhanded going on here. But I don't want to betray the quiet boundaries Julian and I set for ourselves, the unspoken understanding between us that we wouldn't parade our arrangements around. The things we do in our marriage are private, sacred even, and I know Julian trusts me to keep it that way.

Kai's silence is heavy. He doesn't look angry anymore —just hurt, the flash of disappointment evident in the downturn of his mouth, the tight line of his shoulders. The sting in my chest grows, knowing that the last thing I wanted was to disappoint him.

Finally, I find my voice. "Just trust me, Kai. It's not what it seems."

His nostrils flare, and then his face flashes with that unknown emotion from before, and I realize with a start that Malakai Ravage is *jealous.*

"What do you mean by that?" He steps back, his brows drawn in a hard line, as if he's trying to keep himself from unraveling. "Is this some sort of sick game the two of you are playing?" His eyes go wide. "Are you messing with *me*?"

"No!" The word escapes, louder than I intended, and I immediately regret it. I take a calming breath. "It's not like that, Kai. It's just... complicated."

Kai's jaw tightens. "So explain it to me, Sophie. Because right now, all I see is someone who thinks she can have it all without caring about who she hurts along the way."

His words leave me reeling. I open my mouth, then close it, wondering how I can make him understand without actually telling him about the situation. I can't betray the trust Julian and I built—or at least, it feels like Julian should be here too so we can tell him together. I could tell him that Julian knew all along—that nothing ever happens without honesty between us. But my words are stuck in my throat.

It feels like trying to bridge an impossible distance.

He lets out a frustrated sigh. "You know what? Forget

it." His gaze softens, but there's still an edge to it, a look of someone who feels like a fool for ever trusting me in the first place. "I just thought you were... different. The work on the house is done, and I don't want any part of whatever the fuck is going on with you and Julian—"

"And what, exactly, do you think is going on?"

Julian's voice cuts through the quiet hallway, and both Kai and I turn to find him standing a few feet away.

CHAPTER EIGHT
THE FANTASY

JULIAN

"What's going on?" I ask, coming to stand beside Sophie.

Kai stands less than a foot away. His shoulders are tense, and his gaze flicks back and forth between us as though he's witnessing a moment he shouldn't be. He shifts his weight before crossing his arms tightly over his chest, a protective shield. His eyes dart away every time they land on me, then reluctantly return to Sophie, as if he's not sure where to look—or where he belongs in this exchange.

"Kai saw me kissing..." Sophie trails off, and when I look up at Kai, his jaw hardens.

"Ah," I say, smiling as I face him. "And you thought I'd ever allow another man to touch my wife without my explicit permission?"

Kai's lips part. "You knew? So, what? Is it like a game,

or are you guys in an open marriage?" Before I can respond, he holds a hand up. "You know what? As I told Sophie, I don't want or need to know. I don't want to get caught up in whatever the fuck is going on."

Just as he moves, I grab him to keep him from walking away. As my fingers wrap around Kai's hand, an electric current shoots through the space between us, startling me in its intensity. I can feel the rough calluses from him working with his hands. The veins and cords along the back of his hand, thick and bulging.

He stops mid-stride, his body tensing as he glances down at our joined hands, his face momentarily unguarded. For half a second, the angry and frustrated expression is replaced by something softer, something almost familiar. His fingers twitch against mine, like he's deciding whether to pull away or hold on.

I remember the last time I held his hand like this. It was summer. Crestwood was hot, and we'd been tipsy, laughing over nothing in particular, our fingers brushing and lingering in the dark on the grounds of Ravage Castle, weeks before our freshman year at uni together.

Our eyes meet, and it's as if the years between us vanish, pulling me back to late-night talks and the hesitant, stolen moment we'd shared in our college dorm. I remember when he kissed me—how I'd paced the hallway, every nerve buzzing with the possibility of what we could be.

And then he walked away like it never happened.

Like *we* never happened.

For a long time, I couldn't imagine a life without him

in it, and part of me still feels that loss, buried under the years but never entirely gone.

Kai's expression shifts, his guard wavering as he studies me. I can see the confusion there, the wariness laced with a hint of something warmer. He swallows, a hint of something that might be regret or longing passing over his face before he glances away. I know he remembers too. He must.

"Kai... Sophie is a hotwife. Do you know what that is?" I ask, voice softer.

He pulls his hand back, slowly, as if reluctant to break the connection but too wary to let it linger.

"No."

"Julian..." Sophie's voice is sharp with warning.

I shrug. "He thinks he saw something he didn't. I think we owe him an explanation, don't you?"

She swallows, and I can sense the hesitation in her stance, the blush slowly creeping up the fair skin of her neck and onto her cheeks. But there's no going back now.

It strikes me then that Sophie is ashamed to tell him. I can't fault her. Until this moment, we'd managed to keep this secret from everyone in our personal life.

"Tell me," he says, looking right at Sophie. His tone isn't demanding. It's *curious*. Maybe even a little intrigued. And there, in the way he's not hiding his feelings *at all*, I see it—the way his eyes skim over her full lips, the way he takes a subtle step closer to her.

"It means Julian likes to watch me sleep with other men," she tells him.

Kai's body stiffens. His gaze locks onto hers, and for a split second, I watch the realization crash through him.

I watch him. *Really* watch him.

His pupils dilate. There's something in his eyes—possession. *Lust.*

My cock twitches, and I clear my throat to cut through the heavy, tense atmosphere.

Why do I enjoy the way he's looking at my wife like a delicious snack?

I shouldn't. I should hate it, maybe even feel threatened by it. But instead, it coils low in my stomach—something dark and thrilling.

"What you saw was completely consensual and planned by yours truly," I tell him, keeping my voice light. "I like watching her be desired by other men. It's intoxicating. But don't mistake it for something secretive," I finish, my eyes boring into his.

His gaze hardens again, but there's something else beneath it, a trace of vulnerability I haven't seen in years.

"Clearly," he says, his eyes lingering on Sophie a little too long. "I should go. Have a good night." Turning to face Sophie, I see the way his eyes soften for her. "The party is great, Soph. You outdid yourself."

With one last look at me, he begins to walk away.

When he's a few feet away, Sophie takes my hand and clears her throat. She opens her mouth, but before she can speak, I pull her body into mine and kiss her.

She moans, her hands sliding around my waist, pulling me closer, and when my eyes flutter open—just as my tongue brushes against hers—I see him.

Kai stands at the top of the stairs, frozen, his gaze locked on us, his expression a dark storm of emotions. His jaw tightens and yet he doesn't look away. He *can't*. His stare feels like an accusation and a confession all at once, as though he's both furious and interested.

Like he's unable to extricate himself from the scene unfolding before him.

I meet his gaze and, for a brief, reckless moment, I don't stop.

I should stop. I know I should.

But I don't.

I want to see how far this stretches.

My fingers tighten on Sophie's hips as I grind my hard cock against her, lifting her dress just enough for my intentions to be clear. A spark of defiance flares in me as I hold his gaze, a silent challenge I barely understand myself. Her soft gasp escapes as I nuzzle into her neck, feeling her shudder beneath me.

"Julian," she whimpers, her voice a delicate mix of need and surprise. But my attention is somewhere else now. I can barely hear her as I watch Kai's reaction, my own pulse quickening in ways I didn't expect. His lips part, his breath catching as he watches us, his grip tightening on the banister, knuckles white. Sophie moans again, but I'm focused on Kai—the sharp, almost pained expression flickering across his face as he watches me touch my wife.

I swear I see something unraveling in him.

Does he like this? Does it make him angry? Jealous?

I push Sophie against the wall.

If he's jealous, why does that excite me so much? Kai's grip tightens on the banister.

He could leave.

He should.

But he doesn't.

His gaze lowers for half a second, taking in the way her legs part, the way my hand presses between them. It hits me like a punch to the gut. I want him to want this. To want her.

To want *us*.

These feelings have been creeping up on me since he showed up again—these stray thoughts I thought I'd buried. The way his hand brushed against mine in the kitchen last week, the ease in how he touched Sophie when he thought I wasn't paying attention.

The way Sophie's cheek had been smudged with white paint, and how Kai wiped it away with his thumb, so natural and intimate.

The way Kai focused intently on aligning the shelves, his brow furrowed and lips pursed in concentration, had me swallowing hard more than once.

The way he wiped paint from his hands onto an old rag, the veins in his forearms standing out as he worked with meticulous precision, left me unable to focus on anything else for the rest of the day.

The way Kai had stood behind Sophie, guiding her hand as she tried to drill into the wall, his low voice rumbling in her ear, felt like something I shouldn't be aroused by—but was.

The feelings are subtle, but they're there, winding

through me in slow, quiet waves. It happened without me even realizing.

And now? Now it crashes hard and fast, like I've been ignoring it too long. In that moment, I realize I want him to feel this ache—the same wild confusion I feel every time I'm near him. My feelings for him are sharper than ever, simmering beneath the surface, tangled with a sort of anger and desire I can't seem to untangle.

The depth of his gaze shifts, a flash of pain and longing I recognize, the same pull I felt years ago. He looks away then, turning abruptly, and I almost call out, a strange sense of loss tightening in my chest. But before I can say anything, he's gone, disappearing down the stairs, leaving me feeling more exposed than I'd ever admit—even to myself.

Hoisting Sophie up and pressing her against the wall, I pull her knickers to the side, unzip my trousers, freeing my cock, and push into her without any warning.

She gasps and pulls away from my lips, looking at me with hooded eyes. "Julian," she mutters, lips swollen and cheeks flushed. "We should talk—"

"About what?" I ask, grunting as I slide all the way into her.

With parted lips, she groans. "About—about—"

"Kai?" I ask, his name on my lips low and sensual.

"Yes," she whispers, throwing her head back. "God, Julian—"

"It's okay, you know," I tell her, kissing her jaw before pulling out and driving back into her soft, wet cunt. "I see the way you look at him, Soph."

She gasps as I slam into her on the last word. "Julian."

I can't help it. I think of Kai staying instead of leaving—standing behind me instead of running away. It feels dangerous and exhilarating. It's worrying how easily I imagine him stepping closer.

My cock throbs, and Sophie arches against me.

Would she arch like this if it were his hands on her waist?

"It should bother me," I growl, baring my teeth as I roll my hips. Her eyes flutter, threatening to close, so I place one of my hands gently around her throat. "Look at me when I say this," I tell her, my voice earnest as I continue fucking her. With each hard push into her, her tits bounce inside her dress and her eyes spark with lust. I know her well enough to know that a minute playing with her clit will have her exploding on my cock, but I hold off because I want to get this off my chest.

"It should bother me, but it doesn't," I confess. "Sometimes, when he looks at you... and when you look at him... it makes me really fucking hot," I add, squeezing her thighs with my hands.

"I'm not— I don't ever want him to come between us," Sophie says, eyes locking into mine as she wraps her legs around me even tighter. Her hand comes to my cheek, and the faint blush from earlier returns. "You matter more than anyone, and I don't ever want you to feel like I'm betraying you."

Kissing her hand, I fuck her harder. "You won't be, because Kai kissed me at uni. If anything, I'm betraying you."

Her eyes flick between mine, widening in surprise at first before her pupils bloom dark. "I shouldn't find that so sexy, but I do," she says after a minute.

"That day I got a splinter? He sucked it out, and I wanked to the feel of his mouth on my hand."

Sophie grins. "You didn't."

I place a hand near her head to give myself more leverage, and then I dig my nails into her arse.

"I did."

Her eyes flash, and she kisses me—*hard*. "Fuck," she gasps, panting against my lips. "That's—really—fucking—hot—"

"Yeah?" I ask, laughing as my wife's cunt feathers around my cock, drawing my orgasm closer. "You like the idea of your husband having a little crush on his friend? You like the idea of fucking him while I watch, or watching while I fuck him?"

"Yes," she whispers, pleading. "Fuck, Julian."

"You're not alone, baby. Maybe we both want him, and that's okay."

"Yes," she says quickly, whimpering. "God, I'm close."

"You and me," I growl, biting her lower lip as I slam into her over and over.

"Yes. You and me. Oh God, Julian, I'm so fucking close—"

"Nothing will ever change that—"

"Yes, yes, fuck, yes—"

"Come for me, Sophie."

She does, and her pussy grips me as her eyes roll into

the back of her head. The tight squeezes draw my climax out, and my knees shake as my cock pulses into her.

"Fuck!" I roar, coming hard and fast, spilling into her with zero abandon.

She goes limp as the last of it leaves our bodies, and for several seconds, I just hold her, pressing her back into the wall as I breathe heavily into the space between her neck and ear.

I thought I'd buried it, whatever this thing with Kai is. But seeing him now, watching him watch us... it's all starting to come apart at the seams.

Neither of us says anything—we just stand there, catching our breaths, the hallway thick with a silence that feels almost confessional. The party is still going downstairs, but it feels so far away from this moment. There's a charge between us, as if we've crossed into territory we can't retreat from. *Malakai Ravage.* His name lingers unspoken between us, like a spark that's finally caught fire.

For so long, he was a forbidden presence I kept carefully pushed away, a relic of another life, a fantasy I never let fully surface. In the years since I met Sophie, I'd convinced myself I'd let him go, that what we shared was locked firmly in the past. But over time, the idea of him crept back in, tucked into casual remarks, brief mentions of his name that felt electric. At first, I was careful. I only let myself wonder what Sophie might think if she knew I still thought of him. But as we became closer, I noticed how her curiosity about him grew, too. Small, offhand comments about his job as a pastor or seeing him working in our house turned into subtle, unguarded interest.

Somehow, without either of us saying it out loud, Kai had become a shared intrigue, a half-formed desire. A kind of thrill neither of us admitted to but both secretly entertained. It was the edge of danger that came from knowing there was someone else we both craved, a ripple of excitement that stayed at the edges of our lives, out of reach but never entirely out of mind.

Of course neither of us would ever consider cheating —it was unthinkable, and I knew Sophie felt the same way.

But something had changed tonight.

Even though Kai had walked away, his presence had lingered in the air. The look on his face before he'd turned—the quiet fury and confusion—had left an undeniable mark on both of us.

I could feel him in the air between us like a haunting.

He'd become more than a fantasy. He was real now, and he'd turned into a dangerous fascination neither of us could deny.

Sophie meets my gaze, and I know she feels it too. There's a hunger in her eyes, a thrill that comes from knowing the boundaries we'd only teased at have been completely erased.

Kai had become part of our shared fantasy.

It's something neither of us will be able to unsee.

And tonight, he'd infiltrated our marriage bed, without even being here.

What if I let him stay? Would he like that? Would that make him happy?

Would he have watched me touch her? Fuck her?

Or would he have touched us both?

The room is quiet, but the choice hangs between us like a precipice—either we embrace this, let the idea of him move from fantasy into something more real, or we step back, cut the threads, and walk away from whatever might lie down this path. Full steam ahead, or sever the pull we feel, once and for all.

But as I watch her, the hint of a smile, a spark of something electric in her eyes, I know there's no going back.

I tell myself this is just a phase—a fleeting curiosity. But deep down, I know it isn't.

It never was.

I wonder if Kai knows how easy it would be to break the rules.

I wonder if he'd even hesitate to participate.

To involve him in our fantasies... for real this time.

CHAPTER NINE
THE AWAKENING

MALAKAI

I lean back in the chair in my private room in Inferno. Running my hands down my face, my fingers press against my temples, trying to ease the weight of the day from my mind.

"You can go," I say, waving Adrian off.

He stands unsteadily, and I zip myself back up without bothering to offer any pleasantries.

"Did I do something wrong?" he asks, grabbing his coat.

I shake my head. "No. I came, didn't I?"

Too hard.

He shrugs. "All right. See you later."

Once he's gone, I groan as I rest my face in my hands.

For years, I've pushed this down, convinced myself it didn't mean anything. That I wasn't attracted to men, too. But if that were true, why did it feel like I was cracking open something I'd spent years cementing shut? I told myself it was just sex, just curiosity—another experiment. But when his hands were on me, firm and certain, I knew the truth. I wanted this. I wanted him.

And yet, part of me still recoiled at the thought, as if wanting him somehow unraveled everything I'd built my life around. As if admitting this desire would rewrite my past, my identity, my faith. It wasn't just fear of what others would say—it was fear of what I'd say to myself.

And admitting that to myself feels bigger than Julian or Sophie. It feels like finally admitting who I am.

After last weekend, I had to know for sure.

I couldn't keep circling around these feelings—toward Sophie, toward Julian—without facing them head-on.

So I did something I've never done before.

I went looking for someone who reminded me of Julian—tall, broad-shouldered, blond hair that caught the light the same way his did. I found him by accident, leaning against the bar at a place in West Hollywood, and before I could second-guess myself, I invited him back to Inferno with me.

I didn't expect to enjoy it as much as I did.

And I definitely didn't expect my cock to get hard, and to come down his throat while imagining that I was face fucking my friend.

It was pure euphoria... followed by extreme panic.

If I admit it to myself—if I accept it—what does that

make me? Am I still the person I thought I was, or is this some version of myself that I've spent my whole life denying?

It feels like I'm on the edge of something big, and I have no idea what the future holds. I just know that being here—*pretending*—doesn't feel right anymore.

When I got the job as headmaster of Saint Helena Academy—or rather, when Chase, my younger brother, bought the school out and *handed* me the job—it felt perfect for where I was in my life.

And now? Recently... I've felt like a fraud.

It's not that religion is less important; it's more that faith itself has become... complicated. The moral code I've spent my life enforcing feels like it's slipping. Or maybe it's me who's slipping. For years, I told myself it was the scripture that kept me in line. I used to embrace the commandments and expectations without question. That the words of Leviticus, of Matthew, were guardrails. But the truth is, I held onto them like a lifeline—not to save me from sin, but to save me from myself. If I followed the rules, I wouldn't have to face the fact that I never fit neatly into the world they built for me. They used to mean something to me. But they feel hollow now, almost stifling.

I speak to the kids at Saint Helena every day. They're young and impressionable, and they trust me to guide them. I wonder what exactly I'm leading them toward, because I don't even know how to guide myself.

Maybe this is part of it. All these years of feeling like I had to fit into a box—straight, devout, the man everyone expects me to be. But I've never let myself acknowledge how much I enjoyed that kiss with Julian seventeen years ago.

I run my hands over my face again, feeling the roughness of a day's worth of stubble. The things I've done with women, even if they strayed from traditional vows, at least felt natural—still within the bounds of something forgivable. But this? The things I think about now... they feel like an outright rebellion.

I can almost hear the scripture whispering its condemnation.

Leviticus.

Matthew.

I clung to those verses, held them close—not to judge others, but to keep myself in line. I wasn't harsh on anyone else, just myself.

Always myself.

Back then, I thought I needed them to make sense of things, to keep myself on track.

And now? I'm sitting here, drawn to thoughts of him, my friend, the man who knows me better than anyone, and yet not at all. The one I used to call my best friend. And Sophie, the picture of devotion. Together, they exist in my mind like some forbidden relic I'm compelled to touch, even as I know I'll be burned.

But lately, what I feel doesn't match the words of condemnation drilled into me since I started seminary all those years ago. It feels like something I've been missing for years but never dared acknowledge, something that only now makes sense, though it's wrapped in shame.

I can't tell where the lines of belief end and my own needs begin. And part of me isn't sure I want to know anymore.

Part of me isn't sure I *care* anymore.

I quickly pack up and walk out of Inferno. Guilt briefly flickers in my mind for dismissing Adrian so quickly. The thought lingers for a moment before I push it aside. It's late afternoon, and I still have a few things to wrap up in my actual office. The walk is uneventful, and soon I'm closing the door before sitting at my desk. I let my face fall into my hands as I let out a frustrated sigh.

I haven't even acknowledged that being with Adrian felt like I was betraying Sophie and Julian, despite not speaking to them since the housewarming party.

A soft knock on the door has me sitting up. "Come in."

Jackson Parker walks into my office. "Hey. Sorry I'm late. Mark called. Apparently our flight next week was canceled, so we're just trying to scramble—"

"I understand," I tell him, leaning forward. "You've got a lot going on right now. In the cabinet behind you, second drawer, there's a bottle of whiskey. Here's the key," I tell him, tossing a key to him.

Jackson laughs. "Naughty headmaster." He reaches behind him and unlocks the drawer, unscrewing the top before taking a swig. "Fuck, that's good."

He hands me the bottle and I sip it before setting it down. "Better?"

"Much," he replies, sighing and leaning back in the chair. "I just want to be there for the birth of our child, you know? If I miss it... I'll never forgive myself."

I nod, considering his words. He and his partner, Mark, are expecting a child via surrogate due next week. He teaches preschool at Saint Helena and is one of our best and most coveted teachers.

He's also Chase's best friend, so I've known him for most of my adult life.

"Do you want to start your leave early?" I ask gently. "I can certainly arrange for that if needed."

Jackson shakes his head. "No way. My little crotch goblins are the only light in my day." He chuckles. "Besides Mark, of course."

I huff a laugh. "Just let me know when I need to call in the substitute. She's all ready and prepped to go. Your class will be in good hands, okay?"

Jackson nods. "Thank you. I can't thank you enough for helping me with the paperwork. It's not easy being a gay man sometimes. And of course, Rod got involved last week," he adds, rolling his eyes as a flicker of frustration passes over his expression.

I stiffen. "Did he? Doesn't surprise me," I mutter, shaking my head.

"Something about the family values at Saint Helena. He was basically asking me to keep my reason for my leave quiet. As if a bunch of three- and four-year-olds care that I'm gay. Sometimes it's hard having to fight for every inch."

I swallow. "I can't imagine."

Jackson is quiet for a few seconds, but his eyes bore into mine. "You okay?"

I clear my throat, glancing down at the whiskey bottle before lifting my gaze to Jackson. "Before you met Mark, did you ever... think you knew yourself, and then one day realize maybe you didn't know as much as you thought?" I ask, trying to keep my tone light, casual, like it's just an idle thought.

Jackson grins, tipping his head thoughtfully. "You mean like how I never thought I'd want my own kids one day?" He chuckles, running a hand through his hair. "I never thought I'd marry a man. But I suppose life has a way of giving you what you need, not what you expect."

"That's true." I pause, trying to find the words I've been wondering about since I got mixed up with both Sophie and Julian. "Were you always sure about how you felt about Mark?"

Jackson's smile softens. "No, not always. It was quite a process of figuring it out. There was a lot of self-reflection. But then I realized I had this significant part of myself that had been dormant until I met Mark." He leans forward, resting his elbows on his knees. "After that, it sort of just clicked." His eyes search my face. "But for other people, it can take a bit of time to come to terms with it. It's not always a switch you can flip on command. Or at least it wasn't in my experience."

Maybe that's what I was waiting for all these years—a moment when everything would suddenly make sense. But it never came. Instead, I spent my entire life compartmentalizing, convincing myself that if I just kept moving, if I kept focusing on my work, I wouldn't have to face the fact that the things I wanted didn't fit into the life I'd chosen. That I was only punishing myself by pretending I didn't feel them at all.

"Right," I murmur, my eyes drifting to the stained glass for a moment. "Guess some things take their time."

"Is this because of Orion and Layla?" he asks, rubbing his chin as he refers to my youngest brother, who just started dating Layla, our stepsister, three months ago.

"What? No, I'm just... thinking about things. Life. My job. The future."

"I only ask because you're very famously the last single Ravage brother. I'm sure the pressure is on, you know?"

I trace the letters on the bottle, letting his words sink in. "Yeah," I say finally, a soft smile pulling at the corners of my mouth. "I think I'm starting to realize there's more to life than the job. More than just keeping busy, keeping up appearances... being what everyone expects."

Jackson raises an eyebrow, his gaze a little sharper, like he's seeing right through the act I've held up for so long.

"For so many years, I thought my work here was all I needed," I continue, "that as long as I was helping others, I'd be fulfilled." I shake my head, almost surprised to hear the words coming out. "But maybe I've been selfish in my own way. Ignoring the things I want. Trying to be everything for everyone else."

"Selfish?" Jackson laughs. "Pretty sure that's not what anyone would call you."

I meet his gaze. "Well, it's what it feels like. Like maybe, for once, I should stop pretending I have it all figured out and actually... want something for myself."

Jackson levels me with an eagle eye. "It's okay to want something. I know your job carries a lot of guilt and heavy shame regarding certain things, but trust me when I say, as long as you're not hurting anyone, who cares?"

The problem is... how do I explain that to myself?

I've spent so many years thinking I was protecting myself—protecting others—by pushing this part of me away. What happens when I stop hiding from it? I've always told myself it's a sin, something unnatural. But is it really? Or is it the shame I've been taught to feel?

I nod. "Yeah. I wish I saw it that way."

"Life's too short. I'm not saying you should quit your job and join a pop band, but... people change. I've changed. And maybe you have, too." He stands. "I should go. I'll keep you updated about everything, okay? And I'll bring a copy of the family leave paperwork tomorrow."

"Sounds good." I stand and hold my hand out. "Thanks for this. I feel like I'm the one who's supposed to be giving you advice."

Jackson laughs, clasping my hand warmly. "Sometimes we need a little advice ourselves, especially the ones who are used to dishing it out. You're only human. Don't forget that."

"Yeah."

He pats my shoulder. "You've got a lot on your plate,

but don't let it stop you from living, all right? You're allowed to have a life beyond these walls." He gives me one last encouraging smile, nodding once before he heads toward the door. "And hey, if you ever need another drink —or a pep talk—you know where to find me."

As the door clicks shut, the silence settles back around me, though it doesn't feel quite as heavy as before. Jackson's words linger in the air. *Life's too short.* I glance around the dim office, at the crosses and stained glass, and for once, the thought of wanting something just for me feels... almost possible.

I take another couple of swigs of whiskey before I stand and put it away. I think about how far I've come from the guy who used to pray away his thoughts—the guy who couldn't look at another man without feeling disgusted with himself. Why was I scared of this? Scared of wanting someone who isn't exactly what I've been told to want?

Locking up, I walk the halls of the mostly empty academy. Walking past my car, I continue down the main road in Crestwood, needing the fresh air and not wanting to drink and drive. I already know where I'm going when I enter Inferno twenty minutes later, and I'm waved inside as one of the regulars.

My youngest brother, Orion, started the kink club a few months ago, and unbeknownst to him and my other three brothers, I've been a more frequent client as of late. There's an entire religious taboo section on both the *Purgatory* and *Paradise* floors, and I've dabbled with scenes when it was easy for me to take part in them anonymously.

And while the club rightfully doesn't allow any edge play on the premises for safety and liability reasons, I've been able to make contacts here who enjoy those things in their own spaces, like me.

I came here to escape what I was feeling, but suddenly, the pounding music from Purgatory below is too loud. The flickering lights are too much. The air feels thick, weighted with things I've spent years trying to bury. The sound of leather slapping against skin echoes from down below.

Why am I here?

And why is it that I don't want to leave?

At least when I'm here, I know I won't be judged, and maybe that's why I enter the bar area and sit down. I put my one and only drink order in—seeing as Inferno has a one-drink rule. The whiskey burns as it goes down my throat, and just as I swallow, I hear a familiar laugh. My whole body goes still as a dark gray suit comes into my peripheral vision, and I shoot the rest of the whiskey quickly, wincing as I set the glass down.

"There's a joke here somewhere," Julian says, coming to sit down next to me.

I don't look at him right away. "You're not the first to say that."

As I slowly slide my eyes to my ex-best friend, my whole body is suddenly aware of the way the gray suit brings out his blue eyes, and how the five-o'clock shadow makes him seem a little less polished than normal.

"Do you keep the company of comedians often, then?" he says, his voice low and half amused.

"Perhaps." I attempt to keep my voice steady. Tearing my eyes away, my fingers trace the edge of the empty glass.

Julian leans in, close enough that I catch a hint of cedar and something darker beneath it, like expensive leather and faint smoke. And bergamot—*just like he used to smell growing up.* It's too familiar, and I immediately think of Sophie and her not-so-secret smoking habit. I look back at him, feeling like I'm being pulled into a whirlpool of my own making.

Julian's eyes gleam as he watches me over the rim of his glass.

"I didn't think this was your scene," he murmurs, looking around. His eyes linger on my button-up shirt—I'd removed my tie earlier, and I'm sure my hair isn't as neat as it was this morning, considering it's been a hell of a long day.

"It's not."

"And yet…"

His gaze flicks to the empty glass in front of me, as if it holds answers I haven't admitted yet. I shrug, but it feels like a weak attempt to downplay the heat curling low in my stomach. This isn't about the drink—and we both know it.

"Nevertheless, you look like you're here to make bad

decisions," he murmurs, a hint of a smirk playing at the corner of his mouth.

"And you're here to stop me?" I ask, a touch too quickly, almost daring him.

He raises an eyebrow, a flicker of surprise in his gaze. "Now why would I do that?" His voice drops even lower, practically a rumble. His hand brushes mine on the bar, just a featherlight touch, but it sends a jolt up my arm, something I don't think he misses.

I pull my hand away.

"Then why are you here?" I ask, my eyes flicking to his mouth before I can stop myself.

"A business meeting, if you'll believe it. My client appreciates the exclusivity here." His eyes drag over my face. "The piece he's after is very high-value, and he doesn't want to be seen with me in public in case it attracts competitors."

I nod. "I see. How's Sophie?"

"Fine. Still recovering from the housewarming party," he says casually. His knee grazes mine beneath the bar, and I tense—not from discomfort, but from the sharp pull inside of me that I can't shake.

Which part? I want to ask, but instead, I keep my mouth shut.

And maybe it's the whiskey that makes me want to ask the one burning question I've had since Julian returned to Crestwood, or maybe it's what happened a couple of weeks ago at the party... either way, I can't move on without knowing. I can't help myself.

"Does she know about us? About... what happened back then?"

His jaw tightens. "Why wouldn't she know? She knows everything else about me."

Somehow, his answer stings more than it should, and his words linger in the air between us. His gaze holds mine with quiet passion, almost daring me to ask why she knows.

I already know the answer.

Because she loves him—and because they share a connection I can't even fathom.

The weight of the past sits like a stone in my throat.

"Everything?" I ask again, my voice sounding hollow even to me. "So, does she know why I left?"

His jaw tightens, a flash of bitterness in his eyes that's both unexpected and all too familiar. "I imagine you'd know the answer to that better than I would," he replies, his voice cold but low. "You were the one who walked away, Kai. You didn't exactly stick around to explain, so how could I explain it to her?"

I swallow, the burn of his words worse than the whiskey. "I'm sorry, Julian. I couldn't do it. It was a mistake. I should have never..."

I can't even admit it out loud.

I should have never kissed you. Not when I couldn't follow through.

Julian laughs, but there's no humor in it. "Right. A mistake." He leans in, his face inches from mine, his gaze piercing through me. "Funny how that mistake still lingers, isn't it?"

I look down, my fingers tracing circles on the bar, unsure if I'm ready to give voice to the storm inside me.

I can feel his eyes on me, unwavering, and the confession I've kept locked away for years slips out.

"I don't regret it, in case you're wondering. I never said I regretted it."

Julian's breath catches, but he doesn't reply right away. He looks away, his fingers clenching around his glass. When he speaks, his voice is tight, raw.

"I never asked, but since we're confessing our sins... I do. I regret it. I regret thinking that kiss meant something. That maybe, just maybe, I wasn't the only one feeling it."

I feel my throat tighten as his words sink in, each one hitting harder than the last. "Julian, I—"

He cuts me off, his gaze sharp, angry. "You don't get to explain it away now. You kissed me, and then you ran. And I don't know what's worse—that you kissed me at all, or that you acted like it was nothing."

Hearing it out loud from him—how much I hurt him, how much I dismissed something that was real—felt like being gutted. But what hurt more was knowing that for years, I let fear dictate my life. I told myself I was doing the right thing, that I was protecting both of us, but all I was doing was running from a truth that refused to be buried.

His voice dips lower, rougher. "You made me feel like a fool for thinking it meant something. And yeah, maybe I should've been smarter than that. But I wasn't," he finishes, his voice cracking.

For the first time tonight, he doesn't look at me. And somehow, that hurts more than if he'd yelled.

Memories of that kiss crash through my mind suddenly, and I feel like I'm drowning. I remember the way the kiss was hesitant at first, like he was afraid I'd pull away. I was the one who initiated it, after all. But I didn't pull away. *Couldn't.* I let it happen. And I can still so clearly remember what he looked like right after the kiss—flushed, out of breath, eyes dark with something I wasn't ready to name.

He looked at me like I was something holy.

And that terrified me.

Because I didn't want to be worshiped. I wanted to be *consumed*.

The difference between him and me, though, was that I never let myself believe I could want him. I couldn't want him.

Not back then.

The pain in his voice is more than I can handle, and I feel myself unraveling, the walls I've built around this crumbling fast. "I left because I didn't know how to handle it... how to handle *us*. And I couldn't give you what you wanted. Not at the time, anyway."

For a moment, his expression softens, a flicker of the man I used to know. But then he shakes his head, a bitter smile tugging at his lips.

"I think you handled it just fine, Kai. You walked out, moved on, left me to pick up the pieces." He leans back, putting distance between us that feels colder than I expected. "So don't pretend you're here now looking for closure. We're a little past that, don't you think?"

My chest feels tight, and I don't know if it's the whiskey or the sheer weight of everything I left unsaid. "I thought I was protecting you by leaving."

He exhales sharply, his face caught somewhere between anger and sadness. "Maybe next time, Kai, let me decide what I can and can't handle." He stands up, his gaze lingering on me for a second too long. "Was it all just an *experiment*?"

"What? No. It just… happened. I can't explain it, okay? I don't regret it, but…"

Julian huffs a cruel laugh, and then his lip curls away from his teeth. "Well, congratulations. You seem to be doing fine. Happy to be your test subject. Have a good night."

He walks away, and his shoulders are stiff with anger. As I watch him walk out of the bar, something inside of me snaps.

The way he said *experiment*…

I can't help but think of the blond head bobbing on my cock just a couple of hours ago, and the way I rutted into his mouth as if he were someone else.

Not just anyone, either.

One specific blond.

Both the kiss in college and the scene with Adrian earlier flash and overlap in my mind. Despite telling myself it was just an experiment, it stirred something in me that I didn't know existed.

The same feeling from seventeen years ago—a raw ache that settles inside of me.

Something I can't explain.

Like a *switch* turning on.

There's no point in denying it anymore, either.

For the first time in my life, I feel it.

Not guilt, or fear... but clarity. Like I've wiped the steam from a mirror. I've spent too long hiding, too long fighting myself. But this? This clarity feels like freedom. It's not the end of a battle—it's the beginning. I know who I am now. And I'm tired of pretending otherwise.

I've spent years trying to erase a truth I was never ready to face, but that's not true anymore. For so long, I thought that if I ignored it, if I pushed it down, it would go away. That if I pretended I was only one thing, I wouldn't have to grapple with being both. But that was the real lie. I was never just one thing, and I never will be. And for the first time in my life, I don't want to fight it anymore.

It all slams into me like a freight train.

I didn't just want him in college. I want him now.

And judging by the way he looked at me tonight, maybe... just maybe, he wants me.

And Sophie...

Fuck.

I want her, too.

CHAPTER TEN
THE DINNER

Sophie

I stop walking, and the equestrian supplies in my arms nearly slip out of my firm grip as my eyes take in the 'For Rent' sign sitting in the window. Setting the bucket of things down, I look around the quaint street corner. On one corner is an old-school newsstand, and on the other is a British pub. Directly across the street is an adorable-looking coffee shop called Perky Roasters.

"Cute, right?" a woman says, walking by in large sunglasses while she pushes a pram. "I wish someone would buy it and turn it into a bookstore. Crestwood doesn't have one, can you believe that?"

"Unbelievable," I mutter, waving goodbye as she walks off.

Looking back at the small corner shop for rent, my

stomach bottoms out with nerves, and I can't articulate why, exactly.

Except...

The art deco space comes to life before me. I glance into the building, noting the oak herringbone floors, white crown molding, and the large window that could be used for an amazing front display. There's a lot of room inside—but not in an overwhelming way. I envision built-in shelves, a few tables for bookish merch, and perhaps a quiet reading chair somewhere in the back.

I could display my favorite romance books...

Or what if it was a romance bookstore?!

Grinning, I send a quick voice message to Stella Ravage, asking for her opinion. She'd recently recruited me into her romance book club, and I'd met her two sisters-in-law, Zoe and Layla, who were also in the book club.

A romance bookstore.

The idea is wild, but... I like it.

Glancing up at the window and ornate woodwork of the front of the shop, I place my hands on my hips as I brainstorm names.

Prose & Passion
Blush Books
The Story Nest
The Romance Nook
Romance in Bloom...

Someone honks at me, and I realize I'm standing in the street. Jumping back onto the pavement, I laugh as I shake my head. I pick the bucket up and carry on down the street toward my car. I only glance over my shoulder once or twice, and even when I start the car, I don't immediately pull out of my parking spot. A quick Google search brings the listing up, and my eyes scour the details, including square footage—which I then have to convert to meters—as well as the price. There are no pictures, and the window was dusty, so I wasn't able to see inside very clearly.

I pull out the small notepad in my glove compartment, jotting down really loose numbers to see what kind of investment this would be. Perhaps, *maybe*... it's possible.

I place the pad of paper back in the glove compartment and begin my drive home.

Ever since the housewarming party, I've been tossing around ideas for my own business. I even went to that psychic in Laurel Canyon, half joking, hoping she'd just *know*. Her answer? "Books."

Hardly a revelation—I've loved reading since I was a little girl, and Ashford Palace were filled to the brim with books I'd acquired as an adult.

Some people spent a fortune on jewelry... I spend a fortune on books. Paperbacks, hardbacks, special editions, first editions... you name it.

As I drive down the main street, I think back to the tiny bookshop in London I used to frequent when I was at boarding school. My love of romance books started young—too young, probably—and I'd been reading love stories since before I knew what half of it meant.

Opening a romance bookstore would certainly make

my mother furious, and that thought makes me smile even wider when I think of a certain instance of her catching me reading romance books when I was sixteen.

"What's that?" she asks, walking over to where I'm relaxing on the couch. I'm home for the weekend, and I'm too engrossed in the novel to pay much attention to her. "Sophia Grace, is that another one of your trashy books?"

She snatches the book from my hands, and I glare up at her. "The author won a Booker Prize, Mother. It's hardly trash."

My mother closes the worn paperback and in one swift motion, she tosses it into the nearby fire.

I jump up. "Hey! I paid for that!"

My mother snorts, which is very unbecoming of her. Her blonde hair is perfectly smooth, and she places her manicured hands in front of the white linen dress she's wearing. Her lips press together in a placating smile, but the glint in her eyes betrays amusement—like she's indulging a child who just said something foolish.

"Oh? And how much did you spend on such filth?"

I grind my jaw as I cross my arms. "It's not filth! It's a love story."

One of my mother's eyebrows arches up. "Love? Darling, life will get a lot easier once you realize that the kind of love in those books isn't real." Her lips curl back as she assesses me. "It's just a fantasy. Get your head out of the clouds and finish studying for your exams next week."

With that, she turns on her heel and walks away.

I stare at the pile of ashes that used to be my book, watching the pages curl and disappear one by one.

I close my eyes at the next light when I remember how angry my mother was that day—how angry she was when she realized I was never going to stay in the London socialite scene, pop out a few kids, and settle down in Julian's family estate in Brookshire.

Reading was my escape. It was the only place I didn't have to be prim and proper. The only time I remember being happy as a child was riding horses or between the pages of a good book. My parents never really tried to show me love—I had to learn from books, and later, Julian.

Maybe a shop like this could bring that feeling to others, too.

I smile when I remember all the nights I spent reading with a torch in hand—the different genres and tropes that swept me up more than exams, or school, or my duties as their daughter. I remember buying a book about aliens at uni, and my roommate accompanying me to buy an alien dildo.

The memory makes me laugh.

I was brought up so naive, but I found ways to rebel.

And I didn't stop reading—if anything, my mother's judgmental tone about romance books only spurred me on.

The store comes back to the forefront of my mind, and I envision the big front window with "The Story Nest" in delicate, gold letters, framed by lush sprays of flowers and maybe a fresh coat of light pink paint. I could display monthly themes—holiday romance, summer romance, LGBTQIA+ books for Pride month...

I can already picture it. Warm light filtering in through those huge front windows, illuminating shelves crammed with paperbacks—each one a passport to someone else's world. I'd host book clubs in the evenings, letting the cozy hum of gossip and laughter fill the air. Maybe a small café corner with lavender lattes and pastries... a haven.

A safe space for people like me—people who didn't always fit the mold they were born into. People who craved escape, not just from reality but from the weight of expectations pressing down on them.

Here, no one would snatch books from trembling hands. No one would call stories "silly fantasies" or toss them into the fire. Instead, they'd be treasured—stacked high, their spines creased and worn from love.

And maybe... just maybe... this shop could be the start of something I built for myself. No titles, no expectations.

A love story of my own making.

The opportunities are endless, and by the time I pull into the driveway at home, I'm fumbling for my phone and quickly emailing the leasing office about the space. If it's still available, and I can tour it, I'll take it as a sign. And if not, maybe it wasn't meant to be.

I'm so distracted that I don't notice Kai standing there—or the way his car is parked on the other side of the driveway—until I'm walking up to the front door.

"Hey," he says, immediately taking the heavy bucket from my hands, his fingers brushing mine for just a moment longer than necessary.

"Oh, hi!" I chirp, my heart picking up pace despite myself. My eyes drift over his black button-up shirt, the sleeves neatly folded to his elbows, dark trousers, and polished leather shoes that seem oddly formal for a quick house call. His jaw is shadowed with scruff, giving him an unkempt edge. When he catches me glancing, he smirks, dragging his hand—marked by that small cross tattoo—over his mouth.

"Hi," he says again, with the slightest tilt of his head, his gaze knowing and calm. He doesn't say it, but he doesn't have to; he knows I'm flustered, and that he's the reason.

It's just after five, so he must've come straight from Saint Helena Academy. The image of him in front of his students, offering them religious guidance while looking like this—tall, self-assured, and authoritative—flits through my mind, uninvited. I shove the thought aside, telling myself to stay focused.

"Out of sight, out of mind," I mutter as I push open the front door, more to myself than him.

"What was that?" He arches an eyebrow, his gaze glinting with amusement as he steps inside.

"Nothing," I mumble, motioning for him to follow me inside. Once he sets the bucket down, he straightens, his expression softening as he takes in the space, finally landing his gaze back on me.

"I had a couple of hours free and figured I could fix that garbage disposal we spoke about?" His tone is casual, almost too relaxed.

My mouth falls open slightly, caught off guard. I'd

completely forgotten about the disposal—about the contractor's mistake with the pipes. I'd mentioned it the day before the party, and he'd offered to fix it, but with everything that happened, I'd convinced myself he wouldn't follow through.

I had it on my list to hire out, but of course life had been busy.

"Oh. Right. Of course. Come in." I turn quickly, eager to escape the force of his gaze, but I don't get far.

"Sophie, wait."

I stop mid-step, turning to find him watching me with an unreadable expression, his hands resting in his trouser pockets, shoulders slightly hunched as if he's choosing his words carefully.

"I'm sorry," he says quietly. "For what I said at the party. I know you'd never hurt Julian on purpose. I just... saw you with that other guy, and I reacted. Poorly." His gaze is steady, and it softens as he watches me.

The memory returns, stark and stinging, the words he'd thrown at me that night.

Julian deserves better.

The words still hit their mark, even now.

"Thank you," I say shortly, crossing my arms in front of me as if I can physically guard myself from him.

Kai's eyes trace the movement, lingering on my folded arms before meeting my gaze again. He studies me for a few beats, as though he's on the edge of saying something else. Then he takes a step toward me, slow and unhurried. I should move, or say something to fill the silence, but I don't. The moment stretches, the tension between us thickening.

"It wasn't just the kiss with the other guy," he finally admits, his gaze fixed somewhere near his shoes. "It was... everything. Seeing you like that. Seeing Julian trust you so completely."

My brows pull together, but I don't interrupt. He lets out a tight breath, almost like he's holding something back.

"I wasn't angry because I thought you were cheating," he continues, his voice lower now, heavier. "I think I was angry because... I wanted it to be me. And I hate that. Don't tell Julian I said that," he adds quickly. "Fuck, sorry. I just mean... I think I was jealous. That's all."

My heart skips a beat, but I say nothing, letting his confession settle like dust in the quiet entryway.

"Thank you for the apology," I say softly. I want to examine his other words, I want to pick them apart and ask him exactly what he means when he says he's jealous.

Jealous of Julian? Me? Or... both of us?

His eyes gleam with something mirthful as he looks down at me, his shoulders relaxing slightly. "Speaking of Julian," he says casually, breaking the tension in a way only someone in a leadership position can achieve. "How's he doing? Besides being busy trying to take over the world?"

I let out a laugh as my arms loosen at my sides. Kai has a way of bringing Julian into the conversation that feels like there's a hint of something else beneath it—an unspoken warmth that's directed at him as much as it is at me.

"Honestly? He's been swamped with work," I say, shaking my head. "The new projects are practically taking over our weekends. I think he's forgotten what a day off even looks like. You know how he gets when he has a new fixation."

Kai's mouth quirks in a smile, his eyes glinting with amusement. "Classic Julian." He pauses, the corners of his mouth tugging into a soft, thoughtful grin. "And to think, the rest of us mortals struggle to keep up."

I roll my eyes, but I'm smiling despite myself. "Oh, please. You act like you're any less of a workaholic." I glance over at him, and there's something new in his gaze—an intensity I can't quite name.

He shrugs, the barest smirk still lingering. "What can I say? I have good taste in role models." His voice softens just a bit, and his gaze dips, lingering on me with a warmth that's almost... fond. His eyes roam over to the bucket of supplies for Snickers, and my Pilates outfit. "Maybe it's contagious, spending time with the two of you."

It's a lighthearted statement, but I catch a faint note of wistfulness in his tone, a quiet undercurrent that he tries to mask behind a teasing smile. The admission hangs in the air between us, and my pulse quickens, surprised at how his words make me feel—something close to... curiosity.

"What?" he asks, noticing my expression. "Am I not allowed to admire my friends?"

The glint in his eye is mischievous, but his voice is sincere, the words slipping out as easily as his smile.

"How is it that you somehow know how to flirt without crossing any lines?"

He barks a laugh at this, holding his hands up. "No flirting here." He winces. "Okay, maybe a little."

I laugh, and he continues.

"But I'm just trying to be a good friend and apologize."

"Thank you for the apology." I look at the bucket. "I should go take these things to the stables before it gets too dark, and then I need to shower before dinner. Julian will be home soon. You know where the tools are," I finish, giving him a teasing smile as I walk over to the bucket and pick it up. "Would you like to join us for dinner?"

The second the words are out of my mouth, I regret them. But I can't exactly whip around the kitchen trying to make dinner when he's fixing the disposal and *not* offer to have him stay.

"I'd love to," he says earnestly, giving me a genuine smile.

An hour later, I feel like I'm living in some sort of alternate universe. Somehow, despite Julian's chilly reception to seeing Kai shirtless and fixing our disposal, they've both somehow been sitting at the kitchen island together… and arguing about art. I'm not wholly paying attention to the conversation, but Kai keeps pinching the bridge of his nose and sighing. Julian hasn't stopped using his argumentative, sarcastic laugh. Every few minutes, I glance over at them between adding layers to the lasagna, and despite the fact that they're not agreeing on whatever it is they're discussing, they're still *talking*.

And the way they're sitting facing each other, focused only on what the other one is saying...

I can tell they used to be best friends.

My lips quirk as I triple check the recipe.

I don't really cook, but my lasagna is one of the only decent things I can make from scratch. Julian does a lot of the cooking, and the other times, we just order a takeaway.

However, Julian just cinched his largest deal of the year and sold a painting for eleven million dollars, so I wanted to celebrate. I didn't expect Kai to be here as well, but the more the merrier.

"Contemporary art is *not* overrated," Julian scoffs, the aristocratic lilt to his voice evident. He brings his whiskey tumbler to his lips and takes a sip.

Kai holds his hands up. "I didn't mean to imply it's overrated. I just meant that for someone like Monet or van Gogh, a lot more craft and thought had to be put into it."

"Right, but who classifies that as art? Where do we draw the line? Art is meant to make us *feel* something, correct? So if a pile of chewing gum makes you feel something, then so be it. And if a large oil painting makes you feel something, fantastic. We can agree to disagree, but you can't possibly discredit an entire movement because you don't agree with it."

Kai sits up straighter and takes a slow sip from his tumbler, finishing off the last of his whiskey. Before he can set his glass down, Julian reaches over and refills it, the amber liquid glinting as it spills into the glass.

"Are you boys going to share?" I ask, my voice dropping low, silkier than I mean it to. "Or do I have to beg for something to drink?"

Julian's mouth quirks up, his eyes glinting as he leans back and takes his time with another sip. "Might be fun to see you beg," he drawls, his voice carrying a hint of challenge.

Kai's lips twitch, but he stays quiet, his gaze heavy as he traces a slow circle around the rim of his glass with his finger, as though lost in thought—or perhaps, lost in me.

I reach for an empty tumbler in a nearby cabinet, holding it out between them. When I glance up, Kai's eyes are on me, dark and unreadable, something molten swirling just below the surface. He doesn't look away as he grabs the whiskey bottle and pours a slow, generous stream into my glass. I bring it to my lips, matching his gaze as I take a long sip, the whiskey warm as it burns a slow path down my throat.

"A woman who enjoys good whiskey is a woman after my own heart," he murmurs, lifting his glass in a quiet salute before taking a sip himself, his eyes only leaving mine to skim down the apricot-colored sundress I'd thrown on.

I look over at Julian, who's been watching the exchange with a slow smile and a knowing, familiar glint in his eye. There's something possessive about his expression, but also... curious.

Like he's assessing the dynamic between Kai and me.

Like he's clocking how it develops... *studying* us. It's clearly something more than just a casual interest.

I know what he's thinking.

The idea sends a shiver down my spine, and I suddenly feel a bit too warm. My pulse starts to flutter, fueled by something beyond just the whiskey.

The tension between the three of us is palpable, filling the silence.

Clearing my throat, I take another, longer drink before setting my glass down. "Right. Who wants to help me with the salad?"

Julian glances over at Kai, a playful edge in his smile. For a beat, neither of them moves, and then Kai slowly rises to his feet.

"I'll help," he says, his voice rougher, his eyes lingering on me for a moment too long.

I slide my gaze back to Julian. He watches the two of us, his expression unreadable, but there's a flash of something in his eyes—something almost approving, or perhaps he's just a little too entertained. He tilts his head, toasting us with his glass, and takes a slow, deliberate sip, his gaze unwavering.

For the next half hour, Kai helps me with the salad.

We default to our old camaraderie, and when the lasagna is ready, he helps me plate it and bring it to the small table near the back window. Tonight feels too informal for the formal dining room, so I grab a couple of bottles of red wine and we all sit down to eat.

Despite Julian's icy reception to Kai earlier, the two of them seem to be on speaking terms now, even going so far as to discuss old memories of when they were teenagers. I love learning things I didn't know about my husband—specifically, the quirks that made me fall in love with him in the first place.

"Does he still make piles with his clothes?" Malakai asks, leaning back with his glass of wine.

Julian snorts. "Of course I do."

I look between them, wondering if Kai knows about Julian's recent diagnosis, but before I can think any longer on the topic, Julian continues speaking.

"It's ADHD. I was officially diagnosed last year. You should've seen me before I went on medication," he adds, running a hand through his blond hair.

I place a hand on his leg. "The important thing is that *you* feel better."

Julian gives me a warm smile. "It drove Soph up the walls. The piles. The unpaid bills. The forgetfulness, the inability to focus on one thing..."

I squeeze his thigh in solidarity and scrunch my nose in the way I know he adores. "I love you just the way you are."

Kai's eyes flit between us as he studies the way Julian brings my hand to his mouth, kissing it once. I hadn't noticed the sun setting, leaving us alone in the dim light, illuminated only by the romantic candles on the table. But as several beats of silence pass between us, the weight of the evening feels almost oppressive in the dim glow of the flames.

I change the subject to something lighter—something that will calm my racing heart.

"Tell me—did Julian have the same obsession with Cadbury chocolate back when you knew him as he does now? Because the man is a menace when Easter rolls around."

Kai chuckles, leaning against the counter. "That checks out. He used to hoard them in his dorm room like some sort of treasure hunter."

"Cadbury's my one weakness," he says with mock solemnity. "Well, that and Flamin' Hot Cheetos. Did you know they're actually illegal in Britain?"

I snort. "Of course you'd love something illegal."

He lifts his glass in a silent salute, giving me a slow, feline smile. "What can I say? I have a taste for things that shouldn't be indulged."

My voice softens, but it comes out too seductive as I roll my eyes. "Oh? Like what?"

He doesn't answer right away, letting the silence stretch just long enough for me to feel the tension creeping up my spine.

Kai clears his throat, and I know what he's going to ask before he does. "If you don't mind me asking..." he starts, running his fingers over his lips, "how did you get started in the lifestyle?"

Julian goes still next to me, and my lips part as I take a large sip of wine. Despite eating two servings of lasagna, I still feel tipsy, and I'm suddenly eager to spill everything to Kai. I meet Julian's gaze and feel a surge of warmth, the kind of thrill I get only when we talk openly like this. With Julian's silent encouragement, I turn back to Kai, who's watching us with a burning focus that sends a thrill up my spine and sends goosebumps to break out on my skin.

"Well," I say, trying to steady my voice, "we were always unconventional. We dabbled in other aspects of the lifestyle occasionally—things like dominance and submission, bondage, role play, which is where—"

"I am aware of what role play is, Sophie," Kai says, his voice soft yet firm.

My whole body heats up.

"Right. Well, one night Julian brought up the idea. We were out, and a bartender in London had been flirting with me. We'd been in a bit of a rut with our duties, and Julian wasn't happy as Lord Ashford. I was even more unhappy as Lady Ashford. It felt... stifling," I finish, looking at Julian, who only gives me a small smile. "He suggested I let myself explore, so I did. I flirted back. Nothing more happened, but it set a precedent in a way. With each encounter, I got more daring. By the time I was ready to take a man to bed, we'd written up a contract and NDA, and from there, it just... happened."

Kai's eyebrows lift, and he studies me like he's savoring every word.

Julian's hand tightens slightly around mine. "I

wanted Sophie to feel free, to do things she didn't think she could. I guess you could say it's my kink," he says with a slight smirk. "Watching her come alive. Watching other men enjoy what I get to call mine. It's exhilarating."

Kai's eyes flash with something, and he leans back, fingers still absently tracing his lips. "And how did that feel, Sophie?" His voice is low, controlled, but I catch the glint of interest beneath the surface.

"It was... liberating," I confess, voice softer. "At first, it felt strange, stepping outside of the rules we'd grown up with. I mean, if anyone in our circle ever found out... we would've been ostracized. It was also incredibly exciting because of that. I didn't realize how much I wanted to be wanted, to feel that rush of someone seeing me the way Julian does, but differently." I can feel my cheeks heating as I speak, but I don't stop. "It's like discovering new parts of myself each time. And Julian—he loves it as much as I do. Which makes me love it. I guess my kink is watching him unravel in front of me," I finish, squeezing my legs together as Julian gives me a heated, knowing look.

Kai is quiet for a moment, processing, but there's a spark in his gaze. Fascination... mingled with something deeper. "So how do you invite others into this... arrangement?"

"I intentionally choose someone for us," Julian says smoothly, his eyes fixed on Kai.

Kai's fingers stop at his mouth, and his eyes shift

between us, as if he's searching for a hidden meaning behind Julian's words.

It sends shivers down my spine, because all night, he's been looking at me differently. At first, I thought it was because of his apology and confession. But now... I'm not so sure. He's been nothing but polite, but it's not the usual friendly warmth that I'm used to. His eyes linger for a beat too long, and I catch him studying the way Julian touches me when he thinks I'm not paying attention.

It's subtle—so subtle that if I weren't already halfway through a second glass of wine, I might convince myself I imagined it.

"And does this 'someone' usually understand your preferences?"

There's a subtle emphasis on 'someone,' a wisp of interest laced with challenge.

Julian's gaze doesn't waver. "They usually do, yes. We make sure of it. Sophie is... precious to me. And I want her to be adored, in every sense of the word. Not to mention I want her to feel safe. So communication is key."

My heart beats faster as Julian's words sink in. Kai's intensity has always felt charged, magnetic, but now it's laced with the awareness that he's starting to see us—*truly* see us.

Kai leans forward, resting his elbows on the table, his gaze turning serious. "I see."

"And you?" I ask, holding my glass of wine as I give him a wry smile. "Tit for tat, Ravage."

Malakai smirks. "Well, I'm not a stranger to these dynamics. I understand what it takes to build that level of trust." His voice dips slightly, and I catch a note of something darker—something he's holding back.

"Even as a pastor?" I ask, my voice quiet.

"Especially as a pastor," he replies. "Over the last couple of years, my... *interests*... have blended and intertwined with my job. I think, like you, I started to resent the responsibility of it all. Everything is so heavy at work —my job is so important. I needed an outlet. So I found one."

"Well, go on then," Julian encourages.

I swallow, feeling the heat building in the room, and find myself leaning toward him, almost unconsciously.

Kai's expression grows contemplative, his eyes shifting lazily from Julian to me. For a moment he seems almost hesitant to continue, like there's a heaviness that only he carries. He releases a slow, resigned breath, as if he's steeling himself, and his gaze pierces me with a knowing glint.

"Let's just say," he begins, his voice deepening, "that the line between my work and my... desires has gotten a bit blurry over the years. Preaching every Sunday, shepherding my congregation, it requires control and a sense of responsibility. I'm held to a certain standard, you might say." His lips curve into a slight, almost dangerous smile. "But as you might imagine, responsibility like that can feel suffocating."

His words hang in the air, and a thrill runs through me as he continues, his gaze unwavering. If anyone understands the weight of responsibility, it's Julian and me.

"I needed an outlet. I wanted something to let off that pressure. So I turned to the lifestyle. Not like this, exactly," he nods to Julian and me, "but something with a little more... intensity."

Kai pauses, watching our reactions, and the tension thickens. He leans back, his hands draped over the back of his chair, looking every bit the man who knows his own power—and the control it gives him over others. He clears his throat, and his voice lowers even further, almost conspiratorial.

"I enjoy guiding people to the edge, letting them feel their limits and push against them. Some call it edge play," he says, watching me intently, "but for me, it's about helping someone find freedom in surrendering control. I ask them to give up their fears, their expectations, even their sense of self." His gaze flicks from me to Julian. "And sometimes that requires taking them to a place that feels... dark."

A shiver runs down my spine, and I find myself clutching my wineglass a little tighter.

Julian must notice, because he starts to trace slow, lazy circles on my bare thigh. I squeeze my legs together to keep from moaning.

Julian's eyes flick toward me, his hand warm as he digs his fingers in. I'm sure he can feel the way my breathing shifts when Kai speaks, the small telltale signs of excitement I naively think I'm hiding well.

But I've never been a good actress.

He catches Kai's gaze across the table

"I think Sophie's interested in your 'edge play,' Kai."

I choke on my wine, glaring at Julian. "I am not."

Kai leans back, lips twitching. "Are you sure?"

My cheeks burn as I avoid their matching gazes, because he's not wrong.

He knows me well enough.

"And the religious side of things?" Julian asks, his voice soft but probing. "That's part of the play for you?"

Kai nods, an edge of something wicked in his expression. "There's power in ritual. In confession. In submission to something larger than ourselves. I find it fascinating, taking on that role—not just as someone who guides spiritually but also as someone who… demands devotion." His eyes flash as he adds, "I ask them to obey, to trust, and sometimes even to worship."

His gaze lingers on me, and I can feel the air between us heat, like the room itself is holding its breath.

I shift in my seat, letting my dress ride up just slightly. I'm not sure if I do it for Julian or for Kai. Maybe both.

The thought alone makes my stomach flutter.

Julian's hand tightens on my leg. I glance at him, and the corner of his mouth twitches up in that smug, knowing way that drives me wild. He knows exactly what I'm doing. Worse, he likes it.

And Kai?

Kai's gaze flicks down, catching the movement before his eyes meet mine again, darker now. I feel the weight of that look like a slow burn spreading through me.

"And when someone submits to me fully, when they're willing to follow me to that edge," Kai continues, his voice like silk, "that's where they find release. Release from guilt, from shame... from whatever they're holding on to. But it's not for everyone." He leans forward, his eyes gleaming with a dark promise. "It's only for those who truly want to be led."

I sip my wine, pretending like I don't notice the silent exchange happening right here at our kitchen table.

But I do.

And by the time Julian squeezes my thigh three times —our unspoken signal—I realize I'm not just imagining it.

There's something happening here.

And I'm not entirely sure I want it to stop.

There's a long, loaded pause. Julian's ministrations on my leg ground me, and I look over to find him watching Kai with a similar sharpness, something like respect in his eyes.

Julian smirks, leaning forward, his gaze unwavering. "And what about now, Kai? Are you still... guiding people to that edge?"

Kai's gaze grows darker, his smirk twisting into something almost feral. "I try to keep it private," he says. "But with the right people, in the right moment... yes." He lets his eyes roam over us both, his expression unguarded and raw. "If they trust me enough to bring them there."

The weight of his words lands between us, an open invitation wrapped in shadows. I feel a thrill that's equal parts excitement and apprehension, and I can tell by Julian's silent, encouraging smile that he feels it too.

Kai leans back again, his eyes on us both, and he lets out a low chuckle. "I imagine my tastes might be... darker than yours," he says, almost teasing. "But then, I never thought I'd find myself with two people who might actually understand."

"You'd be surprised," I say quickly, shifting in my seat. "Julian and I have experimented with a lot of things, though none of it ever really stuck besides some basic bondage."

Kai's gaze sharpens, and his eyes lock on to mine as his voice drops to almost a whisper. "Have you ever had someone push you to the edge of your comfort zone? To that place where you lose control, leaving you with no choice but to surrender?"

I swallow hard, my heart racing, but Kai presses on. He leans closer, his voice low and steady.

"Have you ever had someone bring you to the edge of pleasure and pain, hold you there, and make you beg to go further, knowing they could either pull you back or let you fall?"

Julian's hand squeezes my thigh, and I feel his pulse quicken against my skin. There's a silent exchange between him and Kai, as if Julian understands exactly what he's asking—perhaps even finds himself drawn to it, as I am.

Kai lets the silence stretch, savoring my reaction. His lips curve into a slight smile. "That's what I mean by edge play," he murmurs, his voice like a dark promise.

"It's about trust, Sophie. Trusting that someone knows exactly how far to take you. And trusting that they know just how much to hold back."

I realize I'm holding my breath, and I let it out slowly, my mind reeling with the weight of his words.

I'm so turned on that every breath has my hard nipples brushing against the soft cotton of my dress. Looking at Julian, he nods once—and then squeezes my thigh three times.

His signal—*again.*

I know what he's thinking. He doesn't have to say it. He's just waiting for me to make the first move.

I shift in my seat as arousal works through me. It sounds wild when I think about what's hanging in the air between us. I *have* been drinking.

Or maybe... I've had just enough alcohol to lower my inhibitions.

Glancing between Kai and Julian, it's like we can all sense the unspoken question that hangs heavily between us. I feel an undeniable pull—the potential of what could happen if we were to step over this invisible line together. I look at Julian and find his gaze steady, yet tinged with something I rarely see—anticipation. He doesn't look surprised, just... intrigued. He turns to Kai, a glint of mischief in his eye, and finally speaks.

He knows I'm too modest to say anything outright—to *ask* Kai to join one of our games.

"Hypothetically," Julian says, his voice smooth but tinged with something darker, "how would this work?"

Kai's expression softens just a touch, but there's still

that edge, that delicious darkness in his gaze. "Hypothetically?" he echoes, leaning back, his hands clasping thoughtfully in front of him. "Well, hypothetically, I'd take my time with her. We'd build that trust together. All *three* of us."

I feel Julian's hand squeeze mine, and a shiver of excitement runs through me as Kai's gaze travels slowly between us.

"Julian," he continues, his tone low and deliberate, "if I were to guide her... it would mean surrendering control to me. Trusting me to lead her where she's never gone, but only as far as she's willing to go." His eyes flick to me, his gaze softening as he adds, "It would mean trusting me to hold you both in the places that scare you and excite you, and knowing that I'd bring you safely back."

I feel a swell of emotion, a mixture of anticipation, nerves, and an aching curiosity. Julian's voice comes again, calm but laced with a hint of eagerness.

He looks at me, and I nod once, the only signal I outwardly give him that I want this.

"And if we were ready?"

Kai lets a small smile curve his lips, finally breaking the focus with a hint of warmth. "Then, we'd start slow. A night just for us to explore, to see where things feel right. To set boundaries and understand each other."

He leans forward again, his gaze steady on both of us. "But," he adds, voice softening, "only if this is what you both truly want. Only if you're both willing to take that step... together."

"No expectations, only a willingness to trust and explore," I add, looking between the two of them.

There's a part of me that already knows Julian and I are both ready. This moment has been building for a while now, though I didn't fully realize it until this very moment.

"So?" Kai asks, looking between us. Somehow, despite everything, he's become the facilitator. "Are we going to do this?"

I look at Julian one last time, but he just smirks at me. "It's not up to me."

Swallowing, I look at Kai. "I would like that."

CHAPTER ELEVEN
THE DANCE

JULIAN

"How do I look?"

Sophie's shy, unsure voice settles over the bedroom and I turn around to find her wearing a white shift dress, sheer black tights, and a leather jacket. She's paired her outfit with the over-the-knee boots that drive me crazy, and her hair is tousled. *Gorgeous.*

"You look perfect, as always," I say, buttoning my white Oxford shirt with shaky hands.

Tonight is the night—exactly two days after we all agreed we'd try a scene with Kai and Sophie. I had to get the contract drawn up, which took until this afternoon, thanks to my distracted mind. And of course, both Sophie and Malakai were tested just to be safe. It also gave us time to come to terms with the fact that we were actually bringing a friend into this for the first time. Normally, the men I chose for Sophie were strangers, people she'd never seen before. It made things easier.

It made things less complicated.

For the first time in a long time, I'm anxious.

Sophie shifts her weight, and I can't help but watch the way her dress flutters over her thighs. She really does look so pretty tonight, and my first thought is how Kai is going to notice it, too.

My stomach tightens, half with anticipation, half with something sharper.

I'm always aroused by the idea of other men finding her attractive—and her giving them a taste of something just out of reach. She is *mine*, after all.

But now, Kai's part of it, and that makes everything more... convoluted.

I glance at the mirror and catch my own reflection, face flushed, fingers fumbling as I continue trying to button my shirt. The trembling in my fingers gets worse, and I curse under my breath when the button slips through my fingers yet again.

Just thinking about Kai sets my nerves on edge. He's invited us to his apartment in downtown Crestwood. I've never been, but I'm anxious to see the place he calls home. I can't help but imagine how he's probably smoothing his hair, getting that cool, unbothered look down like he always does. The memory of that kiss from years ago—a kiss that was a mistake, according to him, but a kiss that still hasn't stopped echoing in my mind—tightens something in my chest.

Our complex history just adds another thorny layer to all of this.

Tonight, I'll only be watching, like I always do. I should be focused on Sophie, but it's impossible to ignore Kai's pull. I already know from the tight knot of anticipation in my gut that Sophie won't be the only person I watch tonight. Even now, when I think I've buried everything, here it is, back to taunt me. I'm *excited* to see him aroused, too.

It's not unusual, per se. I am a bisexual man, and I have, at one point or another, enjoyed watching the men enjoy my wife.

However, those men were not Kai.

They were strangers, and it was easy to say goodbye and never think of them again.

Tonight, though?

I can't promise to forget about how Kai looks fucking my wife.

Studying my reflection, I run a hand through my blond hair. I've been staring at my reflection for too long. My lips are pressed thin, and my jaw is tight.

Why does the idea of Kai touching Sophie feel more personal than with any other man?

There's something else bubbling underneath my cool facade, too, and I would be remiss if I ignored or suppressed it. I'm jealous.

Every time I think about how he'll look at her—how he'll touch her—jealousy prickles up my spine, even if I have no right to feel it.

And the worst part?

Every time I think about how she'll look at him, how she'll touch him, makes me even more envious.

That's a first for me. I've never felt like this before, and the realization hits me like a punch to the gut.

My mind is on a distraction loop, oscillating between different intrusive scenarios for the night—another glorious side effect of my ADHD.

I think about Kai's hands on Sophie's skin, her lips parting under someone else's kiss, her lashes fluttering as someone else gives her pleasure.

Except, it's not *someone*. It's Kai.

That thought tightens something in my chest.

I take a slow, steadying breath, pressing down the knot of jealousy and nerves coiling in my chest. This is what I want. What I agreed to. Sophie, Kai, me—this is exactly how it's supposed to go. If it gets to be too much, I have my safe word; I can call it off anytime. But the thought of pulling the plug feels like admitting defeat, like losing something I haven't even figured out how to hold on to yet.

So I swallow hard, clench my fists, and will myself to stay right here in the thick of it. I need this, even if I don't fully understand why.

"You look handsome," Sophie purrs, placing her arms around my waist. "Are you sure you're okay? You've been quiet all night."

I nod. "I'm sure."

"Because we don't have to do this," she says, echoing the words from earlier when she'd watched me come home after two and a half hours at the gym. I had energy to burn off, but at least my physique will benefit this time around.

All or nothing.

I look down at my doting wife, placing my hands on either side of her face. "I want this. So much."

A slow smile creeps across her face. "Me too."

The car ride to downtown Crestwood is quiet. Sophie plays a Sabrina Carpenter album, and I oscillate between excitement, jealousy, and nervousness.

I have my safe word.

I can tap out.

It'll be okay.

I'd forgotten to take my ADHD medication this morning, which means I've felt extra jumpy and distracted. My left foot bounces against the floor mat as I drive, and the rhythmic sound is comforting somehow. The music hums in the background, but I'm not really hearing it.

My thoughts are too loud.

I know I'm overthinking. I'm good at burying things, locking them away tight so nothing can hurt me. But tonight, it's like my mind refuses to be obedient. Every time the thought of Kai's hands trailing over Sophie enters my mind, I have to quell the jealousy mixed with arousal.

My mind bounces between best- and worst-case scenarios, and I don't even hear Sophie ask me a question.

"Julian?"

"Hmm?" I ask, pulling into the car park underneath Kai's building.

Placing her hand on my leg, she squeezes it once. "You and me, okay? I love you."

I give her a genuine smile. "You and me. And I love you more."

The lift ride up causes my heart to pound against my ribs, and I hold on to Sophie's hand to help keep me grounded. My breathing feels shallow, somehow, so I count the seconds. It helps me, sometimes—especially on days I forget my medication. But I can't find the right tempo. Too fast, and I'll seem overeager. Too slow, and I'll seem hesitant.

Is it possible to feel both those things at once?

I want this, but with Kai, everything feels... heightened.

Sophie's thumb brushes against the calloused part of my palm, and I squeeze her hand back.

It helps.

As we exit on the fifth floor, we quietly walk to the end of the hallway. I've never been here before, but I can't help but feel like Kai's place is going to be modest. Small. Organized.

We wanted to arrange things at his flat to keep it casual and comfortable. A hotel felt too impersonal for the arrangement, and he offered his place up, but I'm now realizing it gives the whole night a raw intimacy that makes me realize just how personal this is becoming.

Will he offer us wine?

Dinner?

Swallowing, I knock on the door once we arrive. The sound is altogether too soft and yet somehow loud in the quiet hallway. My eyes trail over the modern-looking wood door and black doormat. I'm struck by the sudden awareness that we're standing here, on the verge of something I can't control, in front of a door which leads to a place that feels too intimate for what we've planned.

It's like I can already feel his presence on the other side, in his space.

The thought sets off a spark in me that I wasn't expecting, heating my face as I take a shallow breath.

Arousal.

"You okay?" Sophie whispers, her hand giving mine a gentle squeeze.

I nod, forcing a smile, but there's a tightness in my throat I can't shake. "Yeah... it's just... you know."

She smiles at me in that soft, understanding way of hers, and I feel a pang of gratitude.

Just as she opens her mouth to respond, the door opens, and Kai is standing before us. My insides spark with a mix of anticipation, excitement, and nervous energy at seeing his face, and his eyes flare with something similar as he looks between us.

Something in my chest tightens. It's not just his place, but him—here, looking at me with that calm, warm expression that's always managed to both settle and unsettle me. Just seeing him, the familiar strength and quiet confidence in his posture, makes the ground feel a little less steady beneath my feet.

"Come in."

He offers us a soft smile, stepping back to let us in. I step forward half a second before Sophie, positioning myself slightly in front of her.

It's instinct, the same way I always walk on the roadside of the pavement.

Protective.

And maybe a little possessive.

We both cross the threshold into his space. It smells like him, just as I suspected, that familiar, quiet scent that I associate with late-night talks in our dorm room. Everything here reflects him, from the subtle order, the simplicity, the quiet care he puts into things. It's unmistakably Kai.

Not plain or boring, but... simple.

"Would you like a drink?" Kai asks both of us.

My heart's pounding again, and it's all because of him.

Because the way I feel standing here feels like something new and old at once, something that's been waiting for a moment like this to finally come to the surface.

And he's not even going to touch me.

I meet his gaze, and there's a power there I'm not sure he fully realizes. "Sure," I manage, my voice coming out a little more breathless than I intended.

He smiles again, that steady, reassuring smile, and for a moment, I feel like everything else—the nerves, the apprehension—fades into something softer. Just me,

Sophie, and Kai, stepping into a moment that's as unexpected as it is exactly what I've been waiting for.

"Me too," Sophie says at my side.

Sophie and I walk farther into the apartment, and I was right about another thing—it is small.

Except... despite the size, it's curated. There are books placed on tables. A candle on the bookshelf flickering against the leather-bound tomes. A record player sits on a mid-century credenza, lightly playing some nineties music. There's no television, but there's a whole shelf of puzzles and board games.

I hide my smile when I see several puzzles detailing scenes from classic slasher movies. It brings me back to that night in the dorm, and my heart pounds in my chest when I think of how we never did finish watching all of them together.

Sophie's arm snakes around my side as Kai meanders over to a small bar set against one of the walls.

"Wine? Beer? Liquor...?" Kai asks, the last word hanging in the air in such a way that it seems to cut the tension a bit.

"I'll take the liquor," Sophie says quickly, laughing lightly against my side.

"Me too," I tell Kai, and he gives me a quick smirk before pouring some scotch into three crystal tumblers.

As he walks back over to us, Sophie's arm leaves my waist, and I take the opportunity to walk around the living area. There are pictures with his brothers on the wooden mantel, and just as I walk over to the hallway, a small tan... thing... scurries past my legs, making a high-pitched squeaking sound.

I jump back and whirl around just as Sophie's eyes go wide in front of me.

"Don't mind Willy. He's old and not used to visitors," Kai explains, reaching down to scoop up the tiny animal.

I open and close my mouth once before looking at Sophie, who looks half a second away from laughing out loud.

"Willy?" I ask tentatively.

"Yeah. He's a fennec fox. My dad had a menagerie, and when the Feds raided the castle Willy got stuck with me."

"Willy," I say again, trying to rein my inner teenager in. "As in... penis?"

Kai grins as he sets Willy down. "Right. Willy is slang for cock in the UK. I guess I should've seen that coming."

"I think he's cute," Sophie says. "Can I pet him?"

Kai shrugs as he takes his scotch and sips it. "Sure. He's friendly."

Sophie bends down, reaching out to Willy and cooing as he brushes up against her hand and makes another squeaking sound.

The tension feels lighter now, and I lean back against the bookshelf as my eyes flick between Sophie and Kai. The music is soft, filling the silence with a quiet, lilting melody. When Sophie stands up, she smiles at Kai, but she walks over to me.

"Do you remember this song?" she asks, referencing the song playing, "Fade into You" by Mazzy Star.

"I do."

She reaches out for my free hand, and I set my scotch down on the bookshelf as she drags me into the middle of the room.

"Dance with me?"

I smile as my arms loop around her narrow waist, and she rests her head on my chest as we sway to the music.

"I remember how fucking incredible you looked that night," I murmur, ignoring my growing erection as I reference our third date.

It was the first night I slept with her, and the experience changed my life.

Kai walks over to the couch and sits down, scotch in hand. I make eye contact with him over Sophie's head as we move to the slow music, and then I drag my eyes down his chest. He's wearing a navy sweater with a white collar underneath and black trousers. His hair is unkempt and a little wild, and as always, he has a bit of scruff that lines his chiseled jaw. As my eyes rove back up to his face, he's watching me with an almost daring look as he finishes the last of his scotch.

My hands glide over Sophie's back, down to her arse, and she groans as I squeeze once.

Kai's eyes spark with mischief, and he rubs his mouth with his hand. I notice the faint flex in his jaw, though—the way his eyes bore into mine as I drag my hand across her back. His gaze is relentless, the mischievous gleam sharpening every time our eyes meet. The gleam of amusement there—or is it challenge?—stirs something primal in me, something that stokes my need to keep his attention fixed on me. I know exactly what game he's playing, and damn if I won't play it better.

His pupils darken as I shift, rolling my hips against Sophie and drawing her even closer.

I don't look away from Kai—I can't.

His gaze stays locked with mine, intense and unblinking, as I dance with my wife. The longer it stretches out, the hotter my blood runs.

I press against Sophie's abdomen, but my focus never wavers from the man watching us from the couch. Finally, I tear my eyes from his and press my mouth to Sophie's neck, letting my lips graze her skin. My voice drops low, just for her.

"Do you like him watching you, pet? Knowing how hard he's getting just from seeing you move?"

Her breath hitches, and I drag my teeth along her pulse point, savoring the way she melts against me, sighing my name as my fingers tighten on her hips.

I feel Kai's gaze like a physical touch, demanding, hot, and so unwavering it's almost maddening.

I look back up at him.

The air between us thickens, loaded with something unsaid, unacknowledged. Kai's smile twists as if he knows exactly where my thoughts are, what kind of pulse is thrumming in my veins. I can see the glint in his eyes now, an invitation and a provocation all wrapped up in that familiar smirk. He leans forward just slightly, his body language relaxed but his eyes darker, almost hungry, as if testing whether I'll falter, whether I'll break the contact.

I don't.

Instead, I tighten my hold on Sophie, moving my hips in time with hers, a barely-there smirk playing at the corner of my mouth. And still, my eyes don't leave Kai's. He lifts his hand to his mouth again, but this time, he lingers, his thumb grazing his bottom lip as he watches me, deliberate and almost sinful. There's something in the way he looks at me that makes it hard to breathe, something in the silent language passing between us that makes the space around us crackle. It's an invitation, a challenge, and I'm both tempted and damned if I don't meet him where he is.

That *is* why we're here tonight, after all.

When I press Sophie closer, Kai leans back, just enough to let his head tilt to the side, never breaking eye contact. And as he does, that slow, lazy smile spreads across his face—a silent promise that tells me he isn't going anywhere. If anything, he's daring me to take it further. And I'm not sure I can resist the notion of showing him who exactly is in charge of tonight's activities.

"Are you enjoying this?" I ask him, my voice low, almost taunting.

Let him feel it. Let him know.

Kai doesn't say anything, but a flicker of something darkens his gaze—amusement, maybe, or something deeper, something I can almost feel seeping into my skin. He lets his thumb drag slowly across his lip again, the faintest quirk at the corner of his mouth hinting at a silent laugh he's holding back. His eyes roam over me and Sophie, lingering on the way I press her body to mine, the subtle roll of our hips.

Fuck it.

I let one hand come down the side of Sophie's thigh, and she gasps when I move it between her legs. She's wearing tights, so I can't do anything untoward, but I *can* fuel the fire, per se.

My index finger runs along the seam, and I quickly find the sweet bundle of nerves. She gasps again, and this time, I let my other fingers brush against her cleft.

I groan when I feel how wet she is already—even through her knickers and tights.

Kai leans forward just a fraction, one eyebrow lifting in a lazy, almost defiant arch. Tilting his head slightly as if considering me, a challenge simmers behind his eyes. His silence speaks volumes, and the tension between us tightens, humming with an energy I can't ignore. It's as though he's waiting for me to make a move, to see if I'll break first.

And I'll be damned if I do.

"I am enjoying this, actually," he says, giving me a small, amused smile.

"Show me."

My voice reverberates through the room. Sophie stiffens, but I hold her steady, never looking away from him.

I don't break.

Instead, I wait for Kai to show me *just* how much he's enjoying this.

Kai's mouth curves into the hint of a smile, his eyes never leaving mine. "I can show you—in the bedroom," he murmurs, smooth and unwavering.

I remove my hand from between Sophie's legs. She pulls away from me. Her cheeks are flushed and her eyes are glassy, and when I tilt my head in question, she nods once.

"Very well," I tell him. "Lead the way."

He stands, and much to my satisfaction, I see him adjust himself quickly before he reaches for Sophie's hand.

I let her go, and the two of them walk in front of me down the hall.

In any other situation, I would be taking in my surroundings... but right now, all I can think of is how turned on I am.

Once we reach what I presume is Kai's bedroom, my eyes do a quick sweep of the modern walnut furniture, white bedding, and minimal decorations. The bed is simple—modest, even. Not big or ornate, but functional.

As Kai leads Sophie to the foot of the bed, I settle into a chair near the window, my fingers drumming against my knee as I track his every move. I'm buzzing with energy, an almost reckless edge that's making it hard to keep still. This is my scene to control, and he knows it. No matter how smoothly he's orchestrated this moment, he's not the one in charge here.

I am.

Well, technically, Sophie is, but he doesn't need to know that.

Kai and I have always butted heads when it comes to dominance, and if I don't assert myself now, at the beginning of whatever this is, he'll hold it over my head for the rest of the evening.

My ex-best friend glances at me, his expression unreadable, but there's a subtle tension there—a silent acknowledgment. He gestures toward the windowsill. "There's a contract there," he says, voice smooth. His tone is... almost *challenging*.

I look over and see the neat stack of papers—his guidelines and an invitation for formal consent. There's an ironic sense of decorum in that contract, a reminder of where he thought we'd draw the line. But right now, rules are the last thing on my mind. I let a slow, deliberate smile spread across my face as I reach for the document.

The paper feels thin between my fingers, too weak for the intensity of the night. *Fragile.*

It's a barrier, one that stands between me and the restless pull I haven't fully named yet. I know what this contract is supposed to do—set boundaries, make this feel controlled. Safe.

But I don't need paper to control this scene. I already have control.

Without a word, I tear it cleanly down the middle, watching Kai's reaction as the halves flutter to the floor. I don't break eye contact. Let him see it for what it is. This isn't impulsive. It's deliberate. My way of reminding him—reminding *myself*—who's in charge here.

Kai doesn't say a word, but there's something in

the way his shoulders settle. Not defiance. Not irritation. Something quieter. Respect, maybe. Or concession.

He gets it.

I roll my shoulders back, letting the silence stretch as I tip my chin slightly, signaling him to continue. He might be part of this, but he's here on my terms.

Sophie is *my* wife, after all, and this is how we've always done it.

"Julian," she warns, cocking her head. *Behave,* she says with her eyes.

Kai's jaw tenses ever so slightly, his hand hovering near Sophie's, but his eyes flick to mine with a hint of something between submission and defiance.

"I don't need a contract to tell me how you're going to fuck my wife. I'll be here to make sure you do a good job."

His pupils dilate, and I can see the shift in his demeanor as he relinquishes that last sliver of control. This was his game, but he's given it to me now.

"Very well," he says, looking between Sophie and me. He's still smirking, but his movements are careful.

He knows he's operating within my limits.

I hold his gaze, unmoving, letting the weight of my presence remind him exactly who's setting the pace tonight.

With a subtle nod, I offer a final cue, my tone low and even. "Show her what you're here for," I say, leaving no doubt that he's here at my discretion.

Kai's fingers graze Sophie's waist, and I shift slightly

in my seat, the leather creaking beneath me. But it's not her I'm watching. It's him.

There's a heat curling low in my stomach, sharp and insistent, but I bury it beneath something else. Control. Dominance. It's easier that way—easier to frame this as me overseeing everything, guiding the scene like I always do. Like I'm supposed to.

I let my eyes drift over Kai's hand, the way it rests just a little too long against the curve of Sophie's hip.

My jaw tightens, and I lean back, fingers drumming slowly against my thigh.

The charged silence thickens as I watch, fully in command.

And now he knows it.

CHAPTER TWELVE
THE HOTWIFE

MALAKAI

"Show her what you're here for."

Julian's words pierce through me with a fierceness I can't overlook. His tone is meant to provoke—to awaken something I've buried deep inside me that's beginning to stir.

He knows exactly what he's doing, and if I didn't know him so well, I'd be angry.

Him ripping the contract in half feels dismissive—like he knows he can manipulate me before casting me to the side.

But there's a flickering heat in his eyes that tells me there's more here than dominance or control. He's not just testing me—he's watching me. *Gauging me.*

This intensity between us is built on years of familiarity—formative years spent by his side and learning his quirks. Yet, as I watch his jaw tighten and his eyes darken, it's clear I don't know him at all. A glimmer of realization hits me, sharp and sudden. My pulse races under his gaze, and I can feel every cell in my body attuned not just to Sophie, but to Julian. To both of them. I'd spent so long thinking I knew who I was, what I wanted, but this? This is something I never imagined.

The moment is broken when I flick my gaze to Sophie. Running my fingers along the curve of her jaw, I use the softness of her skin to ground myself. Her warmth keeps me steady, but Julian's presence lingers just behind it, chaotic and electric.

Maybe it's Julian's confidence. The way he sits there, completely sure of himself, daring me to rise to the occasion. Or perhaps it's the unspoken permission in his words:

Show her what you're here for.

Saying that revealed something intimate about him, a crack in the armor that allows me insight into their marriage.

It's intimate, what we're all doing, and I'm grateful for the chance to be a part of it. This isn't about scratching an itch or exploring boundaries—it's deeper, more consuming. Something that has been hiding in me all along, waiting for the right catalyst, waiting for the perfect moment.

Seventeen years.

Seventeen years of tension, of trying not to think about the man before me despite trying not to, of pushing these feelings down. Now, the ache in my chest feels impossible to ignore. I'm on the edge of a precipice, staring down into a version of myself I don't know.

As I shift my attention back to Sophie, I let my thumb brush across her cheek, feeling the weight of their eyes on me.

I don't know what this is becoming, but I know there's no going back.

"Don't be afraid to use your safe word," I tell her, my voice a low purr. I'd read their contract and know that she prefers the traffic light system—green for good, yellow for pause and discuss, red for stop.

She nods, her throat bobbing as she brings a hand to my chest. "I know. I trust you."

You shouldn't.

The two words reverberate through my mind as I take in her shiny flaxen hair, her porcelain skin, the tiny freckles on the bridge of her nose, and the way her blue eyes are so bright and wide, it makes me want to call this whole thing off.

I know she's experienced—I know she's not completely naive.

But there's something innocent about Sophie— something I'm so hesitant to corrupt.

The weight of responsibility bears down on me—not just dominance, but the fragility of the trust they've placed in my hands. I can feel Julian's gaze pinning me down.

What if I accidentally cross the line?

What if tonight ruins everything—what if it can't be repaired?

My eyes flick up to Julian, who gives nothing away except for the tight grip on his knee.

It's not a verbal command, or even a nod, but it's the kind of permission I didn't realize I needed.

"Are you sure you want to do this?" I ask, placing my other hand around her waist.

Her lips quirk to the side. "Having second thoughts, Ravage?"

Her boldness makes me laugh. "No. I just want to make sure you know what you're in for. I won't be gentle. And since your husband destroyed the contract…"

In my peripheral, I see Julian stiffen, his jaw flexing as his fingers drum slowly against his thigh, watching closely. Waiting to see if he'll call the whole thing off, I don't move my gaze from Sophie's face, which has taken on the faintest blush.

He doesn't.

"I don't want you to be gentle," she murmurs, her voice nearly a whisper, sending a thrill down my spine. "Father," she adds, her eyes sparking with defiance, and a shiver of anticipation skates down my skin.

My nostrils flare as the hand on her cheek slides back to cradle the base of her skull, fingers threading into her hair as I fist it gently. She's closer now, the faint scent of citrus and something floral teasing me, intoxicating.

"I know what you're doing," I warn, the words a low growl against her cheek.

She gives me a bratty, little smile, eyes glinting, and the urge to break that defiant stare pulses inside me. I smirk and look over at Julian, whose pupils are fully blown as he studies us, hands clenched at his sides, clearly on edge.

"You didn't tell me your wife is a brat," I mutter, tilting her head back as I step closer, pulling her body against mine fully, feeling her chest rise as her breath catches.

"She can be," Julian says, his low voice laced with something dark and dangerous that sends a shock wave of arousal through me. "But she just needs a little reminder to behave."

I arch a brow as I look back down at Sophie, and she pulls her lower lip between her teeth, the challenge in her eyes unmistakable. Doing a scene with a brat is not my typical dynamic. Most of the time, my subs are very obedient. *Too* obedient. It's just part of the religion kink, and when edge play is involved? Bratting out isn't necessarily in the best interest of the sub. And yet, I can't deny how the thought of her disobedience excites me. There's something intriguing about knowing that Sophie is going to push back.

Until I dominate her into submission.

My eyes trace her lips, lingering on the glossy sheen of her mouth, and she notices my hypnotic gaze because she trails her tongue along her lower lip, slow, taunting, daring. And with that lock in her eyes, I lose my mind.

Leaning down, I press my lips against hers, a low, guttural moan escaping me when I get a whiff of her scent, fresh roses mixed with something subtly citrusy. Her lip gloss tastes like vanilla, and her warm body softens against mine as I push my tongue into her mouth, claiming her in a kiss that's anything but gentle.

She groans as I fist her hair tighter, my fingers digging into her hip, and something deep and dark awakens inside me, knowing I'm kissing someone I've wanted to kiss for weeks now. Someone who is funny, and beautiful, and smart, and so damn sexy—yet unpredictable in a way that no one else has been before.

Someone who is technically off-limits.

I could stay like this, tasting her, punishing her, but something inside me wants more.

I pull away, breathing hard, almost reluctant. "On your knees."

Her eyes go wide, wobbling between surprise and defiance, and I ignore the way her lips are perfectly pink and swollen, the way her hair is just slightly out of place, making her look even more irresistible.

Eyes flicking between mine, she smirks, but she doesn't move.

"Do as I say, little dove," I murmur, the words slipping out before I can stop them, and I realize a second too late that I've just given Julian's wife a term of endearment unintentionally.

She notices, too. The smirk fades for a fraction of a second, eyes widening as she catches the reverence in my voice, before her smile returns, even bolder this time. She's just as surprised as I am, but she's hiding it well, the bratty glint in her eye sharper than ever.

Her voice drops to a taunt. "You're going to have to earn it."

My pulse quickens, her challenge stirring something fierce in me. I want her submission, yes. But I *need* her trust. Slowly, I pull her close again, my hand sliding down to rest firmly at the small of her back, possessive, reverent.

For once, I don't know if I want to break her defiance or bow to her fire. But I'm determined to do both.

Her smirk wavers as the air between us grows heavier. I can see her pulse fluttering in the hollow of her throat, her chest rising and falling as she swallows. Her resistance falters, and a softness replaces that defiant spark in her gaze. Her eyes drop, lashes casting delicate shadows on her cheeks as the challenge drains from her expression, leaving behind a quiet vulnerability.

"I'll give you one more chance, but only because this dynamic is new," I say, my tone firm but tinged with warning now.

For a beat, she hesitates. Her lips part slightly as her breath catches. I scowl at her, letting the moment stretch. My silence is deliberate and intended to make her squirm. The corner of her mouth twitches, like she's trying to suppress a grin, but I can see the hesitation creeping in.

She's testing the boundaries, but she must know where this is headed.

"On. Your. Knees." This time, my voice is low and unyielding—the kind that brooks no argument.

Her lips part as if to retort, but something in my tone or my gaze shifts the air between us. Slowly, she lowers herself to the ground. When she finally settles on her knees, her hands rest on her thighs, but instead of the palms-up pose, her fingers drum impatiently against her legs. Her eyes dart up to mine, bold and challenging, as if to say, *Happy now?*

I step closer, towering over her, letting my presence press against her like a weight. "We'll work on that attitude."

She shifts under my gaze, the bratty facade flickering. Still, she doesn't drop it entirely.

"Maybe I just enjoy keeping you on your toes, Father." Her defiance has lost some of its bite, so I decide to press further. Letting the silence draw out, I circle her slowly, letting the weight of my silence press down on her.

"You know, bratty subs don't get to keep their clothes." My voice is soft but sharp, the kind that lingers in the air like a whispered threat.

Sophie stiffens, clearly aroused, but not ready to give in without a fight.

I crouch down, my face level with hers, and reach out to tilt her chin up, forcing her to look directly at me.

"True submission is everything to me, little dove."

It's a command and a promise at once, and for the first time, I see her bravado falter completely.

She's not completely submitting, but she's not pushing back, either.

"Good girl," I murmur, letting the words linger, and I see her shiver, the praise igniting a glow in her eyes. The brat is still there, simmering beneath her skin, but now it's watered down with a willingness that makes me admire her so fucking much.

Without thinking, I let my fingers sweep through her hair, tugging gently, just enough to draw a small gasp from her lips. Her breath catches again, and this time she doesn't fight it. Her gaze stays locked with mine, vulnerable yet fiercely stubborn, as though daring me to see every part of her and still take her as she is.

"Keep your eyes on me, Sophie," I command softly, and to my satisfaction, she obeys without hesitation. Her gaze doesn't waver, and for a moment, I lose myself in the way she's looking at me—half defiant, half surrendered, wholly mine.

I feel Julian's eyes on us, a reminder that he's still there, but even he's faded into the background. Right now, all I see is Sophie kneeling in front of me. I'm tempted to tell her how exquisite she looks, but then with a heavy weight in my abdomen, I remember my temporary role in all of this.

"You're mine tonight," I murmur, my voice a rough whisper. My words cause her cheeks to flush. She nods, biting her lower lip, and I notice the slightest smirk tugging at the corner of her mouth, as if to remind me that she's still not entirely tamed.

I'll have to work on that.

When she hesitates, I step behind her and lower my mouth near her ear, voice dropping. "If you're good, maybe I'll let your husband watch while I edge you for hours. But if you keep testing me... we'll see how well that mouth of yours can beg."

Sophie shudders visibly, and even Julian shifts in his seat.

"Yes, my lord," she finally says, her words laced with mischief but also an unmistakable acceptance.

I tilt my head, letting my thumb brush her lower lip and admiring the way she opens her mouth just slightly, instinctively, as though ready to take any command I might give.

"Such a smart mouth," I mutter, my tone wry. "Now, lose the clothes. I want nothing between us."

This time, she obeys without a word, though the glimmer in her eyes promises this won't be the last time she tests me.

"Tonight is only a taste," I murmur as a reminder, brushing my thumb against her lower lip again and tugging it down slightly. "But next time... we'll see how far I can take you."

Her pupils dilate, and I look over to see Julian's grip on the armrest tighten.

CHAPTER THIRTEEN
THE DEFIANCE

SOPHIE

My chest rises and falls as I pull the zipper on the side of my dress down slowly. Julian is behind me, so I can't see him. Despite that, I can feel his eyes boring into the back of my body, and as I look up at Kai, a shiver works through me at the way he's drinking me in.

Whenever I sleep with men outside of my marriage, there's always a wide range of preferences. No two men are going to approach fucking me the same; they have different tactics and techniques, different ways of doing things. I've been wined and dined while Julian sat nearby. I've also been pressed against a wall and fucked in a matter of minutes. Usually it's somewhere in the middle, and usually, it's Julian giving the commands.

I like that my husband is in charge. It makes me feel safe.

But right now?

I can't look away from Kai as a dark piece of hair falls over his forehead, as he stands there with a heavy, commanding presence.

I've been with soft Dom's before—men who dabble in BDSM. And like Julian told Kai, we've experimented with different kinky things. We're not wholly vanilla, but we're also not as intense as Kai seems to be.

I wasn't sure what to expect tonight, but this?

It's exhilarating.

I know I tend to lean toward the submissive side of the spectrum, at least with Julian, so when Kai tells me what to do—his voice low, steady, and completely in control—it hits something deep within me. The way he looks at me, like he knows he's in charge yet never once crosses the line into disrespect, is... *really* fucking hot. He's somehow figured out the perfect balance that always leaves me breathless.

Authoritative yet not overbearing.

Firm but never cruel.

There's something thrilling about testing him, knowing that he'd never push past my comfort zone. I enjoy seeing that brief hint of irritation when I press against his boundaries.

He never lets it fully show—Kai is far too composed for that—but I can see it in the tightening of his jaw, the faint narrowing of his eyes. And I *like* it. I enjoy the challenge, the game of seeing how far I can go before he quietly but firmly puts me back in my place.

With Julian, it's different. I don't normally act this

playful with him; our dynamic has its own rhythm, one that's softer, more reverent. Julian looks at me like I'm something to be cherished, and while I love that—I need that—this thing with Kai is its own brand of intoxicating. Kai doesn't just cherish; he challenges. He meets my resistance head-on, countering my every move with a calm smirk that tells me he's already thought three steps ahead. It's maddening, and yet it pulls me in, makes me want to push even harder just to see how he'll handle it.

It was the same during the renovations, when Kai was around every day, overseeing every detail with that infuriating, self-assured competence. Our banter back then was sharp and quick, always laced with a hint of flirtation, though neither of us dared to acknowledge it aloud. It felt safe to play with him, to poke at that steady, unshakable demeanor, knowing he could take it without missing a beat. That camaraderie, it's different from what I have with Julian, and I realize now it's carried over into *this*, into the bedroom.

I shouldn't be surprised that Kai's control feels as natural here as it did back then, though now it's layered with a heat and burning passion that leaves me reeling. Even as I push back, as I tease and challenge him, I know exactly how this will end. Kai will take every ounce of my resistance in stride. He'll let me push—maybe even enjoy watching me squirm—but ultimately, he'll take the reins and remind me exactly who's in charge.

And I'll love it. Every second of it.

"May I stand?" I ask, my voice low and sultry, almost challenging but not crossing the line of disobedience.

"You may," Kai says, a hint of amusement in his tone. "Thank you for asking."

Biting my tongue, I stand up and take my boots off. Then I pull the dress down my body. I'm only clad in my bra and knickers, as well as my tights, and Kai's eyes rove freely down my exposed abdomen.

"Fuck," he utters, sighing as he looks back up at my face. My cheeks heat, but he steps forward and places his hands on my hips. "You're perfect."

"Thank you," I whisper.

Using this opportunity, I look over my shoulder at Julian, and what I see makes me inhale sharply.

He's leaning back in the chair, and instead of watching us like he normally does... his hand is palming his very obvious erection over his trousers. He gives me a slow, lazy smile as he continues, and then he gestures for us to keep going.

I swallow.

Julian never touches himself—it's his *one* rule. Once they leave, it's fair game—but he's never involved in this way.

The thought of my husband being too aroused to keep from touching himself makes me want this even more.

"How would you like me, Father?"

Kai's eyes darken as he studies me, and then he walks around me to his bedside table. Opening it slowly, he pulls out a black, leather book, and as my eyes take in the gold cross on the cover, a shiver works through me.

"I'd like you to recite a few passages from the Bible," he says.

My lips part, and I take the book from him as my pulse speeds up. I've never done anything like this, but... I was raised Catholic. Julian and I don't practice any sort of religion, but there's something deeply taboo about playing with religion like this.

I squeeze my thighs together as I flip the book open.

"On your knees, little dove."

Fuck.

That nickname is going to be the death of me.

I bend down to my knees, and my thighs rest on top of my heels. When I look up, he's watching me with one hand rubbing his mouth.

"Is there a specific passage you'd like me to recite?" I ask.

Kai shrugs. "I'm interested to see which passage you choose."

Swallowing my nerves down, I flip the Bible open and skim for the passages that used to resonate with me as a child. My fingers brush the delicate, thin pages of the Bible, and a strange heat rises in my chest. The smell of the old paper pulls me back to Sunday mornings as a child—knees pressed to hard wooden pews, stiff collars scratching at my neck. I hated the silence then, the way it made every fidget, every whispered thought feel like a sin.

But this isn't Sunday school.

This is Kai, his gaze sharp and knowing, like he's

peeling back my layers with nothing but the weight of his attention.

I hate how small I feel under that look, how exposed.

"Well?" he asks, his voice smooth, too calm. My pulse jumps at the audacity of it—how he asks like this is nothing, like it's *easy*. But it isn't. It's a dare, even if he doesn't say it outright.

And I don't want to give him what he wants.

Not yet, anyway.

"You're very sure of yourself, aren't you?" My voice is steady, but there's a slight edge to it, a challenge I'm not entirely sure I meant to issue.

"I didn't realize turning pages was so hard for you," he says, the teasing tone light. "I suppose I should reconsider the other things I have planned for tonight."

His gaze sharpens for just a second, brief but unmistakable. Like a blade glinting beneath velvet, a shadow of something harder, darker, presses to the surface before vanishing just as quickly.

How much is he holding back? The question curls inside me, electric and forbidden.

Instead of being obstinate, I bite down on the inside of my cheek. My thighs press together as I shift my weight, and the tension between us only coils tighter.

I know what he's doing—he's waiting for me to crack, to hand him my obedience on a silver platter. But submission is supposed to be mine to give, not his to take. The realization is a spark, igniting something reckless in me.

I flip through the pages, skimming passages about

humility and obedience, the words pulling at old wounds I'd rather not prod tonight. My skin prickles as memories surface—hands clasped in prayer, sermons about surrendering to God's will. I was always told to *follow*, to *trust*, to *serve*.

But I've spent years unlearning those lessons, peeling off the expectations like a second skin. Both Julian and I have, and it hasn't been easy at times.

For example, my mother's disapproving expression when I told her Julian and I were moving to California, which might as well have been a different planet.

And now Kai wants me to kneel, to recite those same words that once made me feel so small?

I stop on a random passage and glance up at him, meeting his gaze head-on. He's still watching me, quiet and composed, his hand resting against his mouth like he's fighting back another smirk.

Something in me itches to break that composure, to see if he's as calm as he pretends to be.

"Do you want me to mean it?" I ask, my voice low, teasing, testing. "Or are you happy with a performance?"

The question hangs between us, and for a moment, his expression shifts, it's subtle, but enough to make my breath hitch.

It's dangerous, pushing him like this. I know it. But the thrill of it hums in my veins, mingling with the slow ache of anticipation building in my core.

I want to give in. I want to feel the weight of his control, to let him pull me under and quiet the noise in my head. But first, I want him to *take it*. To remind me why I kneel in the first place.

"What do you think?" he asks, his voice a dark purr.

I clear my throat and glance up at him. "All right, how about this one, my lord?" I let my finger trail down to Proverbs and find the verse that feels just outlandish enough. "'Like a gold ring in a pig's snout is a beautiful woman who shows no discretion,'" I read, keeping my tone perfectly matter-of-fact.

I look up to meet his eyes, waiting for his reaction.

I see his mouth twitch as he tries not to smile, clearly catching him off guard.

"Interesting choice," he says finally, his voice careful but laced with amusement.

"Oh, you don't like that one?" I ask, feigning innocence as I turn a few more pages with exaggerated nonchalance. "I'm sure I can find something more appropriate for the occasion."

There's a flicker of something dark in his eyes now, a warning I'm both thrilled and terrified to see. He doesn't rise to the bait—not yet.

"All right then," he says, his voice warm and daring. "Hit me with your best shot."

I let out a small laugh, unable to help myself. "Oh, you asked for it," I say, glancing down at the pages, pretending to search seriously for something profound.

My finger stops on a verse, and I try to keep a straight face as I look back up at him. "'Better to live on a corner of the roof than share a house with a quarrelsome wife.'"

I tilt my head innocently. "Words to live by, don't you think?"

His chuckle resembles a dark purr. He steps closer, the movement slow and deliberate, as if he's giving me time to rethink what I've just done.

As if he wants to make me sweat.

"You're enjoying this, aren't you?" he asks, and there's a glint of amusement in his eyes, though it's tempered by something far more serious.

I shrug, biting back a grin. "What can I say? You handed me a Bible and gave me free rein."

He walks closer, and there's a dangerous glint in his eyes as he snatches the Bible out of my hands.

"Julian said you like to be punished," he says, and I see him look up at my husband. "What's her least favorite punishment?"

I look over my shoulder at Julian, and he's watching this all unfold with an amused smile.

"She has really sensitive nipples."

I break out into a cold sweat, and as a scowl moves across my expression, he winks.

The bastards.

"They're not that sensitive," I say, trying to keep my voice even.

Kai doesn't react immediately, but I notice the subtle way his jaw flexes, like he's filing the information away for later. Julian's eyes flick to him, and for a brief second, it feels like they're speaking without words.

Julian knows exactly what kind of man Kai is—and how far he could push me if I let him.

"Noted," he drawls. "And since you're in the mood to challenge me," he says, his voice low, "I think I have just the thing."

He pauses for dramatic effect, letting his finger settle on one of the pages. "'Whoever stubbornly refuses to accept criticism will suddenly be destroyed beyond recovery.' Proverbs 29:1." He looks up, his expression equal parts smug and amused. *Prick*. "Sounds like you might need a little lesson in obedience."

I cross my arms with a smirk of my own. "Oh, is that so? And here I thought we were just reading Bible verses, not cherry-picking sermons."

He drops to his knees so that we're at eye level, leaning in and closing the Bible with a soft thud.

His voice is a low murmur. "Careful. Keep it up, and I might just have to remind you who's in charge."

I can't help the laugh that escapes me, but something in his tone makes my cheeks warm. There's something in his look that tells me he's definitely not backing down.

"Yes, my lord."

His eyes flash, and then he reaches around my chest to the clasp of my bra. In two seconds, my strapless bra springs off and falls to the ground. Kai's gaze softens, his eyes tracing over me with a quiet intensity. The same hand that undid my bra runs through my hair, and it feels... *really* nice.

There's a stillness to his touch, as if he's saying a silent prayer.

"Stay here," he says, standing up and walking to his bedside table. When he returns, my skin prickles with both dread and anticipation. It looks like a rosary, but there are two clamps attached with a beaded chain.

As he drops the rosary around my head, my body visibly shudders as the palms of his hands brush against my skin. "Sit up straight."

I do as he says, keeping my spine straight. Tracking his movements, unease slithers through me when I see him adjust the clamps.

Julian and I had tried nipple clamps before, and it was altogether an unpleasant experience. I'm not the kind of woman who can get off when someone sucks my nipples, and Julian knows how sensitive they are. The idea of experiencing a clamp again gives me anxiety.

Kai crouches down in front of me, and just as the end of the rubberized clamp touches the delicate bud, I flinch and move away unconsciously.

His eyes come up to mine, brows pulled together. "You know your safe word, Sophie." He's right, I do. And I'm not afraid to use it. I open my mouth to tell him so, but he reaches out with one hand, tilting his head as he reveres me. "But I'd like you to trust me with this. I read the contract Julian sent me. I know your limits, and I know you don't enjoy pain. This might be uncomfortable at first, and it might sting, but I'd like you to try it. For me."

For me.

He tugs on my heartstrings with that—he knows how comfortable we've become around one another. We've gotten closer over the last few months. He's never given me any reason to doubt him.

He's my friend, and I *do* trust him.

"Okay," I whisper.

"That's my good girl," he purrs, smirking as he deftly adjusts the clamps around my nipples.

They harden, tightening with every brush of his fingers, and I find myself squirming before him. He chuckles, and I hiss when he clamps my left nipple. It's not as tight as I remember the last time I tried them, and I realize that Kai must've adjusted them somehow. Relaxing a bit, he does the other nipple, and other than a small quiver, I keep still until Kai stands up.

"Stand up, please."

I do as he says, cheeks heating. There's an element of humiliation to the clamps, especially with the rosary that hangs down to my navel, brushing my skin like a reminder of my submission. Despite the surrender I feel, a trace of shyness rises in me knowing Julian is watching, his gaze steady and appreciative. The clamps make me feel both exposed and *adorned,* every sensation heightened by the feeling of being "decorated"—on display just for him, vulnerable and yet treasured.

"Step out of your tights and underwear."

Again, I obey him this time. A part of me feels like I'm wearing a leash of sorts, and if I defy him now, he might tighten the clamps or do something else I haven't yet thought of.

Rolling the tights down, I step out of them along with my black thong, discarding them somewhere behind me. My eyes instinctively find the floor, but a second later, I feel Kai's finger on my chin.

"Look at me," he says softly.

I lift my eyes to meet Kai's, and in that moment, it's as if something shifts inside me. Julian is my husband, my foundation, the one I've always built my life around. But Kai's gaze, steady and unwavering, stirs something I can't quite name—a warmth I didn't realize I was missing, a pull that tugs at the edges of my heart, making room where I never expected there to be any.

Julian has always been the only person I allow myself to feel something for, but right now?

His gaze feels intense and different from what I've experienced with other men. It might be admiration, or perhaps something deeper. This awareness between us is both unsettling and exciting. I swallow, unsure if I'm ready to acknowledge it. But he's here, and we're doing this, so I can't deny it anymore.

And I feel immediate guilt because of it.

"Turn around and show your husband how fucking good you look right now," Kai says, stepping away.

That same guilt fills me as I turn around, and I work to keep my expression neutral. Julian's eyes track over my unreadable expression with ease, and though this has never happened before, he lifts a hand and crooks a finger, beckoning me over.

I'm torn—because on the one hand, Julian is my husband.

But I'm also doing a scene with Kai, and it feels disrespectful to break the scene when that's not something we normally do.

One of Kai's hands comes to my shoulder, brushing

my hair to one side. His warm breath feathers against my ear, and I look back at him for approval.

"Go on, little dove."

Opening my eyes, I slowly walk over to my husband. As I do, he unzips his pants and pulls his cock out. My eyes go wide as I step between his legs, and his free hand comes to the back of my thigh. That one small contact makes me want to cry—it grounds and tethers me to him, and whatever I was feeling before doesn't feel so scary all of a sudden.

Just as I reach out for his arm, I feel Kai come up behind me.

My body stills.

This has most definitely never happened.

"Spread your legs," Kai says, his breath fanning against my shoulder.

I hear him open a condom package, and though I really want to turn around and watch him roll it on, I keep my eyes on Julian, who is working his cock faster now. Julian doesn't look away from me either, and as I spread my legs, something hot and unfamiliar snakes through me. Kai is in charge of me, but in a way, Julian is now involved.

And I *really* like the idea of that.

"What do you say?" Kai whispers, one hand coming to my arse and squeezing it.

I'm smart enough to know this is also a test. And in my research, I'd discovered that people with a religion kink liked to be worshiped. I also remember what he said over dinner the other night.

I ask them to obey, to trust, and sometimes even to worship.

Though I doubt we'll be dabbling in edge play tonight, just the idea of following Kai off that cliff, of letting him guide me...

I take a breath, my voice steady but soft. "I submit to you, Father. I offer myself to you, to guide, to shape, to worship." The words feel strange as they leave my lips.

But then I look over my shoulder and meet his eyes, and I realize that perhaps I've been waiting for this moment, this act of surrender. There's something powerful in acknowledging the reverence, the devotion he's asked for.

His pupils blow dark, and I let myself look down at his cock, which is now sheathed with a condom.

My mouth goes dry.

It's thick and long, and I can see the purple head of his shaft pressing against the end of the condom. My wide eyes flick back up to his, and just as I ask how he thinks he's going to fit that *thing* inside of me, one of his hands comes between my legs.

Kai's thumb brushes over the cross dangling against my sternum, and his eyes flick to Julian, a small smirk tugging at the corner of his mouth.

"That's a start," he says softly. "But worship... that takes time. This is just the first prayer. There's so much more I could teach you, if you're willing." The words hang between us, dripping with promise. "So fucking wet, little dove."

Without a warning, he presses a finger inside of me, and I turn back around to face Julian.

He's stroking himself, using spit to lube himself up. His breaths are coming in little pants, and he works himself faster the longer I watch him. The sight of my husband unraveling makes me clench around Kai's fingers. And then my mouth drops open when Kai curves the finger inside of me. There's something profound about touching Julian, about standing between his legs with one of his hands on the back of my thigh—as Kai fingers me. In all other instances of sleeping with other men, Julian isn't involved at all. He just watches, and gives commands. But this?

It might be my new favorite way of doing this.

It feels *right* to include him.

Kai inserts a second finger, and my eyes roll into the back of my head as he slowly stretches my opening, curving his fingers and hitting that sacred spot inside of me.

"Oh God," I whimper.

"That's right." His voice is low, commanding, sending a ripple of heat through me. "I am your god." His voice is ragged from working my pussy, and there's something about the way he says it—like he believes it, like he *knows* it—and a part of me can't help but believe him too. Every touch, every command, pulls me deeper into this web of temptation, and I realize with a shiver that I'm more than willing to be caught.

My mouth drops open when he adds a third finger,

but just as a low groan escapes my throat, he removes his fingers from inside of me.

"Bend over."

There's nowhere for me to go other than to hover over Julian, who's watching me with wonder as he works himself faster, his breath stuttering. Placing my hands on the arms of the chair, Julian's eyes flick down to the necklace and clamps. I'm leaning over so much that the rosary part is sitting right over his heart, and if I wanted to, I could bend my neck and kiss him on the lips.

Kai nudges my legs farther apart, and one of his hands comes to my arse. Julian's gaze flicks to Kai's hand between my legs, and for a brief second, something passes through his expression—something protective, almost territorial.

But he doesn't stop him.

He's letting this happen, but he's watching closely. Always watching.

I hear Kai sigh contentedly from behind me. "Deep breaths, little dove. This might hurt."

CHAPTER FOURTEEN
THE SPECTATOR

Julian

Sophie's eyes widen, and her mouth opens in a silent scream as Kai pushes into her. My thumb swipes at the precum gathering on the tip of my cock, and I use it as lube, working my hand faster. Flicking my eyes up to Kai, I see his lashes flutter as he goes still, reveling in the way it feels to be inside of my wife.

I *know* how it feels, and somehow, it only seems to connect us more.

Kai's eyes drop to mine, narrowing slightly as one of his hands fists Sophie's loose hair, pulling her neck back and causing her to arch her back over me. There's no smugness in his expression, but there's also no hesitation. He knows this isn't about him challenging me directly—yet, I can't shake the pulse of competitiveness curling low in my stomach.

It only spurs me on.

Biting my lower lip, I rut my hips up into my hand as Kai continues to slowly fuck my wife over me.

I normally keep my hands to myself, but the whole night has felt different from the other times, somehow. There's something here between the three of us, and I'll be damned if I don't explore it further by pushing the boundaries of the past and present.

My hand tightens around my cock, but the pressure does little to ease the knot winding in my chest. There's a weight to whatever's happening tonight... something that both constricts and enthralls me as it presses against the walls I've built so carefully around Sophie and me.

I tell myself it's just the gravity of the scene, the thrill of watching her come undone by someone I trust. I tell myself this is just another scene. Another stranger, another fuck. But my hand betrays me, pumping faster as Kai's grip tightens in Sophie's hair.

I know better.

Kai isn't just anyone. And the way she melts for him, the way his eyes darken when he looks at her, it carves into something I wasn't prepared to confront tonight.

I should stop this. I could. The safe word sits heavy on my tongue, but I can't bring myself to say it.

"Fuck her harder," I mutter, looking Kai in the eye again. My lips pull into a cocky smirk, and Kai's eyes flash with disobedience. "She can take it."

He meets my gaze, deliberately ignoring my command for a second longer than necessary, his knuckles white where they grip her. A flicker of defiance lingers in his expression, subtle but clear.

I almost admire it. *Almost.*

But the way his hand lingers, possessive in a way that's not entirely playful, strikes something sharp inside me. I clench my jaw.

"I said harder, Kai."

He grunts as he thrusts harder, and Sophie's eyes squeeze closed. Her hands curl tightly around the arms of the chair, and I feel my orgasm get closer.

"That's all you've got?" I ask, my voice low and taunting. "This is all elementary, Kai."

"Are you always this bossy?" Kai asks, his voice ragged. One of his hands comes around her throat.

I huff a laugh. *He has no idea.* "Yes."

Sophie whimpers, but I don't touch her. This isn't my scene, as hard as it is to resist. I shouldn't even be this involved. I shouldn't want to cross this line, not with him. But the way she arches, the way his hand flexes at her throat, it's too much. The air feels heavier than usual, thick with something that doesn't just come from arousal. My toes curl inside my shoes, and I dip my chin as I watch Sophie's arousal drip down the inside of her thighs.

"Good fucking girl," I say softly. My eyes roam back up to Kai, and both his hands are on her hips now, pulling her onto his cock. "She likes praise," I offer. "The right combination of pretty words will have her squeezing you so tight you'll see stars."

Kai groans and fucks her harder, and I match his tempo with my hand.

"Oh fuck," Sophie whines. The mascara she so meticulously applied earlier is smudged underneath her eyes, and her chest is blooming pink with arousal.

One of Kai's hands moves around to the front of her body, and then it snakes between her legs. He lightly circles her clit, and the low sound that escapes her lips has me properly fucking my hand now.

"She likes that," I tell Kai. "But not too hard—just like that," I tell him.

His nostrils flare, and I can't tell if he enjoys my interjections or not. I'm leaning toward not, but that's too fucking bad.

"Yes," Sophie hisses, rolling her hips. "Right there," she adds.

I can smell her arousal, and in a bold move, I reach between her legs. My fingers brush Kai's, and I enjoy the way his whole body rolls with a shock wave at the contact. Using her arousal as lube, I coat my cock and slowly, deliberately, stroke myself to the edge of a climax.

Sophie's tits bounce with every thrust from Kai, and the silver clamps look so fucking gorgeous clipped to her brown nipples. I can tell she's nearing the edge based on the way her face slackens, the way her hands loosen on the wooden arms of the chair.

"She's close," I say. "And so am I."

"Oh f-fuck," Sophie cries out. Her face scrunches up, and I see her lift up onto her toes—

"Now," I tell Kai.

His lips part, and he uses his free hand to pull on both nipple clamps until they pop off. She cries out, and I can tell the exact moment she begins to come on his cock. His breathing turns ragged, and his hips begin to jerk erratically.

Holy fuck, she's making him come.

A low groan sounds through the room, and mixed with Sophie's quiet pants and convulsing body, it is probably one of the most erotic things I've ever seen. Kai squeezes his eyes shut as he fills the condom, his body quivering from head to toe. His hairline is wet from exertion, and his lips are parted as he finishes.

"Shit," I hiss, my balls drawing up. Everything inside of me pulls taut, and I slow my hand, squeezing tightly down at the base of my cock. "Oh fuck, I'm going to—"

Kai steps back slightly, pulling Sophie with him, and then he presses her head down.

She understands his intentions, because a second later, her warm, wet mouth circles my cock.

I spill into her as I roar, my cum gushing against her tongue and dribbling down her throat. "Don't swallow," I rasp.

She does as I say—*good fucking girl*—and I erratically fuck her mouth until the last of it leaves my body.

My eyes find Kai's, and I give him a lopsided smile. "Save some for Kai." My command is heavy and vibrates through the room. Sophie goes still, mouth full of my cum. I've most definitely never gotten to this level of involved in a scene, and it's fucking exhilarating.

I feel unhinged—and the whole situation feels unpredictable.

It's refreshing.

Sophie slowly straightens, and then she turns around to face Kai—who is glaring at me.

"Go on. Give him a taste."

My words are a challenge, and he knows it.

With one hand around the back of her head, he pulls her face to his, and they kiss. I watch with my lips quirked to the side, feeling cocky as fuck when Kai moans.

At kissing her, or the taste of me... I'm not sure.

When they pull away, he wipes his mouth with the back of his hand, and then he pulls his condom off. He walks over to where Sophie discarded her knickers, and he cleans himself off with them without looking away from me.

"I'm going to use the loo," Sophie says quickly, snatching a nearby throw blanket and wrapping it around herself before walking into the en suite and closing the door.

The silence between Kai and me is charged.

I quickly put myself away and then I stand, zipping my trousers. When I get close to Kai, I can see the way his breath stutters. I snatch Sophie's knickers from his hand, giving him an indolent smile. His fingers twitch after I pull them from him, and for a brief moment, I consider letting him have them—just to see what he'd do with them.

But the thought unsettles me in a way I can't quite

explain, like holding on to the last piece of her, like it's something I can't afford to lose.

"Those are for *me*."

I clean myself off with them before I pocket them. Kai's eyes grow darker, but he doesn't respond.

And for whatever reason, I want him to. However, before I get the chance, Sophie walks out of the bathroom wrapped up in a towel. Her eyes find mine before they flick over to Kai, and then she comes to stand next to me.

Usually by now, the men are gone and I perform aftercare with her. But since we're in Kai's house, it would be strange to leave.

Reaching over to her, I run a finger down her jaw. "You did beautifully," I tell her, giving her a genuine smile.

She bites her lower lip before standing on her tiptoes and pressing a kiss to my mouth. And then she turns around and presses a kiss to Kai's cheek.

I track the way his eyes drink in her 'just fucked' look, the way one of his hands curls into a fist as if he's restraining himself.

Fuck... if he keeps looking at her like that...

The kiss is brief, fleeting, but the way Kai lingers makes my throat tighten. I run my hand over Sophie's jaw, grounding myself in the familiar feel of her skin, reminding myself who she belongs to.

"I can order pizza?" I offer, feeling slightly awkward.

"Pizza sounds amazing," Sophie says, and it comes out as a satisfied sigh.

I nod and usher her out of the bedroom, and when I turn, I see Kai's eyes follow her.

There's something unsettling about how easy this feels, like we've stumbled into dangerous territory, but none of us are willing to acknowledge it yet.

I can't decide if I like it or hate it.

"Are you coming?" I ask, trying to keep my voice light.

Kai exhales slowly, his shoulders dropping as if a weight has been lifted, and I notice the faintest hint of relief in his eyes. For a moment, the tension that had been knotted between us seems to loosen, like we're all taking one step closer to something... more. Something none of us fully understands yet. But for now, it's enough.

I mean, if the scene we just did was any indication, we're long past whatever the fuck we expected to happen tonight.

"Yeah," he says, his voice softer than before, almost like he's giving in to the idea—letting himself believe this could work.

Whatever *this* is.

CHAPTER FIFTEEN
THE ALPHA

MALAKAI

As I lift the barbell off the rack, the cold steel presses into my palms, grounding me in the moment. The plates clink faintly as I steady myself, and as I push through each rep, the burn spreads through my chest and arms, sharp and steady. It's a good kind of pain, the kind that silences the voice in my head and reminds me of why I've been hiding out at the gym instead of acknowledging what happened last night.

I'm not even sure what happened, how it went from a fun night with Sophie to somehow involving Julian. As I push my body past the limits I've set for myself, my jaw clenches tighter. The taste of his cum on Sophie's lips... the salty, bitter taste... it was the first time I'd ever tasted it, and I wanted more.

And *fuck*... being with Sophie was addicting. The way

she was so responsive, the way she fought back, only to submit beautifully... it made me feel as if I'd earned her submission. I wanted to do it again, and not just the physical things, either.

I anticipated that being with Sophie would feel transactional. That afterward, they'd be eager to go home and talk amongst the two of them. And I'd be left by myself—plus Willy, of course.

But that's not what happened at all.

After we'd all come down from the scene, the pizza arrived, and we sat around in my living room watching *Halloween*. It felt... normal. Julian and I complained about the carelessness of the characters while Sophie laughed —that half snort she tried to hide—and the way her eyes lit up when she glanced at me felt like we were sharing some secret. Julian sat steady and confident next to her, his quiet intensity filling the room as always.

When he smirked at me, I felt an indescribable ripple of... something. Like an unseen electrical current.

I didn't expect to feel this way about Julian.

That easy connection we had, the quiet respect that simmered into something heavier, something that kept me awake most of last night after they'd left, was impossible to ignore.

I couldn't help but watch the two of them, and how they fit together seamlessly, like two halves of a whole. Julian's hand resting casually on her knee, the way he looked at her like she was everything, and yet, somehow, it didn't shut me out. If anything, it pulled me closer.

I felt included.

Like I'd somehow slipped into their lives in a way that felt effortless, but wasn't supposed to happen. And I hated that I wanted more—of both of them, in every possible way.

Wanting them was a disaster waiting to happen, but it's too late now.

I am so very fucked.

Setting the barbell back on the rack, I run a hand through my sweat-soaked hair. My arms are shaking, so I need to call it quits before I'm rendered useless tomorrow.

Wiping the sweat off my face, I glance at myself in the mirror. I threw on an old T-shirt with the arms cut off, and I'm wearing a pair of gym shorts. For a second, I wonder what Sophie—and Julian—see when they look at me. I know I'm in good shape, and I'd have to be deaf not to hear what some of the older students whisper about me.

Priest Daddy is a new one, which is funny considering I'm a pastor, not a priest.

When I was up for the headmaster position at Saint Helena Academy, I assumed that my background as a Christian pastor might spark curiosity; and not in a good way. Luckily for me, the board liked my background in education and administration as a pastor. Plus, I was very clear about my commitment to upholding the school's values. While I'm not Catholic, I've taken the time to deeply understand and respect Catholic teachings, ensuring I can uphold the school's identity and traditions.

Today, though, I don't feel very righteous.

What I did last night was certainly not very *holy*.

Turning around, I go still when I see Julian laying on a nearby bench doing presses. My eyes scan the area for a spotter, and I don't see one.

Fucking hell.

He should know it's not safe to do bench presses with that much weight and no spotter. Then again, Julian has always been spontaneous and reckless, something I can now attribute to his ADHD. When we were young, he always had grand ideas, fixating on a certain hobby or interest. So it doesn't surprise me that he's on the bench by himself. Why ask someone to spot when he can get it done alone in half the time? Who cares if he smashes his skull in the process?

Grinding my jaw, I stalk over to him and help him reset while cursing under my breath.

"You reckless buffoon," I grumble. "Ever heard of a spotter?"

Julian glares up at me. "I'm fine by myself. I'm not even lifting that heavy today. But if you want to volunteer, by all means..." His words trail off, and he arches a brow.

My jaw tics as I help him with his next rep. I attempt to keep my eyes on the nearby carpet, but he's shirtless and that's not helping things. I can't help but let my gaze wander down to his toned abdomen to the sharp lines of his Adonis belt, cutting like sculpted marble into his hips, drawing my attention downward despite my better judgment.

"Enjoying the view?" Julian asks, his tone arrogant.

I help him place the barbell back on the rack, and then I force my gaze back up to Julian's smug face, my throat tightening as if the weight he's benching is pressing down on my chest instead. His lips twitch into a smirk, and his blue eyes twinkle with mischief that only stokes the fire simmering low in my stomach.

"You're insufferable," I mutter, stepping back and wiping my hands on my shorts like I can scrub away the strange, unwanted heat crawling up my neck.

Julian sits up, rolling his shoulders as if to flaunt the definition there. "Don't be shy," he teases, reaching for his water bottle. "You're welcome to stare all you want. I don't mind." He winks, and it's so blatantly cocky that my irritation boils over, mixing with an ache I can't quite place.

"Why do you do that? Do you enjoy being an asshole?" My voice wavers, betraying me.

I need to leave—now.

As I pivot on my heel, Julian's laughter follows me, low and maddeningly self-assured. "Running away already, Kai? Don't tell me I've scared you off so easily. Especially after last night."

My fists clench at my sides as I make my way toward the locker room, the air feeling heavier with every step. I slam through the door and lean against the cool tile wall, breathing hard like I just ran a marathon. My heart hammers against my ribs, and I press a hand to my chest, willing it to calm.

What the hell is wrong with me?

No—what the hell is wrong with *him*?

Why is he always goading me? Does he think I'm going to somehow bend to his will? It's infuriating he'd think I'd ever let him get under my skin like this.

But... he already has, hasn't he?

The memory of Julian's smirk flashes in my mind, and I groan, dragging a hand down my face. He's just messing with me. That's what he does—pushes buttons, crosses lines, gets under people's skin. He's always been that way, even as a self-assured teenager. But why does he get to me like this? Why did I let myself—

I shake my head violently, as if I can dislodge the thought. It's nothing. Just irritation. Annoyance.

Except the way my pulse spikes every time he looks at me says otherwise.

The locker room feels suffocating, and I head for the sink, splashing cold water on my face. I need to pull myself together. Julian's just trying to get a reaction, and damn it, he's succeeding. But I won't give him the satisfaction.

I won't.

Shoving off the sink, I walk to the showers and close the individual shower door behind me. Stripping my clothes off, I turn the shower on and stand under the hot water for several long seconds. The scalding water rushes down my back, but no matter how hot I make it, I can't wash away the memory of his hands on me. My skin prickles at the thought, my pulse refusing to slow.

I press my forehead against the tile, letting the water

cascade over me, and for the first time, I admit it to myself.

I didn't hate it.

My whole life, I've been the one calling the shots—structuring every scene, every relationship, until I was the center of gravity.

But last night, with Julian pulling me into his orbit, I felt weightless.

I shouldn't crave that loss of control. But the thought of giving in, just for a moment, sticks to me like honey, sweet and cloying in a way I can't shake.

Using the shampoo and bodywash the gym provides, I wash myself and practice keeping my mind calm and still. I focus on the feel of the water falling down my back, the feel of my calloused fingers running down my face, the way the hot water seems to calm and comfort me.

Especially when I turn my face up and close my eyes.

When I'm done ten minutes later, I feel more balanced. Quickly drying myself off, I wrap a towel around my waist and grab my dirty clothes, heading to my locker.

For the second time, Julian is there.

His back is to me, and for a second, I consider turning around and hiding somewhere so that we don't clash again. But he must sense my presence, because he turns around to face me, setting his phone back down in his locker. He's still shirtless, but I don't let the sweat glistening along the hard planes of his chest distract me.

"Good workout?" I ask, keeping my voice even as I open my locker.

"Yeah. It was nice to work through some... frustrations."

I keep my expression even as I put my dirty clothes in my gym bag. "I see," I say slowly, not taking the bait.

"You know, I hardly ever get to talk to the men Sophie fucks after the fact," he says a second later.

My hands still on the zipper of my bag.

Deep breaths.

Turning around, I smirk as I drop my towel.

To Julian's credit, he doesn't break eye contact. Instead, one of his brows arches up, and he crosses his arms.

"So... how was it? For you, I mean."

Don't take the bait. Don't take the bait.

"You sound jealous," I offer, pulling my boxer briefs on.

He scoffs. "Hardly. I have nothing to worry about."

My eyes find his as I step into my sweatpants. "Yeah? You sure about that?"

I don't even know why I'm saying these things. I know Julian and Sophie are solid. But for whatever reason, I feel insecure.

Julian's lopsided smile grows as he walks over to me. He steps so close that he backs me up against the lockers, and the cold metal presses against my hot skin.

"Oh, I'm sure. My *wife* enjoyed her night, and so did I. Thank you for your service."

My nostrils flare. His smirk doesn't waver, but I

swear I see a shadow of something darker in his eyes. Triumph? No—control. He's always been steady like that, unshakable. It's infuriating, really. Because right now, I feel like I'm coming apart at the seams.

Sophie is his. She'll always be his.

And me? I'm just a fun distraction. Something shiny and new until they get bored.

It shouldn't bother me. I should know better than to let it bother me. But the way Sophie laughs when she's around me, or the way Julian's gaze lingers just a second too long when he thinks I'm not looking, none of it feels temporary when I'm in the moment. It feels dangerous. Like maybe I could actually matter to them. Like maybe I'm not just passing through.

But deep down, I know better.

He leans in closer, his breath warm against my ear, and I clench my fists, fighting every instinct to shove him away—or pull him closer.

"What's wrong, Kai? You seem upset," he murmurs, his tone just condescending enough to piss me off. "Is there a problem?"

The way he says my name sends heat rippling down my spine, and I hate how easily he gets under my skin.

"Yeah," I manage, my voice low and strained. "You."

His grin sharpens, like he's waiting for me to break. To lose the upper hand I'm barely clinging to. I can't let him have it. Not again.

He knew what he was doing last night—having Sophie kiss me, pushing his cum into my mouth. The notion of him doing whatever the fuck he wants sends me over the edge.

Before I can stop myself, I grab him by the throat. My fingers tighten just enough to make his jaw clench. His pulse beats steady against my palm, mocking me with how calm he is, even now.

"You're enjoying this a little too much," I growl. "You've always enjoyed taunting me, haven't you?"

Julian doesn't flinch. If anything, he leans into my grip, his smirk softening into something more dangerous. "And what are you going to do about it?"

For a moment, I think he might give in. His gaze holds mine, daring me to push further. My hand is still firm on his throat, and the air between us feels like it's humming with electric energy.

But then he grabs my wrist and yanks it away as if it's nothing. In one swift motion, he spins me around and pins my chest against the cold metal lockers.

The breath whooshes out of me, and I tense, trying to twist free. His hand presses firm between my shoulder blades, holding me in place.

"See?" he murmurs, his lips brushing the shell of my ear. "You like being put in your place."

His words slither down my spine like molten iron, and I grit my teeth to resist the way my body reacts. My muscles coil like I'm ready to throw him off me, but the weight of his hand pressing me into the cold metal... God, it feels grounding.

The humiliation of it should make me snap. I'm not

the type to be held down. I dominate every room I walk into, whether in the pulpit or the bedroom.

But right now, I don't feel like a pastor, or a Dom, or even the version of myself I thought I knew.

Right now, I feel like someone teetering on the edge of something that terrifies me.

A shudder runs through me, equal parts frustration and something darker, something I don't want to name. I hate that he's right. I hate that he knows me well enough to see through the facade.

"How does it feel to be used?" he whispers, his voice low and lethal. "Payback's a bitch, isn't it?"

My stomach drops. The words hit harder than they should, causing my chest to ache with an unfamiliar pain.

Is that how he sees me?

Just another body to fuck and discard when they've had their fun?

My grip on the metal tightens. I could push him off me—end this right now.

But the sick part is, I don't want him to let go.

Because if I'm just being used, why does it feel so fucking personal?

Why do I enjoy it so much?

My throat tightens, my mind flashing back to that night in our dorm room—the heat of his mouth on mine, the way I'd pulled him in only to shove him away like it meant nothing.

I told myself it didn't matter back then.

But now, with his weight pinning me to the lockers

and his voice in my ear, I wonder if it ever stopped mattering.

"I find it funny that you think you're in charge," I offer, my mouth moving against the metal as I attempt to push back against him.

He has me completely pinned, though.

"That's because I am."

I huff a laugh. "You think you are."

I feel him lean in closer, his body impossibly steady, and the weight of his words presses heavier than his grip.

"No," he says, the faintest edge of a smirk in his voice. "I *know* I am."

The way he says it—the certainty, the challenge—sends a heat rolling through me, part anger, part something else entirely. I twist against him again, desperate to regain the upper hand, but he anticipates every move, his hand firm between my shoulders.

Each movement between us carries a weight that has nothing to do with strength, the air thick with something unspoken—something electric. This isn't just an argument.

It's a push and pull, a battle for control neither of us is willing to lose.

"I'm always the one dominating," I snap, even though the words feel hollow with him pinning me like this.

There's a beat of silence, and I hate how my pulse quickens when I feel him grin against my ear.

"Until me," he says softly, the finality in his voice leaving no room for argument.

I go still, the words sinking in deeper than they should. His weight, his voice, his control—it's undeniable.

And for the first time, I don't know if I want to fight it.

For the first time... I think about submitting.

Before I can respond, Julian steps away and releases me. "I should go. Have a nice day, Kai."

I don't turn around to watch him go. Instead, I wait, panting like I've just run a marathon, until I hear the shower turn on in the other room.

The cold seeps into my skin long after his weight disappears, but the imprint of his palm stays, burning like a brand across my back. I force myself upright, dragging in a breath that sticks in my throat.

I press the heels of my hands against the locker, willing myself to feel disgusted.

You should hate this.

But I don't.

I can still feel his breath on my neck, the way he leaned in, and the calm certainty in his voice when he told me he was in charge.

It wasn't condescending. It wasn't a taunt.

It was the truth.

As I tug my shirt on, I feel the weight of his absence settle in my chest.

I want to call Sophie. I want to hear her laugh, the lightness in her voice that cuts through the noise in my head. I want her to tell one of her jokes, or wax poetic about the romance book she's reading.

But I also want to see Julian. Even if we spar. Even if we taunt each other, unsure of where to file these feelings we both seem to be developing.

And that's the part I can't reconcile.

I don't just want to dominate.

I want to be wanted—fully, undeniably—by both of them.

Stepping into my shoes, I grab my bag and rush for the door.

CHAPTER SIXTEEN
THE CONFESSION

Sophie

My phone rings as I click out of one of my many research tabs. I've been crunching numbers and trying to decide if this dream is just a dream or possible to turn a profit. I know I have Julian's money to fall back on, but I want to do this right. Ever since I saw the empty storefront in Crestwood a couple of weeks ago, I've been dreaming about what a place like that could look like—and how it would feel to spend my mornings with Snickers and my days at the bookshop. I hadn't heard back, of course, but I could find another space that worked.

Aside from market research, I've been trying to come up with a realistic number for the monthly running cost, which would entail inventory and merchandise, something I've never dealt with on this scale.

I want people to walk in and feel at home. I want it to

be colorful and inclusive. I want people to stop and stare from the street, curious about what kinds of love stories await them inside. It's more complicated than simply launching a business—I want people to *feel* how I feel when I'm lost in an amazing book. I intend to create a sanctuary where people *can* experience this, with vibrant, inviting displays and overflowing shelves full of colorful spines. I envision fresh flowers all around the store, as well as curated playlists and a cozy reading nook...

I glance at the unknown number flashing on my screen, and at the last minute, I answer.

"Hello?"

"Am I speaking to Sophie Ashford?"

I clear my throat. "This is she."

"Hello, Sophie. You inquired a couple of weeks ago about the available retail space on Main Street, and I was wondering if you're still interested in a viewing?"

My heart speeds up, and before I can think, I respond. "Hi! Yes! I'd love to view it."

"Great! My name is Elisa Jacobs from Elmwood Properties. Before we schedule a viewing, I wanted to go over a few requirements for renting the space. First, we'll need a copy of your business license or proof that it's in process. Is that something you can provide?"

"Oh, yes," I say quickly, making a mental note to look into it tonight.

"Perfect," she continues. "We'll also need proof of funds, typically your most recent bank statement or a letter of credit from your bank, so we can confirm you're able to cover rent and any associated costs. Speaking of which, are you familiar with the lease terms, or would you like us to email them over to you? This is just protocol, of course."

"I'd love an email," I tell her, feeling shaky with adrenaline and excitement so potent that I almost want to stand up and jump around.

"No problem. Make sure you review them fully before the meeting. You'll want to note the security deposit, which is equal to two months' rent, and the liability insurance requirement—you'll need that before signing."

"Got it," I say, scribbling notes furiously.

"Lastly, if you plan on making any modifications to the space, you'll need to provide a detailed proposal for approval. We'll go over those details after the viewing. Does that all sound manageable?"

"Yes, absolutely."

"Great. I'll send you a follow-up email confirming our meeting time, but does this Friday work for you?"

I do the math in my head. Friday is five days away. It's not enough time, but I'll have to make it work.

"Yes, that works!"

"Great! Looking forward to seeing you then."

"Thank you so much!" I say, hanging up and staring at my to-do list, which has just tripled in size.

When I set my phone down, I squeal and spin around in my office chair as I try to contain my excitement. I press my palms against the desk, steadying the rush of excitement flooding through me. It feels like the first time in years I'm chasing something that's entirely mine. Not inherited. Not expected.

Just... mine.

Growing up, I was always meant to inherit something—a legacy, a title, a noble husband. But I never wanted any of it. I wanted to build something from scratch, to shape something with my hands and make it grow.

The bookstore feels like that. It's fragile, yes, but it's alive. A seed I'm planting *by myself.*

I have a lot of work ahead of me, but if I'm looking at the numbers in front of me correctly... I *should* be able to turn a profit right away.

It's just going to take a little bit of creativity and fundraising.

I can do this.

Grinning, I stand up from my seat and take the stairs down to the kitchen. If I'm going to do this, I'm going to need my energy, so a cup of tea is in order.

I'm halfway down the stairs when my phone buzzes again, but this time, the number on the screen isn't unfamiliar.

It's my mother.

My fingers hover over the decline button, but guilt wins out. Sighing, I accept the call.

"Mum?"

"Darling," she greets, clipped and formal as always. "It's been too long since I've heard from you."

Two weeks isn't too long, I think but don't say. I'd

stopped explaining myself years ago, but her voice always manages to stir something restless in me.

"I've been busy," I offer, climbing the last few steps and leaning against the railing. "How are things?"

"Busy, as well. I just had lunch with the Hastings and, naturally, they asked about you. I had to make excuses for why you weren't at the gala last weekend. You know, Sophie, people notice when you're absent."

There it is. The reminder of the life I left behind—the curated image, the endless social events, the suffocating expectations I'd fought so hard to escape.

"I live in California now, Mum," I say, a hint of steel in my voice. "People are going to have to get used to my absence."

A pause. Then, "And Julian?"

"Julian's wonderful."

And we're currently entertaining thoughts about one of his oldest friends.

I don't add that part.

"Well," she sighs, and I picture her swirling a glass of wine in her hand, peering down at the world from the balcony of her pristine country estate. "I hope you two aren't getting too comfortable. You're still young. Don't get complacent. Opportunities don't last forever, Sophie. Once this little *travel bug* ends, I fully expect the two of you to return to London. And I truly hope Julian is happy, so far from his family. It would be a shame if he no longer found your restless energy adorable."

My jaw clenches. It's a thinly veiled nudge, one she's been repeating since I moved abroad. She doesn't say it outright, but I know what she means. *Julian could leave. You could end up alone.* She's been predicting the downfall of my marriage since the day I told her we were moving, and she's somehow gotten it in her head that I'm at fault for dragging us away from that life.

"I'm not complacent, Mum. I'm building something here. A bookstore, actually."

The silence that follows is heavy.

"A bookstore?" Her tone is pure disbelief, like I'd just announced I'd run away to join the circus.

"Yes. I'm looking at a space this week," I say, forcing my voice to stay light. "I'm really excited about it."

"I see. And will this... bookstore pay the mortgage? Or is that still Julian's responsibility?"

"Mum." My voice drops, but the warning is clear.

"I'm just asking, Sophie. You know I want the best for you. You were raised for a certain life—"

"I know exactly what I was raised for," I cut in, unable to hide the sharpness in my tone. The sound of the front door opening is a perfect distraction. "Actually, Mum, Julian just got home. I need to go. I'll call you soon."

"Give the viscount my regards," she says, hanging up before I get a chance to gag at her use of his formal title.

Pocketing my phone, I take a deep breath. I won't let her bring this exciting moment down. I've worked too hard to pull away from that life to let her drag the happiness from me.

The bookstore.

This Friday.

That is exciting, and I can't wait to tell Julian.

Walking into the kitchen, I start my tea. I'm just stacking biscuits on the rim of my mug when he saunters into the kitchen, looking fresh and showered from his time at the gym.

"Hi!" I tell him, setting my mug and biscuits down as I bounce from foot to foot. "You'll never guess who called me! Well, besides my mum, and that conversation went about as well as a fox in a henhouse."

His eyes slowly lift to mine, and my smile drops off my face. He seems distracted.

And... *guilty*.

"Who?" he asks, standing on the other side of the kitchen. "I mean, besides your mum, who I'm sure still believes you seduced me into abandoning centuries of noble lineage for overpriced avocado toast and sunshine."

I smile, but it doesn't reach my eyes. He always comes over and gives me a kiss, no matter what. So why is he still all the way on the other side of the kitchen?

My brows knit together as I shake my head. "Oh, it was just—" I pause, wanting to make sure he's okay first. "Is everything all right?"

He smiles, but it doesn't meet his eyes. "Yes, everything's fine. What were you going to tell me?"

As if a spark reignites the energy inside of me, I bounce as I clap my hands once. "The letting agency for that retail space in town. They've offered to show it to me, and they asked for paperwork... that's a good sign, right?"

His smile widens. "That's fantastic news, Soph."

"I mean, now I have to *actually* file for a business license, show proof of funds, get insurance, and proposals for renovations... all before Friday..."

He arches a brow. "How much do you need?"

I hold a hand up. "I don't need anything. I have an idea for fundraising."

His face softens. "Okay. But you know I'm always willing to help you, right?"

Walking over to him, I wrap my arms around his neck. "I know. But I have to do this on my own."

"I understand," he murmurs, placing his hands on my arms and kissing the inside of my elbow with a delicate kiss. "Can I help with anything?"

"I don't think so. It'll be a busy five days, though." Pulling my head back a bit, I study his expression, which still seems off. My eyes flick between his bright blue ones, trying to decipher why he seems to be in a funk. "Are you sure you're okay?"

He doesn't immediately say yes, and my skin prickles. Pulling away slowly, I look up at his face.

"Julian?" I ask when he doesn't answer.

"I don't know," he says, his voice thick. "I feel like I'm fraying at the seams," he says, running a hand down his face.

"How so?" I ask, titling my head and reaching out for one of his hands. When I begin massaging it, he groans and lets his head fall back.

"I saw Kai at the gym."

I pause my ministrations. "Oh? How is he?" I ask, trying to lighten the mood.

"We sort of got into an argument... or... I don't even know what happened, to be honest."

The prickling feeling works down my spine as I process his words. Or lack thereof. I'd have to be blind not to see the way my husband looks at Kai, or the way Kai looks back at him. Their history is long and complicated—and I know the kiss they shared years ago didn't help matters last night.

I knew that Julian was provoking him last night in nearly every instance, trying to establish his dominance. He'd never done that before when I'd been with another man, so I was just as surprised as Kai.

"What sort of argument?" I ask Julian, my voice steady, though my heart races with the possibilities unfolding before me. I drop his hand and take a step back, sensing the seriousness in his expression.

Julian rubs the back of his neck with his hand, and my stomach sinks.

"Uh... he put his hand around my throat, and then I pressed him against the lockers."

I'm quiet, waiting for him to continue, but instead he just looks at me hesitantly.

"That's it?" I ask, trying to sound casual.

"Yes. No. Well, that's all that involved Kai. But..." He looks down at the ground. "I was sort of stirred up, so I had to relieve myself in the shower."

My lips twitch with the threat of a smile. "Julian, you've wanked to Kai before. It's normal to fantasize about someone other than me, and it doesn't bother me."

He nods once, looking up at me. "No, I know. This time just felt different. And I wanted to tell you. It felt... wrong."

As I process his words, I feel many different emotions. There's a pang of discomfort at the thought of Julian's complicated feelings for Kai—a discomfort that lingers, but doesn't quite evolve into jealousy. It's not a terrible feeling... but more like growing pains. And as the seconds tick by, it morphs into something that almost feels like curiosity.

The tension between them has always been palpable, even before I met Kai. For years, I brushed it off as old wounds or maybe unresolved anger whenever he spoke about his ex-best friend. But now, after last night... perhaps it was an opening to something I hadn't fully allowed myself to consider until now.

I should feel possessive or betrayed, perhaps even angry, despite never feeling those things with Julian. I've never been the jealous type. Instead, there's a strange clarity weaving through my racing thoughts—a sort of quiet understanding that surprises me. Julian's feelings for Kai, no matter how complex, don't endanger our bond—in fact, they could enrich it.

If we let it...

A spark of warmth blooms inside of me.

What if this isn't something to fear? What if it's an opportunity, one that could deepen the bond we all share? I think about Kai, his sharp wit, the vulnerability he hides under his tough exterior, the way he looked at me last night, the soft way he touched me...

There's a tenderness for Julian there, too, one I hadn't fully contemplated until now.

It's a surprising thought, but one that settles firmly into place.

Perhaps this isn't a threat to my marriage. Perhaps it's the start of something new, something none of us expected, but all of us could grow to want.

The prickling tension along my spine eases, replaced by a cautious excitement.

"How did it feel wrong? Why was this time different?"

He shrugs. "Because we've been intimate with him. Last night... it wasn't supposed to happen. This... him and me... it feels like I'm emotionally cheating, Sophie."

My chest aches, but not from betrayal.

From empathy.

"You think *I'd* think you were emotionally cheating?" I ask gently. He nods, and he looks so sheepish that I can't help but smile. I step closer so that we're touching, and I take both of his hands in mine. "First of all, I'd be the biggest hypocrite of all if I thought that, considering..." I trail off.

He huffs a laugh. "Yes, well, we spent weeks going over our limits and the rules. I'm kind of free-falling here, you know?"

I narrow my eyes, smirking. "You want permission? Fine. Let's talk about it now, so if there's ever a time you'd like to pursue things with Kai, you won't feel so guilty."

His mouth opens and closes. "I— That's not what I—"

I squeeze his hands. "I know. You're a good man, Julian Ashford. It's why I married you. If I thought for one second that Kai would come between us, I'd say so."

He studies me for a few seconds. "You don't think he'd come between us?"

I shake my head. "No. I don't. I'm not really sure what's happening with us, but if you'd like to pursue things with him solo, I'd be okay with that." My smile grows. "In fact, I really like the idea of watching the two of you together. Is there such a thing as a hot-husband?"

His expression relaxes. The tension in his shoulders melts into something softer.

Relief.

Gratitude.

His lips twitch into the beginnings of a smile, and I realize in this moment just how much he's been carrying this weight alone. The idea of exploring his feelings for Kai, of daring to step into the uncharted space we're now tiptoeing through together, has obviously been bothering him. But now? Now, we're here, together, unraveling it piece by piece.

"You mean that?" Julian asks, his voice hesitant but laced with hope.

I nod, my fingers tightening around his. "I do. Look, this... it's not exactly traditional, I know. But when have we ever done things the traditional way? What I feel for you doesn't shrink because of Kai. And what you might feel for him? It doesn't take away from us. I think we're stronger than that."

He stares at me for a moment, his gaze searching mine as though he's trying to figure out where my boundaries truly lie—or if they even exist in the way he feared.

"And what about you?" he asks, his voice quieter now. "How do you feel about Kai?"

The question sends an unexpected ripple of warmth through me.

"I don't know," I admit, being fully open and transparent. "But I like him. And I like the way he cares about you, and the way he talks about you. It's hard not to feel drawn to him because of that. I sort of feel like we share something, you know?"

Julian tilts his head, considering my words. "So, you're saying..."

"I'm saying," I interrupt, grinning, "that maybe this doesn't have to be a problem. Maybe it could be something beautiful."

His brow furrows slightly, but there's a light in his eyes now, a flicker of understanding, of intrigue.

"You think we could make this work? All three of us?"

I shrug, though my smile doesn't falter. "We shouldn't get ahead of ourselves. We'd have to talk to Kai. And..." I pause for a beat, my gaze softening as I search his face. "We'd have to make sure you're okay, too."

His expression falters—just for a second—but I catch

it. The hesitation. The old wounds I know are still there, even if he doesn't say it outright.

"I know you, Julian," I continue gently. "I know there's history there, and I don't want to ignore that. This isn't just about attraction—it's about trust. And if there's any hurt left between you and Kai, we need to talk about it before we even think about moving forward. Otherwise, it's not fair to any of us."

Julian exhales slowly, running a hand through his hair. "You're not wrong," he admits after a moment. "There's a lot I haven't let go of. And I don't want to mess this up before it even begins."

I reach for his hand, squeezing it lightly. "Then we take it slow. We figure it out together. But only if it's what we all want—and if we're all ready."

His lips quirk in a small, thoughtful smile. "You always know how to keep me in check."

I smirk. "Someone has to."

Julian exhales a laugh, shaking his head, but there's a brightness in him now that wasn't there before. For a long moment, he just looks at me, like he's trying to see if I really mean it—if this could truly be as simple as I'm making it sound. I can practically hear the wheels turning in his head, his instinct to analyze, to find the cracks in an idea before it even has the chance to exist.

But instead of voicing another doubt, he sighs, dragging a hand through his hair. "You make it sound so simple."

"It is simple," I tease. "You're overthinking it. Just...

let it be what it's going to be. Let's talk to him. See how he feels. No pressure, no expectations. Just honesty."

For the first time all night, Julian smiles—really smiles. He bends down, his face an inch from mine.

"I don't deserve you," he murmurs, his voice laced with affection.

"Don't be ridiculous," I whisper back. "We deserve each other. And maybe, just maybe, we deserve him too. Maybe there's enough of whatever we have to go around."

"Okay," he says, his nose brushing against mine. "What does this mean, then? We've never done this. It's only ever been a one-time thing with other men."

I shrug. "We should talk to Kai. But... I think a blanket permission to be with him—with the caveat that we communicate about it—is a good first step. If he wants to, that is."

Julian nods, resting his forehead against my own. "You're perfect. Is it bad that I want to fuck you on top of this gorgeous marble?"

I laugh. "I'm surprised we haven't already. We've christened so many other places in the house..."

"Oh, fuck. You have things to do," he murmurs, kissing me on the cheek and stepping back.

I groan. "I do. But maybe—"

Julian waves me off. "Go on, then. Your tea's getting cold. I'll make us dinner, okay?"

My lips quirk to the side. "Okay. I love you."

He winks, looking a hundred times more relaxed now that we talked. "I love you more, Soph."

CHAPTER SEVENTEEN
THE HESITATION

Julian

Sipping my whiskey, I keep my eyes focused on my phone. I've been debating how to message Kai for nearly two days, dragging my feet and waiting for inspiration to strike. Of course I'm overthinking everything, and the fact that *he* hasn't reached out only heightens the insecurity I feel around him.

He's the only person I second-guess myself around. It feels so similar to when I met and fell for Sophie. The waiting games. The secret, furtive glances. The second-guessing. *Does she like me as much as I like her?*

And now, with Kai...

It feels like I'm dating all over again.

An incoming email from a client distracts me immediately, and I swipe over, reading quickly.

I hardly notice another man slip into the seat next to

me. I continue skimming the email from a client, quickly replying about an issue we'd run into with shipping an expensive art piece abroad, when the man clears his throat.

I look over at him, narrowing my eyes, and then a smile slowly lifts the corner of my mouth.

What are the chances that I'd run into Kai's brother tonight of all nights, as I'm in turmoil over how to reach out?

"Orion Ravage," I say, holding my hand out. I recognize him from briefly saying hello to him at our housewarming party.

"The infamous Julian Ashford," he says, smirking as he shakes my hand. "Nice to see you again. At my bar, of all places."

I look around the dark, art deco space as my eyebrows shoot up. "This is your place? Nice job, mate."

"Thanks, I appreciate that."

I laugh as he takes a seat next to me. "Sorry, it's just, before the party, the last time I saw you I think you were... twelve? Thirteen?"

Orion chuckles. "Something like that."

He orders sparkling water, and I can't help but think of how he—and all the Ravage brothers—remind me so much of Kai. It's their mannerisms, their intense personas... their good looks. Being a bisexual man, I've definitely noticed the latter.

"So," Orion says after taking a sip. "Can I ask you something? It's been bothering me for years."

I finish my whiskey and gesture to the bartender for another. "It depends," I say, teasingly.

He narrows his eyes as he thinks through what he wants to say. Finally, he turns to face me fully, and his expression is open and curious.

"Whatever happened between you and Kai? One day you were thick as thieves, and the next..." He trails off and shrugs.

What happened?

The memory sits there, dusty but sharp. The feel of Kai's hands gripping my shirt so tightly, the soft graze of his lips—God, I was young enough to think I could stop it from meaning something.

And I was wrong.

I take a deep breath before setting my glass down, tapping my wedding band against the glass. The whiskey feels like it's burning a hole in my chest, and as the bartender sets another tumbler in front of me, I think of what to say to Kai's brother. His question is direct, sure, but I know he's not trying to be rude. There's no malice in his tone.

Still, it throws me off-balance.

It's been a few days since Sophie and I talked about possibly asking Kai to explore this... thing... between us further. I told her I'd take care of it, and yet, I've found myself stalling for time. Making excuses. Letting the days slip by, telling myself the timing isn't right.

Maybe I'm overthinking it. Maybe I'm imagining the hesitation in his eyes that wasn't really there. But every time I think about bringing it up, I remember the way he walked away last time, seventeen years ago—without a word, without looking back—and the question catches in my throat.

What if this time is no different?

"It's complicated," I tell Orion. My voice is quieter, and Orion leans in a bit closer, waiting for me to continue. Leaning back on the barstool, I swirl the rest of the whiskey around in my glass and admire the way it catches the light. Then I toss it back in one long swallow.

I'm going to need to get a cab home.

Orion is looking at me with something I can only describe as patient curiosity, but the silence is heavy. This is Kai's brother. I should talk to Kai first, right?

But... what if he walks away again?

I suppose it couldn't hurt to ask Orion for his opinion. I know he's also in the lifestyle as a Dom. Inferno is his club, and he's fairly well-known within the community.

Plus, as much as I try to push thoughts of Kai away, the more I drink, the more I can't stop thinking about what Sophie and I talked about. She trusted me to bring it up, but I've been avoiding it—trying not to think about what it would mean to open that door after everything that happened seventeen years ago.

Orion sighs. "It doesn't seem that complicated to me." His tone isn't arrogant. It's matter-of-fact. "At least from what I've inferred. Maybe you should talk to him. It seems like something's still bothering you, and in my experience, those feelings only fester the longer you wait."

I nod as I gesture for another whiskey, and the bartender brings it right over. I swallow it in one long sip. It's only then that I realize I probably should've eaten dinner before drinking. Setting the empty glass down harder than I mean to.

"Something happened. Seventeen years ago. And then he walked away like a coward."

I keep it vague. Kai needs to be the one to tell his brothers, not me.

Orion raises an eyebrow, surprised. But then his expression softens almost immediately, like he's piecing something together.

"Ah. That makes sense now."

I glare at him, bristling at his calm response. "It does?"

"Come on," he says, cracking a grin. "You and Kai were inseparable. Do you really think none of us noticed when it all fell apart? I don't think I saw Kai smile for at least a year. He never talked about it, but we could tell something had changed."

"Well, brooding is practically a family sport, isn't it?" I tease, masking the way that information makes me feel.

Orion huffs a laugh, but he waits for me to continue. I look away, feeling drunk and like I want to confess everything to Kai's brother. I never let myself think of how Kai handled what happened. I figured he'd walked away, so he likely brushed it off. But now that I know it seemed to affect him as much as it affected me?

I don't know what to do with that information, and I don't know how to reply.

I catch myself tapping my wedding band against the glass again. I stop when Orion's gaze flicks to it, and I pretend I wasn't just sitting here unraveling like some lovesick teenager.

"Does Sophie know? About what happened?" Orion asks, and again, his tone isn't judgmental. For whatever reason, I feel at ease with Kai's youngest brother.

"She does." I don't elaborate—it's not important, not really. "Sophie and I..." I pause, trying to figure out how to word what I'm trying to say.

Orion chuckles. "I know everything that happens at my club, Julian. I know all about the arrangement you and Sophie have."

I trace the rim of my glass with my index finger. "Right. Well, things got complicated, and now..."

I flinch. Orion continues to listen, and it feels good to talk to someone about this. "It's not just Sophie. I want it, too. Or at least I think I do. I'm just... I don't know. I've been carrying this unresolved knot of feelings for years—anger, embarrassment, longing—all wrapped up in our complicated history. And now, with Kai and Sophie... the knot is pulling tighter, and..."

"You're scared," Orion finishes, sipping his water.

I shrug. "I suppose I am."

Orion sighs. "Look, I know my brother. Kai's not the same person he was back then, and neither are you. If there's even a chance you're still holding on to those feelings, he deserves to know."

I rake a hand down my face. "You make it sound so simple."

"It's not," Orion admits, shrugging. "But it's worth it. You're not going to figure any of this out by avoiding it. Talk to him. Be honest. If nothing else, at least you'll finally know where you stand."

"Right. I'll pour my heart out, and maybe we can settle things with a round of polo afterward," I retort sarcastically.

"Whatever it takes." Orion answers, and I don't expect his words to *weigh* so much.

I sit in silence as I let his words settle. He's right, damn him. I can't keep running from this, not if I want to move forward—with Kai, with Sophie, or even just with myself.

Orion claps me on the shoulder, his tone turning lighter. "Look at it this way: worst case, he walks away again. At least you'll know you've got a strong track record for surviving it."

I let out a reluctant laugh, shaking my head. "Thanks for the vote of confidence, mate."

"Anytime," Orion says with a smirk, standing to leave. "Good luck, Julian. You're going to need it."

As he walks off, I pull out my phone, thumb hovering over Kai's contact.

Type.

Erase.

Type.

Jesus Christ, how hard is it to send a simple text?

I lean my elbows on the bar, rubbing the back of my neck as if the motion alone will knock the indecision loose. The cursor blinks at me like it's mocking my hesitation.

> Hey, want to grab a drink sometime?

Backspace.

> Hope you're doing well. We should catch up.

Delete.

I stare at the empty message field, feeling like a teenager asking someone on a date.

Why the hell does this feel harder than it needs to be? This isn't the first time I've dealt with messy feelings or unspoken tension. Hell, my marriage is built on unconventional boundaries. And yet, Kai... Kai's different. He always has been. There's no script for this, no clean way to approach the man who kissed me once and left me wondering for seventeen years if I imagined the way he held on just a little too long.

I tap the screen again, exhaling sharply.

> We need to talk.

There. No overthinking. No unnecessary weight behind the words. Direct. Unavoidable.

Before I can convince myself otherwise, I hit send and toss the phone onto the bar like it's radioactive.

CHAPTER EIGHTEEN
THE SWITCH

MALAKAI

I stare at the email for several minutes, trembling with barely contained fury.

Despite having a couple of conversations with Chase, my brother, it appears that Rod fucking Dumplant went behind my back and contacted Bradleigh Evan's mother, Victoria, copying me in.

The subject line is insulting enough. **"Concerns Regarding Bradleigh Evans"**—as if her mere existence is simply a logistical issue to be dealt with and forgotten.

The email is overly formal and dripping with condescension, and it makes me fucking angry on her behalf.

In the email, he cites concerns raised by members of our school community regarding Bradleigh, as well as exploring alternative options that might be in Bradleigh's best interest. He goes on to say that the current environment is "clearly challenging for her." As an added insult—aka "after much prayer and reflection"—he goes on to say it would be prudent to consider transferring Bradleigh to a school better equipped to meet her unique needs.

He even attaches a list of nearby institutions and offers to assist Victoria in planning to ease the transition.

Bastard.

My jaw clenches so hard it's a wonder my teeth don't shatter.

If the devil is a person, surely Rod Dumplant would qualify.

Deciding for Bradleigh—behind my back and behind Victoria's back—that she would be better off somewhere else? That we'd be better off without her? He might as well have said outright that she doesn't belong at Saint Helena.

My eyes move down to the next email.

Victoria had responded almost immediately. She rejected his offer and asked for a meeting between the three of us to understand what steps are being taken to address the harassment her daughter has experienced, rather than move her out of an environment she's already adjusted to.

I smile when I read it, thankful she's not going to bow down to Rod's ridiculous suggestion, but it also makes me angrier. She shouldn't have to defend her daughter's right to exist at this school. Rod knows this isn't a practical solution for Victoria—not with her long work hours and inability to juggle even more of a commute. He knows, and he still chose to frame this as if he were doing her a favor.

But the thing that pisses me off the most is that he copied me into the email in the first place. He wants me to be complicit—to nod along to his sanctimonious, little charade.

When I was a pastor, I used to speak on the paradox of tolerance. It's essentially a philosophical concept that goes like this: if a society is too tolerant of intolerance, it will eventually be dominated by intolerance, which will therefore undermine the principle of tolerance itself.

My fingers hover over the keyboard, and I ruminate on Rod's email for a few minutes before deciding to respond.

Fuck it.

I email Rod and let him know that we need to talk, making sure I loop Chase into the email. Then I email Victoria separately, agreeing to her meeting, and ensuring she knows that in *my* school, as headmaster, Bradleigh is and always will be welcome to pursue her education. I'm not shy about stating that I disagree with Rod's email, either.

Just after hitting send, my phone lights up.

JULIAN
We need to talk.

Running a hand through my hair, I let out a long sigh.

Now?

> **JULIAN**
> Yes.

> Okay. I'm at home if you want to stop by.

> **JULIAN**
> Sure. I'm at a bar downtown so I'll walk over.

After sending a thumbs-up, I slam my laptop shut and stand up, stretching. Willy comes trotting into the living room, squeaking as he weaves between my feet.

"Yeah, yeah. Let's go on a quick walk before Julian comes over."

Grabbing Willy's leash, I pocket my phone and keys before wrapping his harness around his chest and securing the leash. Though it took a few months, I'd trained Willy to go on walks. He had his own playroom in my apartment with a large enclosure for when I'm at work, but he's still a wild animal and needs a lot of exercise. I'm about half a mile from downtown, so I know I have a few minutes before Julian turns up. Despite weighing only three pounds, Willy pulls on the leash and attempts to get into every single thing we encounter. I get a few strange looks, as always, because of his size and giant ears. But after a quick jaunt around the block, he's panting and seems content with our shorter-than-normal walk.

As I round the corner of my level, I see Julian leaning against the door of my apartment building. As I walk closer, he lifts his head from his phone, looking at me quickly before dropping his eyes to Willy.

"Tell me you did not train a fox to walk on a lead."

Smirking, I shrug as I walk up to him to open the door. I get a whiff of whiskey and his musky, bergamot scent, and I hate how much I've come to enjoy his smell.

"He can use a litter box, too."

Julian scoffs. "Fuck off."

I chuckle and we take the elevator up to my floor. Once we're inside my apartment, the door closes behind us and I crouch down and unclasp Willy's harness. He yips and squeaks a few times before running wildly into his playroom. As I stand, I look back at Julian, who is hovering near the front door.

Why is it that I'm always aware of his presence now? I don't remember feeling this way when we were teenagers.

Then again, I wasn't fucking his wife while she fed me his cum back then, either.

But right now? He's like a storm cloud, ready to burst. And I suppose he's always been that way—always had an astounding effect on his surroundings. I used to say it was because he had a larger-than-life personality, but now I'm wondering if it's more than that.

Especially as his sharp gaze cuts through the dim lighting, pinning me in place.

"You wanted to talk?" I ask. My voice is steadier than I feel. There's no point in dancing around the fact that he texted me and wants to talk. Also, the fact that he's here on a Wednesday night, at nearly nine in the evening, instead of at home with Sophie, sends a nervous thrill through me. My stomach twists with nerves, and I don't want to examine why too closely.

Julian shrugs off his suit jacket in a singular fluid motion, laying it over the back of my couch with practiced precision. Leaning against the back of it with two hands, he looks back up at me. His expression is relaxed, and I know I didn't misplace the smell of whiskey earlier. *He's been drinking.*

I don't know why that thought makes my heart begin to race.

His eyes gleam with something darker as he huffs a laugh.

"Yeah," he finally says. "I wanted to talk about what happened on Saturday. And Sunday. At the gym."

My hands, mid-motion to set my keys and phone on the entryway table, go still. The memory of what he said in the locker room echoes too vividly in my head. Forcing myself to gently place my belongings down, I slide my hands in the pockets of my pants as I attempt to project the nonchalance I don't feel.

"What about it?" My voice comes out too quiet—too *careful.*

He doesn't answer immediately. Instead, he remains behind my couch, which is probably for the best, considering he pinned me against the cold, metal lockers the last time we saw each other. Everything inside of me tightens when I think of his hand against my back.

When I think of how *in control* he was, and how I could've moved, but instead submitted.

"Well, first of all, I'm sorry for ripping up your

contract on Saturday. And I'm sorry if I made you uncomfortable in any way. I didn't expect to get so riled up, uh, watching."

I stop breathing, fighting the urge to look away, to escape the weight of what he's admitting.

I knew he was riled up. I could tell by the way he touched himself. But to hear him admit it…

"As for the locker room," he continues. His voice has an edge to it now. "I suppose I was…" He hesitates, running a hand through his hair before letting it fall over his forehead. "I was still angry about what happened that night seventeen years ago. And I wanted to hurt you."

The floor feels unsteady, and I swallow hard, unsure of where to go from here. The words from the locker room work through me again, just as sharp and biting as the first time.

My wife enjoyed her night, and so did I. Thank you for your service.

And then the murmur that followed, venomous and deliberate…

How does it feel to be used? Payback's a bitch, isn't it?

The memory burns, but I can't ignore the heat it stirs in me—something jagged and raw, but unmistakably alive.

Julian's voice pulls me back to the present. "It was immature of me to taunt you. So, I'm sorry."

I stare at him as my heart pounds against my ribs. Truth be told, his words hurt more than I'd like to admit. There was something pulling me closer to both Julian and Sophie, and with those words, he'd drawn a line in the ground and treated me like a male escort. Not that there was anything wrong with sex work, but I suppose I just assumed that whatever the three of us had went deeper than that.

He'd made me feel like a mere transaction, and I was still reeling from it.

"Sorry," I echo, the words like ash in my mouth. "That's it? That's why you wanted to talk?"

Julian clenches his jaw. "What do you expect me to say, Kai? That I'm sorry for still being angry all these years later? Do you blame me for that? You kissed me and walked away like it meant nothing." His voice rises in volume, getting sharper with each word. "Or should I apologize for wanting to break you a little? For wanting to see if you'd fall apart under me?"

The air between us crackles with electricity. My breathing turns uneven, and I can't seem to look away from him. His blue eyes—so familiar, and yet not—burn too brightly, too full of truths I'm not ready to face.

"Julian," I start, my voice faltering. I run a hand over my mouth, and I don't even know what I'm trying to say.

"No. Don't 'Julian' me," he snaps, his voice cracking on the last word. It lends a sliver of vulnerability that doesn't match the steel in his words. "I've been trying to move past this. *You.* For seventeen fucking years. But then you came back into my life, and I..." He exhales sharply, like the words are physically wounding him. "I can't seem to help myself."

He steps around the couch, and suddenly he's in

front of me, close enough that I can see the gold flecks in his eyes and the tightness in his jaw.

Close enough that I'm not sure I'll survive this moment if I don't touch him.

Or maybe if I do.

His chest rises and falls as I try to form the right words. "It's complicated. With me... I'm just..."

My control slips away with every second that passes, like sand through my fingers. As his eyes dip to my lips, I forget what I'm fighting against, exactly. Because this? I've never felt anything like this before.

"Maybe you're not the only one who can't seem to move on," I offer, my voice low and shaking.

His expression gleams with something... surprise, maybe. Or *hope*. But it's gone in half a second, replaced by a look so dark and intense that it makes my knees weak.

"Say it," Julian whispers, stepping closer. His voice is a command, but his eyes are pleading. "Say what you want, Kai."

My pulse is roaring in my ears, but I can't seem to find the words. The silence hangs between us, heavy and suffocating.

And then Julian's hand brushes against mine.

The touch is fleeting. Exploratory. But it's enough to shatter whatever fragile hold I had on my composure.

"I don't know what I want," I admit, my voice cracking. "But I think... I think I want you to show me."

His breath catches, and for a moment, neither of us moves.

Then his hand curls around my wrist, firm but not painful. Suddenly, the world narrows to the heat of his calloused skin against mine.

"Kai." My name is quieter on his lips than I expect—soft enough to send a shiver through me. He doesn't let go of my wrist, and I don't pull away. His gaze meets mine, steady and confident. Despite that, though, he hesitates. His thumb brushes over the edge of my palm, sending a jolt of sensation straight to my cock. "You know Sophie and I have an understanding."

My core clenches. "Yes. I'm aware. I was there on Saturday, after all," I add, arching a brow.

Julian steps closer, and I inhale sharply as he slides his other hand down to my free one, lacing both his hands with mine. It's both comforting and electrifying all at once, and I feel like I might spontaneously combust at any moment.

"Right. But I'm not talking about that. You and me? What happened between us? It's not a secret to her." I can't look away—not now, when his voice dips into something softer. Something *raw* and real. "What I mean to say is that she knows what you mean to me, and she's fine with it. More than fine."

His words hit me like a punch to the gut. "She's fine with this?" I ask, pressing my body against his.

I know I'm taunting him right back, but I'm still feeling a little petty from the alpha show-off in the locker room the other day. Plus, admitting... all of this... is leaving me with no filter.

"Not just fine," he murmurs. The heat of his breath

feathers against my cheek. "She's *encouraging* it. This is bigger than just you and me, Kai. But I don't want to push you into anything you're not ready for."

His words land heavily between us, and my breath catches as one of his hands comes to rest on my hip, warm and steady.

"What exactly are you saying?"

His lips twist into a faint smile. "Sophie wants this. All of us, together. But she knows this—you and me, alone—is important. To me. And perhaps to you, too."

I swallow. The meaning behind his words settles in my chest, and they swirl in my gut in a dangerous mix of terror and relief.

"Like last weekend?" I ask, feeling like I'm laying everything on the table.

"Yes. But also... more. Perhaps keeping it casual, but still exploring what this could be. For all three of us."

"And Sunday at the gym? Was that for all three of us?" I ask, the question slipping out before I can think it through.

His gaze hardens on mine, and my stomach twists when it morphs into something uninhibited.

"No," he says firmly, his voice a low growl. "Sunday was for me. Just me."

The scent of whiskey washes over me, and I have the sudden urge to kiss him, to taste it for myself. I'm suddenly reminded of that night seventeen years ago—the sweet, buttery scent of his breath, and the scent of him that always smells slightly of bergamot. It triggers that kiss to flash through my mind violently, and I can't help but hold back a groan.

My apartment suddenly feels too small, and the air feels explosive.

"And what about this?" I ask, my eyes dipping to his lips. His tongue darts out, wetting them, and I unconsciously step closer so that he can feel how hard I am.

"I think we both know there's something more here than either of us wants to admit."

I'm not sure who moves first, him or me, but when his lips press against mine, it's not tentative. It's steady, the kind of kiss that doesn't ask.

It only takes.

Groaning, I move my hand from his wrist to his hip, pulling him into me. I'm suddenly pulled back right back to that moment seventeen years ago again, when we found ourselves in this same exact scenario. This kiss is... *just* as good as it was almost two decades ago, if not better. He moans into my mouth, the sound vibrating through me like a thunderclap. A thousand white-hot bolts of electricity shoot through me as his tongue parts my lips, the taste of whiskey smoky and sharp. Without thinking, I rut against him, desperate and mindless, but it's like hitting a wall of steel.

It feels like temptation incarnate—the kind of surrender I used to preach against.

But there's no altar here, no pews to kneel at. Just Julian, and the way his gaze strips me down to the marrow.

He breaks the kiss suddenly, but his hands on my

shoulders keep me steady and hold me in place. His chest is heaving, but his eyes are razor-sharp, cutting through my haze of arousal.

"No," he says, his voice steady but laced with heat. "You don't get to take over. Not tonight."

His voice grounds me, but the connotation makes me feel dizzy with something I don't recognize. He shifts his body, pressing me back until my shoulders hit the opposite wall of my living room. The cool surface shocks my overheated skin.

I should push back. I should shove him away, remind him who's stronger, who's always in charge. But my body doesn't listen. It melts into the wall behind me, as if I've been waiting for this... for him. That thought alone should terrify me, but it doesn't. It feels like breathing, like some part of me has been holding its breath for seventeen fucking years.

"You want this?" he murmurs, his voice a velvet purr. His knee slides between my thighs, pinning me in place, and *fuck* if I don't love the way it feels to give in to his dominance. I nod, unsure if I'm capable of speaking, and he cracks a dangerous smile. "Then show me."

He presses against me, and the weight of him against my body is unyielding. He places both hands on either side of my head, and I realize that he's caging me in, trapping me here beneath him.

Just like in the locker room.

For the first time in my life, I let myself feel it.

The raw, undeniable thrill of surrender.

I could stop this—I trust him to step back if I needed

him to. I'm not sure if I want to know what it feels like to let him win... or if I'm scared I'll never want him to stop.

My body loosens, and as his eyes bore into mine, I let my eyes dip to the space between us.

"You're used to being in control, aren't you?" Julian's voice is a knife's edge, cutting through the tension. "But not with me."

I can't answer him—can't seem to find my voice. My breath is caught somewhere in my throat, and as his lips brush my jaw, my eyes flutter closed.

"Not with me," he repeats, whispering the words down to the pulse thrumming at the base of my neck.

I shudder as he grazes my skin with his teeth, and a sound that is half whimper, half plea escapes me.

I'm certain I've never made that fucking noise before.

"Admit it," he demands, his knee pressing up and into my cock. It takes everything not to thrust against his warm thigh.

A sharp gasp escapes my lips. "Yes," I choke out, the word falling from me like a confession.

Julian rears his head back just enough to look me in the eye. His expression is smug and triumphant, and I don't even fucking care. I'm under some sort of spell here, and it's fucking terrifying.

But also exhilarating.

His hand slides up to cup my jaw, and his thumb brushes my lower lip. "Good boy."

He takes a step back and his hand drops away. I miss the warmth instantly, and Julian just smirks as he studies me.

"Think about it, Kai. About what this could be."

Just as he turns to walk out, I panic and blurt the first thing I can think of. "I don't need to think about it."

He turns back to face me as he shrugs his jacket back on, giving me a knowing smile. "Good. Because neither do I."

The sound of my front door closing barely registers after he leaves, but the heat of him, the weight of his words, lingers. And for the first time, I'm not sure if I'm terrified—or ready.

I sink onto the couch, the weight of what just happened pressing down like iron shackles. The air feels different, charged, like a storm just passed through. My lips are swollen, and I swear I can still feel Julian's breath against my neck. It's fucking pathetic... but I don't move for a long time.

Because what just happened didn't feel like defeat. It didn't feel wrong. The only thing I feel is relief—that submitting to Julian felt like taking a deep breath for the first time in a very long time.

CHAPTER NINETEEN
THE BOOKSTORE

Sophie

I inhale and exhale to quell my nerves. My hands are sweaty, and I check my reflection in the rearview mirror to make sure I don't have lettuce in my teeth, and then I gather my folio and exit my car. I've barely slept all week as I've spent the majority of my waking hours on the business license application as well as the liability insurance certificate, proof of funding, modification proposal, and a check for the application fee. I'd also included plans for the fundraising events I'm planning before and during opening, as well as a *very* detailed business plan. I doubt the latter two things will be needed, but my mother raised me to always be overprepared.

I couldn't wait to tell her I was opening a romance bookstore.

She was going to lose her mind.

"Please tell me it's going to be pink," a familiar voice calls out.

I grin as I walk up to Stella Ravage. She's hand in hand with her daughter, Beatrix, who is humming to herself adorably.

Smiling, I hug her and then crouch down to say hello to Beatrix, who I know just turned two.

"Hi, Bea," I say, and she smiles and waves at me.

When I stand back up, I take in Stella's fabulous outfit—a bright yellow maxi dress that clings to her curves, and a pink suede jacket with matching sandals. Her glittery, teal backpack only adds another pop of color, and I suddenly feel drab in my black linen shift dress.

"You look amazing," I tell her, taking in her minimal makeup.

A group of people pass us by and stare at her. A couple of them do a double take. I don't blame them.

She's bloody gorgeous.

"Sophie, this isn't a job interview, you know. I mean, don't get me wrong, you always look fucking fit. But maybe take your hair down?" she suggests.

I smirk as I untie my bun, letting my blonde hair fall over my shoulders. She steps forward and tousles it a bit, and then she reaches into her handbag, pulling some bright pink lipstick out.

"Here. You should be wearing lipstick when you sign the contract."

My heart races as I swipe the lipstick on using the reflection of the shop glass. When I'm done, I turn back to her and smile down at Beatrix, who is watching me quietly.

"I appreciate your help today," I tell her, leaning against the side of the building. We're both a few minutes early, and the leasing agent will be here soon.

"Of course. You said romance bookstore, and I immediately knew I had to be here for this. Plus, power in numbers and all that. Didn't you say it would be a bloke showing you around?"

I nod. "Yeah. It was originally supposed to be Elisa, the woman I spoke to on the phone, but..." I trail off, wiping my hands on my dress.

"You'll do great," she says, picking Bea up and holding her on her left hip.

We chat for a few minutes, and just as I'm starting to get worried, a black sedan pulls up and parks right in front of us.

I swallow and stand up straighter, holding the folio in front of me with one hand. A middle-aged gentleman exits the car, and his expression pinches slightly when he takes in the way Stella, Bea, and I are all waiting out front.

"Sorry I'm a few minutes late," he says gruffly. "I'm Jake."

I reach my hand out to shake his, but he doesn't do the same, so I awkwardly drop it to my side. When I glance over at Stella, she mouths, *Arsehole.*

"That's okay. I'm very excited to see the place," I tell him eagerly.

He huffs a dismissive laugh. "You're the only one. It's not exactly a looker, if you know what I mean."

My brow furrows as he unlocks the door, and then we step inside.

Oh.

My smile falls as I take in the crumbling facade. Elisa had sent over the floorplan, but she said pictures weren't currently available.

Now I see why.

The floorboards are disintegrating, the wallpaper is peeling, and there are cobwebs everywhere. When I drafted my proposed renovations, I didn't include new flooring—that would eat into my start-up budget.

"Oh my God, this place has incredible bones," Stella says, her voice encouraging and excited all at once.

"I need to make a call. I'll give you a few minutes to look around," Jake says, leaving us alone in the space.

I bite my lower lip to keep from crying.

Spinning around, I try to find any redeeming qualities, and I can't. Just like when the house was under construction, I couldn't see past the mess.

All I see before me is impossibility.

"Look," Stella says, carrying Bea on the other hip and pointing to one of the walls. "Original crown molding. Plus, some of this floor can be salvaged. I bet we could get Kai to help fix the floors, slap a coat of pink paint on the walls, and call it a day, babe."

I almost sob at her optimism. "It needs a lot of work." The space is certainly large enough for a bookstore—we could even do a fun display in the window, and I'd still have room for a reading nook in the corner. "A *lot* of work," I add.

Stella sighs and sets Beatrix down. "Please don't touch anything, darling," she instructs her daughter, who only nods as she precariously starts to walk around, inspecting the empty space. "These two walls can be built-in floor-to-ceiling bookshelves," she starts, walking over to the two main walls on either side of the front door. "And a few individual shelves back here in the reading nook—themed shelves, special editions, maybe some merch. And here," she says, walking into the middle of the room, "We can put two sofas and a coffee table. The counter can go there," she adds, pointing to where I'm standing, "And we'd still have room for a table in the front window display."

I swallow, attempting to see her vision, but I can't see past the filth.

"Also, how fun would it be to have a giant inflatable cock right here?" she asks, cackling as she points to the space above my head.

I laugh just as Jake clears his throat, having opened the front door without either of us noticing.

"So? What do you think?" he checks his watch, and my stomach sinks. If I want this place, I should say something. It's now or never... "I have another meeting soon, so I should probably lock up."

Before I can overthink it, the words tumble out. "If you knock five hundred dollars off the rent each month —to cover the renovations I'll have to tackle—I'll take it. Right now." I straighten up, surprising even myself.

An hour later, Stella and I are waving goodbye to an annoyed Jake, who is late for his next meeting, and I'm clutching the folio to my chest. He still has to run a background and credit check, as well as verify the funding, but he made it seem like the place was mine if I wanted it.

Even better, he agreed to lower the rent. Despite initially trying to dismiss the idea of a romance bookstore, Stella had won him over eventually with her charm. By the end, he seemed almost impressed with us.

I'm so glad I asked her to accompany me today.

"Hunnry," Beatrix says, pointing at her mouth.

"We're having dinner with Daddy soon, darling," Stella coos. She reaches into her backpack and hands Beatrix a bag of what looks like Cheerios before strapping her into a fancy-looking pram. "I'm very proud of you," she tells me, smiling when she's finished. "You kept your cool, and you're about to be the owner of—what were you planning on naming the bookshop, anyway?"

My cheeks heat. "I filed the business paperback under Ashford Publishing. I still don't have a name in mind yet, but I figured I could use this name for other things, too."

Stella's eyes brighten as she gestures toward downtown. "I want to hear all about those other things. But first... I have a quick meeting with the admissions advisor at Saint Helena Academy. I've got to get this child of mine on a goddamn wait list for preschool two years early," she adds, shaking her head with an exasperated chuckle. "I mean, it's just a formality, of course. Maybe you want to join me on the walk, and you can say hello to Malakai?"

I open and close my mouth. It's late afternoon on a Friday—I'm sure he's swamped.

And yet... I can't help but *want* to see him.

Julian had told me what happened two nights ago, and then I'd asked him to tell me what happened again in greater detail in bed, because it turned me on to think he'd kissed another man.

Turns out, I enjoy the idea of *him* with another guy. Oh, how the tables have turned.

I've always known Julian was bisexual—he was very up-front about it when we met. And truth be told, I love the idea of him getting to explore that side of himself. I have no doubt that he loves me and always will.

"Sure. I'd love to join you," I tell her. "Let me just pop my folio into my car."

A minute later, we're enjoying the warm afternoon sunshine as we walk through downtown Crestwood.

"So..." she says, taking a sip from her water bottle. "What's up with you and Kai?"

I stumble over my feet at her question. I didn't expect her to come right out with it. We're closer now, sure, but her question catches me off guard.

"What do you mean? We're friends."

Stella laughs. "*Just* friends?"

I scoff. "I'm a married woman. Of course we're just friends."

She smirks as she glances sidelong at me. "Okay, then perhaps I should ask, what's going on with Julian and Kai?"

My mouth drops open. "How did you—" Snapping my lips together, I shake my head as I pop my sunglasses on.

The sun feels incredible. I'll never understand how anyone could prefer the cold, drizzly weather in London to the sunshine of Southern California. The way the sun soaks into my skin feels almost healing after thirty years in London, trying to fit in with people who would keel over if they knew what Julian and I were into.

"It's complicated," I tell her.

"I knew it," she says triumphantly.

I sigh. "Please don't say anything to anyone."

She shrugs. "I won't. But Miles suspects something, too, just so you know. He's the one who told me, actually."

I narrow my eyes as we walk past a group of giggling elderly woman power walking.

"Miles knows?"

Stella laughs. "Of course he does. My husband is nothing if not observant," she says, giving me a wry smile.

"I see," I say, my voice coming out quieter than I intended. "Well, now you know."

"So, are the three of you like... a throuple?"

I shake my head. "No. We're just... having fun."

"I can respect that," Stella says. "Love is love, right? I'm much too jealous to share Miles, so I admire you for going after what you want. I don't think I've ever seen him so affected by anyone before," she adds, chuckling. "He's definitely all in, you know?"

I nod, but I'm quiet the rest of the ten-minute walk to Saint Helena Academy.

While I have no doubt Stella is right, I also can't help but feel like I need to explore my relationship with Kai by myself a bit. I can tell he has feelings for me, but when we're all together, it's hard to separate the fact that I'm Sophie versus *just* Julian's wife.

I hadn't really spoken to him since last weekend, but I'd taken initiative and added us all to a group chat. I figured it would allow us to plan anything in the future, and it would make him feel included. We'd all briefly chatted this week via text, but with everything happening with the shop, I'd been too swamped to really open the conversation to anything further, or making plans to see him again.

Still, I can't help but be excited to tell him about filling out the application for the space. He knew this meeting was important, and both he and Julian had sent me good luck texts earlier.

Once we arrive at Saint Helena Academy, the front desk receptionist ushers Stella into admissions, and I'm given a visitor's pass and directions to Kai's office down the hall. It's nearly empty, and Stella mentions it's a half day for the students, so they're all gone. I say goodbye and walk through the office to find Kai.

The school is stunning, set within white stucco walls, terracotta accents, and arched windows. Palm trees dot the front entrance as well as the courtyard I pass by down the hallway. There are vibrant flower beds of jasmine and different kinds of succulents, as well as bougainvillea draped over most of the exterior.

As I walk, I take in the crosses and religious artwork —biting my lower lip when I think of the last time Kai and I used the Bible. I pass the chapel, which has rows of wooden pews and an altar adorned with fresh flowers. Even empty, I can see what drew Kai here. It's serene but it feels almost alive, and despite the fact that I'm not religious anymore, I can see the appeal.

Standing in front of a wooden door that says 'Headmaster Malakai Ravage,' I knock gently three times.

No answer.

I knock harder this time, but there's still no answer.

"He's at the pool," an older woman walking down the hall says. "It's his Friday afternoon ritual."

My lips part. "Oh. Okay, thank you."

Her eyes quickly take me in. "Are you a family member?"

Pressing my lips together, I shake my head. "No. Just a friend." Turning around, I'm about to walk away when she speaks again.

"He keeps the door to the pool locked, but I can open it for you if you'd like to say hi?"

"Sure, that'd be great. Thank you."

She gestures for me to follow her, leading me farther down the hallway. "How do you know Headmaster Ravage?"

"He's, um, friends with my husband."

She nods. "That's wonderful. Between you and me, I think he needs more friends. *Quality* friends, you know what I mean?"

On your knees, little dove.

My chest flushes when I think of last weekend. "I understand completely."

As we stop in front of a pair of double doors, she pulls out a set of keys, carefully inspecting each one until she finds the one she needs. Quickly unlocking the door, she holds it open for me.

"Here you are. I'm headed home for the day. Please tell the headmaster that Susie says hello," she says warmly, turning and walking away.

Stepping into the large indoor pool area, I let the door close behind me. The click of the lock reverberates through the large, warm space. The space is massive, tall ceilings with coffered designs and an open, airy feel while still retaining the warmth. The pool itself is a shimmering, turquoise expanse, tiled in deep blue. The concrete is clean and new-looking, and I admire the way the space feels functional while still being elegant.

Very apt for a private school.

My eyes find Kai instantly. He's doing freestyle, facing away from me, and I can't help but watch the way his muscles bunch and contract with each movement. Slowly walking closer, I attempt to keep my heeled boots quiet so as not to startle him. He moves so smoothly through the water, each sweep of his arms propels him forward. The pool ripples around him, mirroring the quiet power in his strokes. Watching him is almost hypnotic, and as I stop on the other side of the pool, I tilt my head slightly as he comes to the edge nearest to me.

He flips and pushes off the wall, turning his head to breathe. For half a second, I see his profile—sharp jawline, damp strands of hair clinging to his forehead, his expression one of pure focus. My traitorous heart pounds as I scramble for something—anything—to say when he notices me.

And then he stops.

Still facing away from me, there's a shift in his rhythm. Straightening mid-stroke, he treads water for a second, and I freeze. Biting my lower lip, I wait.

He turns, his gaze finding mine instantly, as if he knew I was there all along.

His eyes meet mine, dark and unreadable, and for a second, the air between us feels charged. A slow smile tugs at the corners of his mouth as he pushes the wet hair off his forehead.

"You're not exactly as stealthy as you think," he says, his voice low and teasing, carrying easily over the quiet lap of the water.

I huff a nervous laugh. "Well, stealth isn't exactly my best feature."

He smirks and swims closer, head above water, stopping right in front of me. "That's true. I suppose you have... other talents."

God, it's so *bloody* hot in here.

My heart stutters in my chest. I attempt to keep my composure, but the way he's looking at me is making it hard to think straight.

"I suppose I do," I say, a little breathlessly.

I try to hide the slight tremor in my hands by shifting my weight to one hip, but he's still watching me, all that quiet power radiating from him. And then he does something that makes me feel like I'm melting into the concrete. His eyes slowly drag from my eyes down to my chest, and even farther down until he gets to my feet. And then, even slower this time, his eyes find mine again.

Fuck, he's good.

"So? How'd the meeting go?"

I blink, his question pulling me back from the tension stretching between us. "I think it went well. The place is... a disaster. It needs more work than I thought, but I can't seem to walk away from it."

His head tilts slightly, and the faintest smirk tugs at his lips. "You've always liked a challenge."

I laugh, the sound nervous but real. "Or I just don't know when to quit."

Kai swims closer, stopping just beneath me, his hands resting on the ledge. His eyes flick to mine, unreadable but warm.

"Maybe that's not such a bad thing."

I swallow, heart skipping at the proximity. "Stubbornness isn't always a virtue."

"Sometimes it is," he counters softly, tilting his head to the side like he's studying me. "It's the same part of you that refuses to let anyone decide who you should be."

His words hit harder than I expect, the quiet truth settling over me. I shift my weight, letting out a shaky breath as I drop my gaze to the water rippling beneath him.

"You noticed that?" I murmur, the vulnerability creeping in uninvited.

"I notice a lot of things." His voice is low, intimate in a way that makes it hard to hold his gaze. But I do.

A flicker of something tightens in my chest—acknowledgment, maybe. Or relief. Because I know he means it. In his own quiet way, Kai sees me. All the parts I keep hidden behind carefully curated smiles and small talk.

All the parts I only allow Julian access to.

Before I can respond, his hand drifts from the ledge to the top of my ankle, thumb brushing against the skin just above the collar of my boot. The simple touch sets every nerve on edge, but his eyes stay on mine, patient and expectant.

"You look warm," he says, his voice low and tinted with faux concern. "Maybe you need to cool off?"

I blink, suddenly aware of how I'm starting to sweat from the heat. My breath hitches as his hands come to my ankles. The touch is light, almost teasing, but I know better than to mistake it for anything less than control.

"Maybe I do," I tease, my thoughts scattering.

I've always known where this path leads, especially after last weekend.

Where time spent with *him* leads.

But there's something about this moment—about the way he's looking at me, about how much I've allowed myself to want him—that makes it feel different.

More intense.

Like something has shifted between us.

He cocks his head, eyes never leaving mine, and for a moment, I wonder if he's going to do something that might push this quiet game into something real. But then he pushes off the wall and gives me a knowing look.

Stepping out of my boots, I set my handbag down and sit on the edge of the pool. The concrete is warm, and as I drop my feet into the cool water, I hum in pleasure.

"I forgot to tell you that Susie says hello," I say, leaning back on my palms. It's a distraction, and I know it.

Kai gives me a lopsided smile, treading water a few feet away. "Ah, so that's who snuck you in. I was wondering how you got here. That lock is industrial strength."

"She said you do this every Friday."

He dips his chin. "I do. I find it relaxing. And since Fridays are half days, I *normally* have the pool to myself."

The weight of his words isn't lost on me. He knows why I'm really here. Knows I'm not just making conversation.

But he doesn't call me out on it. Not yet.

Pulling my lower lip between my teeth, I ignore the pull toward him that makes my chest ache. He seems so calm and collected, like always, and I'm already squirming.

Julian's face flashes in my mind, and I almost pull away. But the heat in Kai's gaze keeps me pinned, his fingers skating along the edge of my sanity. Julian trusts me. I trust him. And more importantly, we trust Kai. But this feels like... more.

It's enough to pull me back from this all for a second, but only just. The tension between Kai and me is thick and raw, like it's about to spill over.

Looking down, I allow myself one last thought of Julian.

We agreed this was fine. All of us. No secrets, no guilt. We talked, we set our boundaries, and we chose this together. Besides, Julian kissed Kai two days ago. This is fine.

My focus flicks back to Kai, and his eyes narrow slightly, as if he can sense my hesitation or read my thoughts, and I'm not sure which is worse in this instance.

"You seem distracted, too," he murmurs. His tone is a low purr, almost teasing as he drinks me up with that familiar, dangerous hunger.

"I am," I whisper, my breathing uneven.

He glides through the water and swims right up to me. "I can help with that."

For a second, I think he's going to pull me into the pool. Instead, he places wet hands on either side of my bare thighs.

"What do you need, little dove?"

God, that nickname...

The question lingers in the air between us, heavy

with implications. And as I meet his gaze, I realize that even if I wanted to, I don't think I could stop this now. I don't *want* to stop it.

Water falls from his dark hair onto his face, and then he shakes his head, splashing me with tiny drops of water before slicking it back with his hands. His hair is usually hanging in front of his forehead, so it's nice to see his full face.

"Hey!" I squeal, holding my hands up. "You got me wet."

His gray eyes flick downward to the space between my thighs before coming back up to meet mine. He's watching me with a mischievous expression, and he doesn't even have to say it—I know exactly what he's thinking.

"Are you going to get in, or do I have to pull you in?"

"You wouldn't," I tease, narrowing my eyes as I look down at him.

His hands come to the tops of my bare thighs, and his expression changes in a heartbeat from playful to serious and enigmatic.

I swallow. This was *not* what I thought would happen when I decided to accompany Stella to Saint Helena. I thought I'd poke my head into his office, say a quick hello, and then be on my merry way.

Instead, I'm sitting on the edge of an indoor pool while Kai eye fucks me, and he's insinuating that he wants me in the water with him, all the while being an incorrigible flirt.

"I *would*," he purrs.

"And what would I wear home, then? You'd ruin my dress."

His lips twitch. He knows exactly what I'm insinuating. If I go home to Julian in a wet dress...

A low growl escapes his lips. "Move your dress up and spread your legs."

My mouth drops open. "No. We're in a public place—someone could see us—"

"I take it you're not an exhibitionist, then?" he asks, cocking his head. "Are you worried we'll get in trouble?"

I snap my mouth shut before answering. "Well, yeah, I mean—"

"I'm the headmaster, Sophie. I'm in charge here. So if I want to taste your cunt before sending you home to your husband, who's going to stop me? Plus, the only door into the pool is locked, and everyone is gone since it's a half day."

"But Stella is with admissions—"

"Trust me, Sophie. No one is getting in here."

I stop breathing. "Kai..."

He grins as he darts his eyes down to my thighs and back up. "You take risks, Sophie. You told me just now... you don't know when to quit. Consider this a challenge." He pauses, and his eyes pierce into mine. "The bookstore scares you. So do I. Maybe that's a good thing."

I swallow, unsure of what to say to that. Because he's right.

"Go on, little dove. Show me how *wet* I just made you."

Jesus fuck.

With shaking hands, I shimmy my dress up my thighs, past my hips. And then I spread my legs in front of him, giving him a full, unobstructed view of my hot pink knickers. From his position in the water, his shoulders are at about the same height as my hips, so all he has to do is gently tug my bum closer to the edge of the pool before he runs his hands along the inside of my thighs.

Everything inside of me pulses as he leans closer. His breath is hot against the thin fabric of my knickers, and his fingers dig into my thighs, just enough to make me squirm. Sliding his hands higher, the water on his palms leaves a cold, damp trail against my skin. Despite being hot, my whole body shudders as a shiver claws down my spine.

With one hand, he trails a finger upward, brushing against my seam. Gasping, I bite my lip, and my breathing turns heavy and ragged.

"You're so responsive," he says softly, almost to himself. Moving my thong to the side, I suck in a breath as his eyes flick down to my core. Using his thumb, he gently brushes it against my clit, and I jolt as my hands clutch the edge of the pool.

"Kai—"

"My lord," he corrects sharply, his eyes locking on mine. "Say it."

"My lord," I breathe, the words barely audible.

"That's better," he murmurs, his voice a velvet purr. Sliding two fingers between my folds, he moves slowly—

exploring. *Testing.* "Do you think Julian will recognize the taste of my mouth after I send you home?"

I gasp, and I feel my cheeks flush. Kai's arrogance and confidence isn't a cover—he's truly in control, truly in charge of the scene.

"Answer me," he demands, pushing into me fully.

"I—don't know," I stammer, the words tumbling out unbidden.

"You're honest at least. Good girl."

And then he's pulling me closer. His fingers curl inside of me as his teeth graze the inside of my thigh, and I. Can't. Breathe. Every nerve ending inside of me lights up, and I can feel everything from the warm, wet mouth inching up my thigh to the gritty concrete underneath my bare bum.

"You're shaking," he observes, his voice a mix of curiosity and amusement. "Are you nervous?"

I nod. "Yes."

His lips curl into a smile. "Good. Fear sharpens the senses. Do you trust me?"

"Yes," I answer, though my voice wavers.

"Then give me your fear, little dove. Show me what true surrender looks like. Lay back."

"What?" I ask, hesitating.

"Lie on your back," he adds, pushing me back.

I do as he says, and the warm concrete feels nice on my back. He moves between my legs, and I go still. I can't see him—I can only hear the light splashing of water.

"Hold your breath." His voice is calm but unyielding.

I lift my head to look at him. "What?"

"You heard me. Hold. Your. Breath."

A flash of panic works through me. His eyes bore into mine, grounding me. Nodding, I inhale deeply and hold it.

His hands slide to my hips. "That's it. Now keep still."

Before I can process what's happening, his mouth is against my core, and his tongue laves up my slit. I buck against him, body arching involuntarily, as he works his tongue in slow, deliberate strokes. The pressure inside of me mixed with the sensations of his mouth cause me to exhale sharply, gasping for air.

Kai pulls back immediately, and when I lift my head, his gray eyes lock onto mine.

"Did I tell you to breathe?"

My cheeks burn as I shake my head.

"Then don't." His tone is sharp, but not cruel. "Hold it. Trust me, Sophie."

I nod as I inhale, holding the air deep in my chest and feeling more prepared this time. But this time, when he leans into me, the intensity is magnified by two fingers curling inside of me. The lack of air makes every movement, every flick of his tongue, feel so much more intense. I'm suddenly hyperaware of every sensation, and in seconds, I find myself on the edge of a climax.

My head begins to pound, and then I can't hold it any longer. Gasping loudly, the sound reverberates through the large room.

Kai's free hand tightens on my thigh and he pulls the other one out from inside of me.

"You're fighting me," he asks. His tone is inquisitive—not unkind. "Why?"

"I don't know," I admit, voice trembling.

"Yes, you do," he says, his voice a low murmur. "Tell me why."

My chest aches as the truth comes out before I'm ready to admit it. "Because I'm afraid."

"Of what?"

"Of losing control," I tell him, looking up at the coffered ceiling.

"That's exactly what I want, little dove. I want you to lose control. I want you to let go. I want you to *trust* me. Because next time we do this, it's going be my hands around your throat and you're going to have to trust that I'm not going to go too far." I nod despite the panic lingering on the edge of my mind. "Again. Breathe deep. Hold it. And trust me to know your limits."

This time, when the pressure immediately begins to build inside my chest, I give in to the feeling. When I'm relaxed, it sort of feels like I'm floating, like the air in my lungs might carry me away. And then when Kai gently pushes his fingers between my folds at the same time his tongue swipes through me, my eyes flutter closed as pleasure claws at me. His mouth moves against me with relentless precision. The sensations sharpen every second, and the heat building inside of me demands release.

My whole body trembles as I near the edge, and though I know my body needs air, I trust Kai enough to know that he'll tell me to breathe soon. That recognition

—the *trust*—surprises me. There's only ever been one person I've trusted this much before—only one person who could get under my skin like this.

Julian.

The pressure builds, with the need for release and for air tangling together until I don't know which one I crave more. Kai's tongue moves in slow, deliberate circles, each flick sending a pulse of heat spiraling through me. He's relentless and teasing... like he's savoring the way my body is reacting. It's precise enough that I know he's remembering what Julian taught him.

I clench desperately around his fingers, my hips bucking involuntarily as my body writhes under his control. My thighs shake, and then my whole body goes taut from a mix of pleasure and pressure. Just when I don't think I can take any more, his free hand comes to my abdomen, and he presses down, grounding me.

"Breathe."

The rush of air mixes with the release that tears through me with zero abandon. My back arches, and though Kai's hand remains on my abdomen, I feel myself contract around his fingers. A wave of heat surges through me, pleasure crashing over every part of me like a storm. I cry out, my entire body seizing and shaking with the force of it, stars dancing behind my closed eyes. It's overwhelming, a white-hot rush that leaves me gasping and undone, my fingers clawing at the concrete as I finally let go.

He groans—his mouth working me through my

climax and dragging it out. Waves of sensation crash through me so intensely that I forget where I am.

I forget everything but *him*.

When it's over, I go limp. In a flash, Kai is there, pulling himself onto the deck and running a wet hand over my forehead.

"You did so well, little dove," he murmurs.

I look up at him, and for a second, I understand why people pray to a deity. Because what just happened, the way he guided me through it, felt otherworldly.

"I'm so proud of you."

The weight of his words causes me to close my eyes, and they sink into the adrenaline still coursing through me—calming me.

As he pulls me up and wraps an arm around my shoulder, I feel him kiss the top of my head. For a second, Kai pulls back, like he's about to apologize.

I stop him, curling my fingers into his damp hair, pulling him closer.

"Don't," I whisper, my breath still ragged. "I wanted this. I want you."

"Me too," he murmurs back.

And somehow, I know with absolute certainty that we'd crossed a line today, a line we could never uncross.

Even if we could... I don't think I'd want to.

CHAPTER TWENTY
THE APPETIZER

Julian

I take another sip of my whiskey, listening to the sound of tires crunching on the gravel driveway. It's a nice night, and I have the windows in the receiving room open to let in the early night breeze. And as I lift the glass of amber liquid to my lips again, I let the whiskey sit on my tongue for a few seconds, numbing my mouth as I stare down at Sophie's text from half an hour ago.

> SOPHIE LOVE <3
>
> On my way home. Viewing went great. I signed the contract. I saw Kai... and there's something I need to tell you.

My stomach clenches with nerves as I swallow the whiskey slowly. The sound reverberates through the quiet room, and when I hear her car door slam shut, I sink back into the chair I'm sitting in.

I hadn't responded to her text—I didn't know what to say. I didn't have the whole story, and I wanted to hear what she needed to tell me before reacting.

Something hot slides through me when I think of the two of them together, different scenarios playing before my eyes in my overactive imagination. Did she run into him at the shop? Or did she seek him out somewhere? Perhaps they ran into each other and went back to his place... He doesn't live far from the building she was viewing.

A cold sweat breaks out on my forehead as I hear her come through the front door.

"Honey, I'm home!"

Her voice carries through the house, and I have to ignore the pang of disappointment that works through me. She sounds normal—*unaffected*—and I wonder if I'm overthinking this.

It has to mean something that I *hope* she tells me she fucked him, right?

I suppose it would cancel out the guilt I've been carrying around for kissing him two nights ago.

"I'm in here," I call out.

The sound of her shoes echoes through the large foyer, and then she's before me. She's in a rumpled linen dress, but her face gives absolutely nothing away. Sitting up straighter, I give her a genuine smile before setting my drink down and patting my lap.

"Sit."

I swear her cheeks tinge with color at my command, and I watch her carefully, waiting for her to confess. For a second, I think about blurting it out—*did you fuck him?*—because I need to know. I force myself to sit still, but it feels like my entire body vibrates with anticipation. Patience feels like a luxury I wasn't built for. Even now, the need to interrupt her claws at me, to skip ahead to the parts I don't know yet.

ADHD doesn't care about propriety—it demands *now*. I've learned how to fake patience, but sometimes I'm just holding my breath, pretending to wait.

She sets her handbag down and steps out of her boots. Smoothing her hair, she gives me a shy smile before walking over to me. When she's a foot away, I reach out and pull her down onto my lap. She inhales sharply as I twist her around, pulling her face down and pressing my lips against hers.

She moans as one of my free hands moves up her skull, fisting her hair and pulling it just the way she likes it.

When I pull away a few seconds later, she sways as she watches me with glazed-over eyes.

That's my girl.

"How was your day?" I ask, running the hand that was in her hair down her spine until it's resting on her lower back.

"Good. I signed the contract—Jake said he'd get back to me next week, but he didn't foresee any obstacles. The place is a wreck, and it'll need a lot of work, but Stella painted a vision I can't unsee now. I... I think this is going to be a really amazing thing," she tells me, grinning. "And I can't wait to show you."

Lifting one of her hands, I kiss the back of her palm, and then I lay it against my warm cheek.

"That's incredible, pet. I'm so very proud of you." Her eyes flick between mine, and she pulls her lower lip between her teeth. "Was there something else you wanted to tell me?" I ask, keeping my voice smooth as I attempt not to laugh at her uncomfortable expression.

"Umm..."

Pressing a finger to her lips, I tilt my head as I look her in the eye.

"What's wrong, Soph? Are you worried I'll be mad?"

She pulls her lip farther into her mouth before looking down. "No, it's just... it's always been you and me against the world. It feels strange to tell you that I was intimate with another man."

My lips twitch with the threat of a smile. "Sophie, I've watched you with plenty of other men before."

"No, I know. It's just that you weren't there this time, and I guess I just have to get used to the idea that Kai and I will have something just for the two of us. Like the two of you do. It's the first time I've felt separate from you."

Separate.

The word lingers like an echo in the room. I'm not sure why it bothers me—maybe because I've never feared losing her to anyone else. But hearing her say it now, I wonder if I've been so focused on managing my own feelings for Kai that I forgot to check in with hers.

Maybe I assumed she'd follow my lead, but she's stepping ahead of me, isn't she?

It makes me think of all the times she seemed bored, or restless. All the times she'd latch on to a detail for the housewarming party, and now the bookshop...

She had questioned her place in our life, and I'd dismissed it.

But now?

Now, I can feel the shift—subtle but undeniable. The quiet confidence in the way she talks about Kai, the way her eyes spark with something more when she mentions him. I recognize that look. I've worn it myself.

For the first time, I wonder if this isn't just about sharing her... but about watching her grow beyond me in ways I didn't anticipate.

And strangely, I don't feel threatened. I feel something else—something softer. Pride, maybe.

I cup the back of her head, brushing my thumb over her jawline, grounding both of us in the space between words. "I understand completely. But I think it's a good thing that we're all compatible together, in many different configurations. It bodes well for whatever this is, don't you think? The fact that we all have chemistry together and separately is rare. Now, are you going to tell me what happened?"

She snaps her eyes back to me. "Well, Stella had a meeting at Saint Helena Academy, and she asked me if I wanted to say hi to Kai. I said yes, but when I got to his office, he wasn't there." She takes a deep breath. "A very nice woman showed me to the pool, and he was in there swimming laps."

She shifts on my lap, and I have to wonder if she's aroused just thinking about it.

Because I'm sure as fuck hard as a rock.

"And?" I ask, running a hand up her thigh.

"And," she answers, almost breathless, "I don't even know what happened, to be honest. I've never experienced anything like that before."

A low growl settles in my chest as I run my hand up her thigh, only to find her knickers already wet.

It ignites a smoldering ember of possessiveness. I want to hear every detail, want her to spell it out piece by piece, but somewhere in the back of my mind, a question lingers. Is it the dominance I crave, or the reassurance that I still hold something Kai doesn't?

"Tell me everything." She gasps as I lightly run a finger over her seam, and when a full-body shudder works through her, I chuckle. "Go on, Soph. What happened after you found him swimming laps?"

She whimpers when I add a bit of pressure, and I have to press myself farther into the chair so as not to grind my cock against her arse.

"I sat down on the edge, and he told me..." She trails off, a blush forming on her cheeks. "He told me to lift my dress and spread my legs. He didn't—he didn't give me an option. And then he put his fingers inside of me."

I feel something white-hot flash through me at her words, my cock feels heavy—*aching*. I don't speak. I only wait for her to continue.

"He told me to hold my breath. So I did, but it didn't work at first. I was too nervous. He went down on me at the same time, and then he made me lose control of everything I thought I knew," she finishes, face red as she looks at me.

I take in her words, imagining how she must've looked spread out before him on the pool deck. It's better than the different fantasies I'd been thinking up before she walked through the door.

"Also, he said, 'Do you think Julian will recognize the taste of my mouth after I send you home?'"

A low, guttural groan breaks free from my chest, and before I know it, I'm lifting her off my lap and setting her down on the floor as I hover over her.

"Hm. That sounds like a challenge," I purr, nudging her dress up as I fumble with my belt.

"There's my territorial husband," she whispers, smiling up at me.

I unzip my trousers, freeing my cock. Before I enter her, though, I swipe a finger through her folds, bringing it to my lips and sucking. Her eyes glaze over, and I don't give her any sort of warning before I drive into her. My hand curls near her head, and I drop my chin as my mouth falls open. It feels like she's suctioning me into her, and my whole body shudders as soon as I'm fully sheathed in her tight heat.

"Fuuuck, pet. You're so wet."

She moans, shifting her hips slightly so that I can push in another inch. My arms shake at the sensation of being inside of her just an hour after Kai had his mouth on her—I might actually come too soon.

"Well? Are you going to sit there, or are you going to fuck me?" she asks.

Grunting, I wrap a hand around her throat as I pull out. She gasps, waiting for me to push back into her, but I press the tip of my cock against her instead, not giving her the satisfaction yet.

"Did you come?" I ask, bending down and sucking on the space between her collarbone and ear.

"Y-yes," she stutters, her nails trailing underneath my shirt as she scratches me.

"How many times?" I ask, my tongue laving against her soft, delicate skin.

"O-once," she mutters.

"And did you like being dominated by him?"

"Yes," she sighs, throwing her head back even farther.

I thrust into her, and she gasps, letting out a low, loud moan. It reverberates through me, and I lift myself up to get a better look at her from my knees. Pulling her hips up, I rest the backs of her thighs on mine, holding her close and angled up as I continue fucking her.

"God, yes, that angle is divine," she says through clenched teeth. She tries to roll her hips, but I hold her down. Biting her lower lip, she looks up at me and gives me a bratty, little smile. "Harder, please."

Gritting my teeth, I fuck her with zero abandon. I'm so rough that we actually move across the carpet, and the slapping sound mingled with her loud groans... it's too much.

Especially when I take my thumb and begin to swirl her wetness—or Kai's saliva?—through her folds.

I watch her carefully, half expecting her to fold beneath the weight of my stare. But she doesn't. Instead, she presses a hand to my chest and pushes—just slightly—until I'm the one beneath her. For a second, I consider flipping her back, but I don't. I let her stay on top, even if it feels unnatural.

She rides me, confident and smiling, and my hands move to her hips, gripping the flesh.

A minute later, she shatters, eyes squeezing tight as her cunt grips me over and over. I watch her raptly as she falls apart, mesmerized by the way she goes completely still, just for a moment, before trembling uncontrollably. It's one of my favorite things about her.

"Fuck. I'm so close, baby."

"Come inside of me," she begs, her voice a soft whimper. "Please, Julian. I *need* you."

"Soph, I'm—fuck—"

My cock explodes, and my hips jerk as I empty everything I have inside of her. When the last of it leaves my body, I pull her off me and collapse to the floor.

She follows, rolling over to face me, a satisfied smile grazing her lips, and I'm suddenly struck with an idea.

"Stay there," I tell her, sitting up and grabbing my phone from where I'd left it on the table.

"What are you doing?"

I look down at her, flushed and spent, rumpled and so very clearly *just fucked*.

"Spread your legs, baby. Let me see my cum drip out of you, pet."

Her mouth drops open, but she does as I say. Slowly inching one leg to the side, I growl when I see my seed slowly slide out of her perfect, pink pussy.

I snap a picture—legs spread, hands relaxed at her sides, soft smile—and draft a text to Kai.

I hover over the message for a second longer than I should. It's a game, one I know Kai is smart enough to catch onto. But I can't resist the impulse. If he wants to play with Sophie, he'll have to know I'm still in the game too.

> I did taste you. Thanks for the appetizer.

"Did you just take a picture of my fanny?" she asks, sitting up and grabbing my phone. When she reads what I wrote him, her eyes flash to mine.

"Julian Ashford. For shame," she mutters, laughing.

I chuckle as I stand up to grab something to clean her off, thinking of what Kai will say when he gets that picture from me.

When I return, I clean her up, running a hand down her thigh and smoothing the hair away from her face. She's sated, drowsy in that way that makes me want to wrap her in blankets and keep the world at bay. I don't move right away.

Instead, I stay there, pressing my lips to her forehead like she's the most delicate thing I've ever held.

CHAPTER TWENTY-ONE
THE INVITATION

MALAKAI

I'm tidying up my office when there's a knock at the door. Internally groaning, I walk over to the door and pull it open, not expecting to see Rod Dumplant's suntanned face and too white teeth. It's past six, and I assumed I was the last person here for the day.

"Rod," I say, not immediately letting him into the office. "How can I help you?"

"No hot dates tonight, Ravage?" he asks, smirking as he gestures for me to let him in.

I don't need hot dates because I just ate the best pussy of my life, but of course I can't say that.

The memory of Sophie spread out before me on the pool deck threatens to give me another erection—and I almost gag at the thought of getting aroused in Rod's presence.

"Not tonight, I'm afraid," I tell him, gritting my jaw as he sits down in one of my chairs, unprompted. *Sure, take a seat...*

"Aw, that's too bad. When I was your age—before I met Melanie, of course—I had dates every weekend. You're young. You should be out on the town."

My teeth ache from grinding them so hard. "Yes, well, my job keeps me busy. Did you have something to discuss, or is my dating life an agenda item at our next board meeting?" I ask, not bothering to mask my annoyance.

Rod huffs a laugh. "Apologies, Malakai. It just pains me that a good, Christian man like yourself isn't married with kids yet." I sit down behind my desk and rest one leg over the opposite ankle, leaning back and narrowing my eyes, waiting for him to continue. "Anyway, I'm just here to discuss Bradleigh Evans."

No surprise there.

Leaning forward, I pin him with a hard stare. "No offense, *Rod*, but don't you have better things to worry about?"

His smile falls off his face, and suddenly his expression is what I can only describe as *ugly*.

"I do, actually. Which is why I want to move forward with moving her to another school. This issue has already taken up enough of my time, and I want her gone."

My nostrils flare, but otherwise I keep my composure. As much as I want to tell him to fuck off, that won't help her or any of our other marginalized students.

Because he certainly won't stop with Bradleigh.

I have to get my point across now, because as much as I hate it, he *is* on the board. Unfortunately, his opinion matters. If I lose my cool on him, it will only give him ammunition to pursue his campaign of hate against my other students.

If a society is too tolerant of intolerance, it will eventually be dominated by intolerance, which will therefore undermine the principle of tolerance itself.

"Bradleigh is staying at Saint Helena. I have a meeting with Victoria Evans next week. End of discussion."

Rod starts to open his mouth to retort, but I cut him off, my tone sharp and unyielding.

"Let me make one thing abundantly clear, Rod. Saint Helena stands for inclusivity, dignity, and respect for all students. If you cannot uphold those values, you are welcome to step aside from your position on the board. I will not tolerate any actions, overt or covert, that seek to marginalize or harm any student under my care. Not Bradleigh. Not anyone. Not ever. Do I make myself clear?"

The silence between us is thick, but I hold his gaze until he nods curtly. The message has been delivered.

"You've made yourself more than clear, Ravage, and it's given me a lot of insight into what you stand for," Rod says, eyes narrowing just enough to suggest he knows more than he lets on. "Let's hope the board appreciates your forward thinking as much as you think they do."

Just then, my phone chimes. I glance down, brow furrowing when I see that it's a text from Julian. Picking it up, I give Rod a hard look before opening the message.

Everything inside of me grows hot, and I nearly drop my phone when a picture of Sophie on the ground comes through. Rubbing my mouth, I take in the way Julian posed her to show off her spread legs—and his cum visibly dripping out of it. The caption makes me hard instantly.

> JULIAN
> I did taste you. Thanks for the appetizer.

Fuck.

My.

Life.

Locking my phone, I set it down and look back at Rod, who is watching me curiously.

"Everything okay?" he asks, narrowing his eyes.

"Everything's fine, Rod." I gesture at the door. "If you don't mind, I have some work to do before leaving for the day."

Rod stands slowly, straightening his too big suit and giving me a pointed look. "This isn't over, Ravage."

I meet his gaze with an unwavering calm that I know will infuriate him more than any retort.

"You're right, Rod. It isn't over, because as long as I'm headmaster, there will always be someone here to stand between your hatred and my students. Good evening."

He glares at me as he turns and walks out without another word.

As soon as my door closes, I release a long sigh and run my hands over my face. I'm exhausted, and all of this bullshit with Rod is messing with me. I know people like him exist everywhere, but it makes me angry that people like Bradleigh—and now myself—can't just live our lives. Because if I know one thing, it's that if Rod finds out about my situation with Julian and Sophie—whatever it is that we're doing—he'll paint it in a negative light, and technically, I could lose my job because of it.

That thought suddenly strikes me.

He's on the board, and he's only one member, but I was voted in. It would be very easy for a majority to vote me out. And while Chase owns the majority of shares for Saint Helena, he could be outnumbered if parents complain.

If our funding is threatened, it could get very messy, very quickly.

I have to make sure Rod never finds out about the Ashfords.

Speaking of Sophie and Julian...

Leaning back in my chair, I pick my phone up and slowly unlock it. I zoom in like a pervert, smirking when I see her displeased expression. My guess is this picture and subsequent caption were both Julian's idea.

But is it a summons? Or simply another provocation?

I quickly respond to find out.

> Is this an invitation, or just you showing off?

While I wait for him to respond, I continue cleaning

up my office space. I find that if I spend my Friday evenings tidying my life up, I go into the weekend with a clearer mind. And if the last week has been any indication, I'll need a clear head for whatever this is with Julian and Sophie.

My heart is still pounding from the picture, and I have to adjust my cock a few times as I go. I try not to ruminate on what it could mean that he texted me, about the possibilities behind it.

Is this really something they want? Are they both open to this... to me?

I glance at my phone, half expecting an immediate reply considering the subject matter, but it stays silent. That's the worst part—waiting, wondering if I just overstepped, if I'm reading into this all wrong. Because at the end of the day, I'm here, and they're together. Besides, maybe Julian is testing me. I wouldn't put it past him to fuck with me, waiting to see if I'll cross some imaginary line so he can shut this whole thing down.

What is it that he said? *How does it feel to be used? Payback's a bitch, isn't it?*

Or... maybe he wants me to cross it.

For a second, I consider that this could truly work between us, and the notion has my blood heating all over again. The memory of Sophie on the edge of the pool is still vivid in my mind. The way she pushed back, her sounds, her touch, the way she responded when she finally gave in to me... it was everything I've ever wanted in a submissive, and everything I never knew I needed.

And Julian, his eyes on us last weekend, and the possibilities of what that could mean going forward...

My phone buzzes.

I snatch it up like a drowning man grabbing a life raft. Julian's text is short, casual, like he didn't just flip my world on its head.

> JULIAN
> Why don't you come over and find out?

My breath catches. An invitation. At least, I think it is. But for what? Talking? More? I feel like a teenager again, trying to read between the lines of what he's saying—and trying not to get my hopes up, either.

I type back before I lose my nerve, staring at the screen as my thumb hovers over the send button. My pulse pounds in my ears, and my whole body is alight with possibilities.

One fucking text from Julian, and the ground beneath me feels unsteady.

I wonder if he knows how little it takes to unravel me.

> Be there in twenty.

The second the message sends, I'm already moving, grabbing my keys and shoes. I pause by the small mirror by the door, tugging at my tie and loosening it. *Attempting to appear calm.* Running a hand through my hair, I take a deep breath.

It's useless.

Julian will see straight through me.

My chest is tight, and my hands are shaking, but for once, it's not fear. It's anticipation. Whatever this is, whatever they want, I'm walking straight into it.

CHAPTER TWENTY-TWO
THE COMFORT

Sophie

The warm water feels lush against my skin, and I stay in the shower for a few minutes longer than normal. After Julian and I finished half an hour ago, I started cramping and spotting—a sure sign that my period is coming a couple of days early. And now, as the water cascades down my sore lower abdomen, I know it's inevitable, and before long, I'll be doubled over with cramps.

Just as I turn the tap off, Julian lightly knocks on the bathroom door.

"I'm done, darling," I call out, grabbing a towel and wrapping it around myself.

He steps inside, still wearing his navy trousers and white Oxford shirt from earlier. "Kai is coming over."

I stop mid-step, my eyes going wide. "What? *Now*?"

He shrugs and holds his hands up. "Yes. It wasn't my

intention to invite him over, but it just sort of... happened."

I shift my weight to the other foot and grab another towel for my hair. "Awful timing. I just started my period."

Julian shrugs. "That's okay, pet. We can just hang out and watch a movie."

I frown. "Do you think he'll be disappointed?" I ask, scrunching my hair to get all of the water out.

"If he is, fuck him," Julian says, reaching into the bathroom drawer and handing me a tampon as he kisses my temple.

Marriage.

"I just don't really feel like getting dressed up," I admit, the gnawing sensation inside of me getting worse by the minute.

"Soph, tonight doesn't have to be anything we don't want it to be. You set the tone, okay?"

I nod, not bothering to close the door when I walk to the toilet and insert my tampon. Julian has seen me at my absolute worst, so putting a tampon in while he watches is nothing. When I'm finished, I wash my hands and walk into the bedroom. Julian follows me, and I see him grabbing my favorite period clothes—loose joggers and a baggy T-shirt.

I don't bother with a bra.

Out of the corner of my eye, I see Julian discard his clothes—in the laundry hamper, surprisingly—before grabbing a pair of loose shorts and a crewneck jumper.

Once we're both done changing, he goes into the

bathroom and grabs my hairbrush. It doesn't happen every time I shower, but when I'm not feeling well, he loves to brush my hair and take care of me. I give him a shy smile as I sit on the edge of the bed, and he takes his time brushing through my wet hair.

"Do you need your medicine?" he asks, referring to the spliffs I keep in the cigarette case.

I nod, lying back on the bed when he's done.

Just as he lights one for me, taking a drag before handing it to me, our phones buzz with the doorbell notification.

"I'll go," Julian says, giving me a once-over as he hesitates by the door. "I can send him home if you'd rather not have company."

I shake my head. "It's okay. This should help, and I want to see him."

His eyes bore into mine. "Are you sure?"

"I'm positive, babe. Go let him in. Maybe lower his expectations for the night, too, while you're at it."

He huffs a laugh. "Any man who doesn't want to spend quality time with your sexy arse—period or not—isn't worth our time."

Something warm cracks open in my chest. "I love you."

"Love you too, pet."

"Now go let our guest in before he thinks we're standing him up."

He nods once before leaving me alone in the bedroom. I continue taking drags of my spliff, wishing for the pain to lessen just once.

I let myself sink deeper into the mattress. This wasn't how tonight—or this weekend—was supposed to go, but the flare-ups always did tend to screw up my plans. Exhaling slowly, the spliff begins to soothe the sharpest edges of the pain, but it doesn't ease the disappointment snaking through me. I'm not sure what I hoped this weekend would bring, perhaps a chance for all three of us to be together after everything happened today between me and Kai. Instead, I'm stuck in bed, with my body betraying me yet again.

As I close my eyes and attempt to ride out the pain, I can't help but think back on how far I've come. For a long time, I hated my body for what happened every month, in the days before and after my period. I missed opportunities, had important plans canceled, and even had some hopes shattered. It all made me feel so utterly *broken*. Back when Julian and I were trying for a baby, I pushed myself through endless tests and treatments. I was convinced I could will my body into compliance. I had control issues, and this was the first time something was entirely out of my control. It was absolutely terrifying. But even after the diagnosis of endometriosis, even after knowing why nothing was working, I couldn't shake the feeling that I was failing.

At being a wife, a mother, a *woman*.

It took time and a lot of reflection, but I'm in a much better place now. Both Julian and I have let go of the pressure to conceive, and with it, so much of our stress has disappeared. I've stopped fighting my body. Some days, like today, are harder than others. But somehow,

I've made peace with what I can't control. We plan on adopting children one day, far in the future, when things have settled down, and I've had the surgery I need. But for now, I'm grateful for the life Julian and I share.

Especially now that we live here—now that we've finally let ourselves be happy, and found happiness away from the place that felt stifling for so long.

The bedroom door creaks open, pulling me from my thoughts. I open my eyes to see Kai and Julian stepping inside. Kai looks worried, like he rushed up here the moment Julian finished explaining.

"Hey." His voice is soft and kind. He's standing in the doorway with his hands shoved into his pockets, and my husband is lingering behind him.

"Hi," I manage, my voice quieter than I intend.

Glancing between them, I wonder what Julian told Kai. For a second, I think about apologizing, but then I stop myself. I don't need to apologize for this—Kai has already shown me he's the kind of person who understands. He made that very clear last month when he laid down in bed with me—platonically, of course—until I fell asleep.

"Are you okay?" Kai asks, tentatively stepping forward. I nod, even though I'm not really okay, and something in his expression softens. "It's okay. We don't have to do anything tonight. Maybe we can watch a movie or something?" he asks, looking at the TV Julian set up in here last weekend.

"I'll make popcorn," Julian says, clapping Kai on the shoulder.

Something passes between them—understanding, or solidarity—I can't quite place it. But it catches me off guard, and I feel a wave of gratitude for these men. They're here, and they're not making me feel like a burden.

That alone is a comfort.

Julian leaves Kai and me alone, and Kai steps closer, his movements careful. It reminds me of the last time he was here, how tentative he was, especially since I was naked in a bath. I almost laugh when I think of the look on his face when I stood up… the lazy way his eyes drank me in.

"Want me to sit with you for a bit?" he asks.

I nod again, unable to speak as another wave of pain works through me, radiating to my lower back. Closing my eyes, I attempt to breathe through it, but as always, it's relentless. The mattress shifts as Kai sits on the edge of it.

"I don't know what this feels like, but I can see how tough you are," he tells me, taking the old spliff and discarding it. His warm, calloused hand envelops mine, and his thumb swipes across the top of my palm.

I let out a shaky breath, his words sinking in despite the pain. "It doesn't feel like I'm tough right now," I say, wincing.

"You are," he says firmly. His hand around mine is grounding, and a second later, the pain starts to subside.

It never truly goes away, but the cramps come and go in waves, so I know I have a little bit of a reprieve.

"It's okay to feel like crap. We'll take care of you."

His reassurance settles whatever leftover doubt was left in me, and I feel myself sinking farther into the mattress. Closing my eyes, I squeeze Kai's hand when the next wave comes, and I come out of the haze of pain.

Julian reappears minutes later with a bowl of popcorn in one hand and, of course, a half-eaten Snickers bar in the other. He breaks off a piece, popping it into his mouth with the same reverence he'd give to caviar.

"Seriously? Snickers and popcorn?" Kai smirks as Julian flops onto the bed.

Julian shrugs. "It's the perfect combo. Gas station chocolate hits different, and if I can't have Cadbury..." He trails off, winking.

I laugh softly. The pain dulls just enough to let me appreciate how perfectly Julian straddles the line between decadence and simplicity.

"Julian might care about appearances but he lives like a slob at home," I tell Kai.

Julian snorts. "It's true. I have piles hidden all over the house. Perhaps one day I can show you."

"Never touch the piles," I warn Kai, smirking.

Kai laughs. "He's full of contradictions, isn't he? Splurging on expensive gym memberships but prefers to eat gas station snacks. I always said he was a menace."

Julian smirks, stretching out beside me with all the smugness of a man who knows exactly how ridiculous and adorable he is. Something knowing passes between the two of them at that word, though.

"I'm all about the high-low life, mate," he adds, reaching for another handful of popcorn. "Exclusive gym, but I'll drive two miles out of my way for a ninety-nine-cent hot dog."

Kai raises an eyebrow. "That's impressive. Living like royalty by day and a raccoon by night."

Julian grins. "Balance, Kai. It's the cornerstone of health and happiness."

I nudge him with my elbow, resting my head against his shoulder. "He says that, but you should've seen the meltdown when the gym juice bar was out of dragon fruit puree last week. The man practically rioted."

Kai chuckles, shaking his head. "Gas station chocolate and dragon fruit smoothies. You really are an enigma."

Julian winks at him, tossing a kernel of popcorn in the air and catching it in his mouth. "Keeps you guessing, doesn't it?"

Julian and Kai figure out what we're going to watch, and I curl up as a deep, relentless ache coils low in my abdomen, like barbed wire tightening with every breath, sharp and dull all at once.

Without another word, Julian hops off the bed and comes back with another spliff—passing it to Kai first. I watch as Kai takes a drag, passing it to me between his fingers.

"Here. This will help."

I take a slow drag, the smoke curling into my lungs as I close my eyes. The pain doesn't go away completely, but with Kai's hand holding mine and Julian close by, it feels a bit more bearable.

When I'm finished smoking a minute later, Kai takes the last drag and discards it.

"*Scream*?" Kai asks, flipping through the available channels. "Or *Scream 2*?"

I feel Julian gently moving me to the middle of the California king bed, and a few seconds later, Kai scoots into my left side while Julian takes my right side. I'm small, but they're two large, hulking men—and I'm sure it's not exactly comfortable for them.

"Relax," Julian says, adjusting me so that I'm on my left side. His body curls around mine, and as the horror movie starts playing, I feel Julian place the popcorn behind my bent knees so that Kai can access the bowl. When I look up, Kai is still lying on his back, but he turns and faces me.

As the opening scene of *Scream* flickers on the screen, I feel the warmth of their bodies anchoring me to the bed, like a protective cocoon against the ache in my abdomen. Julian's steady breath against the back of my neck soothes me, his arm draped over my waist just like he does every night, and Kai's presence on my other side feels surprisingly natural.

Like he belongs here.

He slips an arm beneath my jumper, laying it against my lower back. His palm is warm as he applies just enough pressure to ease the tension. His movements are quiet, fluid, like he's done this a hundred times before. The pain doesn't vanish, but the weight of his hand anchors me, dulling the sharpest edges.

Julian nudges him with the popcorn bowl, smirking.

"For someone who broods like it's a full-time job, you've got the bedside manner of a spa therapist."

Kai snorts softly but doesn't stop the slow, steady circles he's tracing against my spine. "I'm just efficient," he murmurs, as if this is no big deal.

But it feels like a big deal. The heat from his palm sinks deeper, grounding me in a way that's intimate but not overwhelming. I exhale, letting the tension unravel just a little more, grateful for the quiet comfort he offers without making a fuss.

"This is honestly rude, and quite frankly, unfair," I grumble from between them, pulling the blanket tighter around my waist. "You two get to lie here unbothered while I feel like my uterus is trying to murder me."

"Oh, believe me, pet. Watching you in pain is absolute torture. We're suffering, too."

"Nice try," I deadpan, tilting my head toward Kai. "And you? No snide comment?"

Kai smirks. "I know better than to argue with a woman's uterus."

"Smart man," Julian mutters through a mouthful of popcorn.

Kai reaches for the popcorn behind my knees, popping a kernel into his mouth with a quiet crunch before setting the bowl back. When he catches me watching him, he gives me a small, lopsided smile, his eyes soft in the dim light.

"You good?" he whispers, keeping his voice low so as not to disturb Julian.

I nod, unable to find the words to express what I feel in this moment. It's not just comfort, though that's part of it. It's the strange but welcome realization that this dynamic—the three of us tangled together on this oversized bed—feels like it's becoming *us*. Like maybe it's not just an experiment or a fleeting phase but something solid. Something real.

A few minutes go by, and the pain eases slightly, both from being high, and being warm and cozy between them.

"Oi, you're hogging the blanket," Julian mutters, tugging at the fabric draped over Kai's shoulder.

"It's not my fault you didn't grab a second one."

I snort, burying my face into Kai's chest. "I'm literally right here. Can we share, please?"

Julian tugs the blanket up dramatically, cocooning me so tightly that Kai's left out in the cold. Kai groans in protest, and Julian grins against my hair.

"Guess it's survival of the fittest, mate."

I muffle my laughter as Kai leans over, tossing half the blanket back over himself without missing a beat.

"I'm not above stealing from you," Kai says, smirking. "Share custody or I'm claiming the popcorn."

Their banter is familiar now, and it comforts me. For so long, I could tell Julian still held a grudge toward Kai for what happened between them. But now, they seem to have settled back into being friends. It came so easily, and a small part of me wonders what it would've been like to know them back then.

The thought of it makes my eyes begin to droop, and

my breathing becomes more even as I feel more drowsy by the minute.

"Try to sleep, little dove," Kai says, his voice a gentle murmur. "We'll be here all night if you need us."

I close my eyes, letting his words settle over me like a blanket. The pain still lingers, but it doesn't feel as overwhelming anymore now. Not with Julian's steady heartbeat against my back and Kai's warm gaze holding me steady.

For the first time in a long time, I feel a quiet sense of belonging, as if this—being here with them—might just be everything I'll ever need in this life.

CHAPTER TWENTY-THREE
THE BEGINNING

JULIAN

I wake up feeling warm, and as I slowly come back into my body, I can feel Sophie's back against my chest. Sighing contentedly, I reach around and wrap my arm around her—but it settles on top of another arm.

My eyes fly open, and I sit up quickly as I take in the scene before me.

Sophie is still asleep... and Kai is cuddling her front side.

Rubbing my eyes, last night comes back into focus. There was *Scream*. And then *Scream 2* and *Scream 3*. Kai and I had laughed and thrown popcorn at the TV a few times when the characters were being bloody pathetic, and we'd even talked long after the third movie had ended—all with Sophie asleep between us. It was nice. It almost felt like old times, with him teasing me about my disorganized habits, and me teasing him about things like naming his fennec fox 'Willy'. Kai had a pet sitter on call, and once he got Willy sorted, he told me all about the other pets his brothers had.

I learned more about how he'd grown closer to Orion in the past couple of years, and how he'd gone to seminary school, followed by graduate school for religion, just for fun. I'd asked him about his faith, and while he was a bit tight-lipped at first, he'd opened up and admitted that there were aspects of Christianity he didn't recognize anymore. That he still believed, but he had grown to resent the hatred some people spewed in the name of religion.

All in all, it was enlightening. I found myself mesmerized by the way he spoke so fondly of his students and his family, while also managing to look so damn sexy laying in my bed. When Sophie had whimpered in her sleep, he'd curled around her body, no questions asked, and had resumed his conversation with me.

Sophie has always been my greatest achievement. I know I'm a lucky fucking bastard because she married me. And while our marriage was premeditated by our parents in a way that only the aristocracy can understand, I couldn't help but fall for her at first sight. I treasure her, and I know the bond we share is rare. I *know* that no matter what, she and I were always destined to be together forever.

And now?

Now, I'm sitting here watching Kai—beautiful,

magnetic, infuriating Kai—hold Sophie with a tenderness I didn't think anyone besides me was capable of. My mind twists around the idea of them, instinctively resisting, like a knee-jerk reaction I can't control. Because letting someone else into this sacred space—*our* space—shouldn't feel like this.

It shouldn't feel *right*.

But it does.

Besides their breathing, the room is quiet, the kind of quiet that feels earned after a good night's rest. Sophie is tucked between Kai and me, her body relaxed in the deep, unguarded way she only ever achieves when she feels truly safe.

From where I lie, I can see the way the early morning sunlight plays across their features. Sophie's hair fans out across the pillow, and Kai's cheek rests against it like he's drawn to her scent, even in his sleep. I see his arm tighten around her just slightly, as if to reassure himself she's still in his arms.

I sling my arm over her shoulder, but my focus is fixed on Kai.

Any ordinary man should hate the way he's holding her. I should feel threatened, jealous, *something*. Right? But instead, there's only a strange sense of calm settling over me as I watch them. His face shifts, pressing closer to Sophie's hair, and the corner of my mouth quirks up into a smile despite myself. I've never known anyone besides me who could hold her like that, like she's something fragile and infinite all at once.

It hits me, suddenly, how much I trust him. Not

entirely, not yet, but enough. Enough to let him in, enough to let him stay.

I never thought I'd see this. Never thought I'd *want* to.

Least of all with the man who once broke my heart.

The thought twists in my chest, unfamiliar and unnerving, but it's there.

Sophie stirs between us, shifting slightly until her hand lands on Kai's chest, her fingers curling there as if to anchor herself to him. I watch the way his body instinctively adjusts, his breathing syncing with hers in a way I know well from years of holding her in my sleep.

And then, his eyes blink open.

It takes him a second to focus, to realize where he is. When his gaze meets mine over Sophie's head, he freezes for a fraction of a second. But there's no tension, no awkward scramble to explain himself. Recognition, and perhaps acceptance, flash over his expression. He lifts his head slightly, keeping his hand steady on her waist.

"You okay?" he asks, his voice scratchy with sleep.

The question is simple enough, but there's a weight behind it that I can't quite articulate, a genuine concern that catches me off guard for a second. I realize then that until last night, I've been giving him a pretty hard time with everything—between what happened seventeen years ago, to the stunt I pulled at the gym last weekend. And despite telling him that we were open to things with him, it must feel strange to enter an established marriage.

Especially because he's still technically in the closet.

I'm not an arsehole, but I can be petty.

And because of that, I decide that *I'm* the one who's going to need to make the next move here.

"Yeah. You?"

Kai nods, and his hand twitches on Sophie's side. "Me too."

His gaze moves to her, his expression softening in a way that makes everything inside of me tighten. He's looking at her like he can't quite believe he's *allowed* to touch her outside of a scene. In fact, the only time I've seen him *not* gentle was during the scene with her.

I observe the way he rubs her lower back in small circles, like it's second nature. He's quiet about it, not fishing for praise. He's just... doing it.

He cares about her.

I suppose I could resent him for that... but instead, I'm reminded that I'm not the only one who can cherish her the way she deserves. And maybe that's not a bad thing.

"You're careful with her," I tell him, the words coming out gruffer than I intend them to.

Kai pauses for a few seconds before answering. "Of course I am. She deserves that."

Looking down at Sophie, I can see how she's still clutching his shirt. Her face is serene in her sleep.

"She does," I agree, my voice barely above a whisper.

Kai doesn't say anything else. His eyes find mine once more, and in that quiet exchange, I feel the first tentative threads of understanding begin to take shape.

I sigh, settling back against my pillow. Adjusting my

arm, my fingers brush lightly against Kai's, and he doesn't pull away. Instead, he watches me with something akin to amusement, or perhaps something else.

"Never in a million years did I think..." he starts, swallowing before looking down at Sophie. "This is all still really new to me. I've never..."

"You never experimented with a guy?" I ask.

His eyes glint with mirthfulness. "Not until very recently."

It feels like a punch to the gut, and as my jaw hardens, I can't help but narrow my eyes. "Oh? Do tell."

He huffs a laugh. "You sound jealous."

"I am."

Kai's gray eyes bore into mine, and it feels like someone's sucked all the air out of my lungs. His teasing smile turns quieter, more vulnerable.

"You don't need to be jealous. It wasn't like... this," he adds, looking back down at Sophie.

"Like what?" I ask. My pulse is beating erratically, and my chest feels tight. I see him shrug.

"Like... this. Like it matters. This matters to me. Or it's beginning to, at least."

The words land heavy and warm, tangling with the jealousy still bubbling beneath the surface of my skin. For the first time in a long time, I don't know what to say, so I just hold eye contact as he sighs, gearing up to continue speaking. Looking away, he opens his mouth.

"I'm sort of figuring all this out as I go. And it doesn't help that every time you look at me, it's as if you want to kiss me and strangle me at the same time. It's fucking unnerving," he adds, his smile faint but unmistakably happy.

I laugh, and Sophie begins to stir. "Well, you are infuriating sometimes."

His eyes narrow ever so slightly. "And yet... you're still here."

I swallow as the silence stretches between us, and everything between us feels taut and electric. Sophie mumbles something unintelligible, breaking the spell. Kai looks away first, his hand brushing against mine again, deliberately this time.

"We've got time to figure it out, I guess," I murmur softly.

"Figure what out?" Sophie asks, stirring as she opens her eyes and looks right at me.

"How are you feeling?" Kai asks, and she turns to face him.

"Better. Much better." She slowly extricates herself and stretches, yawning as she scoots to the edge of the bed. "Be right back. I desperately need a wee."

Kai laughs as she walks to the en suite, and suddenly it's just the two of us laying together in bed.

My mind is spinning as I scramble for what to say.

It's not like he's obligated to stay, but he did, and now I sort of feel like I should make him breakfast or something.

"How are your baking skills?" I ask him, positioning myself on my side with my face propped in my hand.

Kai's lips twitch, and I can't help but let my eyes flick over his face unabashedly.

"They're decent," he answers, eyes bright as he smiles.

I can't help but smile back. "All right. Let's go make some cinnamon rolls."

"Cinnamon rolls?" he asks, and we both climb out of bed on opposite ends.

I don't miss the way he has to adjust himself—I have to do the same.

"They're Sophie's favorite," I explain. "In fact, I should probably give you a list of things she loves—English breakfast tea with a splash of milk and two sugars. She's rarely in a bad mood, but when she is, a cup of tea and a couple of biscuits," I start, making a kissing sound with my lips. We both walk down the stairs together. "Cinnamon rolls, as previously stated. She'll always order the steak at a restaurant, but she'll also want to try what you order, so be prepared for that. Proper chips—you call them fries here—are the cure-all for every one of her ailments. You can take the Brit out of England, but you can't take England out of the Brit, I'm afraid."

Kai laughs as we walk into the kitchen. "I appreciate the notes."

As I head to the refrigerator, I notice him lingering behind the island, his hands braced against the counter like he's grounding himself. His eyes track me, quiet but thoughtful, the way they used to when we were kids and he wasn't sure how to step into my world.

"What are you doing? Grab a bowl. It's not like you don't know where everything is," I say over my shoulder.

Kai had spent the better part of a day helping Sophie and me unpack our kitchen things. He'd been so good-natured about her indecisiveness, and at the time, I saw his adoration of her as good humor.

Now I know better.

However, the way he stays put makes me pause.

Kai shifts his weight, gaze flicking to mine. "I get the feeling I'll need to know a lot about Sophie... but what about you?"

The question throws me off, but I school my expression quickly, shrugging lightly as I pull out the butter and eggs. "Me?"

He shrugs, offering a small smile. "Yeah. I used to know everything about you, Julian. But now... I don't know. Feels like there's a lot I missed."

The weight of that hits me harder than I expect. He's right. He did know me—back when things were simpler, before seventeen years of silence settled between us. It's strange how much can change, how much can stay the same.

I crack the eggs into the bowl, the sound sharp in the quiet. "I guess I've grown up a little."

Kai snorts softly. "A little. But you're still you, right?"

I glance up at him, one brow arching. "What exactly does that mean?"

His smile widens, but there's something softer in his eyes. "Loud. Confident. Everyone's favorite person at the party." He pauses, gaze dipping for a second. "I was always a little jealous of that."

I let out a low laugh, shaking my head. "You didn't need to be. I would've traded half those parties to sit in that tiny dorm room, listening to terrible music and pretending we had life figured out."

Kai's eyes flick up, surprised, like he didn't expect me to remember things that small. But I do. I always have.

"You still haven't answered the question, though," he points out, leaning against the counter.

I sigh, stirring the eggs. "Fine. Art is a big thing for me. I consult now, as you know, but I collect too. I like nice things—good wine, tailored suits. Keeps me grounded... or distracts me. Depends on the day." I shoot him a wry grin. "Cooking's been a more recent thing. It helps quiet my brain. I've tried a hundred different hobbies over the years, but nothing ever sticks for long. The ADHD hasn't changed much."

Kai chuckles. "I remember that. You dragged me through half of your weird hobbies."

"Lucky you." I smirk.

"Do you remember that book binding class you made me take with you? It was fucking horrible," he chimes in.

I laugh. "I do."

"What else?"

I cock my head. "Working out helps too. Drinking. Partying. Causing trouble when I'm bored—some things never change."

Kai's gaze softens, and for a moment, we're not standing in my kitchen now—we're seventeen again, and he's looking at me the same way he used to, like he's memorizing me all over again.

"I missed this," he says quietly.

My chest tightens, but I force a grin to break the tension. "Careful, Kai. You might start to like me again."

"Too late," he mutters, grabbing a bowl and stepping beside me. His hand brushes softly against my lower back.

The moment lingers, familiar but heavy with something new, and this time, there's no hesitation as he moves closer to me—like he belongs there, even after all this time. We work in silence with the dough, and Kai is a fantastic sous-chef. I can tell my messy enthusiasm irritates him, though, because he trails behind me and wipes up the various messes I seem to create everywhere.

He also takes the towel slung over my shoulder and folds it perfectly, setting it down next to the bowl on the counter without even realizing he's doing it.

Twenty minutes into letting the dough rise, Sophie comes down the stairs wearing leggings and a cropped sweatshirt. Her hair is still damp—she must've taken a shower—and she looks fresh-faced and rested.

I open my arms instinctively, pulling her into a tight hug as I close my eyes and inhale the fresh citrusy smell of her shampoo. My eyes snap up to find Kai watching us with trepidation.

I know he still feels like an outsider, and I don't know how to fix that.

"You okay?" he asks her, both hands flat on the island as he looks at her with a furrowed brow.

"I'm good," she says, pulling away from me and walking over to him. She places a hand on his shoulder and squeezes once.

"Absolutely famished, though." Peeking over at the rising dough, she shoots me a furtive look. "Is that what I think it is?"

"It is. Kai helped me."

She looks over at him and gives him a shy smile. "Thanks for staying the night. I don't think I've slept that well in... years."

Kai looks at me, as if he's making sure her words aren't affecting me negatively. But I can't deny that I slept like a baby, too.

"Same," I say quickly, walking over to Sophie and placing an arm around her waist. If he's feeling like an outsider, I'm going to need to make more of an effort to include him. And that means not hiding my feelings, not shying away from saying what I'm thinking. "What are your plans today?"

Kai looks at Sophie, who looks at me. I smile down at her, and her eyes glitter with amusement.

"I don't have plans. I can let Willy's sitter know I'll be home later."

"Willy's more spoiled than I am. I didn't know that was possible," I say offhand, smirking.

Sophie snorts as she shifts her weight, putting one hand on her hip as she looks at Kai. "Well, now you do have plans. With us."

Kai looks between us again, nodding once before crossing his arms. "Okay. And what would these plans entail?"

Smirking, I look down at Sophie. "Well, usually we just hang out and watch movies, in case she gets another flare, so it won't be terribly exciting or anything—"

"Count me in," he says, walking over to the kettle. "Tea?"

CHAPTER TWENTY-FOUR
THE INSECURITY

MALAKAI

"Let me tell you, a paddle in the right hands is practically a truth serum."

I smirk as I sip my whiskey. Orion is recounting some salacious detail between him and Layla, our stepsister and his girlfriend. Letting the whiskey settle against my tongue, I savor the burn before swallowing.

It's been a week since I spent the night at Ashford Palace, and since then, I haven't seen Julian or Sophie. It's not for lack of trying—Sophie was busy getting the keys to the retail space, and Julian was out of town until returning late last night. We'd all been texting, and we had plans to hang out tomorrow night at their house. No pressure, but I knew what I wanted to happen.

Orion leans back in his chair, a smug glint in his eye.

Miles, who is seated across from us, snorts as he sips his whiskey. "Paddling? I dunno, I don't really understand the whole punishment thing. I'd rather just skip to the fun part," he adds, swirling his drink idly as his lips curve into a wry smile.

"That *is* the fun part," Orion says, rolling his eyes. "The buildup, the tension, the sweet satisfaction of breaking her resolve…"

"That's all you, bro. I don't need Stella to beg for it," he adds, his lips form a cocky grin.

Chase huffs a laugh next to me, nearly choking on his red wine. "That's a shame. You don't know what you're missing," he adds, wiggling his brows at Orion as they high-five each other.

Liam clears his throat from his place at the end of the table. "You know, I think I'm with Miles on this one. I don't like punishment. Pleasure can be just as potent as pain if you know what you're doing. No rules or games. Just pure, unfiltered indulgence." He takes a swig of his beer as he leans back.

"Is that what you tell yourself?" Orion asks, his smirk sharpening.

I chuckle under my breath, setting my glass on the table in front of me. "I think we all know that Liam's idea of control is letting Zoe make him think he's in control."

Liam chuckles, completely unbothered as the eldest brother. He's used to our teasing and camaraderie.

"Hey, it's worked pretty well for me so far."

"Amateurs," Orion mutters, sharing *a look* with

Chase. Miles lifts his glass to Liam and they clink their drinks together in a mock toast.

After that, the banter flows easily. Chase and his wife, Juliet, are in town for the week, visiting from Northern California. We always attempt to get together often, and I see Miles, Liam, and Orion often enough. They all live in Crestwood, like me. But whenever Chase is here, we try to make more of an effort to spend time as brothers. Tonight, we're at one of Orion's bars in downtown Crestwood.

As per usual, I stay quiet and observe as my brothers continue discussing every facet of their respective kinks.

"What about Kai?" Chase asks. "He's been awfully quiet over there. Where do you land on the pain versus pleasure spectrum?"

Both, I think.

I glance over at Orion—the only brother who knows what and who I'm into, because he's seen me around Inferno. It's not that I don't *want* to tell them. Hell, they're my brothers, and out of everyone, they'd understand more than anyone. But for me, kink is so personal and something I've always held close to my heart. Not out of shame, but because it feels like a language only I know how to speak. Especially the religious aspects... only someone *in* the church could understand.

And my brothers are most definitely not religious.

They would never judge me, but I know that sharing would mean unraveling something that's always been mine. It's tied to the church, and to *that* part of my life—something I've always held at arm's length from them.

And though I've evolved from a pious eighteen-year-old reciting scripture to a mid-thirties pastor who got off on the same aspects that once made me kneel before an altar, it's still the one thing I have for myself.

Being a middle brother meant I didn't get a lot of things to myself.

In a large family like ours, where every action and choice was scrutinized by our father, it was hard to find something that belonged solely to me.

My kink is a quiet sanctuary for whenever the world gets too loud. I don't intend to keep it hidden, but I suppose I want to preserve the intimacy of it. Being a Dominant anchors me. Especially when the rest of my life sort of feels like it's spinning out of control—especially in the last few weeks.

I catch Orion's subtle nod, a silent reassurance that he gets it, and that he won't say anything.

"What about me?" I ask, leaning back and pinning my younger brother with a hard look.

Chase grins, the fucker. It's as if he expects some sort of revelation to fall from my lips, but instead I let the silence stretch. *Might as well make him squirm.*

"There's not much to tell," I say quickly.

"Not much?" he goads, eyes twinkling.

"I mean, I guess there's one thing," I say slowly, reaching for my whiskey.

Looking down at the amber liquid, I clear my throat. I haven't come out to them as bisexual, because I truly didn't know I was—or couldn't admit I was—until very recently. But I told myself the first step would be saying it out loud, and my brothers are the first people I'd tell anyway. I know, without a doubt, I already have their support.

I can feel the eyes of all of my brothers on me, and I guess it's now or never, right?

"Well?" Miles asks, frowning.

Though, when my eyes dart over to my older brother, he winks at me, as if he already knows. And being the most observant brother, it's possible he does.

"Don't get too excited. It's not as sordid as your stories," I warn, glaring at Chase. Exhaling slowly, I set my glass down without taking a sip. "I've been spending time with Julian and Sophie."

When I glance around the table, I realize they're all waiting. *Expectant.* My lips twitch as I attempt to suppress a laugh.

"By spending time, I mean..." I rub the back of my neck, suddenly uncomfortable with labeling whatever it is the three of us are doing together.

"Go on," Chase says, daring me to continue.

"It's complicated," I admit, choosing my words carefully. "It started with me helping around the house, and then I realized I had feelings for both of them. I like being around them. And now that Julian's forgiven me for kissing him all those years ago—"

"I knew it," Liam says quickly, slapping the table. He points at Miles. "You owe me twenty bucks."

I look between my older brothers. "You took bets?" I growl, glaring at them.

"I'm just insulted I wasn't involved," Orion mutters, looking at Chase. They both scoff.

"You were both minors at the time," Liam says defensively, his smile wide. "And you were, like, twelve," he adds, glancing at Orion. "It was a bet between adults."

"Don't feel too bad," Miles says, chuckling. "Zoe wasn't even born yet when we made the bet."

Liam lets out a long, frustrated breath. "I suppose I walked into that one, didn't I?"

As much as I want to be annoyed, I can't help but laugh at Miles making fun of Liam's age gap with his wife.

"So when you say Julian and Sophie... do you mean *both* of them?" Liam asks, his voice curious, but not judgmental. If there's one thing he's good at, it's not judging us.

I nod. "Both of them." Taking a deep breath, I shrug. "I'm bisexual. And I think I always have been without realizing it. Or, without wanting to say it out loud."

My brothers are quiet as they take in the information, and for a fraction of a second, I panic. After all, as far as I know, they're all straight. I've always felt a bit like an outsider, thanks to my unusual job, and this information could possibly only drive that wedge between us deeper. The table is quiet for a beat, and then Miles is the first to speak, a slow grin spreading across his face.

"So, you're into them as a couple? How, exactly, does that work?"

I roll my eyes. "Exactly how it would work with a

single person. We hang out. We do... other things," I add, thinking of Sophie on the pool deck last week.

"How did it happen?" Chase asks, leaning forward. "Like... did they approach you?"

I look between all of my brothers. "No comment about me being bi?"

They all give me blank stares, all of them shaking their head, and I huff a laugh as my nerves dissolve into nothing. Of course they wouldn't care. I might as well have told them my hair was brown.

"Sort of," I say slowly. "But for the most part, it just happened. None of us expected nor sought it out. Who knows where it'll go, but..." I take a sip of my whiskey, swallowing my second drink clear down before continuing. "I'm excited about the possibilities."

Liam holds his beer up. "I think I speak for all of us when I say we're all dying to know how this plays out."

We all laugh, and I relax back into my seat. "No pressure or anything," I say dryly.

The conversation shifts after that, and the heavy weight of my confession dissipates as my brothers revert back to their usual joking and storytelling.

I know my brothers, though—they'll circle back to this.

Probably sooner than I'd like.

Miles, especially. He loves to meddle.

Truthfully, though, I don't mind. We lost our father earlier this year, and our mother passed away almost a decade ago. We're all we have left of family, and I'm grateful we've only gotten closer over the last few years in the midst of them all settling down with their significant others.

Just after ten, I'm on my fourth drink and feeling a bit more willing to be open. Liam and Miles leave, and shortly after, Juliet comes into the bar to pick Chase up, nuzzling into his chest as they walk out together. I miss having them close, but I also know they're happy up north.

Orion swirls the sparkling water in his glass, watching me with interest before drinking the rest of it. It's just the two of us now, and though I know I should get home soon, I'm also looking forward to being completely open with him since he knows the situation.

"So," he says, setting his empty glass down. "Feel better after your confession?"

I shrug, leaning back in the booth. "Yeah. But I didn't expect you guys to give me a hard time about it."

Orion is quiet for a few seconds. "Is Sophie still a hotwife? You know, now that you're involved?"

It takes a second for his words to sink in. "I suppose not. I mean... we're not exclusive, but I don't think they'd do anything like that without asking me how I felt about it."

Nodding, Orion gives me a pointed look. "And how do you feel about it? About her sleeping with other men?"

My jaw rolls, and I look down at my clasped hands as I imagine Sophie and Julian with another man involved. Even though I know Julian never got physical with them, it still irks me for some reason.

It makes me feel jealous.

She's mine, and so is he.

"Have you done any research? Julian and Sophie are what we call a stag and vixen in the lifestyle. It's worth looking into. They have a reputation."

"Are you warning me or just telling me to be cautious?" I ask, my brows knitting together. If anyone was going to educate me, it would be Orion. He's a popular kink educator, so I know his advice is sound.

"Mostly just to be cautious. In their circles, you're an outsider—what we refer to as a unicorn. With regards to polyamory, a unicorn is a person who is invited into a relationship with an existing couple. It can be problematic because the couple can make demands but the unicorn can't do anything that could cause any inconvenience for the couple. In other instances, a unicorn is brought in to patch any problems the couple might have."

My face is hot as I take a sip of the water I haven't touched all night.

"A unicorn," I repeat under my breath, rolling the word around like it doesn't quite fit.

I hadn't thought about it like that. Not until now. Orion's not wrong—Julian and Sophie were established long before I ever came back into their lives. I'm the addition, the extra... the guest.

Is that what I am to them? Briefly closing my eyes, Julian's words from the gym come back to me.

How does it feel to be used? Payback's a bitch, isn't it?

Without realizing it, Orion has somehow exposed my

deepest insecurity about all of this. Because at the end of the day, they *are* an established couple. They're married, and I'm an outsider.

Just like with my family.

Just like at my job.

I've always been someone on the outside, looking in, and I suppose I just have to hope that Julian's apology and conviction last weekend about bringing me into their relationship was real.

Because it was.

I felt it.

I just can't shake the feeling that at the end of the day, I'll be the one left standing alone.

"You know, some unicorns end up taking over the castle. Don't sell yourself short, Kai. They wouldn't have invited you in if they didn't already want more. It takes work from all parties."

"I appreciate the cautionary advice," I tell Orion, giving him a small smile.

"And just so you don't think I'm trying to be negative, I really like them. Sophie and Julian. I hope it all works out for the three of you."

"Thanks, little brother," I say, giving him a fist bump.

"You okay to walk home?" he asks, standing. "I told Layla I'd meet her at Inferno."

I nod. "Yeah, I'll be fine. But I don't think I'm going home."

We walk out together, and I wave goodbye to him as a warm breeze settles through the air. It's crackling with energy, or maybe it's just me and my nerves.

Pulling my phone out, I send a text to Sophie.

I know I shouldn't need their reassurance. I tell myself I'm fine either way.

But I also know I won't believe it until I hear Sophie's voice.

> Hey, can I come over?

CHAPTER TWENTY-FIVE
THE BOOTY CALL

Sophie

> MALAKAI
> Hey, can I come over?

I stare at my phone as a sly smile curves on my lips. Looking over at Julian, I hand him my phone with the text showing on the screen. Julian leans over on the couch, pausing the foot rub he's giving me, and smirks.

"What do you want to do, babe?" he asks, running a hand along my bare calf.

It's the first night we've had together in almost a week. Julian is reading some art magazine, and I'm curled up with my newest romance book in paperback. This one is interesting, though, because the heroine falls in love with three men, not just one. Stella had pitched it to me as something called *why choose,* which is a genre entirely new to me.

Setting my book down, I pull my lower lip between my teeth. "I don't know. On the one hand, if I say I want to see him, then we don't get a night together. But, on the other hand... I really want to see him. And that makes me feel guilty."

Julian sighs, setting his magazine down on the coffee table and pulling me onto his lap. "Soph, if we're really going to do this with him in earnest, then perhaps we should stop thinking about *us* versus *him.* If you want to see him, don't feel guilty for admitting it. That's not how I want this dynamic to work, you know? We should be open, communicate, and let go of what we should be feeling. Because this whole thing isn't traditional anyway, so fuck what anyone thinks, right? Plus, I'm not going anywhere. Nothing is being *taken away.* Kai just adds to the dynamic."

I grin as I nuzzle into his chest. He always knows exactly what to say.

"You're right. And I do want to see him."

I feel Julian smile as he kisses the side of my head. "I want to see him, too."

He hands me my phone, and I type out a quick response.

> Of course. We're both here. :)

Climbing off Julian's lap, I look down at my leggings

and tank top. My hair is in a loose ponytail, and I don't have a lick of makeup on my face.

"Should I change?" I ask Julian, who's wearing trousers and a soft, light gray jumper.

He shakes his head. "You always look great, pet."

My phone buzzes.

> **MALAKAI**
> Okay, just grabbed a taxi. Be there in ten.

Excitement courses through me, and I do my best to tidy up the living room as Julian helps. We'd ordered sushi earlier, so I recycle the containers and wipe the countertops off.

"Feels a bit like a first date," Julian says, opening the bin for me to dispose of the rest of the rubbish lying around.

I huff a laugh as I finish washing my hands. "Feels a bit like a booty call to me."

My husband walks over to me, pressing his chest to my back. His hands slide around my waist, lips brushing against my ear.

"Well, maybe it's both. But either way, I'm not complaining."

Shivers work down my spine as my phone buzzes, and when I look down, I see my doorbell app notifying us that Kai is here.

"I'll get the door," Julian says, walking away.

I watch him go, barefoot and casual, and... happy. There's been a noticeable lightness to him these past few weeks, like something heavy has shifted. And I know exactly when it started.

It's not just Kai's company that's made the difference. It's also everything he's been part of. For example, when I picked up the shop keys on Tuesday, I should've felt overwhelmed. I mean... what expertise did I have to run a bookstore? However, instead of freaking out, I felt almost excited—because I wasn't doing it alone. Kai had agreed to help with the renovations without hesitation, and knowing he'd be there to help me made the whole process feel a lot less daunting.

Perhaps that's why I've been smiling more, too. It's not just about the shop or the repairs—it's him.

As Julian opens the door, I can hear Kai's low voice greeting him. The idea of him coming over makes me feel like I've been dipped into a warm bath, and I lean against the kitchen counter for a moment, giving myself a minute to let it all sink in.

The thought of the shop finally coming together fills me with a sense of pride, sure, but it's the memory of how Kai had immediately volunteered to help with the shop that warms me from the inside.

The memory of waking up between them, and how we spent all day together watching movies and cuddling up on the couch. It's so *easy* with him. He so seamlessly fits into our life that it's starting to feel like he was always here.

And for the first time in a long time, everything feels... right. Not perfect, but right. Like the puzzle pieces of my life are finally starting to click into place.

For a month or two, when we first moved here, I worried we'd made the wrong decision. I thought maybe we'd just run from our problems, only to end up trapped by the same stifling societal expectations.

But lately... it feels different.

Now, it feels like we were meant to be here.

Like we've finally started to build something that feels like home.

I wipe my hands on a dish towel, glancing down the hall where Julian disappeared, and a small smile tugs at my lips as the two men walk into the kitchen. Kai is immediately commanding in his leather jacket and jeans, and as he shrugs it off, I let my eyes take in the muscles contracting along his arms as he sets the jacket over one of the barstools, revealing a tight black T-shirt.

"Hi," he says, his eyes a bit wild as they search my face.

"Hi," I answer, crossing my arms as I chew on my lower lip to keep from smiling.

He looks like he rushed here, his face is red with exertion, and his hair is messier than normal. Plus, he's breathing heavily.

"I would offer you a drink, but I can smell the whiskey from here," Julian says, coming to stand behind Kai.

Cocking my head, I place my hands behind me on the countertop as a smile breaks free on my face. He walks over to me. "Malakai Ravage, is this a booty call? Did you get drunk and—"

Before I can finish my sentence, one of his hands fists the back of my hair as he smashes his lips against mine.

Everything explodes inside of me, and a searing, white-hot energy flares to life, dropping heavily from my core to between my legs. He tastes like whiskey and something minty, and the combination has impatience stirring through me. I moan as my hands fly up to his face, and I instinctively pull him closer. He cages me in, taking the lead and pressing me against the counter. As his tongue swirls with mine, my body becomes frenzied for him.

"Kai," I whisper, letting my head fall back as his lips trail fiery kisses along my jaw, and down my neck.

Kai's lips are still searing against mine when I feel Julian behind him, his presence looming closer. Kai's grip tightens in my hair, and for a second, I forget to breathe. The heat between us spikes, but before Kai can deepen the kiss, Julian's hand slips between us—flat against Kai's chest.

"Slow down," Julian murmurs, almost lazily. His fingers splay wider, pressing Kai back with a deliberate ease. "Let's not get ahead of ourselves."

Kai's eyes flash with something—frustration, maybe—but Julian isn't fazed. His hand doesn't move, even as Kai shifts like he wants to argue.

"I thought this was a booty call," Kai mutters, though his grip in my hair loosens.

Julian smirks. "It is. But you know the rules."

I swallow hard, watching as Julian lets his fingers trail down the center of Kai's chest, light, teasing. Kai stiffens slightly, though I catch the gleam of desire in his eyes.

"And what rule is that?" Kai asks, his voice rougher now.

Julian leans in, his breath warm against Kai's ear. "I lead. You follow."

The words land heavy between them, and something shifts in the air. Julian isn't just playing with him—he's checking to make sure Kai is truly comfortable with the rules we've all set together. I can feel the tension ripple through Kai's frame, but he doesn't pull away.

Kai's eyes darken, but there's a flash of restraint behind them, like he's holding himself back. I've seen him dominant and in control, but this... watching him struggle beneath Julian's quiet authority, sends heat pooling low in my belly. It's intoxicating, like standing too close to the edge of a cliff, half terrified and half thrilled by the idea of falling.

Julian notices it too. His eyes glint with something knowing.

"She likes watching you squirm," Julian murmurs, his gaze flicking to me briefly.

Kai's lips curl, his chest rising and falling with measured breaths. "I'm not squirming."

Julian arches a brow. "Not yet."

Kai's jaw tightens beneath Julian's hand, his breathing heavier now, measured but on the verge of something slipping. I can see the muscles in his neck flex, the barely contained hunger vibrating beneath his skin.

For a moment, he looks like he's going to challenge Julian, to push back.

I shift slightly, stepping back just enough to give them space, my back pressing against the cool edge of the counter. The heat between them feels palpable, like something I shouldn't be intruding on but can't look away from.

Julian's gaze flicks toward me, his eyes dark with something unreadable, before returning to Kai.

The pause stretches too long.

Then Julian tilts his head slightly, almost in invitation, and something in Kai breaks.

I watch as Kai's fingers curl at his sides, tension rippling through his frame, before Julian seizes his mouth with a kiss that brooks no argument. For a second, Kai matches him, a clash of heat and dominance, but then Julian shoves him back against the refrigerator.

The metal thuds faintly under the impact.

Kai growls, and it's a low and feral sound. Pulling his head back, he presses against Julian's chest in order to regain the upper hand, but it's no use. Julian won't give in.

He never does.

I'm mesmerized and I can't look away. It's the first time I've seen them together like this, and the energy between them is like an alpha showdown playing out in front of me like a movie. I'm caught between wanting to intervene and not wanting to interrupt. My breathing turns ragged as I watch, waiting for the friction between them to reach a breaking point.

"Are you enjoying the show, Soph?" Julian mutters suddenly, his voice even despite Kai testing him. His eyes flick to mine, catching me in place. "He's still got energy to burn."

Kai snaps his head to me at that, and as his lips pull into a sharp, dangerous smirk, I swallow. Julian releases him, stepping aside, and I barely have time to take a breath before Kai's focus locks on me. In two strides, he's on me, his hands gripping my waist and pulling me into him. I can feel how hard he is, and I resist the urge to shift my hips against him.

"Now it's your turn," Kai says, his voice rough, like a command wrapped in velvet.

He kisses me again, and this time it leaves no room for questions or hesitation. It only takes and takes and *takes*. His hands slide to my hips, pulling me flush against him, and I melt completely.

Behind him, Julian chuckles. "That's it, pet," he says, his voice carrying a note of indulgence. "Don't hold back for me. I'm enjoying the view."

But I barely register the words, because Kai is already working my tank top off. I hold my arms up, and he pulls it over my head, along with my bra. He pulls away and leads me into the next room by taking my hand.

The dining room.

I'm lost in the way he's looking at me, and the large table stands waiting in the center of the room, its polished surface gleaming faintly under the low lights.

He pauses for a second, looking over his shoulder at

Julian, who is hovering by the door. "Are you staying there?"

Julian cocks his head. "For now." His gaze shifts lazily to me. "You seem to have this under control."

Kai shifts his attention back to me. "Good."

He kneels and peels my leggings off, followed quickly by my knickers. This is nothing like last time, I hardly have time to wrap my mind around what's happening before he makes his next move. Last time, we were careful—deliberate and slow while we learned about each other's bodies.

Tonight feels more frenetic, like a grenade ready to detonate.

He presses me against the edge of the table, and the cool wood hits the backs of my thighs. I shiver as he steps closer, his body crowding mine. Tilting my chin up, his thumb brushes my lower lip slowly.

"I've waited two weeks for this, Sophie. Two weeks since I've had you like I want to. Two weeks since I've been inside of you."

His words send a shiver down my spine, and my breath catches as his gaze holds mine. His gray eyes are the color of dark steel, and my nipples harden as they brush against his T-shirt. Kai's lips claim mine, and the kiss is deep and consuming. My fingers curl around the fabric of his shirt, and his hands trail down my sides.

"Are you ready to give me everything?" he asks, his voice gravelly.

I nod, completely breathless as his hands guide me up onto the table.

From the doorway, Julian's voice cuts through the haze, smooth and amused. "Careful with her, Kai. I'd prefer her still coherent when I join."

Kai doesn't pause or even indicate that he hears Julian. His hand slides between my legs, spreading my thighs. A low rumble manages to escape his throat, and I swallow as his dark eyes pierce me to the spot.

"You'll wait your turn," he says to Julian, not bothering to turn around.

I can feel Julian's gaze on us, heavy and approving. Kai fists my hair and pulls my head back, his mouth tracing fire along my neck.

"I need a condom," Kai murmurs against my heated skin.

Looking over his shoulders, my eyes find Julian's. We have a stash for the men I sleep with upstairs, but I find myself staying silent.

"Soph?" he asks, tilting his head.

Looking back up at Kai, I know I'm in the moment and it's irresponsible to think of *not* wearing a condom. But I want to feel him bare. I've always loved the feeling of Julian inside of me, and I want to share this with Kai, too.

But before I can tell him this, Kai reaches out for my chin and looks down at me with a look of furtive contemplation.

"As much as I want to fuck you bare, little dove, it's something we should discuss beforehand. Not during a scene."

I nod as his thumb brushes against my lower lip. "The condoms are upstairs. I can—"

"I'll get them," Julian says, pushing off the frame of the door. "Carry on."

Kai watches Julian disappear down the hall, his jaw tight as he adjusts himself in his jeans. His hand brushes against my cheek, fingers lingering as if grounding himself in the moment.

"You're enjoying this," he mutters, though the corner of his mouth twitches into something dangerously close to a smile.

I bite my lower lip, my eyes dragging down his body. "Maybe a little."

He huffs a quiet laugh, but his gaze sharpens as his thumb grazes my lip. "You like watching him pull my strings."

I nod, heart hammering. "I do."

Kai doesn't look away. "Good. Because I'm not done with you yet."

I lean back against the table and look up at him. "Well, then, you heard him. Carry on."

Kai's lips lift into an easy smile. "You're lucky that I don't feel like fighting you tonight, or punishing the disobedience," he murmurs, his hand caressing my shoulder softly. "Get on your knees."

"Yes, my lord."

I'll never get sick of the way his eyes darken whenever I say that, or the way his expression grows just a little bit more menacing. I slide off the table, lowering myself to my knees, and I don't wait for permission to reach forward and unbuckle his belt.

He doesn't stop me, but he also doesn't move to help.

I smirk, thinking of how Kai likes to test the boundaries—the push and pull of our dynamic—and I can feel his eyes boring into me as I work his belt free. His hands remain at his sides, and a slight flex of his fingers is the only indication that he's affected by what's happening. Taking my time, I'm deliberately slow, knowing it will irritate him.

"Are you going to help?" I ask, my tone teasing.

"You're lucky I find that mouth of yours charming, Sophie." Leaning down, his fingers graze my jaw before they tip my chin so that I have no choice but to meet his eyes. "But don't mistake charm for control."

His voice is calm, but there's an edge of warning to it.

I swallow, and the weight of his presence settles over me. Kai's dominance isn't loud or over-the-top. It's like an ocean current, steady, inescapable, and utterly dangerous if you're not prepared. Lowering my gaze, I continue unbuckling his belt.

The tension in the room makes me hyperaware of every sound—the scrape of leather through metal, the sound of the buckle jingling, the faint creak of the floorboards under Kai's feet... and the soft hitch of Kai's breath when my fingers brush against the bare skin above his waistband.

His control might be ironclad, but that shaky inhale tells me everything I need to know: he's ready, and he won't last long.

So many people see submission as a weakness. They don't understand the kind of power it takes to look someone in the eye and offer yourself to them. With Kai, I'm not just giving him control, I'm inviting him to take it. There's power in watching him step into that role, in seeing the confidence build in him as he realizes he doesn't need to hold back.

"You're taking your time," he says, voice low but loaded with warning.

I let a sly smile grace my lips before looking up at him. "I thought you said you didn't feel like fighting me tonight."

A muscle in his jaw tics. "Don't push me."

The warning doesn't scare me. Instead, I pull my lower lip between my teeth, ignoring the low swoop of something heavy dropping down between my legs. Just as I open my mouth to reply with something bratty, I hear Julian's footsteps just outside the door. Looking up at Kai, I see the flicker of anticipation as my husband gets closer. Having spent enough time with Kai, I recognize the subtle shift in his demeanor.

He's torn, I think, between wanting to keep the upper hand with me and whatever uncertainty or curiosity that Julian sparks in him.

Julian's voice carries into the room as he enters. "Am I interrupting?"

I turn my head to see him holding a condom in one hand, his expression both amused and knowing. His hair is slightly mussed, like he's deliberately trying to look casual and failing spectacularly. Julian always has an air of control about him, even when he's trying to let loose.

Kai straightens slightly, though he doesn't step back. His body language changes almost imperceptibly, shifting into something more neutral. I file the observation away, knowing it's something I'll want to poke at later.

"No," I say, my voice light. "Kai was just about to show me if he knows how to work a belt better than I do."

Kai's gaze flicks to me, and there it is, that sharp tension, the push-and-pull that keeps us both on edge. He doesn't respond right away, instead turning his attention to Julian, who has moved closer.

Julian's eyes sweep over the scene, and a faint smile tugs at his lips. "I leave for five minutes, and you're already causing trouble," he says, his tone teasing but warm. It's hard to tell if he's talking to me or Kai, or both of us.

Kai exhales a laugh, low and quiet. "She has a talent for it."

Julian steps into the space between us, close enough that I can feel the heat of his body. His hand brushes my shoulder, and I feel a strange thrill at the way Kai watches him, something unspoken passing between them.

"Is that true?" Julian asks me, his voice dropping a little. "Are you causing trouble?"

Fuck.

I look up at him, wide-eyed and feigning innocence,

though I know I'm not fooling my husband. "I wouldn't dream of it."

Kai huffs a soft laugh as his hand brushes my cheek.

"Well," Julian says, holding up the condom with a smirk. "I think we've waited long enough, don't you?"

Kai's gaze flicks to mine briefly before moving back to Julian. There's a hesitation in his expression—subtle, but there. I wonder if Julian sees it too, the way Kai's confidence falters ever so slightly when he's the one being scrutinized.

I reach for Kai's waistband again, a quiet reassurance, and feel his breath hitch as I tug him forward just a little. "What do you say, Kai?" I ask, letting my voice dip low. "Are you ready?"

For a heartbeat, he doesn't answer, his gaze darting between us. And then he nods, the tension easing just enough to remind me that this is new for him—being seen, being wanted, being caught in this pull between submission and control.

"Yeah," he says finally, his voice low and rough. "I'm ready."

CHAPTER TWENTY-SIX
THE TABLE

JULIAN

It's truly captivating to see someone so typically in control embrace vulnerability. Knowing that I'm the one he willingly turns to fills me with appreciation for that trust. It's clear that he's not accustomed to being teased. It seems he's holding on by a thread with my wife. I mean, Sophie has always had an ornery side, but watching how much it gets under Kai's skin? That's a new kind of entertainment.

"How is this going to work?" Sophie asks, eyes shifting between Kai and me.

I step closer, watching how each of them reacts to my presence. A multitude of scenarios flash through my mind, one of which is using my dear wife like a spit roast. But tonight, I think we need to figure out what we each want out of this. Kai especially, since he's hovering between indulgence and restraint, like he's not sure which part of himself he wants to lean into tonight.

Such a gorgeous switch, I think.

"Well, the two of you look comfortable," I start, my tone light. Sophie smirks up at me, and Kai, for all his bravado, watches me carefully, like he's waiting for his cue.

Yeah, I could really fucking get used to this.

My eyes travel back to my wife, and her eyes spark with something mischievous.

"You're so good at getting him worked up," I tell her, running a hand through her hair to her ponytail. Removing her hairband slowly, I toss it to the side and let her golden hair fall onto her bare shoulders. When my eyes meet hers again, she's watching me with hooded eyes. She likes this. She likes when I'm in control and when I acknowledge her.

So does Kai, though he's too proud to admit it.

As if to prove my point, I reach a hand over to Kai's buckle, which is undone and hanging loosely in front of him. In one swift motion, I pull the belt through the loops roughly.

He stumbles, but I catch him with my other hand. His chest rises and falls rapidly, and I look down briefly to see his cock straining against the material of his trousers.

"I could say the same thing about you," Sophie says, her voice playful and testing.

Kai shifts away from me, the faintest hint of discomfort in his posture. I know he's not used to sharing control, especially not with Sophie. But with me? That's a different story.

That's where things get interesting.

Looking into Kai's eyes, I notice a spark in them—part resistance, part something else that I don't think even he fully understands.

"Don't hold back on my account, Kai," I say, my voice firm.

"I'm not holding back," he says. His voice betrays him, it's rougher than before.

"Ask Sophie how she wants to do this," I say, putting my hand at the base of her neck.

His eyes narrow slightly before roving down to Sophie. The shift in his stance is subtle, and I can tell he's still holding on to that thread of control.

But something in him is unraveling.

Sophie watches him with that daring, ornery look, but it soon transforms into something more understanding.

"We're all in this together, right?" Sophie asks softly.

He looks back to me, and I nod once. "Ask her what she wants, Kai." I keep my voice light, an initiation rather than a command.

Kai takes a moment, his gaze oscillating between Sophie and me. I can see the gears turning in his head. He's only ever played with women, and one man. He's usually in charge. And when we're all together, he can't do that. Relying solely on the strength of our triad is intimidating, he doesn't have his kink or dominance to fall back on. So I get it.

I'd be terrified, too.

Finally, Kai exhales, his shoulders easing just a little bit. "What do you want, little dove?"

Sophie stands up and takes the condom from my hand. Looking up at Kai, she uses her teeth and opens the packet. I watch them, mesmerized, as she pulls his cock out with her free hand. And then she rolls it onto his shaft with both hands. I clock the way he shudders whenever she touches him, and it sends a flash of arousal through me.

My cock is straining against my trousers, and I want nothing more than to keep watching how much she affects him.

Taking a step back, she hops onto the dining room table—the same table that's been in our family for over four hundred years. It's dark Jacobean wood, nearly twenty feet long, and sturdy as fuck. It's rumored that Queen Victoria once ate at this table when visiting one of my ancestors.

Seeing my naked wife about to desecrate it... it's almost too sexy to handle.

"Please fuck me, Kai," she says, spreading her legs so that they hang down. Pointing her toes, she leans back on her hands, and my eyes dart to Kai's.

A low rumble sounds through the room, and then he moves between her legs. I walk around to get a better view, and as Kai hovers over her, I see his cock twitch as he presses against her glistening cunt.

"Yes," Sophie whispers.

Kai looks over at me, and as he pushes into her, his

jaw slackens. I relish the way his eyelids droop, the way his lips part, and the way his whole body seems to quiver. He presses into her, meeting resistance. A red flush breaks out on her chest. Watching her stretch for him, watching the way her mouth drops open...

"Fuck," she hisses, throwing her head back.

Climbing onto the table, I crawl behind her, *needing* to touch her. The old table groans under my weight, but I don't care right now. Kai's hands work down her thighs, spreading her legs even farther. Sophie relaxes back into me, placing her weight on her elbows as I let my hands drift over her peaked nipples. Looking up at Kai, who is eye level with me, I pinch one nipple and revel in the way he hisses, briefly closing his eyes as if trying to regain control.

He must've felt her cunt clench.

With every thrust of his hips, the table creaks ominously, but in a way, it heightens the moment. All of this is so *wrong*—cradling Sophie in my lap while another man fucks her on the table where we eat our meals together as a married couple...

I rock my hips against her back to find the friction that I need, and as I let my eyes slowly drag up to Kai, I find him watching me. Slowly pulling out of her, he snaps his hips and drives into her—*hard*.

"Oh fuck, just like that," she whimpers.

"She likes that," I tell him, using my hands to knead my wife's breasts.

Sophie cants her hips and arches her back the more I

work my fingers, and her head falls to the side as Kai continues his punishing pace.

"I know. I can tell," he says, darkened eyes on me.

"She loves it when you play with her clit. Do it now."

Kai slows his pace, glaring at me. "Why don't you let me decide how to handle her?"

I huff a laugh, pinching Sophie's right nipple a little too hard. "You sure you want to challenge me in my own house? Go ahead, but you won't win."

Kai's hands come to Sophie's hips, and reluctantly, one of his hands moves between her legs. As if in tandem with me, she lets out a long, low groan as Kai takes two fingers and begins to circle her sensitive bundle of nerves.

"That's better," I murmur, watching the way he plays my wife like a fiddle. "Now make her come."

Kai looks down at Sophie, and I can see the way he digs his free hand into her hip, almost pulling her onto his cock.

"Yes, Kai, just like that—"

I open my mouth to tell Kai to up the pressure on her clit, but he does it without me asking. Letting himself hover over her, one elbow by her head, he bends down and kisses her passionately. As he tilts his head, his eyes pierce into mine as if to prove his point. When he pulls away, I can see the way his muscles are bunching and contracting along his arms, and I know he's holding himself back now.

"You're so good at this," I say, and he looks up at me

with wide eyes. "Just like that. Keep going. She looks incredible with you."

Sophie moans. "Oh God, Julian, I'm close—"

"I love watching this," I tell Kai, and his brow furrows as if he doesn't understand. As if he can't contemplate that I'm being nice to him, and it seems to spur him on.

I doubt he's used to being praised in bed, he's usually the one doing it.

This is going to be so much fucking fun.

"I'm coming. Oh fuck," Sophie hisses, back arching. Tipping her head into my chest, her eyes roll into the back of her head, and I bite my lip to keep from groaning. Watching my wife come undone is my favorite sight in the whole world.

But *Kai* being the reason she's coming undone? It's a close second.

"Come for me," I tell Kai, knowing this is the first small step to getting him to submit to me in bed. I may not be the one fucking him, but when's the last time someone told him to come?

A low, raw sound escapes his lips as his body begins to jerk. Pulling out quickly, he pulls the condom off and drops it to the floor just as he comes over Sophie's stomach. Large, thick spurts hit her skin, and I watch as his cock pulses over and over. Closing his eyes, he holds on to Sophie's hips as he rides out his orgasm. I watch, enraptured, as he goes still. His hands are still twitching on the fleshy part of her hips, and when he slowly opens his eyes, his pupils are a dark smoky color.

"Fuck," he mutters, pulling away from Sophie and looking down at the mess he made of my wife.

Sophie slumps back against me, and I can tell from the way she's shivering that she's completely spent. Brushing the sweaty hair off her forehead, I scoot back so that she can lie down on the table fully.

"Come here," I tell Kai, nudging my jaw to the other side of the table behind me.

Slowly, he walks around as I get my cock out. His eyes trail down before coming back up to my face, and I give him a wicked smirk.

"Have you ever wanked a man off?"

Kai runs a hand down his mouth and shakes his head.

"Do you want to?" I ask, positioning myself on my knees over Sophie as I stroke myself a couple of times.

Kai's hand hovers near my cock, uncertain but eager. His breath ghosts over my shoulder, and I feel the slight tremor in his fingers as they curl around me. It's the kind of touch that betrays inexperience—not clumsy, but careful, like he's afraid to take too much.

"Relax," I whisper, covering his hand with mine, guiding him. "I want this. I want you."

His forehead rests against the back of my neck for a moment, and I hear him swallow. Maybe he's thinking about what this means—what we mean. I don't rush him. I let him find his pace, because there's something deeply satisfying about watching him lower his guard, inch by inch. A shaky breath escapes my lips when I move his hand on top of mine a few times, showing him how I like it. And when I remove my hand, I feel him step closer so that his chest is against my back. The tight, raspy breaths escaping his lips have me shuddering in his hand. It's... warm. And big. Sophie has small hands, so Kai's hand around my length feels incredible.

It feels like my own hand, but ten times better because it's Kai.

His grip on my cock tightens just enough to make my breath hitch. His thumb drags over the tip, slower this time, like he's deliberately teasing me—a whisper of his usual dominance breaking through.

A large part of me likes the idea of Kai kneeling at my feet. But there's another part, a dangerous one, that wonders how it might feel to let him take the lead.

That's the part I don't like to think about too hard.

"That's it," I mutter.

Sophie isn't just smirking anymore. Her lips part, her breath coming quicker. The telltale flush creeping up her neck and her chest rises and falls, like she's forgotten how to take a deep breath. When her gaze shifts between us, lingering on Kai behind me, something twists in my chest.

It's not just hunger in her eyes.

It's awe.

Her aroused state sends a jolt through me, spurring me on. It makes me want to push further, to make her fall apart just from watching us.

I look down at her. "Get ready, baby. I'm already close. You want your men to make a mess of you?"

Kai goes still behind me for a fraction of a second. It's subtle enough that I hardly notice, but I do notice.

"Yes," she says, her voice husky. A shiver ripples through her and her thighs squeeze together. "Give me everything, Julian."

Groaning, I begin to rut my hips into Kai's hand. Without thinking, I let my head fall back against his chest, rocking my hips into his hand. His pressure is perfect, and every few strokes he swipes the precum from the tip with his thumb, sending shock waves through me. His breathing turns ragged behind me, and when I lean forward to swipe some of his cum off Sophie's stomach, he lets out a low groan when I add it to my shaft as lube.

"Fuck," he mutters, working his hand faster.

I *want* him to lose control. I *want* to turn him on. Every emotion from seventeen years prior flits through me, even something potent enough to physically rock through me.

I *want* him to want me back.

"For someone who's never done this, you're very good at it," I tease, my voice shaky.

"Yes, well, maybe I just know what you like," he growls.

My eyes flutter closed as everything inside of me pulls taut. "F-fuck, I'm going to…"

My orgasm cuts me off, slamming through me so hard that I let out a string of expletives. My cum flies over Sophie's chest to her stomach, mixing with Kai's, and my body convulses unconsciously as I cover her in my seed. Kai doesn't stop—he only slows—milking every last drop out of me by squeezing my shaft. I tremble and shake like it's my first time, and when I'm finished, I feel him step back.

"Are you going to make him lick it off?" Sophie asks, swirling both of us together on her stomach.

I huff a laugh as I climb off the table. "Not this time."

"Too bad. That was hot."

Grabbing a nearby serviette, I wipe Sophie off and discard it on top of the used condom. Pulling my trousers back up, I chance a look up at Kai.

He's watching us with his hands in his pockets, probably unsure of where to go from here. We've all gotten off, so I'm sure he's waiting for us to dismiss him.

"You okay?" he asks Sophie, walking around to where she's standing.

"Much better now," she says, wrapping her arms around Kai's neck and standing on her tiptoes to give him a kiss.

His hands are resting on her bare hips, and I suddenly have the urge to join them. Taking a step closer, I come around to Sophie's other side, putting my hands on top of Kai's. There's a wrinkle between his brows, and I lean forward and press a chaste kiss to his lips over Sophie's head. Pulling away, I kiss the top of Sophie's head.

We all walk back into the kitchen, and I hand Kai a glass of water. My fingers brush against his wrist. It's a subtle touch, but I catch the way Kai goes still, like he's not used to being looked after.

Like he's not used to anyone checking in on him after a scene.

"You good?" I ask, softer now, my earlier dominance melting into something gentler. Kai nods, but I catch the ghost of something vulnerable in his eyes.

Sophie presses her palm against his chest, grounding him, and he smiles down at her.

"Well, I'm famished," I tell them both, stepping away. Before Kai has a chance to second-guess anything, I shrug and cross my arms. "Do you want to stay the night?"

CHAPTER TWENTY-SEVEN
THE FORMULA

MALAKAI

"I think the thing with these horror movies is they're formulaic," Sophie says, grabbing another handful of popcorn from Julian's lap behind her. I work my thumbs into the arch of her bare foot. She hums softly in appreciation, wiggling her toes to encourage me to keep going. Julian gives me a lopsided smile as she chews quickly. "So yes, it's fine to complain about the character acting like a clown, but every one of these movies has an early murder. We expect it. Usually, it's gruesome and memorable. One by one, other people die, but we all know who the protagonist is going to be early on."

Julian smirks, his free hand lazily running through her hair. "She has a point," he says, sipping his tea.

"I never said she didn't," I retort, smiling as I shovel more popcorn into my mouth.

"You could say romance novels follow a formula too," Sophie muses, eyes flicking toward the paperback novel she set down on the coffee table. "People don't pick up one of these slashers to be surprised. They want the comfort of knowing exactly what's coming. The chase, the screams, the inevitable bloodbath. Same with romance—the characters meet, there's tension, there's sex, and then they get their happy ending."

Julian tilts his head, thoughtful. "Comfort in predictability."

I glance between them, bemused. "Is that what we're doing now? Comparing masked killers to happy ever afters?"

Sophie grins. "Why not?"

The characters on-screen begin screaming as a masked man chases them, and we all turn our attention to the antics of the 'formulaic' movie. I rub along the side of her calf, feeling the warmth of her skin beneath my palms. She changed into an adorable set of baggy silk pajamas, and I let my eyes wander over her bare face and bright, blue eyes. Out of the corner of my eye, I catch Julian watching me. His gaze lingers, soft but assessing.

"What?" I ask, leaning back against the couch and pausing my foot rub.

Julian shrugs. "This is just nice. That's all."

Sophie wiggles her foot against my chest. "He's right. It *is* nice. You give a mean massage, Malakai Ravage."

I chuckle, shaking my head. "Glad to be of service."

I'm still smiling as I turn back to the movie, but I can feel Julian's eyes on me every few minutes. When we're all done eating, I look over and his hand is resting along the back of the couch. Stretching my arm, I reach out for his hand, gripping it firmly once before letting go.

He looks over at me, and something passes between us.

The ease between us feels natural, but even as I play along, there's a weight that sits low in my chest. It sneaks in when I'm not paying attention—when I let myself enjoy this *too much*.

Because this *is* too easy.

And that's the part that scares me.

"I'm knackered and need to go to bed. It's nearly two in the morning," Sophie says, yawning. "Are you boys going to join me, or do you want to finish the movie?"

"We'll finish," Julian says smoothly, fingers brushing lightly over her hair.

She leans over to kiss him softly, then turns and presses a kiss to my cheek. "Don't stay up too late."

"Night, Soph."

"Love you," she murmurs to Julian, and he returns it without hesitation.

Their words hang in the air long after she goes upstairs, and I suddenly feel nervous again. What happened earlier was such a far departure from what I'm used to. For as long as I can remember, I've been in charge in bed. As for the last few years, I've been a Dom. To submit to Julian tonight the way I did... to let him guide me during a scene with Sophie, and then to give him a hand job...

It's a night of firsts for me, and I don't quite know how to act around him.

The Dom in me wants to fight back, but whatever happened tonight was nice—it was *different*.

After that night at the gym, I'd done some research on switches. I always assumed I was fully Dominant, but then I learned that certain people could bring out different dynamics in us. I'd never wanted to submit to anyone before Julian, and I wasn't sure what that meant.

I wasn't sure if I *wanted* to know what it meant.

Because, to be honest, discovering I'm bisexual has already been a life-altering event. I don't need to add anything else to my plate right now.

Julian catches me watching the empty staircase. "Relax, Kai. You look like you're plotting your escape."

I huff a soft laugh, rubbing the back of my neck. "I'm not. I promise."

Julian sets his tea down, stretching an arm along the back of the couch again. His knee brushes against mine as he shifts. I notice he doesn't pull away.

"How are you feeling about tonight?"

I glance over at him. As always, he looks calm and collected, the very picture of someone who's completely at ease with how the night unfolded.

I'm not sure I'm there yet.

"Good," I say absentmindedly. "I mean, it was... different for me. But good." I hesitate, searching for the right words. "I guess I'm not used to all of it yet. I'm not used to the way you and Sophie are so comfortable sharing her... and letting someone else in like this. I keep wondering if I'm overstepping, but it's like the two of you don't even flinch. It's natural for you."

Julian's gaze softens as he nods, but there's a hint of something else, something unspoken. "The physical part might seem easy, but it wasn't always like that." He shifts his gaze to the coffee table, as if sorting through a memory. "We had to figure it out—there were rough patches. Jealousy. Communication issues. But this?" He gestures between us. "This is new. For both of us."

That catches me off guard. I thought I was the only one feeling untethered by all of this.

"There's no right or wrong way to do this, Kai," Julian adds, his voice quieter now. "We're figuring it out too."

I can tell he means it, and I appreciate the reassurance. "Yeah, I get that," I answer, leaning back against the fluffy couch. "It's just a lot to wrap my head around. But I'm okay with it. I like being with both of you."

"Good. We like being with you, too." Julian smiles then, and it's one of those disarming ones that makes me feel like it's just for me.

Maybe it is.

That thought sends something warm through me, something that makes my chest ache a bit.

I push the feeling to the side. This is supposed to be *fun*. That's what we agreed on, isn't it? Fun, no pressure, no expectations...

What feels right.

His words hover in my mind.

That's the thing, though. Being with Julian and

Sophie feels more right than anything I've ever done, and that's what terrifies me about all of this.

Julian shifts closer, and his knee brushes against mine again. I have to ignore the way it sends a maelstrom through me.

"But...?" he asks.

I blink. "But what?"

"Don't play coy, Kai," he says, his smile turning mischievous. "You're mulling something over, and I can tell because you do this little furrowed brow thing when you're overanalyzing. It's cute, but also, it means you're overthinking again."

I laugh and shake my head. "It's nothing bad. I promise."

He studies me for a few beats, and I can feel the weight of his attention on me. "Are you sure?"

"Yeah." Nodding more firmly this time, I turn to face him fully. "I mean, look... I've never done anything like this before. It's just new. And I'm just trying to figure out where I fit in all of it."

"Well, wherever you want to fit, there's room for you," he says, his expression turning soft again. "That's the whole point of all of this. We're not trying to make you into something you're not, Kai. This is about finding what works for all of us, collectively."

His answer is thoughtful, but it's not entirely what I want to hear, either. Deep down, I'm still trying to figure out what works for me—and what I really want.

Orion's voice creeps into my thoughts before I can stop it.

Julian and Sophie are what we call a stag and vixen in the lifestyle. It's worth looking into. They have a reputation.

And...

A unicorn is a person who is invited into a relationship with an existing couple. It can be problematic because the couple can make demands but the unicorn can't do anything that could cause any inconvenience for the couple.

I hadn't thought much about it at the time. I knew what those terms meant—just being in the lifestyle meant that I was familiar with all of it, at least on a surface level. It doesn't bother me—I'd be a hypocrite if it did—but I've always been monogamous, even when playing with a submissive. I've only ever had one play partner at once. And now, after tonight... after being intimate with Sophie *and* Julian, it's hard not to wonder, is this all temporary for them? A passing phase?

Julian nudges me gently with his leg. "Stop thinking so hard. Just... be here. With me."

"Okay," I say, smiling softly.

And as that word leaves my mouth, I know I mean it in this moment. But as he presses play on the movie, I can't shake the quiet voice in the back of my mind.

What if this is all they want from me? And what if I want more?

CHAPTER TWENTY-EIGHT
THE SLEEPOVER

Sophie

I wake up warm, with the space between my legs throbbing. Something warm and hard presses against my clit, and I shift my hips forward slightly, trying to chase the friction I need. Suddenly, a hand comes to my swollen nub, and from the way I'm close to the edge, I suspect that I've been teased in my sleep. My pajama pants are made of pure silk, and they glide against the cotton knickers I'm wearing smoothly. I'm on my side, and as I shift a tiny bit closer to whatever is giving me the friction I need, I feel a warm hand press against my abdomen and pull me back against *another* warm, hard thing.

My eyes fly open, and my eyes land on Kai on his side. One of his legs is hooked over mine, and just as I open my mouth to ask what he's doing, someone moves behind me, pressing what feels like a thick cock against my arse.

Julian.

"Good morning, little dove," Kai says, smiling. "We've been waiting for you to wake up."

"How did you sleep?" Julian asks from behind me. His hand comes to my hair and pulls it over my shoulder. Pressing a kiss to my bare neck, my eyes squeeze shut as Kai works his hand inside of my knickers.

"Am I dreaming?" I ask, my voice a breathy whisper.

"I bet she's already so fucking wet," Julian murmurs.

His words cause my nipples to harden, and I thrust my hips forward into Kai. "That feels g-good," I say, my breath stuttering.

In one swift motion, Kai slides my pajama pants down, and I lift my hips to get them off, rolling onto my back and kicking them off the bed.

Just as I attempt to roll back over to my side, Kai pulls me on top of him, so that my back is against his chest.

"Relax, Sophie," he murmurs.

Julian climbs over us, and he looks so fucking adorable in the morning—his hair tousled, and his face relaxed and sleepy. Reaching down, he begins to unbutton my sleep shirt. With each drag of his fingers against my skin, I let out a small puff of air. Kai moves underneath me, spreading my legs with his knee, and just as Julian works the last button free, Kai's cock slides between my legs. He doesn't push into me—not yet. But it's a warning of what's to come.

"That's it," Kai says, his breath husky as he slides his

cock against my folds. I can hear how wet I am, and it sends a shiver down my spine. "How do you want to do this?"

Looking up at Julian, I pull my lower lip between my teeth. He's kneeling between my legs, wearing only boxer briefs, and my eyes immediately trail down to his straining erection. My mouth waters, and I swallow as I reach out for him.

He smashes his lips against mine, and as his hands come to either side of my head, I feel Kai slide his hands up Julian's arms. Moaning, Kai bites down on my bare shoulder, and Julian pulls away.

"I want both of you. At the same time," I clarify, my voice frayed.

"So, one in your tight, little ass and the other in your perfect cunt?" Kai asks, nibbling my bare shoulder.

Shaking my head, I look up at Julian as I deliver my next sentence. "No, I mean both of you inside one hole."

The effect is instantaneous. Julian stills for a moment, his lips parting as a ripple of heat sparks in his gaze. He takes my hand, pressing a slow, reverent kiss to my knuckles as a low, appreciative groan rumbles from his chest.

"Babe, as much as I'd love that, I don't think you'd be able to take both of us without a little preparation first," he says, his voice huskier now as his eyes drop pointedly between my legs.

Before I can respond, I feel Kai's body tense behind me, his hips pressing forward as if drawn to me by instinct. He lets out a soft, choked moan, the sound vibrating against my skin. His hands tighten on my hips, and I can feel him, hard and insistent, against my back.

"Fuck, Sophie," he murmurs, his voice wrecked, like the very thought of it has unraveled him.

Their reactions fuel me, a heady thrill coursing through my veins at how much power I seem to hold in this moment—how much I've set them off with just a single sentence. My usual submission feels far away, replaced by a boldness I didn't know I could wield.

Julian's grip on my hand tightens, his thumb brushing over my knuckles like he's holding himself back.

"You really know how to drive a man wild, don't you?" he says. His gaze drags over me in a way that makes me shiver.

Kai leans in closer, his breath hot against the back of my neck. "Tell me you're serious," he whispers, the need in his voice evident.

I tilt my head slightly, a smirk playing at my lips as I glance between them. "Oh, I'm serious," I say, the confidence in my voice surprising even me.

And the way they look at me after that—the raw desire in their eyes—makes me feel unstoppable.

"There's lube in the drawer," Julian says. "And condoms—"

"No," I interrupt quickly. I know I'm about to ask something very big of Kai—something that *could* have repercussions. While I'm not fertile, as two years of trying and two rounds of IVF have proved, there's still a possibility I could get pregnant. We've both been tested, so I'm not worried about that aspect, but asking him to fuck me without a condom is a lot to ask. Still... I want to feel him.

All of him.

"What's up, pet?" Julian asks, running a hand over my bare stomach. I lift my head, watching as his fingers casually sneak between my legs, swiping my wetness farther down. My eyes nearly bug out when I see him swipe it over the dark pink head of Kai's cock.

Kai shudders underneath me, and lets out a low groan at the contact, and all I know is that I need them both inside of me somehow.

"I don't want to use a condom," I admit.

Kai's hands, which had just settled around my hips, go still. "Are you sure?" he asks, kissing my shoulder again.

I look up at Julian. "As long as we all agree to be safe... I don't see the issue," I say shyly. "And depending where Kai... is..." I trail off, cheeks heating. "I suppose there is still a chance I could get pregnant—"

Kai groans underneath me, and his hands grip my hips tighter. "Fuck, Sophie. Don't say things like that to me."

My mouth pops open. *Is he worried, or...?*

"What?" I ask, my voice nearly a whisper.

"You have no idea how much that turns me on," Kai murmurs, his grip tightening on my hips as he presses his body closer, holding my hips still as he thrusts up against my wetness. "The idea of fucking you bare... of filling you with my cum... it's so fucking hot. I don't care about the consequences right now, I just want to feel you." His breath is heavy against my skin, clearly lost in the passion of the moment.

Looking up at Julian, I'm surprised to see him watching us with a soft expression. He takes my hand and threads his fingers through mine, bringing it to his lips.

"That's fine with me. But I want her cunt today," he tells Kai.

He crawls off the bed, walking to my bedside table and grabbing the bottle of lube we hardly ever use, except for anal.

My breathing hitches.

"Spread your legs, pet," Julian says, climbing back onto the bed.

"Wait," I rasp, keeping my legs closed.

He looks down at me with a teasing smile. "Open. Your. Legs."

"It's a little early in the day for anal," I tell him with a sardonic tone.

"It's never too early for anal," Kai says.

I spread my legs slowly, and Julian dribbles some lube into his hand before reaching between my legs. Trailing two fingers down my seam, I feel him circle Kai's cock—and Kai's resounding groan at the contact.

"Shift your hips up," Julian directs.

I do as he says, and Kai uses his legs to spread my legs wider.

"So perfect," Kai murmurs. He looks at Julian. "Get her nice and ready for me."

My mouth drops open when Julian takes his index finger and presses it against my puckered hole, inserting it just barely and making sure there's enough lube for an army. He pushes it in deeper, and my eyes roll back when he does.

I fought anal for a long time with him, but I can't deny how amazing it always feels.

"That's it," Julian says, inserting a second finger. "So fucking tight and warm. Kai is going to love it."

He withdraws his fingers, and a whole-body shiver works through me.

"She's ready," Julian says, sitting back.

"Lift your hips, Sophie," Kai mutters.

I do as he says, lifting myself up. He lines his cock up with my arsehole. It feels unnatural—I don't think Julian and I have ever done this position in regular sex, let alone anal. The warm head of his cock presses against me, and it's a huge departure from a couple of fingers.

"Deep breath," Kai whispers against the back of my neck. "Relax, little dove. This only works if you're relaxed."

I take a couple of deep breaths, letting my back lay across his body fully. He shifts underneath me, and in an instant, the tip is inside.

I gasp, my fingers curling against the bedspread I'm gripping with an iron fist.

"Good girl," Kai says, his voice a velvet purr. He pushes in a little bit more, and I ignore the sharp sting of his girth.

Julian leans forward and dribbles some more lube,

circling my opening. It allows Kai to press the rest of his cock inside, and when he's done, he settles inside of me and goes still.

"There we go," he says, though his voice is shaky.

"Have you ever done this before?" I ask, my whole body trembling on top of him.

"Me? Sodomy? Never," he retorts quickly.

It makes me laugh, and when I do, he adjusts himself inside of me.

"Oh fuck," I whimper.

"You feel so good," Kai says, keeping himself inside of me. His hands move up to my breasts, and I groan when his warm hands cup them gently.

"Spread your legs, Ravage," Julian says, and he climbs between us.

God... I have Kai under me and I'm about to have Julian on top of me. This must be a dream, right?

Drizzling a little lube against my slit, Julian shifts his hips and lines his cock up. "If it's too much, just tell me," he says, blond hair messy. His face is etched with arousal, and his tongue presses against the inside of his cheek as he slowly presses into my pussy.

"Fuck," he whispers, hissing.

My mouth drops open. It stings—more than I thought it would. It feels like everything is stretching unnaturally, and I break out in a cold sweat.

There's no way they're both going to fit.

"Wait," I whimper, trying to close my legs.

Julian stops, smiling softly down at me. "You're doing so well, pet. Let me warm you up a little bit," he murmurs, taking two fingers and sliding them against either side of my clit.

Everything inside of me clenches at the sensation, and Kai groans under me. His hands twitch against the flesh of my breasts.

"Holy fuck, Sophie," he says, his voice dripping with supplication. "I felt that."

The sound of his tortured voice sends a flash of arousal through me. Julian must notice, because he moves his fingers against me again, sliding them gently over my clit, over and over. Kai uses the opportunity to shift his hips forward, pulling out ever so slowly before thrusting back into my arse.

It sends a jolt of white-hot heat through me.

"Oh God," I whine.

Kai's right hand comes up to my throat. He leaves it wrapped loosely just below my jaw, but his thumb presses into the side of my neck.

"Do you trust me?" Kai asks. I gasp as he applies a bit more pressure.

Because next time we do this, it's going be my hands around your throat and you're going to have to trust that I'm not going to go too far.

"Yes," I whisper.

"Good. Use your safe word or tap me if it goes too far, okay?"

"Okay."

Julian slips a finger into my core, curving it ever so slightly, and my whole body trembles at the double intrusion. And with Kai's hand around my throat... so many sensations work through me at once that I can't even articulate it. Julian adds another finger, moving them in such a way as to stretch me. The sting doesn't feel as bad now, and when I begin bucking my hips against his hand, he pulls them out.

Inserting his fingers into his mouth, he sucks, grinning. "Mmm. My favorite thing to eat."

I huff a laugh as he lines his cock up with me again. This time, I relax, letting my body completely melt into Kai's chest, who only grips my neck tighter.

"You're perfect," Kai murmurs into my ear. "Yes, little dove. Just relax. *Trust. Me.*"

Julian's cock presses into me, and I feel it the instant he's fully seated inside of me. I'm full of them—and I'm scared to move.

"Fuck," Julian groans, pulling out slightly before thrusting back into me. Kai groans under me, and I can tell by the way his fingers twitch around my throat that he feels Julian, too. "I can feel you, Kai."

Kai moves his hips underneath me, and it's a slow, delicious ache that makes my eyes flutter closed.

"Eyes open, Soph," Julian growls, moving faster now.

His hands come to my thighs, and he runs them along the inside. Everything feels hypersensitive, and every touch—every breath—sends sparks through me. Kai moves his other hand down to my hip, and he presses down on my lower stomach. I gasp, because it intensifies the full feeling. It's maddening in the best way, and each flicker of sensation brings me closer to the edge.

Both Kai and Julian are thrusting into me, and it feels fucking exquisite.

"You're such a good girl, taking everything I'm giving you," Kai says, kissing the back of my neck.

His fingers grip my throat tighter, and everything inside of me gets hotter as a tingling sensation works down to my toes. The sensation of his hand around my throat isn't at all what I expected. I expected to not be able to breathe, but I can. Having his hand around my throat just intensifies every sensation… amplifying every place they're touching me and giving me the most amazing head rush.

"It's true," Julian says, his voice hoarse. "You're handling us both stuffing you full so well," he says, bending down to kiss me.

It's too much, having Julian kiss me, having him move on top of me, all the while Kai moves underneath me with his hand around my throat…

Julian pulls away, and my breathing is ragged. Every one of my inhales is shaky, and as my body tightens, it arches into the pressure of both of them inside of me, chasing it. *Needing* it. The heat spreads through me, low and persistent.

I lose myself completely in the moment.

"I love watching you like this," Julian says, his movements becoming more frenzied. I can tell he's close, the way his skin is glistening with sweat is a big indicator. "So fucking perfect wrapped around me," he growls.

I whimper. "Oh God. Harder, please," I beg,

squeezing my eyes shut. "On my throat and inside of me."

Kai grunts and presses his hand tighter, slamming into me as Julian does the same. His voice drops, dark and teasing. "One day, I'm going to press a blade here instead, feel you tremble beneath it while I take you apart."

The tension winds tighter, almost painfully so. My thighs begin to tremble, and high-pitched, inhuman sounds begin to escape my lips. I'm overwhelmed at the sensation of both of them, at the dizzying euphoria spreading through me. My hands grip the sheets tightly so that I don't fly off the bed when I come.

"God, the noises you make," Kai murmurs, laving his tongue along the side of my neck. "I'll never fucking get enough."

"I'm c-close," I whisper. "Oh fuck, yes, just like that—"

I'm right there, teetering on the edge. And then Kai groans under me, and I can *feel* his cock get thicker, hardening as he comes inside of me. One hand flies to my hip, gripping me so tightly, and the thumb on the side of my neck presses into where my pulse is beating against him, and though it's brief—only two seconds—everything lets go.

It's like a dam breaking. A flood of molten heat and electric pleasure crashes over me in waves as my eyes roll into the back of my head. My body thrashes on top of Kai's, and I feel his hips jerking erratically as he empties himself inside of me. My back arches as a cry tears from my throat.

"That's it, pet. Fuck, I'm coming," Julian says, going still as his jaw clenches, and a loud, low moan escapes his lips as his eyes glaze over. I feel the hot spikes of cum hit my cervix, intensifying everything.

The pulses of my climax continue rolling through me. It feels endless.

And when I come down, I feel absolutely spent. There's nothing but this feeling—my body trembling uncontrollably, fingers still gripping the sheets, the feeling of not being able to breathe. My body is hot and loose, and a lingering hum of bliss ripples through me.

"Holy shit," I whisper, closing my eyes.

Kai chuckles under me, but even his voice sounds shaky as he removes his hand from around my throat. "Yeah."

"We're definitely doing *that* again," Julian adds.

They take care pulling out of me. Julian goes first, and then he helps me off Kai. His hands are steady, like they always are. As I find my footing, I glance down at Kai, and the air shifts.

He isn't just watching me. He's *devouring* me.

For so long, I could feel his attraction to me. I could see the way he longed for Julian, too. But this?

His chest rises and falls with labored breaths, and there's a shadowed darkness in his eyes that freezes me. It's unrelenting—almost *primal*. It's a look I've come to love, but there's something more this time—something raw and unguarded. His hand twitches by his side as if he's fighting the urge to touch me again. His throat bobs as his eyes rove down my body. His gaze softens briefly before that hunger overtakes his expression again.

This isn't just possessiveness. It's something deeper, something he doesn't seem to know how to handle.

Julian doesn't seem to notice. Instead, he murmurs something about cleaning us up, and then he disappears into the en suite.

Kai's mouth tugs into a small smile. "Don't think for a second that I'm done with you," he murmurs. "Not until I'm sure every part of you remembers my touch."

My mouth drops open as a flash of heat works through me, but just as I think of something to say, Julian walks back into the room. My eyes don't leave Kai's as Julian cleans me up with a warm cloth. He licks his lower lip, and for a moment, his gaze isn't just hungry.

It's completely open—like he's waiting to make sure he's not alone in his feelings.

Like he needs to know that this isn't just some momentary conquest, but something deeper.

And that terrifies me, because I have no idea where to go from here.

CHAPTER TWENTY-NINE
THE FIXATION

MALAKAI

The smell of sawdust fills the air, sharp and earthy, as I push the sander across the worn wood floor. Sophie is crouched nearby, focused solely on prying stubborn nails from the baseboards with the conviction of a woman who refuses to let any obstacle get in her way. And she should be damn proud, because this place is coming together seamlessly. I let my eyes wander over her... the messy halo of hair half pulled up, the flushed cheeks from the physical exertion, the way she hums along to a Gracie Abrams song under her breath as it plays over the speakers I installed yesterday...

It feels domestic.

And it feels entirely out of grasp, somehow.

Despite waking up with her and Julian two days ago, it feels like a lifetime ago. Especially since aside from our group chat, I haven't seen them until I showed up this morning to help Sophie with the shop.

It's still a matter of *them* versus *me*.

"Julian's going to love the new floors," Sophie says suddenly, her voice full of warmth. She talks about Julian with the kind of ease that only comes from years of knowing someone inside and out. I wonder if she could ever talk about me like that. "He's already talking about claiming the little corner near the register for a coffee bar. I told him he's not allowed unless he actually sticks with it this time," she adds, her tone light and affectionate.

"Sticks with it?" I ask, keeping my eyes on the sander. The repetitive motion is distracting enough to keep my eyes focused on the floor rather than the woman next to me. "What do you mean?"

"Oh, you know Julian." Her voice is breezy. Too breezy. Yanking another nail out, she tosses it into the growing pile next to her. "He's always had his phases. Things he hyperfixates on until something shiny catches his attention."

I should laugh, but instead my chest tightens. "Hmm."

"You know him. It's just a part of who he is. He's lucky I find it sweet most of the time."

Forcing a chuckle, I ignore the feel of a knife twisting in my gut. I remember the fixations all too well.

"You mean he's never dragged you to a hip-hop dance class? Because *that* was interesting."

Julian had a lot of interests when we were teenagers

—the world fascinated him. He was curious, interested, with a zest for life.

"Oh God, where do I even start?" She sits back on her heels, smudging dirt across her cheek with the back of her hand. I almost laugh because it's adorable. "There was the cycling phase—that one lasted three months, and we still have all the fancy cycling gear to show for it. Then there was pottery. Woodworking. He even tried to teach himself Japanese because he thought it would be fun." She smiles, lost in memory.

She continues. "That's just Julian, though. He gets so passionate about something, throws himself into it completely, and then one day..." She snaps her fingers. "Poof. It's gone, never to return. And he's on to the next thing."

I pause, the sander humming in my hands.

On to the next thing.

Is that what I am? *The next thing?* How long until he moves on? Cycling lasted three months... is that my expiration date, too? I recall the hip-hop dancing fading pretty quickly, too... and the bookbinding, and everything else that seemed to excite him at one time or another. How long until he convinces Sophie to continue being a hotwife with a different guy because he can't get that same dopamine hit with me? After all, I'm not a new, shiny thing.

And I do remember how excited he used to get over shiny, new things.

"It must be nice to have that freedom," I blurt. "To

just move on when something doesn't hold your attention anymore."

I can't help how bitter my words sound, and I almost wince.

Sophie's expression softens, but it only makes everything worse. It feels like she's *pitying* me.

"You know him as well as I do, Kai. You know he loves experiencing things fully. He's always been like that. But when it comes to things that matter..." She trails off. "He's never walked away from the people he loves."

I can't respond. The sander hums angrily beneath my hand, scraping deeper into the wood than I meant to. I ease off the pressure, but the small gouge left behind feels like evidence of the thoughts I can't quite shake.

Because I can't bring myself to ask the question that's bothering me: am I one of those things he loves, or am I just a passing phase?

I could text him, ask him how his day's going. But what would I even say? I already feel like I'm standing in someone else's house, trying to act like I belong.

Sophie seems to sense the shift in me. She stands and brushes her hands on her jeans, frowning.

"Hey, you okay?"

Setting the sander down, I look up and force a smile. "Yeah, fine. Just tired."

What I want to say—what I *can't* say—is that she talks about him like he's some untouchable sun. I can see it in the way her face lights up. And I'm... jealous. I want her to talk about me like that, too.

Sophie and Julian Ashford are their own universe, and I still feel like an outsider. They fit together so perfectly, leaving no room for me unless I wedge myself into the cracks.

She reaches out, and when her hand touches me, it feels like an electric shock. For a second, the tension eases. But the moment she lets go, it creeps back in, like an echo I can't quite silence. Her fingers trail down my forearm, brushing away sawdust I hadn't noticed. I want to believe that means something. But maybe I'm reading into it too much.

"Okay. I'm going to get some water. I think that's enough for today. We can finish this tomorrow," she says, gesturing to the corner I'm sanding.

I nod, grateful for the excuse to step away from the tension in the air. She's always so patient with me—I suppose she's used to it with Julian—but I can't seem to stop spiraling since we were all together this past weekend.

As she walks into the back room to grab water, I glance down at my phone. The screen lights up with a reminder of my meeting.

Shit. I've got to go.

Swiping the notification away, my thumb lingers over the time. The meeting with Victoria Evans is in an hour. I want to stay—I want to tell Sophie everything that's been on my mind for days.

But I also know the fresh air on the walk to Saint Helena will clear my head.

Plus, I have to do this. I have to show up for Bradleigh. I *have* to fight for her.

I stand up and wipe the dust off my faded jeans. I'm filthy—I should probably go home and shower first, but I don't really have time. I shake most of the sawdust off of me, and I walk to the small bathroom off to the side to wash my hands and splash water over my face. Looking up into the mirror, I'm reminded of the first time Julian and I kissed.

I was so worried about what I could possibly offer him. And now?

I'm worried I'm not enough.

Fuck, I sound like a teenager again, I think, running a clean hand down my face. *Maybe I'm more fucked up over all of this than I realized.*

When I walk back out, Sophie holds a water bottle out to me. Her eyes tighten with concern as she catches sight of my jacket.

"You're leaving?"

I nod, giving her a soft smile. "Yeah. I forgot that I've got a late meeting with a parent."

Sophie frowns. "Is everything okay?"

"Probably," I tell her, unsure if I should explain the situation.

"Do you want to talk about it?" she asks, tucking a piece of hair behind her ears. Her expression is so genuine, so earnest... it makes my chest ache.

God... she's fucking perfect.

I sigh. "One of the board members is pushing for one

of my trans students to move schools. I won't stand for it. Her place is at Saint Helena."

Sophie reaches out and takes my hands, pressing her lips together in contemplation. "I'm sorry. That must be really hard. Can't you overrule the board member as headmaster?"

I shrug. "It depends on if I can convince the rest of the board."

She's looking up at me with concern, and I can't have that. Leaning down, I kiss her gently on the forehead.

"It's okay. It's just part of the job."

But it's more than that. I can feel it now, the tension in my chest, the gnawing feeling of everything slipping through my fingers, everything I've built up over the years, everything I thought I understood about myself.

Sophie's gaze on me intensifies, and then she does something that catches me off guard. She steps forward and wraps her arms around me in a tight hug. Her warmth wraps around me, and I close my eyes, letting out a contented sigh.

"You're doing good. You know that, right?"

I can't help it. I bury my face in her shoulder, letting her words soothe something inside of me that's been raw for far too long. My throat feels tight, the words lodged there. I don't feel like I'm doing good. Not right now. Not with the storm inside me that I can't even begin to understand.

I want to tell her everything. I want to tell her that I'm falling for her—and that I'm also falling for Julian.

I want to tell her that I never expected to love two people this deeply.

I want to tell her that it fucking *terrifies* me.

And I want to tell her that it feels like I'm on the edge of something huge—of something that could shatter everything in my life if I'm not careful.

"I have to go," I say a minute later as I pull away. My voice is rougher than I intended. "I'll see you tomorrow, okay?"

She nods, and her hand lingers on my arm. "Okay."

Giving her a shaky smile, I head for the door. It's good that I'm leaving. I need to put my focus on Victoria and Bradleigh Evans, or I'll lose myself in the chaos of everything I'm feeling.

However, as soon as I step out into the warm late afternoon air, I feel the weight of everything crashing down on me.

Sophie.

Julian.

Everything I'm too afraid to admit.

And I can't help but feel like I'm already in too deep to walk away now.

Even if I wanted to.

CHAPTER THIRTY
THE OVERTHINKER

MALAKAI

I get to my office thirty minutes before the meeting is supposed to start, and despite planning on using that thirty minutes for prepping my argument, there's a heavy knock on the door.

"Come in," I say, taking a seat behind my desk.

Julian's face comes into view as he slowly pushes the door open, closing it quietly behind him. "I'm here to see the headmaster?" he asks, his eyes sparking with mischief.

And damn it to hell, because I can't help but laugh, even as my gut twists.

"What do you want, Julian?" I ask. My tone is teasing, but there's a slight bite to it.

I'm not in the mood for his games today, especially since I can't help but feel like a brooding asshole right now.

He locks the door and steps inside my office fully, hands in his pockets as his eyes roam the room. His eyes linger on the rosary sitting on a shelf, and I stiffen as he reaches out, brushing a finger against the beads.

"Please tell me you have plans to use those rosary nipple clamps with Sophie again," he says, his voice light. *Casual.* Wiggling his eyebrows at me, I almost want to laugh at how ridiculous he can be.

But I don't. Instead, I lean back in my chair and cross my arms. "Only if you're nice."

That earns me a grin, sharp and wolfish. I feel that tug of *something* all the way down to my cock. Crossing the room, he comes to stand in front of my desk, placing both hands on the wood and leaning forward. The air shifts completely. My office is supposed to be a safe space, but with Julian standing before me, towering and commanding, it suddenly feels much smaller.

This space is where I'm the one in charge. The one in control. The replica office at Inferno sees all the action, sure, but I based it on this space. Now that Julian is here, perched on my desk like he owns the room, I can already feel the cracks forming in the facade.

"Kai," he says, his voice too steady, as always. As if he's completely unflappable. "What's going on?"

My eyes don't leave his. How the hell can he tell something's bothering me? Then again, I shouldn't be surprised. He used to call me out on my moody shit all the time when we were teenagers.

"It's nothing. I'm tired, and I have a meeting soon—"

"For Christ's sake." He sighs, rounding the desk before I can stop him. He perches on the end, close enough that I could reach out and run my hand up his thigh. "You've always been a terrible liar, do you know that?"

I swallow. The words are in my throat, ready to spill out. His presence is suffocating—all-consuming—in the best and worst ways. Sophie's words from earlier play through my mind in a loop. *Julian's phases. His hyperfixations.* And me, the one thing he hasn't fully committed to, but also won't let go of.

Pottery. Cycling. Japanese. Hip-hop dancing. And now... me. A phase to be worn until it no longer fits.

"You're overthinking something again," he says, his tone softer now. Almost coaxing. "Talk to me."

I think of telling him everything. What the hell, right? It would save me the torture of getting more invested only to get my heart stomped on.

But I don't. I can't. For some reason, I feel the need to keep these feelings to myself. Not forever, but for now. I mean, what does he expect me to say? Does he expect me to hypothesize about the way he and Sophie have completely upended my life? Or the way they've carved a space in my heart that I didn't even know was there? Or perhaps about the way I'm terrified that I'll never really belong to them—not the way they belong to each other?

When I don't answer, he sighs again, his frustration clear. "Kai, this relationship will only work if we're open and communicating. Do you understand?"

The word "relationship" hooks me like a fish. It's not

the first time I've wondered if that's what this is, but hearing him say it out loud throws me off-balance.

Looking at him now, so self-assured, so at ease, I suddenly feel hot all over. "Is that what this is? A relationship?"

Julian arches a brow, his expression bemused. "I suppose so. What else would it be?" I open my mouth to respond, but he continues before I can get the chance. "We're having fun, right? It doesn't need to be more complicated than that."

And... there it is. That easy, casual tone he always defers to. The one that somehow feels like sandpaper against my raw nerves. I remember how he'd brush over any vulnerable feelings as teenagers. How he'd change the subject, or make a joke to diffuse the situation.

We're having fun, right? It doesn't need to be more complicated than that.

He says it like it's obvious, like it's the only way to approach this, and for the first time, it hits me just how different our perspectives might be.

"Right. Fun," I echo, my voice flat.

"Isn't it?" he presses, a hint of concern creeping into his expression. I force myself to nod, even though my stomach churns. "Kai?" His voice is firm now, pulling me out of my thoughts. He cups my chin, forcing me to look at him. "What do you need?"

The question lingers between us, and something inside me clenches.

I don't know the answer. Maybe I don't want to know.

But I know how to stop thinking.

Before I can stop myself, before I can unravel whatever this ache in my chest is, I slide off the chair, sinking to my knees in front of him.

I need to stop thinking. The only way to quiet the storm is to let him anchor me.

My heart hammers so loudly, I swear he can hear it. But I don't look away.

Julian's eyes darken as surprise flashes across his face, but it's fleeting. His hand slips from my chin, trailing down to brush through my hair, gentle but deliberate. The touch is grounding, but it still feels like I'm grasping at smoke.

He's right here, but I can't shake the feeling that he's inaccessible.

"Is this what you need?" he asks softly, his voice smooth, calm. Like he knows. Like he's letting me have this even if neither of us fully understands why.

"Yes."

The word escapes before I can think too hard about it, before I can drag myself back to whatever emotion I'm trying to outrun.

And as his fingers tighten ever so slightly in my hair, grounding me, I let the tension ease. Even if just for a moment.

His answering smile is slow, predatory—and it makes my stomach tighten. "Good."

The door to my office is locked. I'm usually more cautious—it's why I don't play here—but it's late, nearly five or six p.m., and the building is quiet, everyone else long gone for the day.

The meeting is across campus, anyway.

Lighten up, I tell myself. *You've been grumpy all fucking day.*

Julian slides his hands through my hair, gripping it just firmly enough to make me gasp in surprise. My heart is fucking *galloping.* I've never done this before, and until recently, never thought about doing this before. But I don't hesitate as he unbuttons his pants. The sound of his belt and the rustling of fabric echoes loudly in the quiet room.

This all feels sacrilegious.

And that thought only spurs me on.

I shouldn't want him this much. I can feel the heat simmering beneath my skin, and it's too much, too fast, like I'm chasing something I know will disappear.

"Kai—"

I pull his boxer briefs down and stare at his cock. It's pretty. Thick, veiny, with a pink head—a pink head that's leaking precum. The thought of turning him on so much that he's already leaking precum only makes my cock harder.

Looking up at Julian, I let my hand slide over his length. It's smooth and hard all at once, and it feels both familiar and foreign to me. His lashes flutter for just a second before his eyes bore into mine, steely and hard.

"Suck," Julian orders, his tone commanding.

It sends a jolt of arousal straight through me, and I don't hesitate to take him fully into my mouth.

The act of sucking, of letting my tongue explore the texture and soft feel of his shaft, feels strange. Everything is different from what I expected it to be—the salty taste, the heavy weight, the rhythm of my mouth as I move to take him into the back of my throat. It feels overwhelming, but not in the way I thought it would be.

And the sounds he makes—low, guttural—vibrate through me and send a tingling sensation down my spine.

"Fuck, Kai," he murmurs, his voice frayed. His hand fists my hair tighter, guiding me deeper. I let him do it. *I want him to.* "Fuck, that's it," he adds.

My cock throbs with need at the noises he's making. He sounds completely indecent, with the small whimpers that escape his throat and the low, deep growls that I can feel before I hear. Rocking his hips into my mouth, I let my tongue swirl around his length. And, because I know how amazing it feels, I use one hand to grab onto his ass, holding him deep inside my mouth, and the other to cup his balls.

The way his body shudders, the way his cock hardens just slightly, makes me cant my hips forward against nothing.

I need a release, because this is so much hotter than I thought it would be.

"I'm going to come soon," Julian warns, squeezing my hair and trying to pull me away. "Kai, fuck, I'm so close—"

I suction my cheeks, and he groans too loud for comfort before his cock spills into the back of my throat.

I heave and gag, but I attempt to take it all, swallowing quickly. The salty, bitter cum coats the back of my throat, and when he finishes, he pulls out with a 'pop' and a mouth that's hanging open.

I wish I could capture his face right now, because I'm pretty sure I could get Julian Ashford to do anything at this moment.

Pulling me to my feet, his hands keep me steady as I sway. My knees feel weak, and I adjust myself. The way he's looking at me, a mix of awe and perhaps something he didn't expect, sates me.

"You okay?" he asks, brushing a thumb over my scruff.

I nod, but what just happened settles over me, heavy and suffocating. I thought this would help—I thought it might clear my mind if I just submitted to him.

Like perhaps I'd find the answers between dropping to my knees and tasting all of him.

But now I feel like I'm caught somewhere between belonging and breaking.

As his hand cups my jaw, I let my stoic expression slide off, giving way to something I'm sure resembles vulnerability. The truth is impossible to ignore now. Especially when I close my eyes and lean into his touch.

I need them.

But not like this—not like a passing visitor. I need more.

I need to be their everything, too, or I don't think I can do this at all.

"You're overthinking again," Julian says, his voice pulling me back to the present.

I want to tell him he's wrong, that I'm fine, that I can handle this. But I can't. Because the truth is, I don't know how to balance what I feel for them with the life I've built. The life I'm supposed to live.

The rosary on the shelf catches my eye, and I can't help but laugh softly—bitterly. The pastor. The Dominant. The brother. I've spent years keeping those parts of myself separate, hidden behind walls of control and self-preservation. But Julian and Sophie have undone all of that.

"Something funny?" he asks.

"Not really," I say, my voice hollow.

He studies me for a moment, his amusement fading into something softer. "We're not going anywhere, you know," he says quietly. "Whatever's going on in that head of yours, you don't have to deal with it alone."

The words are meant to be comforting, but they only make the ache worse. Because I know the truth: I *want* them. Both of them. But I don't know if I can ever really have them.

That's becoming clear with each passing day.

When Julian leans down to kiss me briefly, his lips warm and sure, I let him. Because for now, it's enough.

But I don't know how long it will be enough.

CHAPTER THIRTY-ONE
THE FEAR

MALAKAI

Julian puts himself away, and then he walks to the door, unlocking it. For a second, I think he's going to leave, but then he walks back over to where I'm standing.

A second later, his lips press against mine for a second kiss, soft and firm at the same time. An electric shock zings through me, sending a shock wave behind my hip bones. It's the kind of kiss that makes me forget the torrent of thoughts threatening to spill out of me, the kind of kiss that makes me forget the tightrope I'm walking, the worry, and the contradictions that are slowly pulling me apart. As Julian groans into my mouth, there's only him—the velvet feel of his lips against mine, the sensation of his tongue sliding against mine, and the quiet promise of the way he's gripping me.

"*Mine*," he growls against my lips, his teeth grazing

just enough to make me shiver. "You're fucking mine, Ravage."

His hand slides up the back of my neck, tugging me closer until there's no space left between us, his forehead resting against mine.

"I don't care how long it's been. I don't care who's touched you since. You were mine then, and you're mine now."

The weight of his words settles deep in my chest, and I swear he can feel the way my heart hammers against his.

"Say it," he whispers, his thumb brushing along my jaw. "Say you're mine."

I do, because, in this moment, I can't imagine belonging anywhere else.

"*Yours,*" I nearly whimper.

His hand comes around my neck, and I let out a low groan.

And then the door flies open.

"Malakai."

The voice is sharp and full of disapproval, slicing through the quiet intimacy that we've created in this moment like a knife.

I pull away instantly, and as I wipe my mouth with the back of my hand, the room begins to spin when I see Rod standing in the doorway. My heart drops down into my stomach. The look on his face can only be described as thinly veiled disgust. His mouth is open in surprise, but his eyes are as sharp as an eagle.

For a few seconds, none of us speak. The room

remains quiet—*charged*. It's fucking deafening. Then Rod steps into my office fully.

"I didn't realize you had company," he says, his tone cold and each word clipped. Flicking his eyes to Julian, they linger on him long enough for me to shift my weight uncomfortably.

This is bad.

Julian straightens, and he looks at me with something akin to pity. "I was just leaving," he says, his voice devoid of any of the warmth from earlier.

"Were you?" Rod asks, his eyes narrowing on Julian. "It looked to me like the two of you were perhaps... busy."

My neck burns. "That's enough, Rod." Somehow, I manage to keep my voice calm and steady. "Julian, I'll see you later."

Julian hesitates, his eyes searching mine—for what, I don't know. But then he nods, and his expression softens just enough to remind me of what we were just doing. Brushing past Rod without a word, he leaves the office.

The silence is too overwhelming.

"Are you ready for the meeting?" he asks, standing up straight.

I stare at him. Is he going to ask me about Julian? This seems like it's too good to be true. I thought for sure I'd get a verbal lashing from him.

"Yes," I answer, my voice brusque.

Following him out of my office, I close and lock the door. We make our way to the boardroom in silence, and I wait for him to bring it up.

He doesn't.

The bastard knows how to keep me on my toes.

Victoria is already waiting for us. I wave to Bradleigh, who is playing on her Nintendo Switch a few yards away, with headphones over her ears.

Her bright, goofy smile makes me huff a laugh, and it reminds me of why I'm here.

And why I'm doing this.

The meeting is short. I hardly pay attention, too frazzled from what just happened, and too worried that Rod is about to be a big dick to Victoria Evans.

In the meeting, Victoria states that she doesn't want to move Bradleigh to another school, and I agree. Rod gives his side of the argument, but it's over soon. Victoria starts to pull legal documents out, and I have to hide my smile when she passes us both a section of the code of conduct for Saint Helena. The passage highlighted is about discrimination, and when she leans forward, practically burning Rod alive with her ferocious expression, she tells him that she's very happy to get the opinion of her lawyer—or rather, the lawyer I put on retainer for her to use, should she need legal advice.

So, the meeting is adjourned.

Rod huffs about it, and I can tell he's pissed.

But Victoria and Bradleigh both give me a grateful smile before they head home.

Much to my chagrin, Rod follows me back to my office. Like before, we walk in silence, though I can feel his irritation radiating from his body as we walk across campus.

"Is this what Saint Helena has come to under your leadership?" he asks just as we walk up to my office door.

I stop walking, meeting his glare head-on with one of my own. "If you have a point, Rod, I suggest you get to it."

His lips curl into something that might possibly pass for a smile if he weren't so full of malice. "Oh, I have a point, Mr. Ravage. Several, in fact, after that flagrant injustice of a meeting just now. But let's start with the incident from earlier." Gesturing to my closed door, I nearly break my teeth clenching my jaw so hard. "I'm concerned about the image you're presenting to our community. To the parents. And to the donors, who keep this school running."

My jaw tightens even further. "Whatever you think you saw is none of your business."

"Oh, but it is very much my business," he counters, stepping closer. "You're the headmaster. This is a religious institution. Parents entrust their children to this school because they believe in its values. If they were to find out that their headmaster is... how should I put this... diverging from those values, it could cause quite an uproar."

He means for the implication to hang heavy between us, but I don't flinch or take the bait. Rod's mistake is simple, he thinks I'm playing by the same rules he is. He forgets that I've been headmaster long enough to know every backdoor deal and every name that carries weight in these halls. I don't need to shout to be heard.

"Funny thing about values, Rod," I say softly. "People

like to think they're set in stone, but they're more like scripture—open to interpretation. And right now, I'm the one holding the pulpit. And as long as I'm here, Saint Helena's values will always be about education, inclusion, and compassion," I say firmly.

Rod's eyes twinkle with something predatory. "That might be your interpretation, but I can guarantee that others might not agree. And while your brother's policies may have tied my hands on certain matters, you can't control what parents choose to do with their children if they were to find out," he finishes, his voice dripping with bitterness.

The veiled threat lands right in the middle of my chest, but I refuse to give him even more fodder. "Is that a threat, Rod?"

"Of course it's not," he retorts, arching a brow.

I stare at him. "If you're trying to intimidate me, you're wasting your time," I finish, my voice hard as steel.

Reaching around to the handle of my door, I hear Rod clear his throat. "As for the matter with Ms. Evans, I can assure you that she will not be the only student with these issues. We have now set a precedent, it seems. I trust you understand the concerns that might cause—"

"Let me be clear," I growl, stepping close enough for him to feel my breath on his face. "If you threaten my students again, I won't stop at policy changes. Bradleigh Evans is and always will be welcome at this school as long as I'm headmaster. As will any other student, no matter their gender identity, race, ethnicity, or religion.

Saint Helena is committed to creating a safe environment for all students," I practically yell. "And while we're at it," I add, stalking closer to Rod and getting in his face. "You should know that you're not the only one with connections, Rod," I say smoothly, leaning back. "The board and I have had very productive conversations lately. If you so much as think about pulling this shit again, I will fuck your life up so hard that you won't know what's up and what's down. Trust me when I say, I have my ways."

Rod's eyes flicker, just for a second, betraying the first glimmer of doubt. He thought I was the kind of man who prays away confrontation. He forgets I've spent years wielding the faith he hides behind like a sword.

"Mr. Ravage, I must say—" His chin wobbles as I huff a cruel laugh.

"I'm done having these conversations with you. If you have any other issue with our policies, take it up with the board. Otherwise, I suggest you stop wasting my time."

Stepping back, my eyes bore into his. I watch with glee as his jaw tightens, and for a minute, I think he might fight back. Instead, he smooths his jacket as though regaining his composure.

"I'll leave you to your day, Mr. Ravage," he says, his tone icy.

Turning on his heel, he walks down the hallway. His shoes echo for what feels like forever, but finally, the silence finds me again.

When he's finally gone, I close the door, leaning my

forehead against it as the adrenaline drains out of me. I won this round... but why doesn't it feel like victory?

My hands are trembling. My chest feels tight, as though I've run a marathon but never had the chance to catch my breath.

This has been a long fucking day.

I sink into my chair, running a hand over my face as the weight of everything I've been holding at bay crashes down on me. I've always been able to keep my cool. Even in the worst moments, I've prided myself on my restraint, my ability to outthink, outlast. But now? Now I've lost control completely.

Rod's words circle in my head like vultures.

You can't control what parents choose to do with their children if they were to find out... certain things about you.

I know his threat isn't empty. This isn't just about my job, it's about my integrity. My identity. How can I be entrusted with these kids if the parents don't approve of who I love, or how I choose to live my life?

And God, the hypocrisy of it all. These parents don't know anything about me. Not really, anyway. How could they, when I barely know myself? When I'm still fucking figuring it out?

Julian's kiss flashes through my mind, the warmth of his lips, the way he didn't hesitate to claim me. I can still feel the ghost of it, but instead of comfort, it brings a fresh wave of panic. Rod *saw*. He saw me kissing Julian, and I can only imagine what conclusions he's drawing, what whispers will ripple through the school if he decides to share what he saw.

I've spent my life living in service to others. To the church. To this school. To my family. And now? Now I'm caught between a love I'm still trying to understand and the impossible expectations of a community that would crucify me if they knew the truth.

I glance at my shelf, where the rosary Julian had brushed earlier sits like a relic of some distant, simpler version of myself. *What would they think if they knew the headmaster is bisexual? That I'm in love with a man and a woman? That I'm still trying to make sense of what it all means?*

It's not just the parents. It's me. My doubts. My contradictions.

My whole life is so different than what I expected it to be. I'd kept myself in this box for almost two decades, finding comfort in the simplicity. Finding release in a way that *I* could control. And now? The Ashfords turned my whole world upside down, and it feels like everything I once knew is slipping away.

And that scares me to the very depths of my bones.

I walk over and pick up the rosary, turning it over in my hands. The smooth beads press into my palm, grounding me in the same way they always have. Despite not being Catholic, I do find the rituals to be beautiful, and the meaning behind things to be in line with what I believe as a Christian.

But the weight of them feels heavier now. And the silence of the room feels oppressive, like it's swallowing me whole.

I've always believed in a God that loves all humans. My faith will always be here.

But my job? My students? Kids like Bradleigh, who need me to fight for them?

I'm not convinced the powers that be will see it the same way.

When my phone buzzes with a new message, I walk to my desk and reach for it automatically. It's from Sophie, a picture of the shop floor, half finished but brimming with potential. Her text is short and sweet.

> SOPHIE
>
> Thanks for helping today! Couldn't have done it without you. Hope your meeting went okay.

I stare at the screen, my thumb hovering over the keyboard.

I want to reply.

I want to tell her how much it meant to be there, how much she and Julian mean to me.

But the words won't come.

Because the truth is, I'm scared—scared that I'll lose everything I've worked for if I let myself believe I deserve more.

I set the phone down without typing anything and press my hands to my face, willing myself to breathe. But the tightness in my chest doesn't ease. Because no matter how much I want to believe otherwise, I know the truth.

Right now, alone is exactly what I am.

CHAPTER THIRTY-TWO
THE LIBRARY

JULIAN

The instant Kai walks into Inferno, I can tell something's bothering him. His shoulders are stiff, and his expression is pinched in a way I haven't seen since we were teenagers. He's wearing black trousers and a white Oxford shirt, no tie. His brown boots match his belt, and as always, his hair is artfully tousled—but his usual ease is gone.

I'd been worried about him all day, knowing yesterday had to have shaken him. Having Rod walk in on us wasn't just a private moment exposed... it was his entire career hanging in the balance. I'd texted him earlier to check in, but his responses had been short, guarded. Now, seeing him like this, I know he's likely still spiraling.

When his eyes find mine above the crowd, there's a

hint of something in his gaze—worry, distraction, or maybe both—as he walks over to us.

My chest tightens. He needs this tonight. I can feel it in the way he carries himself, in the way his expression is strained.

I can take care of him.

I can give him a space where everything else disappears, if only for a little while.

Nudging Sophie, who is chatting animatedly with the bartender, we both turn to face him.

"Hey," Kai says, taking a seat next to my wife. Turning to the bartender, he orders a single whiskey.

"Thanks for coming tonight," Sophie says, reaching out for his fingers. I notice the way his hand goes stiff underneath hers before relaxing. "I know it was last minute, but I—*we*—really wanted to see you."

Kai looks at me, and his emotions are shuttered behind his eyes as he nods once, smiling down at Sophie.

"There's nowhere else I'd rather be."

Sophie's not wrong. After I got home from Kai's office yesterday, Sophie and I hung around at home, wishing we could be with Kai. And because of what happened with his colleague, Rod, I'd wanted to give him some space. But then Sophie had gotten a package this morning... a wearable vibrator. She insisted she wanted to try having both of us inside of her tonight, and thought meeting at Inferno while wearing it would be a good way to get herself ready.

She has the remote control, and my only stipulation

was that she get herself nice and wet for us before we even attempt it.

Kai doesn't know. It's our surprise for him.

"Everything okay with..." I trail off, looking at Kai.

He nods once, and then he slams the entirety of his drink. "Yeah. I took care of it."

I huff a laugh. "Where'd you hide his body, then?"

This puts a genuine smile on his face, and my whole body tingles with warmth. *God, he's fucking cute when he smiles.*

"Very funny."

"I can help dig a grave," Sophie chimes in, grinning. "I have excellent upper body strength from brushing Snickers, and also from Pilates."

This makes Kai's smile broaden. "I might take you up on that one day, little dove."

His use of her nickname makes her blue eyes glaze over. "Whatever you need... *my lord.*"

Kai's eyes go from mirthful to something darker, a glint of possession in his gaze. The air shifts, and Sophie squirms next to me as she quickly finishes her wine.

"I thought we could go upstairs to Paradise," she explains, looking at Kai.

The whole club is based on two levels—Paradise and Purgatory. Orion Ravage owns the place, and I enjoy how exclusive it is here. I know Sophie does, too.

"No Purgatory for you tonight?" he asks, his voice teasing.

She leans back in her chair, crossing her legs. Her

answering grin is slow and deliberate, and her fingers trace the rim of her wineglass.

"Not tonight. I'd rather skip the penance and go straight to the reward."

Kai leans forward, his eyes dipping down to her crossed legs. "Careful, little dove," he says softly. His tone has an edge to it. "Paradise isn't as safe as it sounds."

The weight of his implication hangs in the air between the three of us. Sophie shivers, and my own pulse thrums at the way he's able to control her, the way she seems to unravel without so much as lifting a finger.

Kai is an anomaly, a contradiction I can't stop turning over in my head. With Sophie, I know where I stand, the rhythm of us well-worn and familiar—equal parts give and take, though I do prefer being in control.

But Kai? He's fluid, shifting between roles with a grace that unsettles me in the best way. When he submits, it's deliberate, an offering that feels earned, like he's letting me in on a secret no one else gets to see. And when he dominates, like when Sophie yields to him, it stirs something almost primal in me. A test. A *challenge*. Maybe even admiration.

I want him under me, completely mine, but it's more than that. I want to unravel him, to understand how someone so controlled can let go so entirely.

It's intoxicating in the best way.

And I feel damn lucky in the moment to have both of them in my life like this.

"I'll take the risk," Sophie says after a beat, her voice

more defiant than steady. "Shall we?" she asks, standing from her barstool.

Kai takes in her outfit—a short, plaid skirt and a fuzzy, white jumper with over-the-knee, heeled boots. She looks incredible, as always, and I drink in the way Kai studies her.

I know, I want to tell him. *We won the fucking lottery.*

Kai shifts his focus to me, his gaze dragging like a physical touch. "Let's go."

Sophie's eyes dart to mine as if to gauge my reaction. I can feel the heat creeping up my neck from the promise of what's to come.

We all walk upstairs with me leading the way. Sophie's hand is in mine, and Kai trails behind her. Once we get to the top floor, Sophie places something in Kai's hand, whispering in his ear. From the way he stares down at her, and the way his neck flushes, I can tell she just handed him the remote.

"I changed my mind," she says to us. "I want to go straight to our room."

Kai's eyes find mine on the landing, and I arch a challenging brow in his direction. We'd booked out a private room for tonight, and it required a few strings to be pulled because everything was already booked out.

Kai answers her by clicking the remote on, and her tiny inhale is the only indication that it's working. He looks at me again, his expression serious.

"Lead the way," he says.

I pull Sophie down the hallway, and when I look

back, her other hand is entwined with Kai's, her fingers laced with his.

I can't speak for other couples who open their marriage, but I'm starting to understand the appeal. Seeing the person you love, *loving* someone else and happier than ever? I can see why people do this. It's almost addicting, this feeling of compersion.

Once we get to our room, I reach into my pocket and unlock the door, labeled *The Library*.

When I looked into renting a private room for tonight, I'd seen that they had different themed rooms to rent out. And I thought that Sophie would enjoy this one.

When I push the door open, she gasps behind me.

"Oh, this is lush," she says, coming to stand next to me.

There are two walls of books, floor to ceiling. There's a desk and an armchair, and on the other wall, an extra-large king bed adorned in red, satin sheets.

Kai comes to my other side, and when I look over at him, that same expression from earlier is back on his face.

It's... vulnerable. Open. *Scared*.

Without thinking, I reach over, my fingers brushing against his wrist as I take the remote from his hand. The touch is brief, but I let it linger just long enough for him to feel it, just long enough to let him know I see him.

Kai's eyes flick to mine, searching, and I meet his gaze with something steady, something I hope tells him it's okay. I don't move. Neither does he.

But the tension in his shoulders eases, just slightly.

I turn the vibrator all the way up, the hum of the speakers filling the space between us.

"Oh fuck," Sophie whispers, knees buckling.

Kai's eyes bore into mine, and all I can do is shrug nonchalantly.

"No point in waiting." Looking at Sophie, who looks like she's about to pass out, I kneel down on one knee and begin to unzip one of her boots. Her legs are trembling, so I make sure to let my fingers drift over the insides of her knees and thighs.

"Julian," she growls, knowing exactly what I'm doing.

Once I'm done with the other boot, she steps out of both as I stand.

I'm just about to make a quip about moving to the desk or bed when Sophie turns around and pulls Kai in for a kiss. Her arms work around his neck, and she moans as she presses her body closer.

Yeah, I could get used to this.

I step behind Sophie and work my hands underneath her jumper.

And God, it's not just her—the soft, familiar feel of her skin or the heat of her body beneath my hands—that has my heart pounding in my chest. It's the sight of Kai, his tentative hands settling on her waist, and the way his breathing hitches as she deepens the kiss.

For a moment, I just stand there and take it all in. My hands rest on Sophie's hips, watching my best friend kiss my wife. The way his lips part beneath hers, the way his lashes flutter as if he's caught in some dream he doesn't know he's allowed to have.

But he is.

Because as much as Sophie is mine—always has been, always will be—I can feel it in my chest like a second heartbeat: *Kai's mine too.* Or could be, if he'd let me.

My hand shifts, fingers trailing along Sophie's side, and she leans into me with a soft sigh. Her head tilts slightly, giving me just enough room to press a kiss to the curve of her neck.

But my eyes stay locked on Kai.

He catches me staring, and for a second, he looks like he might pull away. But then, something changes. His gaze sharpens, his brows drawing together, and it's like he's daring me—challenging me—to say or do something.

Instead, I lift a hand and let it hover near his cheek, not quite touching but close enough that he knows he could lean into it if he wants.

And he does.

It's subtle, just the barest tilt of his head toward my palm, but it's enough to send a jolt of heat straight to my core.

Sophie notices, of course she does. She always sees everything. Pulling back just slightly, they end their kiss and she looks at me over her shoulder, her lips curving into a wicked grin.

"You boys need a minute?" she teases, her voice low and rich with amusement.

Kai lets out a nervous laugh, but I just smirk, my fingers flexing against Sophie's hips. "Maybe later," I say, stepping closer, until we're all pressed together. I click the remote down to give Sophie a reprieve.

She hums, pleased, and tugs her jumper over her head, tossing it somewhere behind her. She's in nothing but her bra and skirt now, and when she turns back to Kai, it's like she's giving him permission to look, to touch, to *be*.

But his eyes dart back to me instead, searching.

I reach out without thinking, my fingers tangling with his. His hand is warm, hesitant, but he doesn't pull away. Instead, he tightens his grip, and the way his thumb brushes over mine sends a shiver racing down my spine.

I don't know when it happened, but I'm falling. For him, for this—for *us*.

It feels right. All of it.

When Sophie's head falls back against my chest, Kai's eyes linger—not on her, but on me. There's something sharp in his gaze, something that makes the hairs on the back of my neck stand on end. It isn't jealousy, not exactly.

It's hunger... but for what, I'm not sure he even knows.

"Julian," Sophie whimpers. She starts circling her hips, and I drop to my knees again. "I'm getting close."

"Down," I say, tugging lightly on Kai's trousers. His eyes darken, but he obeys, sinking beside me. When he hesitates again, I slide a hand down his back, applying just enough pressure to make him move. "You can take care of her, can't you?"

When I slowly unzip Sophie's skirt, I see him lick his lips in my peripheral vision. A low, steady humming noise is coming from between her legs, and when her skirt pools at her feet, I lean back on my heels.

"Go ahead," I tell him. "Take her knickers off."

Kai reaches forward and slowly tugs the black, lacy material down. He sucks in a breath when the purple toy comes into view, held in place by a black harness.

"Fuck," Kai whispers.

He trails a hand over the clitoral stimulator, and when he presses it down against her clit, her hips jerk forward erratically.

I trail a finger up the inside of her thighs, groaning when I realize she's leaking arousal. Swiping it onto my fingers, I turn and hold it up to Kai's mouth.

"Taste our girl."

He bends forward, his warm mouth suctioning around my two fingers. His eyes are hooded, and as his tongue swirls around the tips of my fingers, my lashes flutter.

I resist the urge to moan, resist the urge to let my eyes roll back so he knows how fucking good his mouth feels. I remember the feel of his tongue on my cock, the way his tongue moved expertly for someone who'd never given a blow job in his life.

Kai lets out a guttural sound, popping off my fingers as he looks up at Sophie. "Delicious," he murmurs. Kai's tongue glides along Sophie's inner thigh, but his grip on her hips feels too light, like he's holding back. His eyes flick to me, searching for something I can't quite name. I watch as he hesitates, just for a fraction of a second, before he continues.

Even now, I can see it—the tight coil of restraint winding through him.

Pulling her knickers all the way down, he swipes his tongue up her seam, meeting the tip of the vibrator. Reaching around her hips, he unclasps it. The vibrator falls to the floor, and I click it off just as Kai looks up at Sophie with both of his large hands on her arse. "Do you mind if I taste you again, little dove?"

"N-no," Sophie whispers, her hands already running through his hair.

Kai leans forward and suctions his mouth around her clit. The sounds he's making, and the way her mouth drops open in bliss, has me trailing a finger between her legs. I push my finger into her tight cunt, and Kai's scruff brushes against my knuckles as he feasts on my wife. Without thinking, I bend forward and press the side of my face against Kai's, licking my wife in tandem with him.

"Oh fuck, yes, both of you," Sophie whimpers. "God, this is—"

I cut her off by adding two more fingers inside of her. She lets out a high-pitched, pleading sound, and it only makes Kai groan in response as he continues his ministrations. It's messy and wet, and every time Kai's tongue brushes against mine, I let out a low growl.

I've always loved the way Sophie tastes—salty and a bit sharp, with a hint of sweetness. Mixed with Kai?

It's fucking delectable.

"Oh God, I'm close," Sophie says. She has one hand in my hair and one hand in Kai's, and she's pulling us both closer.

"Yeah? Come for us, Soph. Show us you're ready to take both of us at once," Kai says, his voice hoarse.

"Yes, yes, fuck, just like that," she begs us. "More, harder—"

I add a fourth finger, diving most of my hand inside of her now. I'm not gentle, either, but she's more than prepped now.

And as her knees buckle, she cries out. Her skin is trembling, and her breathing turns ragged as she clamps down on my fingers—over, and over, and over. I can feel the way it pulses through her entire body, and it only spurs both of us on.

Sophie collapses against me, panting softly as I run my fingers through her hair. Kai lingers nearby. He starts to pull away, but I reach for him, fingers wrapping around his wrist.

"Stay," I murmur, tugging him closer to us. He hesitates for a second before settling beside me, the tension in his body softening as Sophie's hand slips into his.

"I think I'm ready for both of you now."

CHAPTER THIRTY-THREE
THE SHIFT

Sophie

I drag Kai over to the bed, and he lets me lead him. He situates himself beneath me, his broad chest rising and falling beneath my palms as I straddle his hips, grinding slowly against him. His eyes are dark, stormy, watching every shift of my body like I'm something sacred, like I'm the only thing in the room that matters.

He's been in a strange mood all night, and just the fact that he's letting me lead him is almost disconcerting. I push the thought aside, though—for now, at least.

The soft satin against my knees and calves slides against my heated skin, and when I work my hand under Kai's shirt, he feels like a furnace.

"I want you," I whisper, not bothering to hide the edge of desperation in my voice. "I need this."

Julian comes behind me, straddling Kai as well and

pressing his chest against my back. His hands glide over my waist as his lips brush along the curve of my neck.

I feel worshiped. Consumed. But more than that—I feel powerful.

Kai's hands grip my hips, his fingers digging in as though he's afraid I might slip away. His eyes drift shut briefly, and when he opens them again, there's a glimmer of something else behind his gaze. Reverence.

Reaching down, I slowly unbuckle his belt. He shifts his hips up, pressing his bulge into my bare pussy. I snap the belt off, tossing it to the side. Everything inside of me is pulsing, and I don't try to hide the way my hands work quickly—desperately—to free his cock. It springs free when I pull his pants down, and I slide up so that I'm sitting on top of him, his length pressed against my folds.

I roll my hips against him and a low groan escapes his lips. "Jesus Christ," Kai mutters under his breath, his head falling back against the pillows as he grips me tighter.

Julian hums behind me, his lips curling against the shell of my ear. "She's divine, isn't she?" he murmurs, trailing his hands lower, parting my thighs just slightly to brush his knuckles against Kai's cock as he feels how slick I am.

Kai's breath catches, and his eyes snap to mine, wide and dark beneath the low light. His hands press into the small of my back, grounding himself in the feel of me, but there's a tremble there, barely noticeable, but I feel it like a ripple beneath his skin.

"She's made for this," Julian continues, his voice

curling around us like silk. His lips brush the shell of my ear, each word pouring into me like honey. "Made to take us both."

I slowly start to unbutton Kai's shirt, and as I do, he swallows hard—the movement of his throat drawing my gaze. The soft flicker of candlelight catches the faint sheen of sweat at his temple, the flush creeping along his collarbone where his shirt hangs open. His chest rises and falls beneath me, each breath shallow, ragged, as if he's holding something back, like he's on the precipice of losing control but hasn't decided if he's ready to fall.

I shift slightly in his lap, grinding down just enough to feel the ache of him pressing against me, and his eyes flutter closed for half a second. When they open again, they're molten.

"Kai," I whisper, cupping his face between my hands. His skin is hot beneath my palms, his stubble rough against the soft pads of my thumbs as I trace the line of his jaw. His gaze wobbles, the faintest crack in his armor, but it's there—a flash of hesitation, of vulnerability.

"I—" His voice catches, rough and raw, and he swallows again, searching my face like he's looking for permission, or maybe something deeper than that. His fingers trail up my sides, reverent and deliberate, tracing the curve of my ribs until his palms cup the swell of my breasts, thumbs grazing over my nipples. I arch into him, a soft moan spilling from my lips, but I don't take my eyes off his.

Kai's grip falters for half a second, his chest heaving

beneath me, but I kiss him before he can pull away, dragging him up into the heat of my mouth.

And he lets me.

His hands slip into my hair, tangling at the base of my skull as his tongue slides against mine, soft at first but growing hungrier, like he's chasing something he didn't know he needed until now.

Julian's hands slip lower, parting my legs farther as he settles between them, his cock hard and insistent as it presses against me from behind. I gasp into Kai's mouth as Julian tilts my hips up and back, aligning us.

Kai pulls away just far enough to watch, his lips swollen, his breathing shallow.

"You see that, Kai?" Julian growls, his voice darkening. He tosses a condom next to Kai. I hear him open a bottle of lube before he pushes into me, slow and deliberate. "How perfect she is like this? Feel it. She's full now, but you get to be the one to stretch her."

Kai's eyes drop down to where I stretch around Julian, his expression shifting, raw and unguarded in a way that makes my heart ache.

His mouth parts as if to speak, but instead, he lifts his hand, pressing it flat against my lower belly, feeling the way Julian fills me.

"Christ," he mutters under his breath, his fingers pressing just a little harder.

Julian thrusts deeper, groaning low in his throat. "I think he likes watching you take it," Julian breathes against my ear. His hand joins Kai's, pressing down until the sensation is overwhelming. "Is that it, Kai? You like watching her come apart on top of you?"

Kai's grip tightens, his knuckles white against my skin.

"I do," he growls, his control snapping like a thread pulled too tight.

"You ready for both of us, pet?" Julian growls, his fingers digging into my hips.

"Yes," I breathe, rocking my hips slightly, feeling Kai twitch against me at the movement.

Kai's eyes flutter shut again, his grip tightening.

"Give it to her," he groans, his voice thick and heavy with need. "She can take it."

He grabs the condom Julian had tossed to him earlier, sheathing himself.

We'd discussed this, and though I was disappointed to be using a condom again, we all decided it would be best, just until I'm able to see my new doctor next week. Last time was fine because he was in my arse, but this time, there's more of a risk for pregnancy.

He lifts me effortlessly, shifting beneath me until his cock presses against the slick heat of my entrance, and he presses into me with steady pressure, holding it in place so it doesn't move. After a couple of seconds, the head of his cock slips in, stretching me alongside Julian in a way that feels like too much and not enough all at once.

I cry out. The overwhelming fullness blurs the edges of pleasure and pain, and I cling to Kai, nails digging into his shoulders as I gasp his name. It takes a couple of seconds for him to sink in, for him to get past the tight ring that Julian is already filling so well. But when he does...

My mouth drops open.

His forehead presses against mine, and I can feel his breath shaking as he moves beneath me.

"You're fucking incredible," he groans, his voice fraying at the edges.

Julian's pace quickens behind me, matching Kai's movements until I can't tell where one of them ends and the other begins.

It feels endless.

"Fuck," Julian mutters, his breath hot against the back of my neck. "She's so tight like this."

Kai's eyes flick down, watching where they both sink into me, his jaw tightening as if the sight alone might undo him.

"You feel that?" Julian whispers, his breath ghosting over my shoulder. "That's us, filling her together. Taking her apart."

Kai groans deeply, his hands trembling as they cup my face, pulling me down for a kiss that feels almost desperate.

"This feels fucking amazing," he growls against my lips, his voice ragged.

Julian sets a slow, punishing rhythm behind me, grinding his hips forward in time with Kai's thrusts beneath me.

I can feel them everywhere, stretching me, filling me, unraveling me piece by piece.

It's overwhelming in the best way, the pleasure tipping me dangerously close to the edge.

Julian's hand slips between my legs, finding my clit with ease, and he circles it slowly, drawing soft gasps from my lips.

Julian presses his mouth to my ear, and his voice lowers to a dark, indulgent whisper. "It's my favorite thing, you know," Julian says, his tone deceptively casual. "Watching another man worship my wife. Can you imagine it, Kai? Watching someone else take her while we fuck her together?"

Kai stills beneath me.

It's subtle, the way his rhythm falters—just enough for me to feel the shift.

Julian doesn't seem to notice. He thrusts harder, snapping his hips forward until I gasp and brace myself against Kai's chest.

But Kai's breathing changes.

I feel it beneath my hands, the tension coiling in his muscles.

His gaze drops, and though his hands stay on my hips, there's a distance in his eyes now, a hesitation that wasn't there before.

I reach for his face, brushing my thumb along his jawline, silently willing him to stay with me.

But something's already shifted.

A shiver racks through me, but not from the cold.

"Goddamn," Julian hisses, his movements becoming erratic. "I love the feeling of your cock against mine, Kai," he growls. "I can't wait for the day we can both come inside of her."

"Fuck," Kai whispers, all pretenses gone.

Watching him unravel beneath me is intoxicating, and the sight of him losing control is enough to make me roll my hips. I arch against him, grinding down harder, and Kai's head tilts back, exposing the long column of his throat. His lips part in something that resembles prayer, soft, inaudible words spilling from his mouth as if he can't contain them.

Julian shifts behind me, his lips brushing against my temple as he hears the words too. "That's it," he whispers, his hand curling under my jaw, tilting my head back against his shoulder. "Pray for her, Kai. Let her know exactly how much you need this."

"Thy kingdom come," he groans, his hands trembling as they grip my hips, guiding me to move. "Thy will be done..."

The sound of him—so raw, so close to unraveling—sends molten heat pooling low in my belly. But something shifts beneath his words, something darker. His grip tightens at my waist, rougher now, and suddenly I'm not guiding the pace anymore. Kai takes over, pulling me down onto him with deliberate force, dragging me over the thick length of his cock until I gasp.

"Oh, fuck—"

His control breaks open in front of me like a floodgate. He thrusts up hard, driving deeper, his hips snapping beneath me in desperate, unrelenting strokes. Julian groans low against my ear, his arms banding tighter around my torso as if holding me in place to take everything Kai is giving.

"She's so close, Kai," Julian murmurs, his breath warm on my neck. "Can you feel it?"

"Yes," Kai growls, his voice strained, reverent and wrecked all at once. One hand slides up my spine, curling around the back of my neck, holding me down as he pounds into me, chasing that high. "I can feel her tightening—Christ, she's going to fall apart on us."

My body trembles, caught between the rhythm of Kai's cock driving into me and the relentless, teasing drag of Julian's cock sliding into me from behind.

"Please," I whimper, pushing my head back against Julian's shoulder, my legs threatening to give out. "I—"

"You're ours," Kai breathes, the words vibrating through me like a command. His eyes lock with mine as if he's daring me to break under him. "Come for us, Sophie."

Julian's hand slips lower, pressing down on the bulge at the base of my stomach. "You heard him," Julian growls, his voice rough with need. "Come now, let us feel you shatter around our cocks."

The pressure is unbearable, the heat curling tighter and tighter until I can't contain it anymore.

I break.

I unravel between them, caught in the space where pleasure burns so brightly it almost feels like pain. My walls clench around both of them as I cry out, my body arching between them like a bowstring drawn too tight.

The tension snaps, and the orgasm rushes through me, all-consuming.

"Oh God—"

Kai groans deep in his chest as he feels me pulse around him, and something inside him snaps. His thrusts grow erratic, his hips slamming up into me one final time before he gasps, head tilting back. I collapse, pressing my chest against his and dragging my lips down the front of his throat.

"Yes—fuck, Sophie," he chokes out, his hands bruising against my hips as he holds me down, buried to the hilt. His body trembles, and I feel his thick cock pulse with his climax inside of me. His hands grab my head, bring my lips to his as his forehead presses hard against mine—as if anchoring himself to this moment.

Julian isn't far behind. His nails drag over the sensitive skin of my lower back and arse, and then I feel him stiffen behind me, his cock jerking as he empties himself, hot and deep, alongside Kai.

A rough sound escapes him, something between a growl and a curse. His hand tightens in my hair, as if he can't let go until he's wrung every ounce of pleasure from this moment.

The three of us collapse together, breathless and tangled, our bodies slick with sweat and satisfaction.

I feel Kai's heart hammering beneath my palm, his arms wrapped tight around me like he's afraid I might disappear if he loosens his grip. Julian rests his forehead against my shoulder, his breathing ragged, his lips tracing lazy patterns over my skin as if savoring the aftermath.

For a long moment, no one moves.

I'm weightless, held securely between the two people I trust most in the world, and for the first time in weeks, I feel whole. Grounded.

Loved.

Julian is the first to break the silence, his voice soft but teasing as he nips at my shoulder.

"Goddamn," he rasps, his breath still uneven.

Kai laughs, breathless and hoarse, pressing a kiss to my temple. "Yeah. I think I've lost the ability to speak."

Julian hums in agreement, his lips curving into a grin against my skin. "That's my favorite thing about watching someone else with her. Watching them lose themselves."

There it is—the shift.

The words are light, teasing, but I feel the way Kai tenses beneath me, how the gentle strokes of his fingers on my hip slow, then still.

I tilt my head slightly, catching the shadowed expression before he smooths it over with a quick smile.

But I know him. I know when he's pulling away.

"Yeah," Kai says quietly, his hand slipping to my lower back, no longer possessive, just steady. "It's... something."

Julian doesn't notice the shift—his focus is on me, pressing kisses to my bare shoulder like he's worshiping me with his mouth.

But I notice.

And when Kai's hands start to drift, when his weight shifts like he might pull me off of him, I reach down, lacing my fingers with his.

"Stay," I whisper, squeezing his hand.

He hesitates for only a second before nodding, exhaling quietly as he pulls me tighter against his body.

But even as Julian murmurs soft praises against my skin, even as Kai's body molds to mine, I feel the distance between us—subtle but growing.

And I know, in the quiet corner of my mind, that this isn't over yet.

CHAPTER THIRTY-FOUR
THE FREEDOM

Sophie

When we get back to Ashford Palace, I'm not nearly as sleepy as I was when we left Inferno. Julian says good night to our driver, and the three of us go inside. I'm sore—and every step I take is a heavy, aching reminder of what we did tonight. Still, it was... incredible. And I want to do it a thousand more times. Lacing my fingers with Kai's, I pull him into the foyer and set my handbag down.

"Shall I make us some pasta?" Julian asks, stepping out of his shoes.

"I'm starving," Kai chimes in, looking down at me.

A full-body shiver works through me at his double entendre.

"I should go check on Snickers," I tell Julian. "Barbara left early today."

Barbara is someone I hired to help with most of the

daily upkeep for my horse. And because I've been so busy with the shop, I haven't had the chance to go see her today.

"No problem, pet. I'll take care of making us a late dinner," Julian says warmly.

"Do you want to come with me?" I ask Kai.

"I'd love to," he says, squeezing my hand once.

"There, it's settled. I'll get us some much-needed sustenance and Kai can help you shovel shit."

I bark a laugh. "Julian!"

He's chuckling even as he walks into the kitchen, whistling a song I don't recognize.

"There's no shit," I tell him, rolling my eyes. "I have someone who does all of that. I mostly just brush, ride, and feed Snickers. My favorite things."

"Listen, little dove, I'd shovel shit all day if you were by my side."

Giving him a shy smile, I shove his shoulder playfully with my free hand. Then I bend down to unzip my boots, stepping into my trainers instead.

"I like this look," Kai says, gesturing to my plaid skirt and bare legs. "You look like a naughty student."

"Is that so? I bet you love that, you dirty headmaster."

This makes him laugh, and the sight of him laughing like this—of letting go—is addictive.

"Come on. Let's go."

I open the door and Kai follows me out into the cool night. One of the stipulations of buying this house was that we had to build a barn. I've always had horses—I can't remember a time when I didn't have my own horse, as posh as that sounds. And Snickers is special to me, because picking her out was the first time I remember defying my parents.

She was my first taste of freedom.

Kai is quiet as we walk around the side of the house and down a lit pathway now flanked by magnolia trees.

"My house growing up was called 'Magnolia Estate.' My parents aren't part of the aristocracy like Julian, but we were definitely upper class. They called themselves driven, but I think they were merely ladder climbers, always on the outside waiting for an invitation inside. That's why they brokered a deal with the Ashford family. Our marriage was informally arranged, meaning we were introduced with the expectation of furthering each family's agenda. For the Ashfords, it meant a hefty dowry as well as a pretty wife for Julian. For my family, it meant that I would become a viscountess. Lady Sophia Grace Ashford."

Kai hums in acknowledgment. "Your parents sound... interesting," he says sarcastically.

I snort, stopping next to one of the baby magnolia trees I'd planted around the palace. I press my palm against the trunk, and look up at the large, blooming, white flowers.

"My mother always told me that magnolia trees represented nobility and purity. And that's exactly how they raised me—not a hair out of place, not a word out of line. It wasn't until we moved here that I learned magnolia trees also represent perseverance."

It's quiet, so quiet that the only sound is the faint rustle of magnolia leaves swaying in the breeze. For a moment, it feels like the world has shrunk down to just the two of us.

I glance sideways at Kai, catching the soft crease in his brow as he listens. He doesn't interrupt, doesn't press me to elaborate, but I can feel his attention wrapped around me.

I exhale, letting my fingers drift over the waxy petals of one of the magnolias. "Perseverance," I repeat, tracing the outline of a flower with the tip of my finger. "I didn't realize how much that word would mean to me until I left England."

Kai watches me carefully, his head tilting slightly. "How so?"

I let out a quiet laugh, shaking my head as I brush my hair back over my shoulder. "Leaving felt like stepping off a perfectly laid path into... well, the wilderness. Everything was so clear-cut before. Marriage, titles, expectations—predictable. But here? Julian and I built this place with our own hands. It feels earned in a way nothing else in my life ever has."

Kai's gaze softens. He looks at the house behind us, the soft glow of light from the kitchen window spilling out over the lawn, and then back at the barn in the distance.

"It's beautiful," he says. "And it feels like you."

I swallow against the sudden lump in my throat, caught off guard by how easily he seems to understand.

"It is," I murmur. "I feel more like myself here. But

sometimes..." I hesitate, the words hovering just on the edge of admission. "Sometimes I miss it. Not the life, but the little things. Silly things, really."

Kai doesn't look at me like it's silly. His expression holds nothing but quiet patience.

"Like what?" he asks.

I step away from the magnolia tree, continuing toward the barn with him beside me. "Sunday roasts. The smell of mulled wine at Christmas markets, or even just the festive lights around my village at Christmastime. Watching football with my dad, even though I never really cared about it. The tiny village pubs that somehow still exist, even though they look like they're about to collapse at any moment."

I smile faintly, feeling the bittersweet pang of nostalgia settle low in my chest. "It's not so much the place. It's the memories. I guess I miss who I was when I was there. Or maybe... who I thought I was supposed to be."

Kai doesn't respond right away as he considers my words. "I get that. It's strange, right? You leave, thinking you're running toward freedom, but you end up carrying pieces of the past with you anyway."

I glance up at him, and my curiosity gets the best of me. "Is that how it feels for you?"

His jaw tenses for a second before he answers. "Sometimes." His eyes stay fixed on the barn ahead, but I see the trace of something deeper behind his expression. "Being estranged from my father for years before his death didn't negate the memories. I still thought about him all the time—even now. Taking the job at Saint Helena a few years ago... I wanted to escape who I used to be. But there are days when I wonder if I'm just circling back to it, no matter how far I try to run."

We slow as we reach the barn doors, and I turn to face him fully, reaching out to brush my fingertips lightly against his arm.

"It's okay to change," I say gently. "You've always been the kind of man who carries the weight of the people you love. Your brothers, for example. Your students, and the rest of the staff at Saint Helena. It means you care, Kai."

His eyes meet mine, and for a long moment, he just looks at me, like he's searching for something in my face that he isn't sure he'll find.

"Maybe," he murmurs. But then his lips curve into the faintest smile, and the tension in his shoulders eases. "I think I'd like to see your home someday," he adds quietly. "The village, the lights at Christmas... all of it."

"Have you ever been to England?"

"Twice," Kai answers, smiling down at me. "But only London."

I huff a laugh. "London is fun. But one day, I'd love to take you to get you a proper chippy."

"A what?" Kai asks, grinning now.

God, his smile is addicting.

"You lot call it fish and chips."

"Ah, but chippy is so much cuter when you say it."

I cackle as warmth spreads through me at the thought. The idea of Kai standing in the middle of my childhood village, snow falling around him, feels like something I never realized I wanted until now.

"I'd like that too," I admit. His fingers brush against mine, a fleeting touch, but it lingers long after we continue walking.

We're both quiet the rest of the two-minute walk to the barn. Once we get there, I open the door, and Snickers neighs loudly, her voice echoing in the stillness.

"She's loud," Kai comments, a faint smile tugging at his lips.

"She's lonely," I admit, running my hand over her mane. Guilt prickles at me as I say it out loud. Horses don't live alone. They need companions, just like we do.

I glance at Kai and shrug, trying to keep my tone light. "It wasn't supposed to be this way. When I brought her here, there was another horse. Ace." I pause, my chest tightening. "But he passed away not long after we got here. Colic."

Kai's expression softens. "That's rough. For both of you."

"It was," I say quietly, my fingers stroking Snickers's neck. "She's adjusted better than I have, honestly. I've been meaning to get her a friend—she deserves that—but I've been waiting for the right time. Or maybe I've just been putting it off because I feel like I failed her."

Kai's hand brushes mine, grounding me. "You haven't failed her. You're here. You're taking care of her. That's what matters."

"Thank you." Snickers neighs again, and I laugh. "She knows I have treats," I say, stepping into the barn.

Snickers—a beautiful Holsteiner—leans her head over the stall door. Her big, brown eyes are bright with anticipation.

"Beautiful," Kai says, reaching a careful hand out to pet her. Snickers huffs against his hand, but she's gentle—and she accepts him immediately by rubbing her face against his open palm.

"She likes you," I tell him, hanging on the barn door and smiling.

"How long have you had her?" Kai asks, smiling as Snickers continues to rub against him.

"I picked her out in Germany when I was twelve. My father wanted me to get something fancier, like an Arabian, but Snickers reminds me of a unicorn with her white coat."

Kai goes still. "A unicorn?"

I laugh. "It's silly."

Kai's eyes soften as he looks at me. "No, it's cute. I love that."

His words hang heavy between us, and I swallow thickly before looking back at Snickers. "Anyway, it was the first time I'd gone against my father's wishes. He was strict—both my parents were, seeing as they were raising me to be a *lady*," I add, rolling my eyes. "So, it's special to me that Snickers is here. With me. She's happier—the warm air, the sunshine..." I trail off wistfully.

"And you?" Kai asks, brushing up against my side.

Looking up at him, I pull my lower lip between my teeth. "And me. Because I'm free now."

Kai's brow furrows slightly. "You mean... because of the hotwife stuff?" he asks, stepping away and brushing his nose with his hand.

I check Snickers's water bucket first. It's still half full, but I top it off anyway before fluffing the hay in the corner to make sure she has enough to last the night. The cool air feels steady in the barn, and I run a hand along her flank to check—neither too warm nor too cool. Satisfied, I give her a quick pat before moving to the next task.

"Yeah, that. I really do enjoy meeting the men Julian chooses. I love watching Julian's reaction when they see me, and keeping it one night only makes it easy to carry on with our lives. I suppose doing it *is* freeing. I'm free from societal pressure, free from judgment, free to be and act however I want to."

I pause, watching Snickers for a moment. I can feel Kai's gaze lingering, his silence stretching out just a little too long.

When I glance over, his expression is hard to read, his lips pressed into a thin line.

"It's like stepping into this version of myself that doesn't have to apologize for taking up space—for being desired. There's something powerful in that. Knowing I can be both soft and bold, both a wife and... something else. I get to reclaim parts of myself that the world tries to shame women for. It makes me feel powerful. In control. *Beautiful*," I add, blushing.

"You are," Kai says, looking at me with that same guarded expression. "Beautiful, I mean. My heart nearly stopped that first day when you opened your front door."

I chew on the inside of my cheek as I look down. "Thank you. You're not so bad-looking yourself," I add.

I glance over at Kai, a small smile tugging at my lips. "And honestly? I like the attention. I like being admired, being wanted. Not in a way that threatens my relationship with Julian, but in a way that enhances it. Seeing the way Julian watches me with someone else, the way his eyes darken, that possessiveness he can barely contain... it drives me wild."

Kai shifts on his feet, dragging his thumb along the edge of his jeans pocket. "Yeah. I get that." But his voice is softer, a little distant, like he's turning the words over in his head and not quite sure what to do with them.

"But?" I press gently, leaning against the wall.

His eyes flick to mine, and for a second, I catch a flash of hesitation, something guarded beneath his usual calm. "No, it's nothing," he says, looking away quickly.

I don't press him.

"It's not just about the sex, you know," I continue. "It's about being seen, feeling alive in that moment."

Kai exhales softly, nodding as if he wants to believe it—needs to. "I understand. You feel alive here, and you didn't in London."

"Exactly. Here, there's no stuffy parties or boring afternoon teas with the wives of the aristocracy. Julian and I couldn't do anything without ending up on page six of the tabloids. But here? No one knows or cares who we are."

Kai nods, but he stays quiet.

While Snickers eats more of the treats I feed her, I run

my hands over her back again. Her soft, light-gray hair gleams under the dim barn lights. She nudges me with her nose a few times, probably looking for more treats.

Kai is quiet, but he watches me with something that makes my nerves thrum with anticipation.

When she's finished eating, I stroke her neck gently—just the way she likes it. "Good night, girl," I murmur, adjusting the blanket over her back before shutting the stall door. Snickers lets out a soft snort, and I hear her settling into the hay. The quiet rustling tells me that she's content for the night.

Kai follows me out as I flip off the barn light, the darkness swallowing us as I step outside, the scent of fresh hay permeating the cool, night air.

Crossing my arms, I look up at Kai as we slowly walk back.

He's quiet as we meander down the lit pathway. Taking a deep breath, I break the silence, though something intuitive and unsettling coils low in my belly, like I almost don't want to know.

"A penny for your thoughts?"

He hesitates, placing his hands into his pockets. "I've just been thinking about all of this. You and Julian. The whole dynamic."

I nod as nervous butterflies flit through my stomach. "What about it?"

He shrugs, his steps slowing. "It's a lot to process. Don't get me wrong," he says quickly. "I knew what I was getting into, but actually experiencing it?" He shrugs. "That's different."

I look up at him, studying his vulnerable expression. He's usually so stoic and calm. Seeing him like this only enhances those nervous butterflies.

"What do you mean?" I ask softly.

Kai huffs a quiet laugh. "Listen, Sophie. Don't get me wrong, I'm happy to be here. With you... and with Julian. But sometimes..." He trails off, shaking his head. "Sometimes I feel like I'm standing on the outside looking in."

His words make my chest ache, and I stop walking, turning to face him. "Kai, you're in this. *With* us. Not an outsider."

He looks at me, his eyes searching mine. "Aren't I? You and Julian have this whole history together. You've built a life, routines, traditions. I'm trying to fit into something that's already so solid."

"We're trying to make room for you," I say earnestly. "It's not just Julian and me anymore. You're a part of this. I hope you know that."

Kai's lips press into a thin line, and he glances away. "I don't know. I can't explain it."

"Try," I urge, my voice sharper than I intend.

He sighs, rubbing the back of his neck. "I guess it doesn't always feel like I'm a part of whatever this is. But maybe it's my own insecurity." He looks at me, and his expression is so defeated that it feels like my heart cracks in half. "Forget I said anything, all right?"

I swallow, the warmth from earlier still lingering on my skin, but now it feels distant, like a fading echo. I nod once, and we resume our walk in silence.

It's hard to reconcile this version of Kai with the one I

had beneath me just an hour ago. Back at the club, he was there—present in a way that felt unshakable. His body melted against mine, every touch pulling him deeper, every sound unraveling him until it felt like nothing else existed outside of us.

But the more I think about it, the more I remember the moments I brushed aside.

The way his hands hesitated on my hips, lingering without the same surety as before. The flicker of doubt that crossed his face. The way he'd pulled away slightly, his body stiffening just when I thought he was fully lost to the pleasure between us.

I hadn't really paid attention then, too caught up in the moment. I thought maybe he was overwhelmed—too much sensation, too quickly. But now, as we walk side by side, his steps heavier and slower, it feels like something else.

It feels like he's retreating.

Like he's already halfway out the door in his mind, second-guessing every part of himself that he let us see.

I replay Julian's words in my head, the offhand comment about watching me with another man. The way Kai's eyes had faltered, something dark and uncertain flashing behind them before he buried it beneath a kiss.

I hadn't thought anything of it then. But maybe I should have.

Maybe this isn't just about tonight. Maybe this is about what happens after.

I don't reach for him, even though I want to. Even though it feels like I *should*.

Because something tells me he needs to sit on it for a minute. And maybe, just maybe, he needs to see that we aren't going anywhere.

We reach the house two minutes later, and the warm light spilling from the windows contrasts with the tension hanging between us. Inside, Julian is sitting on the bottom of the stairs, a glass of whiskey in one hand and a book in the other. He looks up as we walk in, a smile spreading across his face.

"Hey, you two. The pasta is done. How's Snickers?"

"Good," I reply, unsure if I should sit down next to him or stay next to Kai. My tone is clipped, though. Julian picks up on it immediately, setting his glass down.

"What's wrong?" he asks, his brows knitting together.

Kai leans against the doorframe, crossing his arms over his chest. "Nothing. Just... talking."

Julian looks between us, his frown deepening. "Okay. Talking about what?"

I look over at Kai, and he shrugs. I can't read him right now, but I do know that open communication is the best way forward.

"Go on," I urge, ensuring my voice stays soft and inviting. "Tell him what you told me. We can't fix this if we don't know what's wrong."

Kai lets out a slow breath, his eyes fixed on Julian now. "We were just talking about how this works. Or doesn't work. For me."

My hands start to sweat, a quiet panic settling in the pit of my stomach. *This feels like he's breaking up with us.*

Julian straightens, his posture sharpening like he's bracing for impact. "What do you mean?"

"I mean... it feels like I'm just tagging along half the time," Kai says, his tone honest and calm. "You two are married. You make decisions, talk about things as a unit, and I'm just... there. Like a guest."

Julian's frown deepens. "That's not what we want, Kai. You're not a guest."

Kai's lips press into a thin line as he shrugs. "Maybe not intentionally. But it's hard not to feel like I'm always playing catch-up. Sophie loves being a hotwife, and you support her. I love that for you guys, it's something you've built together. And I get it, I really do. But it's just another thing that makes me feel like the odd one out."

He pauses, his fingers tapping idly against his thigh before his eyes flick between us. "I guess what I'm saying is... are you sure I'm not just your unicorn?"

The room goes still, the weight of his words settling heavily between us.

Being in the lifestyle, I'm familiar with the term. I know what it means, but I've never associated Kai with being a unicorn—someone we were seeking out to use then discard.

I never intended to fall for him. And I know Julian didn't, either. It all just sort of... happened.

"What?" Julian asks, his voice quieter now, cautious.

Kai exhales slowly, rubbing the back of his neck. "At the club tonight... there was a moment. When you said something about how much you love watching Sophie with another man. And you two just—looked at each other. Like you were the only ones in the room."

I open my mouth to argue, but Kai's gaze pins me in place. "I know what that was. I wasn't part of it." Kai shrugs again, but there's no humor in it. "I mean, let's be honest. I'm the new, exciting thing. I fit into your dynamic now, but that's easy when I'm not asking for more. I'm here for the sex, for the fun—right? But if that's all this is, tell me now."

My heart twists painfully as I watch him stand there, vulnerable and guarded all at once.

"Because if that's the case," Kai continues, forcing out a dry laugh, "adding more guys into the mix down the road... I don't know. It just makes me feel even more like an outsider."

Julian shakes his head immediately, stepping forward. "Kai, that's not—"

"I know it's not on purpose," Kai cuts in, his voice softening just slightly. "But I can't help how it feels."

I catch Julian's eye, and for a moment, there's nothing but silence between the three of us. Then Julian reaches out, curling his hand around Kai's wrist, grounding him.

"Kai, this isn't about you fitting into something we already had. We're building something new with you. And maybe we can discuss Sophie being a hotwife. Together. *The three of us.*"

Kai's lips press into a thin line, and he looks down for a moment before meeting Julian's eyes again. "I understand. But it doesn't change the fact that I'm not... I... I can't see myself being okay with it. With her sleeping with other men."

My heart twists at his words, and I take a step closer to him, my voice soft. "Kai, are you saying you want me to stop?"

He shakes his head quickly, running a hand through his hair. "I'm not asking you to change who you are. I know how much it means to you. The confidence it gives you, the way it makes you feel alive. The way it makes you feel *free*. I wouldn't want to take that from you."

Free.

Just like I told him earlier.

Julian frowns. "Then what are you saying?"

Kai takes a deep breath, his shoulders stiff. "I'm saying I don't think I can do this if it keeps going the way it has. I thought maybe I'd adjust, that I could learn to be okay with it. But I want... something different. Something exclusive. This isn't just *fun* for me anymore," he adds.

I blink, thrown off. "You mean... a closed relationship?"

Kai nods, his voice quieter now. "Yeah. Just the three of us. No one else."

The room falls silent, and I glance at Julian, whose expression is unreadable. My mind races as I try to process what Kai is asking.

"Kai," I say carefully, "you know that being a hotwife was a big part of my life. I'm still trying to figure out what it means to me now, but... I don't know if I'm ready to give it up completely. And Julian..." I trail off, unsure how to finish the thought.

Julian picks up where I leave off, his tone thoughtful. "We've always been open, Kai. That's been our foundation. But I never want you to feel like you're less important or like your feelings don't matter. This is something we have to figure out together."

Kai's jaw tightens, and he looks away. "I just don't know if I can wait while you figure it out. It's already hard, because I'm..." He trails a hand through his hair and looks away. "I don't know. I'm just confused. Plus, knowing Julian would probably want to keep going, even if I don't... I know he loves it, so it feels unfair to ask him to stop, too."

"That's not fair," Julian says, standing. He runs a frustrated hand through his hair, his calm slipping just enough for me to notice. His voice drops lower, rougher. "This isn't about what I want. It's about what we all need. And if exclusivity is what you need, we should have that conversation."

Kai shakes his head, a small, tired smile tugging at his lips. "I'm not sure talking is enough. It's not just about boundaries, it's about whether this can actually work for me. I don't want to be... used. I think I jumped into all of this too soon."

Julian's face pinches with hurt, and I feel a pang of guilt. I attempt to reach out toward him, but he steps back, his expression conflicted. His words feel like a punch to the chest, and I feel the instinct to defend myself, but the ache in his voice keeps me silent.

Julian shifts, his hand flexing at his side like he wants to step in, and Kai notices.

"I need some space," Kai says, his voice quiet. "Just for a little while."

"Kai, wait," I start, but he cuts me off gently.

"I'll see you guys later," he says, turning toward the door.

Kai's hand lingers on the doorknob, and for a second, I think he might turn around. But he doesn't.

The door closes softly behind him, but the echo feels louder than it should.

CHAPTER THIRTY-FIVE
THE HOMEWORK

Malakai

As I sit on the armchair and twiddle my thumbs, I can't help but feel like I'm fully on display. The office is nice—it's modern and warm, with personal touches here and there. Monica, my therapist, is an older woman with short, gray hair and a flowy, colorful outfit. She's not sitting behind her desk, but rather on the couch across the room, so it feels less like a therapy session and more like two people talking casually.

That's probably the point.

"Tell me about your job," she says, smiling.

I clear my throat. "Well, I'm the headmaster of Saint Helena Academy. Before that, I was a pastor and I worked for various churches around Crestwood."

She nods once. "So spirituality is important to you?"

I nod. "It is." The words feel hollow, almost

rehearsed. I frown and lean forward, clasping my hands together between my knees. "Or, it used to be."

The session is already half over. The first thirty minutes, I spoke about my childhood and growing up at Ravage Castle. I told her about my father, and how close I was to my brothers. I thought she'd say something about the infamous Charles Ravage, but she didn't. Instead, she only smiled and told me how wonderful it was that I was close to my siblings.

Monica's expression doesn't change. She simply tilts her head, like she's waiting for me to fill the silence.

"It feels like I'm evolving," I admit, the weight of the confession settling over me. "And in doing so... religion has become less important. At least, not in the way it used to be. I mean, when I first got into this profession, I found a lot of personal fulfillment. I still remember the sense of pride when I got my first job as a pastor at a tiny church on the coast. And even accepting the headmaster position at Saint Helena was one of my greatest achievements. I *fully* believed in the school mission, and though some of the people in my bubble were more close-minded than me, I knew I was doing good. I believed in helping my students. I was the person they knew they could trust."

"You're speaking in past tense," she notes, sitting up straighter. "I see people from all walks of life, Malakai. Children and teenagers, young married couples, men in their eighties, rape victims, you name it. And the only consistent thing between all of these people—and often why they seek therapy—is because they've changed.

Something or *someone* has disrupted their status quo—whether it be an extramarital affair, or perhaps a burglary that leaves them with PTSD. As humans we are allowed to change. We are allowed to change our mind about things like religion. Nothing about life is stagnant."

I swallow. "I suppose that's true."

"So, what disrupted the status quo?" she asks thoughtfully.

I exhale slowly, tracing the faint pattern in the carpet beneath my feet with the toe of my shoe. "I had an old friend move back to town. Julian. He and his wife have become... important to me."

Monica nods. "Important to you? How so?"

I hesitate, the words lodged in my throat like stones. But this is why I came here. If I can't say it aloud, how am I supposed to fix it?

"Well... we've all sort of entered into a romantic relationship."

Smiling, Monica clasps her hands together on her lap. "It's very important to have these romantic relationships, you know. To foster connection. It's wonderful that you've found two people to share that with."

I nod slowly. "It is. But I can't help but feel like... I don't belong."

"Do they make you feel that way?"

I think back to last weekend—the soft brush of Sophie's fingers through my hair, the press of Julian's lips against my skin.

"Mine."

"You're fucking mine, Ravage. I don't care how long it's been."

"I don't care who's touched you since. You were mine then, and you're mine now."

The way Julian's gaze had shifted when he said, *"Imagine watching her with another man together."*

The shadow of doubt. The space that opened between us even as we stayed physically close.

No, I realize. *It's not them.*

And, of course, the looks on their faces when I walked out of their house last week.

I hadn't seen Julian, but I had kept my word and helped Sophie with the shop after I got done at Saint Helena. Our time was spent in near silence, but I could feel her eyes on me constantly. And every evening when I said goodbye, she looked like she wanted to say something. Last night, I swear I saw tears in her eyes when I left.

"No, it's not them," I tell Monica. Sighing, I lean back and run my hand down my mouth. "I suppose I just don't feel worthy of them. Like they're too good to be true. Like I'm waiting for them to move on."

Monica's eyes sharpen, and she leans in slightly. "Malakai, that sounds less like a relationship problem and more like something you've been carrying for a long time. Has that feeling—of being unworthy—always been there?"

I hesitate. My hands come together in my lap, and my fingers twist and untwist nervously.

"Maybe. I guess that's possible." Sighing, I continue.

"I've always tried to do the right thing, but it always feels like it's never enough. Like maybe... *I'm* never enough. For God. For my students. For Julian and Sophie."

Her kind expression doesn't falter, but there's a thread of empathy woven into her calm demeanor now. With her, though, it doesn't feel like pity. It feels like she understands.

"That's a heavy burden to carry. But here's the truth, Malakai—you don't have to earn your worthiness. It's not something given by others, nor is it something you lose. It's inherent. And that feeling of being 'not enough'—that's the piece we'll work on together. It's not something we can untangle in one session. It's certainly not an *easy* fix. This work you're doing—the work of understanding and accepting yourself—it's a process. It's not always linear, but it is deeply worthwhile."

Nodding, I feel both relief and frustration. Relief that there's a reason for this constant knot in my chest, and frustration for the daunting task of doing something that feels insurmountable.

Monica continues. "For now, I want to give you some homework."

I arch a brow. "Homework?"

She smiles. "Yes. Before our next session, I want you to write down one thing every day that you like about yourself. It could be something you did that day, something about your personality, or even something you notice about yourself physically. Whatever feels right. The point is to start identifying these pieces of yourself that are already enough—already good."

I blink at her. "That sounds... hard."

"It might be," she admits. "But it's also practice. And like anything else, it will get easier with time. I also want you to spend a few minutes reflecting on what Julian and Sophie see in you. They've chosen to include you in their lives, Malakai. They see something in you that's worth loving. What do you think that might be?"

Her words land heavier than I expect, a knot forming in my throat. I manage to nod, swallowing hard. "Okay. I'll try."

"That's all I ask," she says, her smile kind and warm. "I don't expect you to have all the answers right away. But you have to be willing to explore the questions."

The session winds down after that, and Monica thanks me for my honesty. She reminds me for the second time that it's okay to feel uncomfortable with these truths I'm uncovering.

Perhaps this time, her advice will stick.

As I leave her office, the weight on my shoulders feels a little different—not lighter, exactly, but less suffocating.

The homework she's given me feels daunting, but as I step out into the brisk evening air, I think maybe it's a step I can take.

Pulling my phone out, I type in a number I have memorized. It rings a few times before a female voice answers.

"Kai? It's Juliet. One sec, let me grab Chase. He's in the garage working on one of his damn cars."

I chuckle. "Thanks, Jules."

"How are you?" she asks. I can hear the creaking floorboards of their old town house just outside of San Francisco.

"I've been better," I tell her honestly.

"Who do I need to beat up?" she asks, and there's the sound of a door opening.

Huffing a laugh, warmth fills me at her words. I never had a sister, but Juliet feels like one now that she's married to Chase, my younger brother.

"No one. It's all on me this time."

"I see," she muses. "Well, I'll hand you over to Chase. And, Kai?"

"Yeah?"

"You can always talk to us, you know. Or maybe come up here for a visit. Maybe the fresh, foggy air would do you some good."

I stop walking. "Yeah. Maybe I will. Thanks, Jules."

After we say goodbye, I hear her mutter something to Chase.

"Hey," he says, sounding out of breath. "What's up?"

"We need to talk about Rod Dumplant," I say firmly.

Chase exhales. "Yeah. I heard about what happened. The whole board heard, actually, because Rod sent a very angry email about the situation with Bradleigh, and then something about 'moral decay within leadership' and the risk of setting a dangerous precedent for the school's values.' I meant to call you about it."

"Wonderful," I mutter.

"Don't worry about him, Kai. He's made a lot of

enemies. The last thing he wants is for us to vote him out."

"And how much would you be paying the rest of the board members to do that?" I ask, grinning.

"That's neither here nor there, but they'd be remiss to forget that I have the most sway with the board of directors, and I could replace them all if I wanted to."

"You don't have to do that," I tell him.

"Why? You're my brother. If he's making your life hell, then there are ways to take care of that. Bigotry has no place at Saint Helena, or anywhere."

I sit with his words for a few seconds, feeling unexpectedly emotional.

"Should I call an emergency meeting?" Chase asks. "I can probably get on a flight over the weekend, and we can sort it out together..."

"Actually, can I come up to you?"

He's quiet for a second. "You're always welcome, Kai. Just let me know when so I can take some time off work."

"Sure," I answer, forming a tentative plan in my head.

"Everything else okay?" he asks, his tone tinged with concern.

I run a hand through my hair. "Not really. But I can tell you in person."

"Okay. I'll see you soon, yeah?"

"Wait," I rush out. "How did you know?"

"Know what?" Chase asks, a tinge of amusement in his voice. I realize I'm probably making zero sense.

"That Juliet was the one for you."

He pauses for a beat, and I can hear the faint creak of floorboards. "Because even when I pushed her away, she stayed," he says quietly. "She showed up. Over and over."

I nod, even though he can't see me.

"That's good to know."

"Come up," Chase urges. "It'll make Juliet's week to host you. No one ever comes to visit us," he adds petulantly. Classic little brother. "Do it for her," he teases.

"Yeah," I murmur. "I'll send you my flight details."

We hang up, and I sit there for a long moment, staring at the darkened screen of my phone.

The weight in my chest feels a little heavier now, like something fragile I've been balancing for weeks is starting to crack.

"Because even when I pushed her away, she stayed."

Chase's words echo louder than I expected, lingering long after the call ends.

But with Julian and Sophie... I left. And they let me.

That thought sinks its claws in deep, twisting.

Maybe that's what's been gnawing at me this whole time. The idea that if I stepped back far enough, they wouldn't follow.

Because maybe I'm not as essential to them as they are to me.

The low, persistent noise of downtown presses down on my shoulders, and for the first time in years, the solitude feels suffocating instead of comforting. I glance around the groups of people out and about—the couples and friends, the college students, the people scurrying to their night shifts.

I rub the back of my neck, exhaling sharply.

Maybe I do need to get away.

A few minutes later, I'm back in my apartment, setting Willy's food down in his porcelain bowl. I sit down on the couch, and it doesn't take long to find a flight up to San Francisco.

Before I can second-guess myself, I book it.

For the first time in weeks, I feel like I'm moving toward something instead of running away.

But even as I close my laptop and lean back against the couch, I can't shake the image of Sophie's eyes lingering on me as I left the shop last night—or the way Julian didn't try to stop me.

CHAPTER THIRTY-SIX
THE BOTTOM

Julian

I tell myself I'm fine.

I tell myself I'll get over it, just like I did when we were eighteen.

I remind myself of all the reasons Kai needed space, and why he probably isn't ready to come back—not to me, not to us.

But fuck, it's been over a month since I last saw him.

I can't stop reaching for my phone—like muscle memory, my thumb hovers over his contact. The texts are still there. I haven't deleted them. I scroll up, staring at the ridiculous things I've sent him.

> (Tuesday, 6:42 AM): Morning. Hitting the gym at 7 if you want to come.

> (Friday, 8:15 AM): I can spot you if you need it. Sophie's busy with the shop today.

> (last Saturday, 10:04 AM): You good? Haven't seen you around the gym.

> (two Mondays ago): Had a craving for some Flamin' Hot Cheetos, and happened to stop by the petrol station near you. Are you home?

> Or perhaps I can entice you with an entire pan of cinnamon rolls?

No response, but they're all marked as *read*.

There's a part of me that wants to say *fuck it*—to stop texting him altogether. I could blame pride, or maybe the ache that forms in my chest every time his silence stretches on too long.

But I can't let it go—not this time.

Sophie catches me one morning halfway through typing out another text to him. She pauses by the kettle, watching me with those bright, blue eyes.

"Julian."

I glance up, feigning innocence. "Morning, pet."

Her gaze drops to my phone, and I swear it's like she can see through the screen. "You're texting him again, aren't you?"

I shrug, locking the screen as if that somehow erases the evidence. "He's probably just busy."

She steps closer, leaning against the counter, her eyes softening. "You know he's not."

I don't respond, because I know she's right.

I see it in her too, the way she lingers in rooms where his absence is most obvious, the way she glances at the front door after long days, as if expecting him to walk in unannounced.

We've built a solid life together. But this? It feels like we're both venturing into uncharted territory, trying to figure our way through something neither of us is familiar with.

Sophie's voice cuts through the silence. "Maybe we just need to give him more time."

I nod, even though I know time isn't the solution.

Time is the enemy.

Time drags.

The gym is quieter than usual this Saturday afternoon, but the weight pressing down on me has nothing to do with the barbell.

I've become an expert at staying busy—early workouts, house projects, helping Sophie with the bookstore, closing deals. Anything to distract me from the ache that hasn't left since Kai walked away.

Seventeen years ago, I could dismiss it—convince myself I wasn't that into him, that I imagined the pull between us or the growing feelings I'd been containing for years. But now? I've had him. I've felt what it's like to share him with Sophie, to touch him, kiss him, envision something more. Losing him this time stings in a way that feels permanent.

Keeping busy helps. Making love to Sophie helps. But the sadness in her eyes mirrors my own. Neither of us knows how to untangle the mess he left behind.

Sophie hasn't seen him much either, buried in preparations for the shop's grand opening. But she misses him. I can see it in the way her gaze lingers on empty spaces he used to occupy, in the soft sighs she thinks I don't notice. It's the same way I miss him, like I'm missing a part of myself I didn't realize I needed.

I thought I was lucky when he came back into my life. Losing him twice feels unbearable.

And yet, there's that voice, the one that urges me to let him go. To stop before I risk unraveling everything Sophie and I have built.

I love my wife. That will never change. But I wonder if there's a limit to how much love I can give, if loving Kai means taking something away from her. If this desire I can't seem to shake is dangerous, threatening the foundation Sophie and I have spent years fortifying.

I've resisted the pull of Malakai Ravage for almost two decades. I tell myself I can't risk losing Sophie—not even for him.

But maybe it's already too late.

This morning, Sophie cried after sex, trembling in my arms as she admitted how much she misses him. And I know. I feel it too.

We're not just afraid of losing him. We're terrified that, somewhere along the way, we already have.

I finish my last set, catching my reflection in the gym

mirror. The weight of the last month is carved into my posture, the worry etched deep in my face.

Sophie and I will always be solid, that much I know. But without Kai... the life we're building feels incomplete.

He's not like the others. The men Sophie's met before were fleeting—forgotten by morning, no strings attached, never to be thought of again.

But Kai fits. With Sophie. With me.

And the thought that he might be the only one who can complete us, that we might never find this balance again, fucking terrifies me.

I need to get him back.

I just don't know how.

As if the universe is answering my siren call, I catch sight of Kai on the other side of the gym in the mirror. He's at the leg press, wearing joggers and a fitted T-shirt.

I stop breathing, and my pulse speeds up. Everything feels hot, and I can feel my neck flushing at the sight of him. Of course he looks good—better than I remember. His muscled arms grip the sides of the chair as he pushes his legs against the flat platform. His brows are scrunched in concentration.

He hasn't seen me yet. I could walk away—leave him be.

But I don't.

His gaze shifts in the mirror, locking on mine.

Shit.

I see the flicker of recognition, the tension that

hardens his posture. He doesn't smile. Doesn't wave. He just watches me, unreadable as ever.

I wait for him to make the first move, but he doesn't.

Of course he doesn't.

Grabbing my things, I slowly walk over to the leg press. He finishes as I walk over, swinging his legs over. I attempt to avert my gaze from the way his abdominal muscles poke through the thin T-shirt, or how good he looks with a bit of heavy scruff. His hair is longer, too, and I'm finding that I very much enjoy this version of him.

His eyes slide up and down my body, too, and it sends a shiver through me.

"Hey," I say, standing awkwardly a few feet away.

"Hey," he answers. His face is blank, neither happy to see me, nor upset.

His gaze lingers on me for a long minute before he tilts his head slightly, as if he's come to some sort of conclusion in his mind. The air between us feels charged, like it always does.

But even more so now because it's been so long since we've seen each other.

The tension stretches between us like a taut wire.

Kai wipes his face with his shirt, the flash of his abs making my breath hitch. He doesn't seem to notice, or if he does, he doesn't acknowledge it.

"Didn't think I'd see you here," I try again.

He shrugs. "Needed a change of scenery."

He's about to stand, but something in me cracks.

"Wait."

I wince at how ridiculous I sound. My fingers tighten around my gym bag, and Kai notices. His eyes narrow slightly.

"I know I messed up. I know we should've made our feelings for you more clear," I start, gripping the towel across my neck like it's suddenly the most interesting thing in the world. "We didn't check in with you, and that's on us. But I…"

Kai's eyes flick up lazily from the bench press, pinning me in place without saying a word.

It's infuriating how much ground he gains just by existing.

I roll my shoulders back, squaring them under his gaze. "I've been thinking about you," I continue, voice rougher than I intended. "A lot. More than is probably healthy for a grown man."

Kai leans against the weight rack, crossing his arms. I can see the muscles shift beneath his shirt, annoyingly distracting, but I stay focused.

"And?" he prompts, like he's flipping through a boring magazine.

I exhale through my nose, my jaw tightening. This is already going spectacularly.

"And I miss you," I admit. The words come out gruff, like they're being dragged kicking and screaming. "There. Happy?"

Kai's face doesn't move, his gaze steady and unwavering.

"You don't seem like the flowers-and-apology-card

type," I add, scrubbing the back of my neck. "So I skipped the bouquet."

That gets me one raised brow. Progress, I suppose.

"You sure about that, Julian?" His voice drops lower, deliberate.

I nod, stepping closer. "Yeah. I'm sure."

His gaze drifts over me, slow and deliberate. I know the look. It's the same one he gave me that first night with Sophie. Except this time, he's letting me sweat.

I sigh, letting the towel drop around my shoulders. "Listen," I say, dropping my tone a notch. "I'm not great at this, feelings and all that. Let's blame the ADHD, but it's probably just because I'm kind of an arsehole, okay? So if you're waiting for me to get down on one knee and deliver some long, heartfelt monologue, you'll be sorely disappointed. My ego can't take that hit."

Kai's lips twitch at the corner, but he doesn't give me the satisfaction of a full smile.

I narrow my eyes. "See, that's the problem right there. You love this, don't you?"

"Love what?" he replies smoothly.

"Watching me grovel."

"Maybe," he says, and his voice is a little too casual.

I huff out a dry laugh, shaking my head. "Jesus Christ."

For a second, neither of us says anything. The weight of the last month lingers between us, heavier than the barbell resting on the rack.

When I finally look at him, there's no humor left in my voice.

"I do mean it," I say quietly. "I miss you, Kai. Sophie does too. This thing without you—" I gesture vaguely. "It's not working. We're not working. And I know I handled it poorly. I should've gone after you. I should've called. *Something*. Truth be told, I wanted to give you space. And I'm here now, feeling like a complete fucking fool. So if you want to make me sweat a little longer, fine. But just... don't walk away again."

Kai's eyes tighten, and I catch it—brief, but there.

"I should make you sweat," he says, though his voice lacks conviction. "I'd pay to see more of this horrible groveling."

I step closer, just enough to invade his space. He doesn't move away.

"You won't," I counter smoothly.

Kai studies me for a beat longer, then sighs, running his tongue across the inside of his cheek.

"Locker room," he mutters, already turning toward the door.

I smirk as I follow him.

"Should I have brought champagne?" I tease under my breath.

"Shut up, Julian."

"Just trying to set the mood," I mutter, not bothering to hide the grin tugging at my lips.

I follow Kai into the locker room without hesitation.

He doesn't look back, but I know he knows I'm there. The door swings shut behind us with a soft thud, locking out the world behind it.

Kai walks over to a set of lockers a few feet away, his movements unhurried. Deliberate.

I stay by the entrance for a beat too long, the weight in my chest pressing heavier with every step he takes away from me.

Like he might vanish if I get too close.

"Julian." His voice pulls me from the spiral. Calm, but threaded with something I can't quite place. "Are you just going to stand there and hope I'll strip for your benefit?"

The dryness in his tone coaxes a faint huff of laughter out of me. "Would it work?" I shoot back, moving toward him at last.

Kai's mouth twitches. "You're a menace."

His old nickname for me makes me grin. He'd used it once in front of Sophie, but that word pulls me right back to when we were teenagers. His teasing smirk, the way he'd shove my shoulder whenever I acted out.

I miss that, our old closeness.

I fucking miss *him*.

When I stop a few feet away, the shift in the air is palpable, like standing at the edge of something vast.

The smile drops off my face and I clear my throat, tugging my towel tighter over my shoulder. "We really should talk."

Kai leans against the locker, crossing his arms in that casual way that somehow feels anything but relaxed.

"About what?" His gaze flicks over me, unreadable. "Words don't mean much, do they? It's actions that count, Julian. At least, that's what I'm learning about all this."

The weight behind his words lands square in my chest.

He's not being cold, just honest. Which somehow cuts deeper.

I rub the back of my neck, suddenly unsure of what to do with my hands. "I didn't know what to say. I let you go. *We* let you go. I messed up. I know that now," I say quietly.

Kai lifts a brow. "I'd say that's accurate."

The corner of my mouth pulls into a half smile, even if it feels a little out of place. He's one hundred percent loving that I'm groveling.

That thought sends a swarm of something light and warm through me, and for a second—only a second—it gives me hope that we haven't lost him forever.

"Right. Straight to the point, then."

His eyes sharpen, narrowing just slightly as he steps closer.

"I'm serious, Julian." His voice dips lower, each word deliberate. "You told me this was just payback. How am I supposed to know it's not still that?"

I swallow, hard. "It wasn't. It's not." His silence stretches between us. "I think about you every day," I admit, the words rough around the edges. "Every damn day. Seventeen years, and nothing's changed."

Kai stays rooted, jaw tight, but I catch the flicker in his expression—the part of him that wants to believe me.

I take another step closer, filling the space between us.

He stays rooted, jaw tightening, but I swear I can feel the emotions radiating from him.

"I'm sorry," I tell him earnestly. "For everything. For not knowing how to handle this. I've never..." I swallow, running a hand over my mouth. Kai's eyes track the movement. "I didn't know how to make room for... you."

I pause, the words catching in my throat as a realization strikes me. Maybe it's not about the sharing that's been hard—it never really was. It's the change. I've always thrived on the thrill of orchestrating something new, the high of control, the rush of it. But this—this is different. It's steady, loving, intimate in ways I hadn't anticipated.

And for the first time, I can see the beauty in it, the trust that comes with letting someone else in. Of sharing the dominance for once, not because I need to, but because I want to.

I meet Kai's eyes again, feeling the weight of my own vulnerability in the moment. "I'm learning," I say quietly, my voice steadier now. "And I want to keep learning—with you."

His expression wobbles, like he wants to believe me, but something is still holding him back.

I step closer, careful but deliberate, until I'm near enough to feel the tension radiating from him. "You were never payback," I continue, the words rasping out of me like they cost something. "You matter to me. To Sophie. This—" I gesture between us, and my hand lingers in the space between his chest and mine. "This was never temporary for me. I'm telling you this because I need you. *We* need you."

For a long second, he just watches me.

But then he takes a step toward me, closing the distance until I can feel the warmth of his breath on my face.

"How can you be sure of what you want when it changes so quickly?" he murmurs.

His words sting, but I can't deny the truth they carry. "Because love doesn't change. You're not some hobby I want to conquer." I press my body into his. "You never have been, Kai."

His eyes search mine, flashing with something I can't quite name—desire, anger, doubt. Slowly, he reaches up, his fingers brushing the side of my jaw.

"I lied earlier," he growls. "I did want to hear you grovel a little bit."

"You're such a prat," I murmur, mesmerized by the way his pupils bloom dark.

"I'm learning to account for my worth," he says, voice serious. "Journaling, talking to a therapist, visiting my brothers more often... I know it wasn't all you and Sophie. I know I pushed you away. So I'm sorry, too. I didn't know how to ask for what I wanted. But I'm learning. I'm going to try."

"And what is it that you want?" I ask, voice soft.

"You. Sophie. If I do this, I want all of it," he starts, voice low and rough and brooking no argument. "There's no going back for me. I want you and Sophie, and all of us together. I want cinnamon rolls in the morning, and cheesy horror movies on the couch at night. And I want an equal say in this relationship."

He exhales sharply, his gaze burning into mine. "But I also want this to be real. I don't just want to be an addition to what you and Sophie already have—I want to build something with both of you. That means time with you, time with her. One-on-one, figuring out what this looks like for us as individuals before we shape it as a whole."

I nod, something warm unfurling in my chest. He's right. This isn't just about fitting him into a space that already exists—it's about making space for something new.

"Good," I whisper, hardly able to breathe. "I want all of that, too. And so does Sophie. We're not going anywhere, Kai."

But he doesn't move, his gaze locked on mine, unyielding. "Words aren't enough, Julian," he says quietly, but there's steel in his voice. "You're going to have to prove it, to show me that this isn't just about control or convenience for you. That you're ready to meet me where I need you."

I swallow hard, his challenge cutting straight through me, but I don't flinch. Instead, I take a step closer, lowering my gaze deliberately, baring myself to him in a way I never have before. My hands fall to my sides, open and unguarded, as if to say, *I'm yours to command.*

"Tell me what you need," I murmur. "I'll do it. Whatever it takes, Kai. I'm yours. Fully. I'll prove it as many times as you need me to."

For a moment, the air between us crackles, charged and heavy, Kai's sharp gaze searching mine. And then, just when I think he might walk away, his hand grips the back of my neck, pulling me closer, his lips a breath away from mine.

His voice is low, unsteady. "That's all I needed to hear."

And then Kai's mouth crashes against mine, and I stumble back against the lockers from the force of it. His hands grip my hips, pulling me closer. And his lips move against my own with a fervor I've never felt before. *Like he's been starved.* My hands move up to his shoulders, then they move to his hair. I moan when I run my fingers through his soft strands, and his musky smell is intoxicating. Everything about this makes me feel raw—exposed. *Vulnerable.* It's a mix of need and heat and frustration, all rolled into one.

He pulls away just long enough to speak. "Showers." His voice is a husky growl that sends a shiver down my spine.

I grab his hand and lead him to one of the shower stalls, setting my bag down on the bench. Once he locks it behind him, he turns to face me.

"Turn around," he commands, looking at me with something dark and primal.

For a second, I hesitate. He's got the look of someone ready to take charge, and I've never done it like this. *I'm* always the one calling the shots. But then I see the way his chest rises and falls. The way his eyes darken as they hold mine.

And I quickly realize that I want this.

I want him to take control.

Because my surrender is what he needs. He needs to take charge, needs to *dominate* me. And I have to show him that I'm serious about this—about him—by submitting to him.

Slowly, I turn around, pressing my palms flat against the cool tile of the shower. Behind me, I hear Kai move closer so that his chest is against my back, and when his arm reaches around for the shower lever, I'm suddenly being drenched by warm water.

"This should drown out your moans," he murmurs, his mouth brushing against my ear.

My T-shirt and shorts stick to my overheated skin, and my cock is so hard that it's almost painful.

There's something beautiful in this surrender, I realize. There's no verbal confirmation of it—nothing is said, or alluded to. Kai just... *is*. And I suppose he's always been that way.

I've just been too stubborn to see it.

My beautiful, handsome switch.

Behind me, I hear the rustling of fabric and the quiet scrape of his shoes on the tiled floor. My breathing turns ragged as his palm comes to my arse, squeezing it once before he pulls my shorts down to the floor.

Fuck, he's really doing this.

"I have some coconut oil. In my bag," I tell him. My voice quivers slightly, and he goes still behind me.

"Coconut oil?" he asks, a bit of amusement in his tone.

My lips tug into a smile. "Yeah. I use it after a shower sometimes. It makes my skin really soft."

He huffs out a chuckle. "Okay." I hear him rummaging through my bag, pulling out the bottle of oil. The lid snaps open, and my knees are doing a shit job at holding me up. When he gets closer, I inhale sharply when I feel one of his fingers slide between my arse cheeks.

"You're shaking," he murmurs.

I roll my eyes. "Well, yeah. I've never bottomed for a guy before."

Pressing his finger into my arsehole, I arch my back. *Fuck, that's...*

Leaning forward, he interrupts my thoughts by kissing my earlobe. "Thank you for letting me be the first."

"Tit for tat, Ravage. One day I'll be your first, too."

"I'd like that," Kai says, nibbling on the skin just below my ear.

I can't help but let out a low groan as he curves his finger toward my cock so that he's pressing against my prostate.

It sends an incredible, electric jolt through me. My cock throbs—and I realize I could very easily come on just his finger.

"Video it," I rush out on a moan. "For Sophie."

Kai laughs behind me. "You think our little dove will enjoy watching me ruin your asshole?"

"Fuck," I hiss. "Yes, I do. I really, really do."

He steps back, and when I look over my shoulder, he grabs his phone from the bench with his clean hand and taps the screen a few times.

"Say hi," he says, his voice a guttural sound. When he steps against my back again, he immediately pushes two fingers in, and my mouth drops open.

"H— Oh, fuuuuck," I whisper, my eyes rolling back as his calloused hand massages that same spot again.

"That's it," Kai growls. "I think you're ready for me, baby."

I nearly collapse at the pet name. It sounds so fucking hot coming from his mouth, and I realize that I'd never submit to another man, but I don't mind submitting to Kai.

Perhaps I'm a bit of a switch, too.

He removes his fingers, and I hear the oil bottle lid snap open again. Looking over my shoulder, I shudder when I see the way he generously oils his thick cock. And then that same hand is on my hip, pulling me back, rougher this time.

All I can do is close my eyes and let him.

"Deep breaths, Julian."

I inhale once, twice. On the third inhale, I feel the head of his cock start to press into me.

"You've got to relax," he says, his voice gentle.

I nod vigorously. "Okay, okay. Give me a second." Reaching down, I begin to stroke my cock. It already feels ready to explode. My balls are aching and heavy, and when I envision fucking Kai just like this one day…

"Fuck," I whimper. "Okay, do it now."

Kai doesn't give me the option to second-guess it. Instead, he pushes into me quickly—firmly—and stays there for a second. My head drops back, and I know it should sting or hurt, but all I feel is fullness.

"Deeper," I beg.

Kai chuckles. "Look at my good boy begging for more cock. You sure you're not a bottom, Julian?" he taunts.

I want to laugh, but I'm afraid I might come immediately if I move, so I stay still.

"Fuck you, Ravage."

"You will," he answers. I clench around his cock, and he groans. "Fuck yes. You feel so good."

"Deeper," I repeat.

Despite never doing this before, I know the second his cock bumps that spot against my front wall, I'm going to be spraying the shower tiles. He moves his hips forward slightly, pushing into me another inch, and my whole body lights up.

I arch my back as he thrusts farther into me, and *fuck*, there it is—

"Holy shit," I mutter, my voice garbled.

"You like this?"

At this, he pushes the rest of the way into me, and a deep, low sound escapes my lips. My whole body is quaking, and my toes curl inside my now soaking wet shoes.

"Yes," I whisper. "Yes, fuck me, *fuck*—"

Kai pulls almost all the way out, adding more oil before driving back into me.

He's not gentle this time, and my whole body rocks forward as he thrusts back into me in one, smooth motion.

"God, that feels... so good..." I mutter, seeing stars.

Everything inside of me is sizzling with white-hot electricity, like someone turned my pleasure receptors up from one to one hundred. My hands curl against the tile, and I don't even need to touch my cock. It's rock hard, bouncing with every thrust.

"Come for me. I want to feel it," Kai says, biting the side of my neck. "Give your wife a show."

"F-fuck," I stutter.

Everything bunches inside of me, and then the pleasure explodes through me unexpectedly. I cry out at the force of it. Kai is muttering something behind me as it feels like I tumble down a steep cliff. My cock leaks cum at first, and it merely dribbles down, but then Kai reaches around and wraps his hand firmly around my shaft, and it's suddenly like a fountain. I'm shaking, convulsing, jerking... I come for what feels like an entire minute. And maybe I do. There's so much cum, so many aftershocks. Every time Kai moves inside of me, another pulse has it hitting the wall.

It's fucking endless.

"Fuck yes," Kai says. "That felt incredible. I'm going to come."

I don't have it in me to do anything but moan when his cock curves and bows. My eyes roll back, and I can feel him pulse deep inside of me. His free hand digs into the flesh at my hips, pulling my arse onto his cock as he jerks. And then he sighs, staying inside of me as he catches his breath.

I hear him press stop on the video, and then he pulls out of me slowly. I bite my tongue at the strange sensation. Expecting him to pull away, I stand there with my arse exposed. But instead of leaving or saying goodbye, he helps me out of my shoes, and then my clothes. When I turn around, he's naked, too.

And he's holding a bottle of bodywash. "Do you want me to wash you?"

There's something acutely intimate about it—just us. Him and me. His version of aftercare. I nod, smiling. And then he comes to stand under the shower with me, pulling us both under the spray of the warm water.

My heart is still pounding, and as Kai begins to clean me, I realize that maybe, just maybe, this could all work out.

CHAPTER THIRTY-SEVEN
THE VIDEO

Sophie

"Oh my God, it's huge," Stella says in awe as I hand her the neon, flashing sculpture above the register, an abstract design made entirely of flowers. The shape is unmistakable, the curves and lines arranged just subtly enough to make people look twice. "I love it!" she adds, laughing as she takes in the vibrant, cheeky arrangement shaped like a cock. It's bold and playful, but just subtle enough to leave anyone who doesn't *get it* blissfully unaware.

I adjust the angle. "It's certainly... bold."

"Bold? This is a masterpiece. You're going to have the horniest bookstore in Crestwood."

"Not sure there's much competition in that area," I reply, stepping down from the stool to admire our handiwork. The warm glow of the pink-and-red interior is cozy and kitschy—exactly the balance I envisioned.

"Now imagine a giant poster of tits and fannies in the loo," Stella adds, waggling her brows. "I'm telling you, nothing says feminism like anatomically correct vaginas at eye level."

I roll my eyes, but the grin won't leave my face. "We are an equal opportunity bookstore, after all."

Her arm slips around my shoulders in solidarity. "I love it. Are you nervous?"

I chew on the inside of my cheek as I look around. The bookstore is complete—aside from the books, which are arriving bright and early tomorrow, and the bespoke sign painter I'd hired for the name. But the shelves are built, secured to the walls, and painted a light pink. The floor is gleaming, thanks to the wood polish Julian picked up the other day. The side tables are red, as is the cash register. There's a pink-and-white checkered rug on the floor, and a teal chaise lounge. Stella even managed to find the giant, light-up cock, as well as matching leg lamps.

The area behind the register has an electric fireplace, a cozy, magenta-colored velvet couch, and a fluffy, cream-colored rug. There are plants in every available corner, and all that's left is to get "The Story Nest" painted onto the light pink facade above the front door in gold, and then to decorate the window display—something Stella promised to help me with tomorrow.

"I'm excited," I tell her honestly. "It feels like I've

been waiting for this moment forever. To have something of my own, just for me..." I trail off.

Stella's knowing eyes drift over me like she's reading every thought I haven't said aloud. She squeezes my shoulder, understanding.

"I'm proud of you," Stella says, squeezing me once before walking into the back room.

I should feel proud. I *do* feel proud. But that pride has been shadowed by the ache I've tried—and failed—to ignore since Kai left.

I miss him. And not in the soft, fleeting way you miss a friend. It's bone-deep, a hollow ache I carry around like an unwelcome houseguest. It lives in the space between every breath I take.

It's pathetic, really. We told him he could have the time he needed. I meant it. I want him to figure things out. But no one warned me how much it would hurt when he actually walked away.

I thought I could handle it.

I thought I was tougher than this.

But I'm not.

I can't count how many times I've replayed his voice in my head, dissecting the way his gaze lingered a second too long over the last few weeks, the way his lips parted as if he wanted to say something but never did. Having him near me working in the shop was pure bloody torture. I thought maybe—*maybe*—he'd text. Call. Something.

Instead, silence.

Julian buries himself in distractions—working late,

pushing himself at the gym. It's how he copes. But I don't have that luxury. When I'm not working in the shop, I sit in our quiet house and let the weight of it sink into my bones.

I didn't expect this to feel like heartbreak.

I thought I could survive without him.

Now, I'm not so sure.

He left, and I think that's what stings the most.

Not just the absence, but the fact that Kai was the one to walk away.

It shouldn't feel so personal, but it does.

I swipe at the tears gathering at the corners of my eyes before Stella comes back.

Having Stella's help has been paramount to getting the shop ready in only a couple of months. And though Kai helped with the harder manual labor, like laying new flooring, the rest was done with Julian and Stella, and occasionally her brooding husband, Miles.

I still couldn't tell if Miles liked me, he doesn't seem to like anyone except Stella.

Of course, all the Ravage men reminded me of Kai, which only made the whole distance and space thing harder. I knew he needed this. Kai carried his own burdens, his own fears about what it meant to be part of something this complex. But knowing he needed time didn't make it any easier to wait for him, or to hope he'd come back to us when he was ready.

Because the truth was, Julian and I would be fine. We always had been, and we always would be.

But *fine* wasn't enough anymore. Not without Kai.

The soft hum of my phone vibrating against my pocket pulls me from the spiral. I glance down—Julian.

I almost ignore it, but something about the message catches my eye. It's a video.

"Something juicy?" Stella asks, returning with a box of tiny, plastic willies. She dangles them in front of me. "Hide these around the store. Whoever finds one gets a free book."

I snort. "Of course you found those."

"Never underestimate my ability to locate miniature genitalia."

I chuckle faintly, already distracted as I press play on Julian's message.

The screen flickers to life, blurry at first. I squint, but as soon as the audio kicks in, I freeze.

"*Say hi.*"

Kai's voice.

The edges of the world tilt.

Then—

"*H— Oh, fuuuuck.*"

My husband's broken moan echoes through the shop, and Stella bursts out laughing.

"Oh my God, did Julian send you a naughty video? And who's the other bloke—"

Kai's voice cuts her off again.

"*That's it. I think you're ready for me, baby—*"

I fumble to pause the video, cheeks burning. My heart pounds against my ribs like a war drum.

They're together.

I can barely string the thought together through the haze of disbelief and... relief?

The ache in my chest shifts, like the weight has momentarily lifted, but the longing rushes in twice as hard.

They're together. Without me.

A part of me feels left out, ridiculous as it is. But mostly, I just want to be there.

I grip my phone tightly.

"You okay?" Stella asks, tilting her head.

"I—yeah. Just surprised."

"It's okay. Miles accidentally sent a picture of his spunk coming out of my fanny to my gynecologist last month."

This makes me burst out laughing. "What?!"

Stella shrugs. "Yeah. It was awkward. To be fair, he meant to send it to me, but her name is *Estrella*, and the old man needs glasses. But on the bright side, she congratulated him on knowing when my fertile window was."

I bend in half from laughing so hard, and when I stand up to look at my friend, she's watching me with a soft expression. Stella is the best at diffusing any situation, and right now I'm so grateful we've gotten close over the last few months.

She makes me feel like I have a little slice of home right here in Crestwood, and I'm sure if I'd known her in London, we would've been fast friends.

"You should go. Leave me the key and I'll lock up. I

won't be long—I need to pick Bea up from Liam and Zoe's house soon anyway."

"Okay. Yeah. Thank you," I say, still feeling frazzled.

Where are they? And are they still together?

I hand the key to Stella, and she pockets it with a bright smile. "Go have fun. And for the love of God, I hope this means you'll all stop moping around."

"What? I'm not moping around—"

She lets out an exasperated chortle. "Okay, whatever you say. I saw you crying the other day when 'Take Me to Church' came on."

"That's— I— It's a sad song."

Arching a brow, she points to the door. "Go get your men. Lock that shit down, because Kai's been moping even harder."

Her words cause me to swallow thickly. "He has?"

Nodding, she tugs me toward the door. "But no more. Go suck some cock and put those sexy lips to work."

I laugh as she shoves me out the door. Just as it's beginning to close, I realize what she was saying earlier.

"Wait, what do you mean your fertile window?" I ask, brow furrowed. "Are you and Miles…"

She nods shyly. "He's on a mission to knock me up before the end of the year."

This makes me smile. I know how much she loves Beatrix.

"I'm happy for you, Stella."

"Thanks, love. Now go."

I wave goodbye as I walk to my car, clutching my

phone against my chest as if people can see the video I have just behind the locked screen. My thoughts race as I replay what I've already seen and heard in my mind—a moment unlike any I've witnessed before. Julian, always so in control, letting go completely. There's no trace of his usual commanding presence, only vulnerability and trust.

Watching him in that moment, I can see how deeply he trusts Kai, how much he wants to experience something in a way he hasn't done before. For Julian, I know it's not about losing control—it's about choosing to share it, to let someone else take the lead.

My chest tightens just thinking about it.

Once I'm inside my car, I play the rest of the video, and I swear I don't breathe for the next eight minutes.

"Deep breaths, Julian. You've got to relax,"

"Okay, okay. Give me a second."

"Deeper," Julian begs.

"Look at my good boy begging for more cock. You sure you're not a bottom, Julian?"

"Fuck you, Ravage."

"You will. Fuck yes. You feel so good."

"Deeper."

"Holy shit."

"You like this?"

"Yes. Yes, fuck me, fuck—"

"God, that feels... so good..."

"Come for me. I want to feel it. Give your wife a show—"

I pause the video, panting as everything inside of me throbs. I shift my weight in my seat, and the movement presses the seam of my denims against my clit, and I'm pretty sure I could rock myself into an orgasm right now. That's how turned on I am.

With shaking hands, I text Julian.

> Where are you?

I let out a stuttering breath when I see him typing a response almost immediately.

JULIAN LOVE <3
> At Kai's. Come over. Now.

I don't even stop to think.
I just drive.

CHAPTER THIRTY-EIGHT
THE REUNION

MALAKAI

I feed Willy as Julian walks into the kitchen to grab a glass of water. His clothes were soaking wet—as were mine—so we both had to wear my backup clothes. Watching him walk around in my old *Saint Helena ROCKS* shirt from a preschool concert a couple of years ago, plus my favorite athletic shorts... it messes with my head.

Kneeling down, I pet Willy as he eats his special food mixture. He makes a growling sound, so I lift my hand and chuckle.

"So territorial," I mutter, quickly texting his sitter and thanking her for watching him earlier today when I was at work.

Fennec foxes need a lot of attention, and it doesn't feel right to kennel him all day long. So I pay a Crestwood

University student to come in and play with him for a few hours every day. She also stays overnight if I'm not here, and knows how to feed and walk him.

I look over at Julian, and he's looking over the notes I have taped to the fridge.

> *I AM WORTHY OF HAPPINESS.*
> *I AM PROUD OF MYSELF.*
> *I CHOOSE POSITIVE THOUGHTS.*
> *I AM ENOUGH.*

Fuck, I forgot those were there. Heat pricks the back of my neck, and I suddenly feel exposed in a way I hadn't braced for. I can't tell if it's worse that Julian's reading them so openly, or that he hasn't said anything yet. His silence is somehow heavier than words would be.

My instinct is to laugh it off, to make a dry comment about how even foxes need daily affirmations. But the words stick in my throat. I glance down at the tile instead, scuffing it lightly with the toe of my sock like that might magically dissolve the lump rising in my chest.

I feel Julian walk closer to where I'm standing by the island.

"I like them," Julian says, pointing to the handwritten notes and tapping them with his knuckle.

"Yeah, thanks. I've been seeing a therapist twice a week. Her name is Monica. She's helping."

I sound casual—too casual, maybe. Like I'm brushing it off before Julian can get any closer to the truth of it.

But it *isn't* casual.

This—all of this—feels like laying out every fragile piece of myself and asking him not to touch anything too hard.

I brace myself for him to make a joke, but he doesn't.

"That's good," he says after a beat, his voice softer now. "Soph and I need to find a therapist here. We had an amazing one in London."

I blink, head lifting. "You've done therapy?"

Julian gives me a look—half amusement, half something else. "What, you think I just magically have my shit together?"

"No," I admit, cracking the smallest grin. "But I wasn't expecting you to admit it."

He laughs, but the warmth behind it isn't sharp. "You don't get to be this fucked up in the head and not go to therapy." He pauses before continuing. "Before I went on medication for ADHD, I just thought I was an anxious, depressed mess. I thought I was simply lazy. Being a viscount didn't bode well for me. The responsibility destroyed me, and I desperately needed someone to tell me I was going to be okay."

His bluntness chips away at my awkwardness, but it doesn't completely erase the way my heart is thudding too hard against my ribs.

Julian shifts, glancing back at the notes again. "I get why it feels weird. I had to do something like this, too. In London, as a teenager."

His eyes flick to mine, like he's daring me to press further.

I don't.

Because I *get it*.

My eyes bore into his, and it suddenly feels heavy. Weighted. And for the first time since we were teenagers, I feel like I know my friend again. Not just surface level Julian Ashford—but the *real* man behind the happy exterior.

He continues. "I'm glad you're going to therapy. I think everyone should, honestly. My parents especially. They could use years of it, truth be told. Sophie's parents too, though they might be a lost cause."

I laugh, and his dashing smile disarms me completely. "Yeah. Monica is having me work on myself. Because I think I realized the reason I pulled away from you and Sophie wasn't because of anything you did. But because, deep down, I don't think I deserve the same happiness that my brothers have."

Julian's brows pull together. He steps closer, placing his hands on my shoulders. "But it was a little bit our fault. We could've been more clear about our intentions and feelings. We could've reassured you. I realize now, looking back, that we were this dynamic force that sort of came into your life like a tornado."

"That's exactly what you did," I tell him, my voice soft as one of my hands cups his cheek.

"It was very easy for us to make you feel left out unintentionally. But never again. I should've noticed the night at Inferno, when you pulled away. I saw it, and I told myself it was nothing. I won't miss it next time. Okay?" he asks, turning his head and kissing my wrist.

"If Sophie and I realized one thing over the past month, it's not how much you add to our marriage, but rather how much you were always meant to be with us. With her. With... me."

His voice breaks on the last word, and I swallow as his eyes turn glassy.

"Yeah, I'm beginning to realize that, too," I tell him.

Just as he starts to drag my face closer to his, my phone vibrates in my pocket.

"Sorry, one sec," I say, pulling it out. "It's my brother, Chase."

"Take it. I'll wait for you on the couch and try not to kidnap Willy."

I laugh at this as I walk into my bedroom. The faint sound of Julian's footsteps retreating follows me.

"Hey. So, is it done?"

Chase chuckles. "Oh, it's done."

There's something weary in his voice, laced with satisfaction. I sit on the edge of my bed, resting my elbows on my knees.

"How bad was it?"

"Bad enough," he says, sighing. "Rod's off the board, effective immediately. We'll frame it as him stepping down for 'personal reasons,' to save face, but I made it clear that he didn't have a choice in the matter."

I let out a sigh of relief, and my shoulders immediately feel less heavy. "Thanks, Chase. I mean it."

"You don't have to thank me. You may be older than me, but it's my job to protect you. Even when you're too stubborn to protect yourself. Remember when Dad kicked me out of the house for wrecking his car?" Chase's voice softens.

I huff a laugh. "Yeah. I covered for your sorry ass until he found out the next day."

"You didn't have to. But you did, because you're my older brother. I owe you, and this is just me paying you back. I'll keep doing it, Kai. As many times as it takes."

The weight of his words lingers between us. "Thanks." Rubbing my mouth, I let out a heavy sigh. "So, what did he say?"

"Rod? Oh, he was flustered. Talked about Saint Helena's moral values and some bullshit about setting examples. He claimed he was thinking of the school's reputation. As if Saint Helena would ever be associated with that kind of intolerance."

"Right," I say, my voice light.

"He crossed a line, Kai," Chase says, his voice harder now. "Not just with what he said about you or how he handled the situation with Bradleigh Evans, but also how he tried to wield his bigotry like a weapon. I told him there's no room on the board for someone who can't uphold the basic dignity of every student and staff member. I mean, you know why I bought the school all those years ago."

"Jackson," I murmur, thinking of his best friend, who was still on paternity leave with his husband and newly adopted son.

"And now my brother."

My throat feels tight all of a sudden, but Chase continues. "Anyway, you know how Rod is. He tried to turn it back on me, calling me hypocritical for 'silencing the opposition,' while placating me with Bible verses. So, I taught him a lesson on tolerance."

I huff a laugh. "Oh no. You lectured him? He hates that."

"Damn right I did. He wanted to talk about values, so I threw it right back in his face. I told him it's not about silencing dissent; it's safeguarding decency. He didn't like that, and when he tried to push back, I... well, let's just say I didn't mince words about how Saint Helena would look in the media if it came out that a board member was using homophobia as leverage."

I bark a laugh. "You're ruthless."

"I'm thorough," he corrects over the phone. "And I'd do it all again for you. For any of you, actually. That's what brothers are for."

The line goes quiet for a moment, both of us letting the situation settle before us. Then Chase speaks again, softer this time.

"Kai, you deserve to be happy. To be yourself. No one gets to make you, or anyone, feel like that's wrong. Least of all some outdated asshole claiming his last shred of power."

His words catch me off guard, and I swallow past the lump in my throat. "Yeah, I'm working on it. Being myself. It's a process." I look toward the bedroom door. "Actually, I should go. Talk later?"

"You're with them now, aren't you?" Chase asks, his tone shifting to something warming, almost teasing. Something *brotherly*. "Julian and Sophie, I mean."

I blink. "Julian's here, yes."

"Good." There's a smile to his voice, and it's contagious. "He seems like a good guy. And Sophie, from what you've told me, sounds incredible. We're looking forward to the bookstore opening next week."

"She is incredible," I tell him. "So is he."

"Then don't let anyone ruin that for you. There's something special between the three of you. And if Rod or anyone else tries to get in the way, just say the word. You know any one of us will handle it."

"I think you've done enough for one day," I tease.

Chase laughs, but when he speaks again, his voice wavers. "I mean it, though. I'm proud of you. And I love you."

I choke up. "I love you too."

He clears his throat. "Okay, I'll let you get back to Julian. And, Kai?"

"Yeah?"

"Be happy. That's all any of us want."

The call ends before I can respond, and for a moment, I just sit there, the weight of his words pressing into my chest. When I finally step out of the room, Julian's waiting on the couch, Willy curled up in his lap.

"Everything okay?" he asks, looking up.

I nod, a small smile breaking through. "Yeah. Everything's good."

"Sophie's on her way over," Julian says, stretching.

"You hungry?" I ask, walking into the kitchen.

Julian follows me, and just as I open the fridge door, his arms wrap around my torso. "Yes, but not for food."

I chuckle and turn around, finding Julian watching me with hooded eyes. "You're insatiable."

"With you?" he says, his breath caressing my face. "You're right. I've never been able to get enough of you, Kai."

His words cause my heart to stutter, and despite wanting to kiss him, I know we should probably eat something before Sophie gets here. We both worked out—and then we *worked out.*

"I told Sophie I don't want anyone else but you. No more scenes. No more guests. Just us."

My fingers twitch against him. "Are you sure? That's a big part of her identity. And yours."

"It was," Julian agrees. "But we all evolve, right? We want you. She's said it. I've said it. Believe us."

Believe us.

That's the hard part, isn't it?

But I'm trying. *Always* trying.

"Sophie's been mine for a long time," Julian admits. "But maybe she can be yours too. If you want her."

"I do," I tell him earnestly. "I want both of you."

"Good. So, about that food," Julian says, his hands coming to the bottom of my shirt.

"I can make a salad? Grill some salmon?" I suggest, winking.

Julian pouts. "Fine. Real food, then." He walks back over to the couch, and I can't help but smile as I think of how to phrase what I'm about to say.

Because he deserves some reassurance, too.

"And, Julian?"

He turns to face me. "Yeah?"

"I'm not going anywhere either. I want this. I'm sorry I walked away, but I promise not to do it again."

Julian's expression softens. "I know. But thanks for saying it out loud."

Turning back around, I grab the fresh salmon filets and quickly throw together a salad and some rice. Julian lounges on the couch, Willy curled up like some smug little prince in his lap. He's flipping absently through channels, but his eyes flick toward the front door every few seconds, like he's waiting for something.

Or someone.

I focus on slicing salmon, but my ears are tuned to the quiet hum of the room, the undercurrent of something that feels heavier than the sound of the TV.

Then Julian's phone buzzes on the armrest, and he lifts it lazily. A grin spreads across his face.

"She just texted," he says, stretching his legs out. "She claims she's a few blocks away, stuck at a light."

I glance over from the stove, flipping the fish with practiced ease. "Really? That was fast."

Julian's grin sharpens, eyes dancing. "Yeah, well. Did you *see* the video?" He smirks. "What did you expect? You basically summoned her with that."

I huff out a soft laugh, shaking my head, but the truth is, I'm watching the door, too.

My heart's been rattling around my chest ever since Julian hit send.

I don't realize I've been holding my breath until the front door bursts open like she's kicking it down.

Julian barely has time to sit up straight.

"Jesus Christ, woman," he calls out, laughing. "I said you were *leaving,* not barreling down the motorway mowing people over."

Sophie stands in the doorway, flushed and wide-eyed, chest heaving like she ran the last block.

"What did you *expect*," she snaps, breathless, "sending me a video *that filthy?*"

Her eyes lock on me across the room, and something in her face crumples.

"Hi, little dove," I manage, but my voice feels thick.

She *sobs.* Actually sobs, her hands flying to her mouth for half a second before she's across the room in five strides, launching herself at me like she's trying to crawl inside my ribs.

I barely manage to catch her, salmon forgotten on the stove as her arms clamp around my neck. Her legs wrap around my waist, and she *crushes* her lips to mine.

It's not soft.

But it's *everything.*

Julian whistles low from the couch. "You're lucky I *like* watching, or I'd be insulted."

Sophie breaks away long enough to glare at him over her shoulder. "You *started without me.*"

He spreads his hands, grinning unapologetically. "*You* took twenty minutes."

"And thank you for the video," she fires back, running her fingers through my hair, tugging lightly. "I'm going to cherish it for the rest of my life."

I chuckle against her neck, but my hands grip her thighs tighter, grounding myself in the weight of her.

"I missed you," I murmur, pressing my forehead to hers.

"I know," she whispers back. "I missed you too."

Her voice breaks, and she kisses me again, softer this time, slow and deliberate.

I open my eyes briefly to peek at Julian, and he's smiling from the couch.

I hold her tighter, hoping she can feel it—how much I mean it.

And how much I *don't* plan on letting go.

CHAPTER THIRTY-NINE
THE THROUPLE

Julian

I lean back against the couch, watching Kai fold himself onto the rug beside Sophie. There's something about the ease of it that makes my chest ache.

"I thought maybe you'd ghost us forever," I admit, swirling the wine in my glass, eyes pinned to the ceiling like it makes the confession easier.

Kai smirks, but the humor doesn't quite reach his eyes. "Not my style. Forgiveness, the Bible, and all that."

"It still felt like you might. I didn't want to say it in front of Soph, but... you walking away scared the hell out of me. I haven't felt like that since... well, the first time you walked away."

I let my chin drop, looking back at the two of them. Sophie is sitting next to him—practically in his lap, which makes me chuckle—and she looks so fucking *happy.* Pushing my empty plate away, I look back at Kai, who is watching me thoughtfully.

He lets out a slow breath, running his hand over Sophie's thigh absentmindedly. "I think... I needed to figure out where I fit in all this," he says finally.

My stomach twists. "Kai..."

"It's not your fault," he cuts in quickly, shaking his head. "I get it now. I mean, hell, I've been in therapy twice a week working on this stuff. But I think I realized I was the one holding myself back."

Sophie lifts her head, turning to look at him. "How so?"

He pauses, running his thumb along the inside of her wrist, thinking through the words.

"I kept waiting for you both to tell me where I fit. For some sign that I wasn't just the guy you were having fun with." He glances at me, his gaze steady now. "But you never treated me that way. It was just... me. I didn't believe it."

The admission twists something inside me, because I get it.

I set the glass down and shift closer, leaning my elbows on my knees.

"Can I say something without you shutting me down?" I ask, locking eyes with him.

Kai arches a brow, that faint smirk tugging at his lips. "You can try."

I huff a soft laugh but meet him with the same level of honesty. "You keep saying we have this whole life together. But you've been in every crack and corner of it since the day you walked through the door. Sophie texted you first half the time before you went MIA. You talk to her about things she doesn't even tell me until days later. I mean, you guys read the same books together... something she's been trying to get me to do for over a decade. And the nights you stayed over? She slept deeper than I've seen in years."

Sophie flushes, but she doesn't deny it.

"It's not just her, either. I still do those midnight workouts you dragged me into that one week. You told me it'd help me sleep. And you were right—damn you for being right. That night Sophie was having a flare-up? You stayed up with me and kept me sane. And when I lose my temper or feel like everything's spinning out, you're the one who grounds me. You don't even have to say anything. Just you being there... it's enough."

I lean back, dragging a hand through my hair. "You've always fit in, Kai. You *are* part of our dynamic now. You're just too polite to push your way in like we expected you to."

The room goes quiet, and I see it, the shifting of something behind his eyes that wasn't there before.

He moves closer, pulling Sophie fully into his lap now, his chin resting against her shoulder as he looks at me.

"I hear you," he says quietly.

And I know he does.

Sophie brushes her nose against his cheek, the warmth of her smile pulling at something in my chest.

"So," she hums, voice teasing but gentle, "are we officially a throuple now?"

I laugh out loud. "Facebook official?" I ask, wiggling my brows as Kai smirks. "Oh, your mother would *love* that," I tell her.

"I'm serious!" she says, sitting up straighter. "If it helps Kai, we should define what *this* is," she suggests. Turning to face him, she pulls her lower lip between her teeth, and she looks so sweet and innocent with her jeans and white prairie shirt. "Did Julian tell you we both decided to stop the hotwife stuff?"

He nods, but his expression is reserved. "He did. But you don't have to—"

"How about we re-evaluate in six months?" she suggests. "Let's settle into this, and if it's something we're all open to exploring, we can discuss options and boundaries. If not, we'll just continue doing this."

He dips his chin, resting it against the top of her head. "You won't be missing out?"

She snorts. "Missing out? On what? I have everything I need right here, Kai," she finishes, her voice soft.

I wink at him as he presses a kiss to her forehead.

"Just to clarify, are we the kind of throuple that takes throuple's trips? I *really* need a holiday once the shop gets up and running."

"Only if I get to pick the destination," he replies.

"Done," I answer without hesitation, tipping my glass toward him. "Though I can't promise she won't pack twelve pairs of shoes for a weekend."

"Arse." Sophie flicks a crumpled napkin at me from the coffee table, narrowing her eyes.

"It'll have to be somewhere with an extra-large bed, though. You know you sleep like you're trying to claim the entire bed," I add, unable to stop myself.

"I take up a perfectly reasonable amount of space," she argues. "You two are the giants."

Kai hums, kissing her shoulder lazily. "It's fine. I'll just sleep between you both. Problem solved."

The simplicity of it curls warmth low in my stomach.

"You know we're just going to keep dragging you to the middle," she teases, poking Kai's chest gently. "Like a human pillow."

Kai smirks down at her, his gaze heavy-lidded but warm. "Fine. As long as Julian isn't snoring directly in my ear again."

I laugh, shaking my head as I remember the camping trip that went awry when we were seventeen. "That was one time, and I had a cold."

Kai arches a brow, his tone all dry amusement. "One time too many."

Sophie grins but doesn't open her eyes, settling deeper against him, her head tucked beneath his chin. I watch the way Kai's arm tightens around her, grounding her in that quiet, steady way he has.

I scoot down the couch to shift closer to them, letting my foot bump against his thigh. "We'll figure it out," I say softly, reaching forward and brushing my knuckles over Sophie's shoulder before trailing them down to

Kai's hand, lacing our fingers together. "Bigger bed. Whatever it takes."

Kai hums in agreement, and there's something different in his expression—something settled, like the weight of the last month has finally started to lift.

Sophie sighs sleepily. "Mm. Yes. And I vote we never let you leave again, Kai."

He doesn't answer right away, and I feel the way his body tenses just slightly beneath her.

I squeeze his hand, grounding him the same way he anchors us. "You heard her," I say lightly, but there's a thread of quiet certainty beneath the words. "No getting rid of us now."

His gaze shifts to mine, something vulnerable but unguarded in his eyes.

"Good," he finally whispers, the word barely more than an exhale.

I press a lingering kiss to Sophie's temple, letting the moment stretch. Then, slowly, I drop to the floor and scoot closer to Kai, brushing my mouth against his in a kiss that's soft and steady. Not rushed. Just... there.

Sophie hums between us, eyes still closed but a lazy grin tugging at her lips. "Thanks for the video, by the way. I will enjoy the precedent you both set with that. The possibilities are endless."

Kai groans softly against my lips. "Don't encourage him," he mutters.

I chuckle, deepening the kiss just enough to hear the soft catch in his breath. "Too late for that," I murmur.

Sophie's arm slides over Kai's waist, pulling him closer as if she can't stand the idea of any space between us.

And for the first time in weeks, I realize, neither can I.

CHAPTER FORTY
THE WORSHIP

Sophie

"That's it. Good girl. *Suck*."

Kai's words reverberate through me, sending a sensation of white-hot heat straight down to my pulsing core. His voice is calm, steady, but there's an edge to it, like he's holding back something darker. Something that I've desperately wanted to see for months now, since he told me about the kinds of things he likes to do in these scenes.

I hollow my cheeks around him, tongue sliding over the smooth, sensitive head of his cock as he tightens his grip in my hair, holding me just shy of where I know he wants me. His restraint makes me ache. I feel it in the way his thighs tense beneath my hands, in the slight tremble of his breath when I hum around him.

And I definitely feel it when I suction around him, pushing him up against the roof of my mouth and making his whole body shudder.

Behind me, Julian's eyes burn into every inch of me, following the slow drag of my mouth along Kai's length. I can feel his gaze lingering where I'm stretched out over the sheets, bare and exposed, every subtle shift of my body on full display.

I pull back slowly, letting my lips drag over Kai's cock until I'm barely kissing the tip, meeting his gaze as I do. His pupils are blown wide, dark gray swallowing the molten silver flecks in his eyes. There's something dangerous lurking beneath that calm exterior, and I want to pull it out of him.

"Look at you," Kai murmurs, brushing his thumb over the corner of my mouth, collecting the moisture gathered there. "So eager to please. Such a good, little servant."

My skin flushes at the praise, but I can't ignore the way Julian shifts behind me, the faint rustle of his clothes betraying how much he enjoys watching this.

"Isn't she?" Kai asks, though his eyes never leave mine. He tilts my chin up, pressing his thumb lightly into the hinge of my jaw. "Our little dove. Always so willing to sin."

Julian chuckles from behind me, low and rough. "She does love when you take control."

Kai's grip tightens, just for a second, before he releases me completely, sitting back against the headboard with an infuriating amount of calm. He strokes his cock lazily, watching as I stay kneeling between his legs, waiting for his next instruction.

The air feels thick, and Julian's hand brushing my lower back with the pads of his fingers makes anticipation curl low in my stomach.

"On top of me," Kai says softly, and I obey without hesitation, crawling over him until I'm straddling his lap, his cock pressing hot and heavy against the slick heat between my legs.

His hands drift slowly down my sides, his touch featherlight, making me shiver. When he reaches my hips, he lingers, holding me just above him, not letting me sink down, no matter how much I want to.

"Patience," Kai whispers. One hand comes to the back of my neck, and he pulls me close to his face. His lips brush the shell of my ear, and the heat of his breath sends a violent shiver down my spine. "Good things come to those who wait."

Behind me, Julian's voice is soft but firm. "I don't think she wants to wait."

Kai hums, and I swear I see the faintest smirk tug at his lips. "She doesn't have a choice."

I start to protest, but the sharp kiss of cool metal against my inner thigh makes the words die on my tongue. My breath hitches as the edge lingers, a tantalizing promise and threat.

"Are you ready for this?" Kai asks, his voice smooth and dark, like velvet over steel. "Because once I start, I won't stop until you're begging for more."

My breath stutters, and my eyes drop down to where

Kai holds the blade of his knife against my skin, dragging it slowly, carefully, along the sensitive flesh. The knife catches the dim light, illuminating the intricate gold filigree along the handle and the sharp edge. Near the base of the blade, an elegant *R* is engraved, the letter gleaming in the faint glow like a mark of authority. *Ravage.*

The sensation isn't painful—it's a delicious sting, just enough to send a surge of heat pooling between my legs.

Julian shifts closer, and I feel his breath on the back of my neck as he watches Kai's every move.

"Look at her," Julian murmurs, brushing his lips over the curve of my shoulder as one of his fingers trails down to the arousal dripping down my inner thighs. "So perfect. So fucking wet for you."

Kai's eyes darken, his grip tightening around the knife. He presses it just a little harder, enough to leave a faint red line in its wake.

I moan softly, rolling my hips forward to chase the friction, but Kai's free hand snaps up, gripping my throat and holding me still.

"Not yet," he growls, his voice dropping lower. "You'll take what I give you. Nothing more."

I can feel how hard he is beneath me, and the sight of him—so calm, so in control—makes me lightheaded.

"Say it," he commands, tightening his hold just enough to make me gasp.

"I'll take what you give me, my lord," I whisper, my voice shaking.

Kai's thumb brushes over the pulse fluttering beneath his hand, and he leans forward, pressing his lips to mine in a slow, bruising kiss.

"That's right. You will," he murmurs.

His grip eases, and I can feel the press of the blade again, higher this time, dragging along my waist to the curve of my breast. The faint sting of it makes my head drop back, and I sigh, relishing the sensation.

Julian groans behind me, his hands sliding up my waist, cupping my breasts as Kai's knife carves another thin red line along the soft swell of one.

"She likes it," Julian says darkly, his lips brushing the shell of my ear. "She always likes it when you hurt her."

Kai tilts his head, considering me carefully.

"Because she knows she's safe," he says quietly, dragging the blade up until the tip rests at the base of my throat.

The metal is cool, but his eyes burn hot.

"She knows I'd never let anything happen to her," he adds, almost as if he's reminding himself as much as me.

I nod, letting my hands drift up his chest, fingers curling around the back of his neck.

"I know," I whisper.

And with that, he lets me sink down onto him in one smooth motion—slow, deliberate—his cock stretching me open until I can't think of anything except the way he fills me completely.

The knife doesn't leave my skin.

His other hand rests heavy on my hip, guiding me

down inch by inch, like he's savoring every second of this. And maybe I am too. More than I expected.

The slick heat of him against me—bare, unfiltered—makes the sensation all the more intense. There's nothing between us this time. No thin barrier, no buffer to dull the friction. I can feel the faint pulse of his cock, the ridges, the raw stretch that leaves me trembling as I take him deeper.

It's the first time we've done this without a condom, and that fact lingers between us like a whispered confession neither of us speaks aloud.

I'm now on the pill. I made the switch to a low-dose birth control last month, partly for this, partly to ease the brutal weight of endometriosis that used to keep me in bed for days. It's helped—more than I ever thought possible. The pain isn't constant anymore. There are days I barely remember it's there at all.

But right now? Right now, I don't feel like a woman burdened by pain. I feel like a woman worshipped.

The thought of Kai—my steady, unshakable man—filling me like this, nothing separating us, sends a shiver down my spine.

It feels... primal.

His eyes stay locked on mine, dark and burning as I sink lower, the blunt head of his cock pressing so deep it steals my breath.

"Breathe," Kai murmurs, his lips brushing against my collarbone. "Let me in, little dove."

I exhale shakily, my fingers curling into his shoulders. His words anchor me as I relax fully, letting gravity pull me flush against his hips.

The knife drags lightly down my ribs, just enough pressure to make me keen.

"Look how well you take it," he whispers, voice like gravel and silk wrapped into one. "So beautiful like this."

The praise strikes low in my belly, pooling molten heat between my legs where I'm wrapped tight around him. His cock twitches inside me, like he feels it too—the same unbearable closeness. The same overwhelming ache that comes with knowing there's nothing separating us anymore.

"You feel that?" he rasps, letting the blade trace the curve of my waist. "Every inch of me inside you. Just you and me. Nothing between us."

I nod, unable to form words as he grips my hip tighter, holding me still.

For a moment, he doesn't move.

Neither of us do.

The world shrinks down to the space where our bodies meet, where I'm stretched and trembling around him, where the sharp edge of the knife keeps me on that delicate line between surrender and anticipation.

Kai's lips press to my temple, the warmth of his breath fanning over my skin.

"This is mine now," he murmurs.

His hips flex, just a fraction, and I gasp at the molten slide of him inside me—bare, thick, and unrelenting.

Mine.

I hear Julian come behind me, his belt clinking as Kai thrusts up into me—*hard.*

"Oh fuck," I whimper, rocking my hips. Kai's free hand is guiding me, moving me up, back, and down with a hard pull. "Yes," I hiss. "Just like that."

The knife comes back up to my throat, and it only enhances the sensation of feeling Kai inside of me. I can hear Julian stroking himself behind me, and as I bend forward to take him, Kai clucks his tongue as the blade presses farther into my neck. I can feel the way Kai controls the pressure of it against my skin—always there, but never dangerous.

I trust him.

"No. Fill her mouth. My little dove is going to recite some Bible passages."

"Mmm, yes she is," Julian says, reaching over and handing me the discarded Bible from earlier.

I grip the leather-bound book to my chest as I grind down on Kai, focusing on the feel of his warm length inside of me. It feels... indescribable.

Julian comes around on his knees next to Kai, and I can tell by the frenetic way he's stroking himself that he's close.

"Open up, pet."

I obey without hesitation, parting my lips as Kai watches with quiet authority. Julian's cock presses against my tongue, heavy and leaking, and I take him fully, hollowing my cheeks as he groans above me.

Thick, hot spurts of cum hit the back of my throat,

but I hold it, locking my jaw as the taste of him coats my tongue—salty, bitter, and grounding.

"Fuck," Julian rasps, shuddering as he slides out of my mouth. "That's my girl."

I lift my eyes, but it's not Julian's gaze I find.

It's Kai's.

There's a heat in his stare that threatens to unmake me. The sharp edge of his knife glinting faintly in his palm. It drags slowly over my abdomen as his eyes flick to the Bible at my side.

The metal's edge catches faintly against my skin, not enough to break it, but enough to promise he could.

"Read." Kai's voice is both prayer and sin, curling around my ribs as I pull the Bible into my lap with trembling fingers. He shifts beneath me, his cock hard as he pulls out, sliding between the lips of my pussy.

I know he's close, it's why he pulled out of me. Despite that, he drags my slick center along his shaft for some much-needed friction.

The soft crackle of the pages fills the silence as I flip through, not even needing to search. It falls open like it's been waiting for this moment.

Kai hums in approval as he presses the blade flat against the inside of his wrist, the dull side resting just below his pulse.

"Go on."

It takes me a second to start, because I have to keep my mouth mostly closed so Julian's cum doesn't dribble out of my mouth.

"'Come, let us bow down in worship, let us kneel before the Lord, our Maker.'"

I barely finish the words before Kai leans forward, gripping my chin roughly between his thumb and forefinger. He pulls me in, his lips hovering just shy of mine.

"Is that what you're doing now?" he whispers, dark and reverent. "Kneeling before your maker?"

"Yes," I breathe, my body trembling with the weight of it.

The blade drags down the line of my collarbone, and I arch into it, the faintest sting blooming as he presses just enough to prick the surface.

Kai's gaze burns through me, both punishment and praise.

"Good," he murmurs. "Because you were made for this. Made to be filled. To take everything I give you."

I whimper as the knife traces the curve of my breast, his other hand already guiding me over his lap. I have the safe word should I need it, or should this be too intense for me. His cock is hard against my pussy, slick and hot, and he bumps his hips up so that he hits my aching clit.

Kai's free hand slides up the back of my neck, and his eyes are softer now. "Keep going."

My lips part slightly to keep from swallowing as I force the next verse from my lips.

"'For He is our God, and we are the people of His pasture, the flock under His care.'"

I barely make it to the end of the verse before Kai's hands grip my hips, lifting me effortlessly. His tip slides against my entrance, wet and needy, as he presses inside with slow, aching precision.

"You're not just kneeling anymore, are you, little dove?" he rasps. "Now you're letting yourself be filled by your god."

Kai thrusts up as I read, his cock sinking deeper, stretching me in a way that borders on divine pain and pleasure. The book slips from my trembling hands, landing beside us on the bed as I brace myself against his chest.

"Say it again," he demands, driving into me harder. His eyes burn with something unholy, something that feels as if it could consume me whole.

I choke out the verse, barely able to focus as his pace quickens, forcing me to ride the line between devotion and debauchery, all the while trying to keep my mouth closed enough.

"'For He is our God—'"

The blade presses just under the swell of my breast, teasing but never cutting, as if he's carving me into something new without ever breaking the skin.

Julian shifts behind me, watching with a faint smirk as his cum still lingers on my tongue.

"Look at her," Julian murmurs. "Dripping, stretched around you. She looks like she was made to worship, doesn't she?"

Kai hums in agreement, his fingers trailing over the faint line the knife left along my breast.

"She's perfect," Kai breathes. His eyes burn with something unholy, something that feels as if it could consume me whole. "My little dove," Kai whispers darkly, leaning up to capture my lips.

I sink deep into the kiss, moaning softly as his hips thrust up again. His tongue swirls around mine, tasting Julian. I hear him swallow, and the low, reverberating growl he pours into my mouth sends me buzzing.

"Who do you belong to?" Kai asks, his voice a low rasp. His soft lips graze mine, teasing, as he thrusts deeper, each roll of his hips deliberate, like he's carving his claim into me with every motion.

His hand presses firmly into the small of my back, forcing me down, anchoring me to him. The other trails the cool metal blade over my left breast. The sharp feel of the knife leaves shallow, stinging lines against my skin, just enough to make me gasp, the dizzying mix of lust and submission flooding every nerve in my body.

"Say it," he demands, breath fanning over my lips, his eyes dark and unrelenting.

I swallow hard, pulse thundering against the blade. "You, my lord," I whisper, the words leaving my mouth like a prayer, each syllable trembling.

Kai's gaze wavers with something dangerous as the knife tilts ever so slightly, dragging up to the center of my chest, stopping just above my heart.

"That's right," he growls. His grip on my waist tightens. "Now show me."

And so I do.

Body trembling, I arch against him, rolling my hips to take him deeper, letting the knife press closer, a sweet edge of pain laced with pleasure. My head tips back, a soft moan escaping as I offer him everything—every inch of skin, every breath, every fractured piece of myself.

His lips find the hollow of my throat, warm and open-mouthed, as he marks me with his tongue, his teeth, his blade.

Piece by reverent piece.

The word falls from my lips before I can stop it, broken but whole.

"Yours."

CHAPTER FORTY-ONE
THE LOVE

Julian

I watch the two of them, heat building low in my stomach. I just came, but I can feel my cock waking up again. Sophie rocks her hips against Kai's, taking him deeper with every roll. She's breathtaking like this—flushed, trembling, completely at his mercy. But it's the way Kai watches her, his silver-gray eyes burning with reverence, that undoes me.

The sight of them together—the raw connection, the unspoken trust—sends a jolt of longing through me. I want to be part of it.

All of it.

"She belongs to you," I say, my voice low and dark, as I step closer to the bed.

Kai's eyes flick to mine, the knife still in his hand as

he drags it slowly down Sophie's side. "She does," he says softly, his voice vibrating with unshakable certainty. "But she's not the only one."

My breath catches, and for a moment, the weight of his words presses down on me. Kai watches me, his gaze sharp and unrelenting. Everything narrows down to this exact moment, and I stroke my cock a few times until I'm fully hard again.

"Switch with me," I murmur to Sophie, leaning close enough to feel the heat radiating from her skin.

Sophie whimpers as I guide her off him, her legs shaking as she shifts to the side. Her eyes meet mine, wide and glassy, her chest heaving as she watches me slide down between Kai's legs.

My hands move to his thighs, spreading him wider as I lean in, my tongue darting out to taste the slick heat of my wife on his cock. Kai's breath hitches. I take him into my mouth, my tongue swirling over the head of his cock before sliding down the length. I groan, loving the taste and feel of him in my mouth.

"Fuck," Kai mutters, his voice low and rough. His hips jerk slightly, but I hold him down, my hands gripping his thighs as I set a slow, deliberate rhythm. The weight of him on my tongue, the way his body trembles beneath me, it's intoxicating.

Sophie moves closer, her hand tangling in my hair as she watches, her lips parted in awe. "God," she whispers, her voice thick with arousal. "You're both so beautiful."

"Julian," Kai rasps, his voice tight. "I need—"

I pull back, my lips wet and swollen, and meet his gaze. "I know. On your knees, Ravage."

He exhales slowly, his broad shoulders rising and falling in steady rhythm as he settles onto his hands and knees in the center of the bed. I watch the subtle shift in his body, the way his fingers flex into the sheets, gripping them like they might anchor him to something solid.

I climb behind him, deliberately slow, letting the mattress dip beneath my weight. My hands skim up the strong lines of his back, fingertips ghosting over his spine. His skin is warm, covered in a light sheen of sweat, and when I rake my nails lightly across his shoulders, I don't miss the way goosebumps rise in my wake. He's bracing himself—not just for me, but for the way this is shifting something inside of him. I drag my hand down his spine, pressing firmly, urging him to relax.

"You don't have to hold onto control so tightly," I whisper against the nape of his neck, pressing a kiss there. "You can let go with us."

He doesn't answer right away. Instead, he tilts his head slightly, like he's mulling my words over.

I reach for the lube on the nightstand, coating my fingers, and run my free hand over the dip of his lower back, tracing slow circles. "Tell me if you want me to stop," I say, voice low and steady. "Okay?"

A beat of silence, then a clipped nod.

He exhales sharply, his head falling forward as I move one finger between his arse cheeks, trying to stay patient. I press a single, slick finger against his tight entrance, teasing, not pushing inside just yet. He inhales sharply, his body going rigid beneath my touch. Sophie crawls on her knees until she's right in front of him. She runs her hands through his hair, and his whole body shakes at the contact.

Something shifts in his expression—uncertainty, pride, need, all tangled together. His Adam's apple bobs as he swallows hard. Then, finally, he exhales and lets his body go slack.

That's my cue.

I press my finger inside him, slow and patient, easing past the tight ring of muscle. The sound that leaves his mouth is nearly a growl, low and breathy, more surprised than pained. His knuckles tighten around the sheets, and I feel him fighting the urge to tense up again.

"That's it," I murmur, rubbing soothing circles against his hip with my free hand. "Relax, Kai. Let me take care of you."

Kai's head drops forward, his dark hair falling into his eyes as he focuses on his breathing. His body trembles, fighting the urge to resist. When I twist my finger, stretching him gently, he shudders so violently that Sophie has to steady him with both hands.

"Shit," he exhales, voice wrecked. "That feels—"

"Good?" I ask, adding a second finger before he can second-guess himself.

He doesn't answer, but the way his body jerks tells me everything I need to know.

Sophie leans in, her lips brushing against his cheek. "Julian's got you," she whispers. "I've got you. Just let us do this for you."

His breath is ragged now, his muscles twitching as I scissor my fingers, loosening him. I feel the moment his resistance crumbles, the moment he stops trying to hold onto control and just lets himself feel. His thighs shake, and his back bows slightly as he pushes back, taking my fingers deeper.

"There we go," I murmur, pressing a kiss to his lower back. "Look at you, taking it so well."

He huffs out something that sounds like a curse, but it's breathless, broken, barely there.

When I curl my fingers inside him, searching for that perfect spot, his entire body jolts, his hips snapping forward involuntarily. Sophie grins, smoothing her hands over his trembling thighs.

"Oh, you like that," she teases, her voice thick with amusement.

Kai groans, dropping his forehead onto Sophie's shoulder. "Shut up."

I smirk, brushing my lips against his hip. "You're in no position to be making demands, Ravage."

He mutters something under his breath, but his hips push back against my hand again, and I can't help but grin.

"You're beautiful like this," I whisper, my voice dipping lower. "Completely undone for us."

His breath stutters, and I swear I hear him curse again, but this time, there's no fight left in it.

There's just need.

"Sophie," I say softly.

She orients herself so that her back is pressed to his

chest. "Fuck me again, Kai," she says, craning her neck and looking back at him.

My fingers are still inside of him as he pushes her down in front of him, lifting her arse to his pelvis and lining his weeping cock up with her cunt.

"F-fuck, Soph," he says, pressing into her slowly.

The sound he makes, the way he cries out, sends a jolt straight through me.

I slick myself up, aligning the head of my cock with his entrance, and as soon as I press forward—just the barest nudge—Kai goes completely still.

His breath catches, his fingers tightening against Sophie's hips like she's the only thing keeping him grounded. I pause immediately, my hands squeezing his waist in reassurance.

"Kai," I murmur, my voice low and steady. "Breathe for me."

He exhales shakily, his back rising and falling beneath my palms.

"That's it," Sophie whispers, voice warm, coaxing.

I feel the exact moment the tension in his muscles begins to unravel, when he stops holding himself back. His thighs stop trembling, his weight settles fully against Sophie in front of him, and he breathes out another shaky sigh.

"Good," I murmur, pressing a slow kiss between his shoulder blades. "That's my good boy."

Kai makes a sound low in his throat—something between a groan and a curse—but he doesn't pull away.

Instead, his hips tilt back the smallest fraction, a silent invitation.

I take it.

Pushing forward, inch by agonizing inch, I sink into him, my grip on his hips tightening. The tight, hot grip of him steals my breath, and I feel his entire body tense again.

Kai's head tips back against my shoulder, his mouth falling open as I slide deeper into him. He pulls Sophie up so that we're all on our knees, the three of us connected in a way that I never could've imagined before this moment.

The heat and tightness of his body pulls a groan from deep in my chest, and I grip his hips, holding him steady as I thrust forward. His breath stutters, his fingers digging into Sophie's waist as he grinds into her from behind.

Sophie gasps beneath him, her spine arching as Kai thrusts into her, slow and deliberate. Her fingers reach back and curl around my hands, knuckles white as she chokes out his name. We find our rhythm quickly, moving in tandem, each thrust timed with his movements inside Sophie.

"Good girl," Kai murmurs, his voice low and dark, as he fucks her relentlessly, his hands bracketing her hips. "Take me. Just like that."

I lean in, pressing my chest against Kai's broad back, the heat of his skin searing against mine. My lips brush the shell of his ear as I murmur, "You're doing so well, love. You feel so good wrapped around my cock."

Kai groans, his hips jerking forward as he takes Sophie deeper, his rhythm faltering for a moment before I guide him back into place with a firm hand on his lower back. The three of us move together—every groan from my lips, every gasp from Sophie layering over the other, weaving a cacophony of raw pleasure and connection. Sophie's noises rise in volume with each thrust, her body trembling as Kai drives her higher and higher, his hips rolling against hers with unrelenting precision.

"Kai," Sophie gasps, turning her head to catch his gaze over her shoulder. Her cheeks are flushed, her lips swollen and parted.

"I know," Kai rasps, his voice trembling as he thrusts harder, deeper, his control fraying at the edges. "I've got you, little dove. I'll take you there."

His words hit me like a lightning bolt, and I tighten my grip on his hips, thrusting deeper into him as he loses himself in Sophie. His body clenches around me, the sheer power of it forcing a groan from my lips.

"Fuck, Kai," I murmur, my voice low and strained. "You feel so good. So perfect."

Kai's head tips back against my shoulder again, his silver-gray eyes blown wide as he meets my gaze. There's something raw and vulnerable in his expression, a mix of surrender and reverence that makes my chest ache.

"Julian," he whispers, his voice breaking. "I—"

"I know," I cut him off gently, pressing a kiss to the side of his neck. "I love you too."

His breath catches, and I feel the tremor that runs through his body as the words settle between us. For a moment, time seems to stop, the world narrowing to the three of us tangled together, every touch and sound and breath a testament to the unshakable bond we've built.

Then Kai surges forward, his hips snapping against Sophie's with a force that makes her cry out, her whole body trembling as she shatters beneath him. Her moans echo through the room, raw and unrestrained, as she rides the waves of her climax, her body taut and trembling.

Kai isn't far behind, his body tensing as he spills into her, his release shuddering through him in sharp, pulsing waves. His head drops forward, his breath coming in short, ragged gasps as he grips Sophie's hips, holding her flush against him.

The sight of them—the way their bodies fit together, the way Sophie melts into him—sends me over the edge. My hips jerk against Kai's, a deep groan rumbling from my chest as I come inside him, the intensity of it stealing the breath from my lungs.

For a moment, the three of us collapse into each other, our bodies tangled and trembling, the room filled with the sound of our ragged breaths. Sophie turns her head, her gaze soft and glassy as she smiles at me, her hand reaching back to tangle in Kai's hair.

"I love you, Kai," she murmurs, her voice hoarse but steady.

Kai nods, his arms wrapping around Sophie's waist as he pulls her against his chest. His head tilts back, resting against my shoulder as he exhales a shaky breath.

"Me too, little dove," he murmurs, pressing a kiss to

Sophie's temple. Then, shifting slightly, he turns his head just enough to glance at me. His expression is open, raw in a way that makes my chest ache.

"And you," he adds, his voice softer but no less certain. "Both of you."

I press another kiss to the side of his neck, my hand sliding down to tangle with Sophie's. "Forever."

CHAPTER FORTY-TWO
THE CONCLUSION

Sophie

I breathe it in, leaning against the register with a soft smile as sunlight pours through the front window. The pink facade reflects against the glass, casting a rosy glow over everything. Chase and Juliet are curled up on the teal chaise lounge near the cowboy romance section, half hidden behind a tower of new releases I haven't shelved yet. Stella and Miles are by the fireplace, arguing over which of the leg lamps needs to be repositioned:

"It looks crooked," Miles grumbles.

"It's meant to look like that," Stella fires back, hands on her hips.

Liam is at the back, whispering something into Zoe's ear as she flips through one of her own romantasy books, the corners of her lips tugging upward. I can't wait to display it front and center, with a handwritten note next to it that reads *local legend*.

And Kai—

Kai stands by the front window with Julian, their heads bent together as they laugh about something I can't hear. I know that sound, though. It's soft and easy, as if seventeen years of weight has finally slipped from Julian's shoulders. It's a sound that feels like home.

"Stop staring," Stella teases, nudging me in the side. "You look like you're about to start reciting poetry about your beautiful men."

I swat her with the back of my hand, laughing. "Can you blame me? Look at them."

She sighs dramatically. "Yeah, well, I look at Miles the same way. Sometimes I cry about how handsome he is while he's sleeping."

From the fireplace, Miles deadpans, "I can hear you."

Stella smirks. "Good. I meant for you to hear it."

Juliet snickers from the chaise, and Chase pulls her closer, dropping a kiss onto the top of her head. The sight of all of them here, crammed into this tiny, chaotic bookstore, makes something twist tight and warm in my chest.

The doorbell jingles as Orion and Layla walk in, carrying a box of custom Kindle cases Layla's been designing for me. "I hope you don't mind," Layla says, grinning as she sets the box on the counter. "I might've added a few with naughty quotes on them. You know, for your more adventurous clientele."

"Oh, please. I *love* those," I reply, already rifling

through the box. One of the cases reads: *I like my books like my men... thick and hard.*

"Perfect," I say with a grin, turning to Kai and Julian. "Look! This one practically screams your name."

Julian hums thoughtfully. "I think the one that says *Sinfully yours* might be more fitting, don't you, Kai?"

Kai smirks but doesn't answer, his eyes on me instead. There's something in his expression—quiet, steady, the way he watches me like I'm the only thing in the room.

That look still undoes me.

Before I can respond, my phone vibrates on the counter. I glance at the screen.

Mum.

I raise an eyebrow, waving the phone slightly in Julian's direction. He leans over, reading the contact name with mild amusement. "She must've seen the feature in the *LA Weekly*."

Stella whistles low. "Is this the part where she tells you she's proud, but in the same breath insults you?"

"More like telling me that pink bookshelves are scandalous," I mutter, swiping to accept the call.

"Hello, Mum," I say brightly.

"I saw the article." No greeting. Classic.

"Oh?"

The line crackles for a second. I brace myself.

"You know... I suppose it's *charming* in its own way," she says begrudgingly. "Though I don't understand the fascination with displaying large neon cocks—"

"It's whimsical!" I protest, biting back laughter.

"Your grandmother would faint."

Julian, overhearing, snorts softly. Kai's shoulders shake with silent laughter.

Mum sighs, the sound distant but somehow fond. "Regardless. I saw the photo of you and Julian with his friend. What's his name? He's very handsome."

"Mum, I can't really talk right now," I tell her, trying to hide the amusement from my voice.

"I just wanted to tell you that you look happy."

I glance toward the front window where Julian is now perched on the arm of Kai's chair, leaning against him like he belongs there. Because he does.

"I am," I say softly.

She pauses. I wait, half expecting some sort of unsolicited advice about propriety or how "ladies don't open sex-positive bookshops."

But instead, she says, "I'm glad, Sophia. I mean it."

My throat tightens unexpectedly.

"Thank you," I whisper.

There's another pause, but this time it feels lighter.

"Well. I'll let you go. Tell Julian I expect him to send something nice for Christmas this year."

"I will," I say, smiling.

I hang up just as Julian strolls over, hands in his pockets. "So... what did Her Majesty have to say?"

"Oh, she *loved* the flashing neon cock, obviously," I tease, wrapping my arms around his waist.

"Obviously." He presses a kiss to my forehead, and then lowers his voice just enough for only me to hear.

"Wait until she finds out about us being a throuple. It might kill her."

I laugh softly, pressing my face into his chest.

Kai joins us a second later, sliding his arm around my shoulders and pulling me in the rest of the way. "If it helps, my brothers love you and we're all incredibly proud of you," he murmurs against my temple.

I tilt my head up to meet his gaze. "Thank you."

Behind us, I hear Orion grumble something to Miles about book placement, Liam teasing Zoe as she flips through an age gap romance book, and Stella already planning the next window display.

Julian sighs, nuzzling into my hair. "We should have a name for these family gatherings. Like a fraternity."

"Or a cult," I joke.

Kai hums thoughtfully. "*The Ravage Cult* does have a nice ring to it."

I lean into them both, soaking up every second of this. The bookstore. The people. The family we've built.

Maybe I'll tell Mum about the throuple someday.

Or... maybe I'll save that conversation for another year.

As the afternoon wears on, I mingle with everyone here. I'm introduced to Luna, who works at Ravage Castle, and her lovely wife, Emma. Jackson and Mark show up with a tiny newborn in tow, Theo Parker. He's adorable and I can already tell he's the light of their life. Beatrix runs through the store carrying her Batman action figure, making exploding noises as Miles chases after her. When Stella tries to get up, he makes her stay seated, the product of her finding out she's pregnant with their second child just a couple of days ago.

Juliet and Chase tell us about an old house they just bought across the bridge in Marin County with massive amounts of land. They plan to fix it up before moving in. Zoe and Liam tell us about a possible, tenured creative writing position at NYU for Liam, and Zoe hints at trying for a baby soon, too. Her aunt Carolina is here as well, and I'm grateful for all of the family support.

"Did someone order pizza?" a man jokes as he steps through the front door, grinning. He's carrying ten boxes of pizza.

Layla and Orion walk over, taking the boxes from him, and Stella nudges me. "That's Scott, Layla's dad."

I nod, watching as Scott claps Orion on the back. I remember the story, how Orion moved in with their mum and Scott as a teenager, making Layla his stepsister.

He notices me, walking over and pulling me into a surprised hug before I can shake his hand.

"You must be Sophie. Orion has told us all about you and your husband."

I glance at Orion over his shoulder. The youngest Ravage brother just winks as we make introductions, and then Scott is hugging Stella.

"Where's your old man? Still gallivanting all over Europe?"

Stella laughs. "Of course he is. But he promised to come visit next month. He can never stay away from his granddaughter for too long."

After Scott congratulates her on the pregnancy—prompting an eye roll at Miles and a muttered "gossiping meddler"—Stella taps her glass of nonalcoholic champagne with a nail, the soft chime cutting through the chatter.

"I'd like to say a few things, as Sophie's newly appointed favorite person."

"Um, you're going to have to fight me for her," Juliet jokes from the couch, already cradling another glass in her hand.

"Oh, please. Sophie's heart is big enough for all of us," Zoe smirks, sticking her tongue out. "If you're good, I'll allow you to be her limited-time sidekick when I'm not around."

Laughter ripples through the room, warm and easy, but the playful banter does more than make me smile, it makes me feel included.

The Ravage family isn't just something I've stumbled into. They've claimed me. Just like Julian did all those years ago. Like Kai has, in his own quiet way.

Stella lifts her chin, her eyes scanning the room as if daring anyone to interrupt. "I was here when Sophie came to tour the place for the first time. And let me just say, it did not look this good two and a half months ago," she starts, drawing chuckles from around the crowded bookshop. I feel my cheeks flush as my eyes dart around the shop—my shop. The soft pink bookshelves, the cascading plants in the window, the little corner with mismatched chairs and a cozy sofa for book clubs... it looks so put together now. Pride stirs quietly in my chest, a fleeting but powerful reminder of what this moment means to me.

"And I know when The Story Nest officially opens tomorrow," Stella continues, her voice softening just a touch, "there's going to be a queue around the block—"

"We call it a 'line' here in America," Orion interjects from the armchair, grinning as Layla elbows him hard in the ribs.

"Queue, line, whatever," Stella retorts, rolling her eyes dramatically but smirking all the same. "My point is, I don't think I've ever met anyone who works as hard as Sophie. She put her blood, sweat, and literal tears into this space, and you can see it. You can feel it. This isn't just a bookshop; it's a love letter. To the books we devour, to the stories that make us believe in love again, and to the people we choose to share those stories with."

My chest tightens as she speaks, and I have to blink against the sudden sting behind my eyes. *Damn it, Stella.*

"I know she thinks she's the lucky one," she adds, glancing over at me, "because she's with Julian and now Kai—and because, let's be honest, who wouldn't want to bang my husband's ridiculously hot brother?"

Kai barks out a laugh from the kitchen, and Julian arches a brow in mock offense. "I'll take that as a compliment."

"It was," Stella replies breezily, lifting her glass higher. "But in reality, you're not just lucky, Sophie. You're also brave. I've never seen anyone dive headfirst into a new life with so much vigor and heart, with so much passion. And let me tell you," she adds, looking at

Julian and Kai. "Love stories like yours belong in books. The steamy, messy, and beautiful kind. The ones that don't just have a happily ever after, but the ones that *fight* for it."

A soft sound escapes my throat, but I swallow it down quickly, forcing out a watery laugh.

She isn't finished.

"Which brings me to my actual point," she says, her voice gentler now, as though she knows she's brushing up against something fragile. "I think it's safe to say that you're one of us now. Officially. We're a lot, but"—she grins, glancing around the room at Chase and Juliet, Liam and Zoe, Orion and Layla, Miles sipping a beer on the windowsill—"you fit right in. I mean, you opened a romance bookshop. You practically manifested your place in this family."

I can't hold back the soft laugh that spills out, but the tears gathering in my eyes betray me. I sniff quietly, but Julian notices—because of course he does. He walks over and wraps his arm around my waist from behind, pulling me against his chest.

"I'm proud of you, pet," he murmurs, pressing a kiss against the crown of my head.

Kai moves beside me, pressing his palm against my lower back in silent solidarity. The weight of their attention—their *love*—makes me want to cry harder, but I bite my lip and try to hold it together.

Stella lifts her glass one final time. "To Sophie. To The Story Nest. And to the happiest of ever afters."

Everyone cheers, glasses clinking together in bursts of sound that echo across the cozy shop.

Julian's voice dips low beside me, just for me to hear. "I hope your parents come visit sometime. Wait until they notice the 'Staff Recommendations' shelf has a whole row of nothing but why choose romances."

I snort, half gasping as I wipe my eyes. "Oh God. She'll definitely need to lie down for a week after that."

Kai chuckles softly, brushing his knuckles against the small of my back. "I'll pray for her."

"You might need to," I whisper, leaning into him. "Especially when she sees the title *Seven Brothers and a Baby*."

Julian hums thoughtfully. "I thought *Claimed by the Team* was bolder, but sure, we'll ease her into the shock. Or you could just put a 'For Mum' sign on it and let nature take its course."

I swat at him, laughing despite myself. "You're lucky I love you."

Kai squeezes my waist gently. "We're both lucky."

The moment stretches, warm and easy, and as I glance around the shop—at the people who have become my family, the men who love me, and the life I never imagined for myself—I feel whole.

Glancing at Julian and Kai as they bicker softly over something or other, I realize this isn't just happily ever after.

This is the beginning of something even better.

EPILOGUE
THE LEGACY

MALAKAI

Twenty Years Later

I open the front door of the house and gesture for Sophie to walk in before me. It feels empty and... quiet. She walks into the foyer, setting her purse down on the table and stepping out of her sneakers. I close the door behind us, and the sound echoes so loudly that I almost flinch. When she turns to face me, there are tears running down her face, and my heart clenches at the sight.

"Come here," I say softly, holding my arms open.

She doesn't hesitate. Walking over to me, she collides with my body and begins to sob. My hands squeeze at her sweater, and my throat aches with unshed tears.

"God, I miss him s-so much," she says, her voice hoarse.

I kiss the top of her head, squeezing my eyes shut. It's

futile. Before I can stop it, my body shakes as I cry. Sophie squeezes me tighter, her fingers grabbing at my torso. I can *feel* her pain, and it nearly knocks me over.

"I know, little dove. I miss him, too."

"What are we going to d-do without him?"

I sniff, blinking rapidly to clear the tears. "I don't know."

"Nothing w-will ever be the s-same," she adds, hiccupping as she cries.

"It won't be, but we'll adjust. Okay? We'll adapt. We'll find a new routine, and we'll be okay. Because we have to be."

"I didn't think..." She trails off. "I didn't think it would be this hard."

"I know, Soph. I didn't, either."

"I mean, you p-prepare yourself for this day your whole life, but..."

"I know. But nothing can prepare you for this feeling."

She continues to cry, resting her cheek against my chest as I rub my hand down her back. Kissing the top of her head, I pull away slowly.

Her eyes are bloodshot, and her lips tremble as she lets out a small laugh. "God, I'm a mess, aren't I?"

I give her a gentle smile as I run a hand down the side of her face. "Still as gorgeous as the first day I saw you."

It's true. Other than a few fine lines, Sophie looks incredible for fifty. I still think she's the most beautiful woman I've ever laid eyes on. Her hair might be a little shorter now, just below her chin. And there may be a few gray strands mixed in with her honey blonde locks, but watching her still takes my breath away, even now.

She gives me a watery smile and runs a hand through my hair. "I know you're just trying to flatter me because I'm sad."

Taking her hand, I bring it to my lips. "So what if I am?"

She sniffs and shakes her head, and her smile drops off her face immediately. "It helped momentarily. Thank you."

Reaching into her back pocket, I pull her phone out. "Do you want to call him?"

This perks her up. "Should we? I mean... is it too soon?"

I huff a laugh. "I don't think so. If it'll make you feel better, why not?"

She pulls her lower lip between her teeth and nods vigorously. "Okay. Let's call him."

I try to hide my smile at the hopeful tone in her voice as I dial. Holding it in front of me, I put it on speaker as it rings a few times. When it finally picks up, Sophie jumps once and reaches for the phone.

"Rowan?"

"Mom?"

"Hi, sweetie," she says, her voice breaking. "I'm just calling because, well, I missed you."

I hear Rowan huff a laugh on the other end. "I miss you too, Mom. A lot."

Sophie's eyes leak more tears, but she holds it together. "Make sure Dad doesn't eat too many Flamin'

Hot Cheetos before your flight, okay? It'll upset his stomach."

"Too late," Rowan says, laughing. There's an announcement in the background, and I hear Julian say something to Rowan in the background. "Mom, I have to go. We're boarding."

"Okay. I love you. Have a safe flight. I've already sent your first care package, so it should arrive at your flat sometime this week. And then of course we'll be there to visit in a couple of weeks—"

"Mom?" Rowan's voice is softer now. "You're spiraling. I promise I'll be fine. Dad's here to help me get settled, and I'll see you in a couple of weeks."

Sophie nods, squeezing her eyes closed. "Okay. I love you."

"Love you too, Row," I chime in.

"Love you, Dad," he replies. "Do you want to talk to Dad?"

Before Sophie and I can answer, Julian's voice flicks through the speakerphone. "Couldn't even wait an hour, could you?" he asks, amusement tinging his voice.

Sophie chokes out a laugh. "I know."

"He's fine, Soph. I promise. I'll get him all settled and show him the lay of the land."

"You mean take him to all of your favorite pubs and get him his first pint?" I chime in.

Julian laughs. "Probably. He's eighteen, it's legal to drink there."

Sophie snorts. "Give him a kiss and a hug from me."

"I will. I promise. But we really do have to go because

we're boarding. See you two in a few days when I get home. Love you both."

"Love you more," Sophie and I echo together as the call ends.

Handing her phone back to her, she gives me a tight smile. "That helped. Thank you."

I take her hand. "Do you want to go sit on his bed and have another cry?"

This makes her laugh again. "God no. I'm not stepping in there for at least a month or two. I'm not a masochist."

Bringing my hands to her shoulders, I rub them gently as I look down at her. "He's only off to college. He's not going to be gone forever. There's Christmas break and summer break… he'll be back. All right?"

She scoffs. "I know I've said it a thousand times, but why did he have to go to London? Why couldn't he stay here?"

I give her a knowing look, and she lets out a sharp gasp before placing her hand over her mouth. "Fuck, I sound just like my mother."

"Yeah. I wasn't going to say anything, but…" I tease.

She swats my arm. "Don't be cheeky."

"I'm always cheeky."

"I need a distraction," she declares. "Bea's at the shop, and Twix is on stall rest after his vaccinations."

I wiggle my brows. "I'm here."

"You don't have to get back to Saint Helena today?" she asks.

I shrug. "I can take a day off."

"Okay. What if we made some cinnamon rolls and cuddled in bed?" she suggests.

"That sounds perfect."

Sophie

Later that evening, as the scent of cinnamon rolls lingers in the air, I find myself sitting in Rowan's room. I know I told Kai I wouldn't step in here for a month, but I couldn't resist. The space feels like him, like all the memories we've built as a family. His bookshelf is a mess, overflowing with novels Julian and I gave him, with dog-eared pages peeking out from nearly every spine. There's a photo on his desk of the four of us at the grand opening of The Story Nest in Larchmont Village, all grinning like idiots, holding up copies of our favorite books.

The ache in my chest from earlier is still there, but it's gentler now. Sitting on his bed, I pick up one of his worn notebooks, thumbing through sketches and notes. He's always had Julian's eye for detail and my flair for creativity, though he's far more disciplined than either of us. I smile to myself, wondering if that's the Kai in him, the steady, grounding presence that holds everything together.

I glance at the corner of his desk, where a small,

framed quote rests. *"A family is a nest of stories, woven together with love."*

Julian gave it to me when I opened The Story Nest in San Francisco. He said it reminded him of what we've built, what we've shared. With seven locations of The Story Nest now under my belt, the last several years have been chaotic and busy. If I'm being honest, life's been chaotic—in the best way—for a very long time.

But I wouldn't change it for the world.

The bed dips beside me, and I look up to find Kai. He's holding two steaming mugs of tea, his hair damp from the shower. "Thought you might need this," he says, handing me one.

"I said I wouldn't come in here," I admit, a little sheepishly.

Kai chuckles, leaning back against the headboard. "You lasted longer than I thought you would."

We sit in companionable silence, sipping tea and letting the quiet of the house wrap around us. My fingers trace the rim of the mug as I glance at Kai. "Do you think we've done enough?"

He looks at me, his brows knitting together. "Enough?"

"For him. For Rowan. To make sure he knows how much we love him, how proud we are."

Kai sets his mug down and takes my hand. "Sophie, we've spent eighteen years loving him with everything we've got. He knows. And if he ever doubts it, he's got three parents who will fly across the world just to remind him."

I swallow the lump in my throat, nodding. "You're right. I just... I can't believe he's grown up. It feels like yesterday I was holding him for the first time. Do you remember when we got the call from the adoption agency? God... I can't believe that was eighteen years ago."

Kai's hand tightens around mine. "It goes fast. But we've still got a lifetime of memories ahead. And hey, maybe one day he'll give us grandchildren to spoil."

I laugh, swatting his arm. "Let's not rush him. He's still my baby."

"Always will be," Kai agrees, his voice soft.

As the quiet surrounds us, I feel the ache of Rowan's absence start to shift. It's still there, but now it's joined by something else—hope. Because even though he's off to London, starting his own story, the nest we've built will always be here, waiting for him to return.

Julian

Two Weeks Later

"I don't mind it. Tastes like coffee," Rowan says, grinning as he sips his Guinness.

I hold my Guinness out to him and we clink glasses. "That's my boy."

Sophie laughs next to me, her cheeks pink from the crisp autumn walk we all just took through Mayfair.

Kai's arm is around her shoulders, and the pub is noisy for a Wednesday afternoon.

"So, how are your classes?" I ask, leaning back in the vinyl-covered booth.

Rowan shrugs. "They're all right. My art history professor is strict. He doesn't like me. But Bronte's been showing me around London on the weekends," he adds cheerfully, referring to Liam and Zoe's son, who moved to London earlier this year and is two years older than Rowan.

"That's nice!" Sophie answers cheerfully. "Must be great to have your cousin so close."

"Beatrix and Adaline will be visiting in November, right?" Kai asks, sipping his whiskey. Rowan nods. Beatrix is twenty-two, and her younger sister is nineteen. They're the troublemakers of the family, and the reason we all suspect Miles was the first brother to go fully gray.

"Yeah. They want to bring the whole American experience to London," he muses, rolling his eyes. God, when he does that, he reminds me so much of Kai. "Aunt Stella and Uncle Miles have been emailing me every day to figure out how they're going to cook a twenty-four-pound turkey in my tiny oven. I guess Rose and Hugh are mad they're too young to come visit alone," he says, referring to Juliet and Chase's seventeen-year-old fraternal twins.

"That'll be lovely," Sophie says, Squeezing Rowan's hand across the table. "Sounds like you've got lots of visits from family to make sure you don't get homesick."

"I promise I'm not homesick, Mom," he says,

squeezing her hand back. "I really like my classes and I've made a few friends. Plus, Aunt Layla, Uncle Orion, and little Sebastian aren't that far away if I ever need some family time. Just a short train ride to Paris," he says, his voice reassuring as he refers to Kai's youngest brother and their family, who now live in Paris. Again, he reminds me so much of Kai when he has to talk Sophie and me down like this.

"And with Bronte being here…" He smiles at Sophie. "I know you're worried about me. But I promise I'm fine. Okay?"

Sophie nods once, tears pooling in her eyes. "I know."

He kisses her hand. "Love you, Mom."

"Love you, too, Row."

I wink at Sophie as she swipes a stray tear from under her eye. My heart clenches that she's so distraught about our son spreading his wings. But it's also adorable to watch how much he cherishes her, and how much she loves him in return. The day we picked him up at the hospital in California when he was five days old was the day both Kai and I became second in line to her heart. She's an incredible mum—motivated, hardworking, and yet still present and caring.

A few months before we adopted Row, the three of us had a commitment ceremony. Although we couldn't legally get married to Kai, it was important to us that we all have some way of making vows to each other. Kai completes us in ways we never would've been able to find without him. And raising Rowan in the sunshine of California, at Ashford Palace where all three of us left our own marks, surrounded by all of his cousins, aunts, and uncles nearby...

I am a very, very lucky man.

"Rowan?"

All four of us look up to see a man in a blazer looking down at Rowan with a furrowed brow.

"Um, hi, Professor Blake."

Professor Blake looks between Rowan, Kai, Sophie, and I, placing his hands in his pockets and rocking back on his heels.

"Oh, sorry, these are my parents," Rowan explains, gesturing to the three of us. "Mom, Dad, Dad... this is my art history professor."

Ah, the one Rowan thinks doesn't like him.

"Nice to meet you," Kai says, his American accent standing out in the quiet hush of the pub. We all reach out to shake his hand, and he reciprocates, but his eyes don't leave Rowan's. He's young. Early-thirties, if I had to guess. Handsome. He has that brooding professor thing down pat.

"See you in class tomorrow?" Professor Blake says, arching a brow.

"Yes, sir," Rowan says, cheeks turning pink.

"Nice to meet you all," he says, his voice low. "Perhaps I'll see you around as well?"

"Yes, we're staying for the week," Sophie adds.

Professor Blake just nods once and looks at Rowan again. "Have a nice night."

He's gone before any of us can utter a goodbye, but when I look back at Rowan, he's staring down at his

Guinness with a flustered look. I smirk as I look between Kai and Sophie, who are both trying not to smile.

"That's the strict one?" I ask, watching Professor Blake walk out the front door of the pub.

Rowan lets out a loud sigh. "Yeah."

"Hmm," is my only answer.

Kai's eyes are twinkling as I look over at him, but none of us say anything else about Professor Blake as the night wears on.

When it's time to say goodbye to Rowan for the night, we all walk him back to his dorm building. We're not allowed inside, so we say goodbye at the door.

"I love you. I'll see you after class tomorrow, okay?" I murmur, placing my hands on Rowan's shoulders. He's nearly as tall as me now—and with wavy light brown hair and blue eyes, he looks the part of my biological son, despite being adopted.

"Okay, Dad. Love you too."

Sophie hugs him for several seconds, and he just chuckles softly as he pats her back. Kai is next, and as they hug, I can't help but feel like I've never been happier. Seeing my son take after me, finding an interest in art and wanting to study art history at uni is somehow healing. Seeing him thrive *here,* in the place that Sophie and I left twenty years ago, is also wholly ironic yet vindicating. We walked so he could run.

At the end of the day, all you want for your children is for them to be happy. And as Rowan turns and walks toward the door of his dorm, he's grinning and radiating joy. He's *happy* here, that much is evident.

"So, shall we all go get absolutely smashed to drown out our feelings?" I ask.

Sophie laughs as she wraps an arm around my waist. Kai comes to my other side, and we walk off campus arm in arm.

"I think I'm too old to get 'smashed'" Kai replies, turning his head and looking at me. "You remember what happened on my fiftieth."

Sophie snorts. "Let's not repeat that. I can't handle a hangover that bad again."

"One drink?" I ask, walking into the early night air of London in late September. Sometimes I miss it. On nights like tonight, when the air has the promising chill of autumn, and you can see your breath in front of you, I feel like I might've found a way to be happy here.

But without Kai in the picture... I can't imagine we'd be as happy as we are now.

He balances us in ways I never expected—steady where I'm impulsive, grounding where Sophie is wild. Sophie softens him, teases out the warmth beneath his restraint, while he gives her the kind of unwavering support she's never had before. And me? He sees parts of me even I've never understood, holding them up to the light with quiet certainty, like he's always known I was meant to be his.

"One drink," Kai says, dropping his arm and taking my hand instead. He laces his warm, calloused fingers with mine. "Just one."

Sophie squeezes my waist and glances up at Kai with

a knowing smile. "You're both terrible at stopping at 'just one.'"

Kai hums softly, his thumb brushing over the back of my hand as we stroll down the cobblestone path leading off campus. The faint sound of laughter and music filters through the crisp night air, the kind of noise that feels alive, brimming with possibility.

"Maybe tonight's not about stopping," I reply, looking between them. "Maybe it's about celebrating."

Sophie's smile transforms into that mischievous smirk I know so well. "Celebrating what? The fact that I only cried three times in front of Rowan?"

I bark out a laugh, squeezing her closer. "Something like that."

Kai chuckles low in his chest, and it rumbles through the cool evening air. "Let's call it a toast to all of it. To this life we've built. To Rowan. To us."

"To us," Sophie echoes softly, leaning her head against my shoulder.

"To us," I agree, warmth blooming in my chest as we walk together, arm in arm, toward the nearest pub. The city's lights twinkle above us, and the three of us move as one, steady and certain.

Whatever comes next, I know this much: we'll face it together.

And that's enough.

Always enough.

Thank you so much for reading Malakai, Julian, and Sophie's story!

The Ravaged Castle series might be over, but I have a BRAND NEW series in the works, and the first book is now available for preorder!

https://mybook.to/FywC5FA
(Release date to be brought forward, don't worry!)

If you want to sign up for release news, updates on this mysterious new series, as well as receive excerpts and teasers before anyone else, be sure that you're subscribed to my mailing list. It's the best place to follow me!

www.authoramandarichardson.com/newsletter
(Psst... you also get a free student/teacher novella as a thank you for joining!)

And to answer your question about Rowan and Professor Blake... yes. That's all I'm going to say for now. ;)

ACKNOWLEDGMENTS

We made it! The final book in the Ravaged Castle series. I've been teasing Kai's story through the other four books, and I hope it delivered. I know as an author I shouldn't have favourites, but... I think Kai has a permanent soft spot in my heart. I think we can all relate to his feelings of unworthiness. Plus, Julian is one of my favorite characters I've ever written. If I could have a spin-off of just him and his gas station adventures, I would (lol).

I have a lot of people to thank for bringing this book to fruition!

First, my husband, who made me cut at least two "arseholes" from the DP scene in favour of other words. IYKYK. Apparently it gave him the ick. HAHA. Also, thank you for being my biggest supporter, my meal provider, and my life companion. I love you.

To all of my early readers: Erica, Macie, Kerrie, Jasmine, Em, Bryanna, Audris, Jess... thank you all for your input! Your insights made this book so much better than it was in the first draft.

To Rumi, THANK YOU for being the best m-dash wrangler! Thanks for making it possible for me to accept all changes and move on, lol.

To Shelbe, for keeping me organised and helping with every aspect of this book.

To Emma, aka Moonstruck Cover Design, thanks for this cover and reading my mind when I said Kai had a finger tattoo!

To Wander Aguilar for the gorgeous photo! And once more to Jess who showed this photo to me, despite already having another model set aside for Kai.

Michele, thank you for being such a thorough proofreader!

To my author friends, who let me vent about the writing process, and to those who inspire me everyday by kicking ass and taking names. I wouldn't be here without your constant support.

And to my readers, THANK YOU. This series would not be what it was without you spreading the word about Chase, Juliet, Miles, Stella, Liam, Zoe, Orion, Layla, Malakai, Sophie, and Julian. Thank you for loving these brothers so much. I'm not done with this world, so don't worry. This isn't the last of the brothers!

Xo,

Amanda

ABOUT THE AUTHOR

Amanda Richardson writes from her chaotic dining room table in Yorkshire, England, often distracted by her husband and two adorable sons. When she's not writing contemporary and dark, twisted romance, she enjoys coffee (a little too much) and collecting house plants like they're going out of style.

You can visit my website here:
www.authoramandarichardson.com

ALSO BY AMANDA RICHARDSON

For a complete and updated list of my currently published books, you can visit my website here:

www.authoramandarichardson.com/books

Printed in Great Britain
by Amazon